THORN

Book three of the *Engine Ward*

S.C. GREEN

GRYMM & EPIC PUBLISHING

ISBN: 978-0-473-35135-9

Grymm & Epic Publishing

Auckland, New Zealand

www.steffmetal.com

Cover Design: Vail Joy

Author Photo: Jess Manning

To James

Who believes in me, even when I don't believe in myself

CONTENTS

PROLOGUE

1832

Even through the layers upon layers of steel, wood and earth, Isambard Brunel could hear the screaming. The sound seeped through the streets above, pushing its way through every crack and crevice like a compie in search of food. Every man, woman and child in London screamed tonight. Their cries echoed through his underground chambers in a cacophony of agony and rage.

Brunel tapped his brass-plated knuckles against the arm of his chair, listening for the mechanical wheezing that meant one of his Boilers had fallen. Even as the Londoners hacked their bodies to pieces, his machines could drag themselves from the streets into the secret tunnels and return to their master for repair. He'd created them thus – his reusable army.

On the workbench, a damaged Boiler unit hissed and spluttered. Brunel leaned over and pushed another shovel of coal into the furnace. As the flames flared and the rotation wheels and mechanical arms Brunel had designed continued their repair work on the Boiler, the machine leaned back against the steel bench and fell silent, letting the heat and steam wash over its mangled body.

Hundreds of his machines waited in the nave of the Chimney in various stages of disrepair: casualties of his battle to keep London from Stephenson's grasp. Brunel was their father, their doctor, the healer of their pain.

Brunel sighed. He should be sitting on the table right now, letting the tines and pistons of the engines restore his own weary body. But he was flesh and blood, damnable mortal ingredients and organ slurry. He'd been so close to perfection; a gleaming iron body, an interior that clanged and churned and wound itself for eternity. *Before Nicholas stole the plate...*

Over the screaming, the bells rang. Someone living had breached the interior door. Brunel wound the tines on his mechanical earpiece, a device that allowed the engineer to discern footsteps through thick walls and hear conversations across a crowded room. The mechanism was so small he'd successfully hidden its presence from even his closest advisors, and he'd used it to weed out some of his more untrustworthy colleagues. Now, as he gave the tines another twist, he only heard one pair of feet shuffling down the metal stairs. He knew who it would be.

Sure enough, a few minutes later the two Boilers guarding the door parted and James Holman stumbled through.

"Stephenson's Navvies hold the southern Wall, and the populace have taken back the city. They've piled a great pyre of Boiler bodies on Bishops Bridge. Engine Ward is no longer in your control, Isambard. Just now, they put the Boiler workshops to the flame, and the Chimney will be next." He didn't step into the light of the fire. James – blinded in his youth by an unknown illness– had no need for the light.

Brunel did not reply.

2

"Sir, are you listening? They have you surrounded. Eventually, they will break down these iron doors."

Brunel spoke, raking the words across his scorched throat.

"And by then, I will be long gone. I am not concerned for what those men of flesh and blood can do to me. If you seek your own preservation, James, leave the city tonight, before they implicate you in my crimes."

"But sir, my eyes! You *promised*..."

"You had my plate, and you lost it again. Do I have the plate, James? Do you see me clasping that precious object to my bosom?"

"No, Messiah—"

"Then you have your answer."

"But—"

Above their heads, something crashed.

Brunel smiled. "James, won't you get the door for our guests?"

Holman's gaunt face contorted in fear, and he fled the room.

Brunel settled back in his chair, twisting his earpiece one final time. He could hear their feet crashing through the church above, and their screams as they met his Boiler guard, ready with jets of scalding water that suppurated their flesh from their bones.

He let the screams fill him, serenading his short-lived victory. He had only a few moments to enjoy the sound before he fled into the tunnels. *It's maddening that they should turn on me now, when I was so close to completion. Still, I built all this; I can build it again...*

"Brunel," a familiar voice spat through the gloom.

He jumped in surprise. Strange, he hadn't heard anyone approach. Brunel turned, but could only just see the outline of a man's shadow in the corner of the room.

Brunel wondered how long he'd been lurking there in silence.

"Ah, Nicholas. I'm so pleased you could join me."

"Don't sully my name on your traitorous tongue," the intruder hissed. "You're a coward and a liar, Isambard, sabotaging your own train to frame Stephenson for murder, and hiding down here to escape your judgement. The city is burning, our own people are dying or fleeing to the swamps, but you care for naught but yourself and your precious machines. My own family—" He gulped.

Brunel smirked, his lips cracking. "Surely the Stokers don't expect their own Messiah to throw himself into the fire? Have you breached my sacred quarters merely to berate me, Nicholas?"

The man stepped out from the shadow, moving under the stream of light flickering from the furnace. He looked wretched – patches of his skin burnt and blistering from his body. His face was tight with fury. Blood leaked from a sliver of shrapnel protruding from under his ribcage. Nicholas raised his hand. Light danced off a glinting sword blade.

"Nicholas—"

Stunned, Brunel could only hold up his arm in protest as Nicholas swung. The steel flashed and tore through Brunel's robe, slicing his right arm through the elbow. The severed arm hung in the air for a moment before thudding to the floor.

Brunel stared at his discarded limb for a moment, numb with surprise. Then the pain arced through his whole body, starting at his shoulder and seizing his right side in uncontrollable spasms. The pain exploded through his brain. Blood gushed from the wound and splattered across Nicholas' determined face. He leaned over Brunel, poising for another cut.

Brunel stumbled back, desperation seeping through his agony. *If I don't reach the tunnels, I will die this night, and I will never be remade.*

His own blood clotted his eyes, blinding him in his gloom. Brunel fumbled for his workbench, but missed and toppled forward. His steel boot caught on a clip, and he fell in a writhing lump at Nicholas' feet.

"You don't know what it's like, *Messiah*." Nicholas spat. "Every hour, every minute I hear your Boilers inside my skull, begging me to kill them, to save them from their agony. If you heard what I heard, you wouldn't wish yourself inside those steel cages."

"And if you knew what I know, Nicholas -" Brunel raised his head. "You wouldn't have come here tonight with murderous thoughts."

Nicholas lunged. Brunel rolled to the side and drove his boot into Nicholas' groin. As the man doubled over, Brunel lashed out again, shoving the man onto the nearby grate covering the air vent to the tunnels below. Nicholas clamped his hands around Brunel's neck and pulled him into his shoulder, adding his weight to the flimsy steel grate. With his one remaining breath Brunel thrust out his foot and pushed the pin from the latch. The unsecured grate clattered away and both men fell into the abyss below.

PART I:
GRAVEYARD

1851

JAMES HOLMAN'S MEMOIRS, FIRST EDITION

For nineteen years Brunel's Wall lay abandoned; from 1832 – the second year of the Metal Messiah's reign – until 1851. Brunel's defeat came only two years after London's citizens fought off the Vampire King's sanguine children. Finally, England was free of the vampires and the machines.

During this time, the royal line was re-established, and the city grew and prospered, becoming once again the shining star of England. And though Brunel's inventions remained in use, his name was forbidden to be spoken and all vestiges of the Metal Messiah's cult were banished from the city.

Among these were the Stokers – the train workers and Wall builders who were Brunel's people. Unable to return to Engine Ward – their home for many decades – the Stokers remained at Graveyard, a wasted landscape of scrap metal and disused railway carriages deep in the fog and the fens of southwest England. Here they worked, and waited for the country to forgive them for the sins of their engineer.

The years passed. The hulking structure of the Wall stood abandoned. The people began to forget the horrors of the Wall; the screams that issued from within when Brunel sabotaged his own train, the stench of suppurating flesh that rose with the steam and clouded the surrounding villages in eternal night; the emaciated and wholly inhuman features of the Sunken – offspring of the Vampire King – who tore the city to pieces in their frenzied feeding; the cold precision of the Boilers, the furnace-masters.

People tore away sections of the steal façade for use in other projects, and vines crept through the holes bored by rust and weather and rats. The Wall became another faded memorial on the London skyline, a monument to those who died in a war no one remembered.

Meanwhile, within the Wall, a light flickered, and the gears began to turn.

My introduction ends here, for the rest of this story belongs to Thorn. Because Thorn herself cannot write, nor has any desire to learn though I have offered on many occasions, I have taken it upon myself to record her adventure.

It will be my last work, for as my name and freedom fades my pain returns, although now it sits behind my eyes, gnawing at my brain like a rat possessed, draining my body of life.

For those who've followed my previous works, it may be of interest to know that I am no longer blind. There are days – especially when the pain rides so great that all the explosions of a steam engine seem to go off inside my skull – that I question the worth of my new sight. This contraption cost me too much, and without my selfishness we all may have been spared much pain and suffering. For my betrayal, I endure my personal hell, so that this tome may be written.

Now that I again form letters with quill and ink, and – after I wind my clockwork eyes – I can enjoy the printed word at my own pleasure, without need of another to read for me, my love of words and witticisms continues to flood my veins.

While in the employ of George Wombwell's Travelling Menagerie, I was blessed to visit Buckingham Palace and meander through whole rooms – three and twenty times the size of my own apartments – filled with nothing but books. Many were coated with dust, a layer for each year they went unread. As a man who lived without books for nearly thirty years, I found that saddest of all.

The books told the history of England; from the founding of the great cities through its rise from the ashes of the Roman occupation, her monarchs and her architects and her clockmakers and her pie sellers. Shelves were devoted to her most recent history: the booming trade in tricorn ivory, Brunel and Stephenson and the engineering sects and their churches and ceremonies, the building of the Wall that kept the dragons out and the citizens in, the Vampire King and his lead-scoured children who terrorised the city, the Gauge War that was Brunel's undoing, the banishment of the Stokers.

Though I pored for hours and days over those volumes, never once did my eyes fall upon the words of a Stoker. Nicholas Thorne's volumes on architectural theory were not even in evidence, though I myself own a bookshelf of his fine leather-bound scripts and know them to be some of the finest work in the field.

I intend this volume in part to remedy that. Maybe it won't be as eloquent as the God Blanchard's treatise on dirigible flight, maybe it won't portray our beast wars with the blood curdling suspense of Herodotus' account of Thermopylae, maybe it won't expound magical changeling animals like the God Darwin, nor depict a God so arrogant and changeable as the damnable Bible. But it will be Thorn's story, and maybe it will be read in future years, and Stokers will know that their history contained great triumph and great sacrifice.

And maybe, if I truly capture her within these pages, Thorn will forgive me, and I will forgive myself.

James Holman, Esq.

***

Deep in the murk of the hanging fog, two eyes glowed like London streetlamps. Along the western edge of the bog a string of paraffin lamps bobbed over the muddied grasses; mere fireflies in comparison to those monstrous orbs. Thorn heard the low grumble of the beast as it sank into the mud. It sensed their presence.

Thorn's shoulders tensed, her finger tightening around the trigger, but the moaning stopped before she could react. She let out a breath.

Not yet.

The fog obscured the beast's form, but from its moans she could place its position. She tugged her goggles off her head and wiped the layer of sweat from the inside, but this did nothing to increase her visibility over the dark, smoky fenland. She crouched lower behind the bulky mainframe of the Gast-Engine, checking the spring-column was stable and the steam-powered weapon was pressurised.

She waited.

Though Thorn could not see him, she knew that several feet away towards the tricorn's left flank waited her friend Lurgo, his Gast poised at the same target.

The cramp in her leg twinged, and her knee buckled, splashing her tunic with soggy peat. Thorn pursed her lips, willing her body to behave, concentrating on the gloom. On the far bank she heard the bell chime thrice.

At the sound the tricorn lurched forward. Mud and peat sloshed at Thorn's feet. The beast growled – fifty feet to her left, whereas before it had been on her right – and Thorn fired.

The pistons slammed in the cylinder, and hot steam rushed past her face. Since the beast still wallowed in the darkness she couldn't tell if she'd landed a hit. Thorn released the pressure valve and another bolt rolled into the chamber. She used her left hand to slide open the vent pins, allowing water to rush through and cool the mechanism.

The bell sounded again, and as Thorn swung the Gast towards the charging animal, she heard Lurgo's bolt slice through the air. The beast let out a great bellow, and a wave of peat splattered the lamps. The already low light grew dimmer.

Thorn reached with her mind through the darkness, searching for a connection to the animal. *Where are you? Let me sense you—*

The ground shook as the tricorn rose again. At last Thorn saw it emerge into the dim semi-circle of lamplight. Oswald's bells became urgent as the great head rose from the water, the dark silhouette of its peat-encrusted hide tumbling forward as it stampeded towards the clanging bell. Weeds draped its bone collar and thorny branches clung to the tough skin on its cheeks. Amongst the eldritch spectacle poked two curved ivory horns – as long as Thorn's outstretched arms and the prize for which they fought – and the ivory stump on the nose, now caked with mud.

Thorn squeezed the trigger, and felt the kick in her shoulder. This time her bolt definitely hit. The beast bucked, rising eight feet in the air and collapsing in the bog. The bell clanged again; *keep shooting, we're not sure if it's dead.*

Thorn tipped out the empty magazine and fed another through the clip rotation, twisting the mainframe towards the lamps. Her mind fixed on the tricorn – slotting between his thoughts like gauge rails on a railway - and its rage and fear poured into her skull.

Got you.

She squeezed the trigger.

"Thorn, behind you!"

Bloody Lurgo, now it knows where you are—

Suddenly, another mind forced itself into hers. The new thoughts rushed her body, and she could smell what it smelt, could *taste* the rage and terror. *How could I have been so careless?* She'd missed the second tricorn, and now it was heading right for her.

Thorn heard the growl on her left – less than ten feet away – and felt the ground swell as the second beast rushed her. She dived backward, the trigger lever snapping off in her hand. The connection in her mind snapped, and pain thundered inside her skull. Rolling over her left shoulder and digging her boots into soft peat, she rose in time to see the second tricorn crash through her abandoned Gast.

The pressure valve arced through the air, whistling and spitting as it slapped into the mud. Sparks flew in all directions, and she leapt back as twists of steel fell at her feet. The mainframe was driven under by the force of the beast, and cogs and gears snapped and buckled. The tricorn barrelled onward, groaning as it struggled to slow its momentum and turn back on her.

Thorn willed her legs to move. Slowly, achingly slowly, she stepped backward, but her boot slid into a boggy hole and she fell. The beast rose and rolled towards her, blood blurring its glowing eyes.

Holy Conductor, save me—

Her stomach sank. Burning rose in the back of her throat. She uttered a final, silent prayer.

The air rang with hissing as Lurgo pumped bolts into the charging creature, and Thorn saw the shadow of its great head fall beneath the surface, until its glowing eyes and great horns disappeared under the mud.

Lurgo took a suicide run within a foot of the second beast – still thrashing in its death throes – and grabbed Thorn under the shoulders. He tugged and her foot slid out of her boot, which – heavy with dripping peat – sunk into the mud with a *plop*.

They tumbled backward. Thorn spat blood and peat onto Lurgo's overalls and held up the broken lever. "I saved this."

"Quartz *will* be glad." His eyes darted across the swamp where the hunting party pulled in the lamps and gathered around the first carcass. "Do you need my arm?"

She shook him off. "I can manage." Perhaps too sour a tone for someone who just saved her life, but it was imprudent to give Lurgo any encouragement. Lurgo had been her only friend for longer than she could remember, but since she turned sixteen – four years ago now – his attention had shifted, most notably to her chest area.

Weeds scraped across her bootless foot as she stood up, and peat sank between her toes, gluing them together. Thorn picked her path back through the swamp, grabbing at the glints of metal on the bog surface. When she came within arms' reach of the second retiring beast, her stomach muscles contracted.

It was almost dead. Blood bubbled from wounds where Lurgo's bolts bore fissures in its belly, but its chest still heaved and the forelegs twitched. Thorn's hands shook as she bent to retrieve the trigger spring, and it fell from her fingers and disappeared under the peat.

Quartz is going to have my head. It'll take months to construct a new Gast, and we have no other weapons powerful enough to penetrate tricorn skin.

Sloshing footsteps behind her meant Lurgo was close. She gathered up the scraps in her skirt, held the corners together and slunk towards the group, keeping her eyes low and hoping in vain no one noticed she was short one boot and one Gast-Engine.

When they entered the circle of light, Lurgo grabbed her arm again, but she yanked it away and shot him a filthy look. In the lamplight he could not pretend he didn't notice her reproach. She saw the hurt in his eyes and turned away, knowing it best to ignore him.

Lurgo left to help the team reposition the lamps around the carvers. She deposited her scraps on the rear of the wagon, tucked her grubby frock coat over them, and stooped over the chassis, picking the debris from between her toes and trying to appear busy.

She watched the action from the corner of her eye; the sheen of hatchet blades in the gloom, the carcass sagging as they tore the ribcage away to expose the bulbous organs. The stench began to flood over the wagon, though no one else seemed to notice. Thorn was one of the few Stokers who retained her sense of smell.

She pulled her peat-encrusted scarf from under her collar and pressed it to her nose and mouth, but it could not alleviate the unforgettable fragrance of blood-leeched peat, or the acrid stench of faeces as the intestines were severed, or the cloying smell of fresh meat. Thorn watched Lurgo help the carvers load the rear of the sled with slabs of dripping meat, and too often she saw his eyes shift to her.

They won't allow me to mourn Rex much longer. I have to convince Oswald I'm a decent hunter, despite this disaster, or he won't allow me to remain in Graveyard. With Rex gone, Lurgo is the only boy who will have me, if I can't convince him otherwise.

In her secret prayers she hoped, of course. But after nine months of no word she knew Rex's Stoker heritage must have been discovered, and the London schoolmasters would have had him killed for his deception. By Great Conductor's blessing he waited for her at the Station of Life.

The others didn't think so, of course. Even Aaron, Rex's father, thought him merely captivated by London's splendour. "He'll come back when he's ready, Thorn. A young man has to explore the world before he settles down and takes a wife."

"He's found himself a bangtail in Whitechapel. He won't be back," Bill Riley, Lurgo's father, said with a scoff. "They never come back."

She shuddered. *Please don't let that be true.*

Compared to *that*, marriage to Lurgo would be heaven.

The carvers returned with the last of the meat, and Oswald stacked six ivory horns behind the boiler mount. His grizzled face bore a broad grin; he was the only one pleased with the night's hunt. The carvers grumbled about the wasted meat; the wagon could only carry one carcass and by the time they returned the other would either have spoiled or be crawling with compies. Thorn heard whispered conversations as the men clambered aboard:

"Oswald should nae trust a woman with this job. He's a weak Chancellor to concede to Quartz's whims. The child is clearly no hunter."

I've killed more tricorns than you've killed rats, Robbie Paxton, and yet you get second helpings before my plate is even filled. It's me who feeds your greedy gullet. And don't forget that black eye your son Walter had last week – told you he walked into a steam valve again, did he? That will teach him for speaking ill of Rex.

"—she should be tending the cooking fires, not here in the marshes. She'll be marrying soon—"

That's what you think, William Haddock. I'll be six feet in the peat bog before I let any of your sons near my lady bits—

"She won't be marrying anybody, because no one will 'ave the witch, not even your lads, William." Bill Riley sneered. "We should have been rid of her years ago. Nicholas' spawn must surely carry his traitorous blood, and for all Aaron's talk of her special skills she's been naught use to us. Why, her third time out and she lost a Gast and a good leather boot! Rex was lucky to escape her. Even if the school's booted him out, I'm sure he's much happier in London."

I wanted Rex to succeed more than anyone. I wanted to have a new life with Rex. Maybe Aaron is wrong, maybe Great Conductor did curse me…

Thorn fingered her pendant – a Stoker cross Rex had made for her before he left – uttering an apologetic prayer. *I am not angry with you, I'm angry with them.* But even that wasn't entirely true. She loved these people, and deep down she was sorry she'd disappointed them again. Her anger turned inward, and she dug her fingernails into her palm till she felt a sting of pain. *You deserve much worse...*

There'll be words with Quartz tonight, and after I'd begged for this privilege. Please don't let him take me off the hunt.

Thorn gritted her teeth as Lurgo lowered himself down beside her, gripping the buffer beam over the boiler chassis and patting her shoulder. She ignored him, squeezing droplets of blood from the nicks in her hand where the steel had cut.

Oswald stoked the boiler. Steam hissed from the valves and Thorn's seat juddered with the familiar slam of the pistons. The engine pushed the skids over the slick peat and the wagon lurched forward. Thorn set her jaw as it began its ascent of the disused broad-gauge track, out of the bog and into the Narrow.

When Isambard Brunel had been Messiah and Lord Protector of England, he had first sent the Stokers into the swamps to extend the South Devon stretch of his Great Western Railway towards Plymouth, cutting across miles of peat-rich fenland. Instead of steam locomotion the trains were moved by the Clegg system of vacuum traction.

As Brunel's loyal followers, the Stokers had worked tirelessly cutting the peat to form the Narrow where the trains would run. The workforce built up a shantytown from abandoned railway carriages and other rubbish they found rotting in the swamp. They laid the gauge and fitted the fifteen-inch pipes for the atmospheric train, only to have the entire system fall into disuse before it was even complete. The technology required leather flaps to seal the vacuum pipes. The leather was softened with tallow, making it a favourite snack for rats and compies, who devoured the flaps in swift succession. The line ceased operation and Brunel moved on to more lofty ambitions. But he ordered the workforce to remain in the swamps, assuring them he would welcome them back into the city as soon as they'd helped him defeat Stephenson. And so the Stokers had fought in the Gauge War, using Brunel's Boiler machines to attack Stephenson's army. But despite all odds being in their favour, the Boiler army malfunctioned and the Stokers were defeated. Aaron Williams had led many of the men into London to confront Brunel, but after the truth behind the wreck of the *Thunderer* emerged and Brunel was defeated, the people blamed the Stokers for the actions of their leader, and banished them back into the swamps. And here in the swamps they remained for twenty years, dwelling in the landscape of their greatest folly.

The wagon juddered over the exposed gauge, and the slopes of the Narrow shone slick with running water. A ramshackle Clegg pump station – its rusted square chimney stained white with compie faeces – marked the northbound stretch of the disused atmospheric railway. The damage from the latest tricorn stampede was obvious; several of the lamps had burnt out or fallen from their sconces and smashed. Two sections of the cut wall had collapsed. Thorn saw the new administrator attempting to note these damages on his slate, though thick globules of rain smudged the chalk.

Icabod had died of cholera last week, and she hadn't yet introduced herself to his replacement. She didn't recognise his curled moustache or probing eyes, but then, Thorn didn't spend her time socialising around the cooking fires, so it was possible she just hadn't noticed him before. He was young for such responsibility, not more than twenty-five or so, with smooth skin and strong shoulders that pulled at the fabric of his greatcoat. His lapels were singed with intricate designs and encrusted with filth, identifying him as part of the Williams clan, the self-appointed aristocracy of Graveyard.

That's interesting. Aaron never would have trusted his family with the accounts. This must be Oswald's influence.

The administrator looked up then and caught her eye. His handsome features broke into a wide smile. Thorn whipped her head away, embarrassed and confused. Why was he *smiling?* Didn't he know who she was?

She concentrated on the path ahead. When she saw the outline of the abandoned Clegg carriage on the gloom-shrouded horizon, Thorn squeezed her eyes shut. She counted to twenty, enough time for the wagon to clatter past without her laying eyes on it. The carriage still held memories she didn't want to face. She opened her eyes again and let out her breath. Lurgo put his hand on her shoulder, *again.* She shrugged him off. *Doesn't he ever give up?*

He knows he's nearly got me, whether I want him or not. Why would he give up now?

Quartz had the watch tonight. He lit the signal lights as they turned into the outer boundary of Graveyard, marked by the high wall of sharpened steel spikes and other scrap. Oswald signalled back that the hunt was successful, and the gate swung open. Thorn sighed; there was no signal for a bittersweet victory.

Within minutes the cutting widened out, and they passed through the outskirts of Graveyard. The oldest carriages littered this area – abandoned over twenty years ago as newer, faster, better models were created. Brunel's first GWR locomotives rotted here, their steal frames and ten-foot drive wheels dwarfing the rusted goods carriages and half-finished sleeper carriages.

Although Stoker society prohibited ownership, there was definitely a hierarchy within Graveyard. While other Stokers lived in newer, watertight units (some even had little garden plots and running water), the poorer Stoker families lived here, huddled inside the broken train shells. Some toppled sideways, some stuck end-up in the mud. All unwanted, all neglected, just like the Stokers who occupied them. Haphazard piles of twisted metal rose and fell from the peat, and the broad gauge tracks buckled like saplings between flaming pools of oil. Steam leaked from various funnels and valves, and the sound of creaking and hissing filled the night. Thorn sucked on her wool scarf, but she had no hope of escaping that smell. Her head reeled with the reek of human filth and waste, of wet, bubbling oil, of bile and sickness and death.

Smells like home.

Oswald slowed the wagon as it passed under the light of the Turret. Quartz kept the exterior of the watchtower in impeccable condition – remarkable, considering the squalor he usually lived in – and its vertical steel walls gleamed as if new. Although Stoker society forbade ownership and others on the watch did duty there, the Turret unmistakably belonged to Quartz. He'd built the interior platforms and designed the clockwork system and mercury bowl that ran the argand wick lamp, which swivelled like a lighthouse over the Southern stretch of Graveyard.

Quartz's Fresnel lens spun the light over the wagon, bathing it in a green glow. Thorn rubbed her eyes and sat up on her heels, ready to jump off. Quartz jammed the clockwork with the assembly weight and the light stopped. He bent over the sill, his features drawn. Raindrops rolled down his hooked nose.

"I see only one Gast Engine."

"Thorn lost hers," snapped Oswald. "I warned you about letting her—"

"I can build another."

"But until then, we're reliant on the stores. Your esteem for Nicholas has clouded your judgement, Quartz. Of course I will be removing Thorn from the hunting party."

Thorn's cheeks flushed with anger. She inched towards the edge of the wagon, keeping her head bowed.

"It wasn't her fault!" *Shut your mouth, Lurgo. You'll make this worse.* "We didn't know there was a second—"

"If she had the *sense*, she'd have known," Oswald snapped. "Aaron would've known."

Thorn squeezed her eyes shut, trying not to cry. He was right, of course. Aaron would've sensed the second beast. *I'm sorry Aaron, I'm not you. I'm not what you think I am.*

Quartz grunted and disappeared inside. The clockwork clacked to life and the green light resumed its cycle. The wagon lurched forward, and Thorn leapt from the side and splashed through the mud to the door. She pulled the cord protruding from the lintel.

Quartz' face reappeared at the window.

"You really buggered up, Thorn."

"I'll help you work on the new Gast."

He spat. The glob of spittle rolled down the funnel and floated in a puddle.

She held up the trigger lever. "I saved this, and a few other pieces. Unfortunately the spring's at the bottom of the bog."

He mumbled something impolite, and pulled on a

lever. A jet of steam shot from the Turret roof, and the iron door swung inward. Thorn ducked inside and pulled off her coat, wringing out the water on the slick steps. She scraped a layer of peat off her bare foot and found another boot in the pile under the stairs, wincing as she pulled it on.

Too small, but it'll have to do.

"Quit dallying," he called down. "Let's see what you've got."

She scrambled up the spiral stairs. Quartz sat in the parlour on the third floor landing, his fingers weaved around a flask. The pungent smell of soot and mecks clung in the air.

Thorn emptied her haul over the grating on the table. "The tricorn crushed the mainframe and the boiler; I had no hope."

Quartz lifted his monocle to inspect the debris. "You've got the steam injection lever though. That's something."

"And Oswald got six horns. By my calculations that's the next six months of supplies paid for. He should be thanking me, not kicking me off the hunt."

"Don't harp on about the *supplies* to me. You know my thoughts on that front." Another glob of Quartz's spit rolled down the wall. "If Aaron were still Chancellor—" he sighed. "Aaron knows the contract with Bristol is crap. The Williams clan take all the profits and feed us on porridge and stale bread. Meanwhile, the Navvies pull up all the broad gauge track we laid and put down Stephenson's flimsy crap, with a shilling a week for their trouble! Soon, the last stretch of the Great Western Railway will belong to Stephenson and Co., and they'll sweep in here and send us all packing. Did Aaron ever tell you what he was planning before he got sick?" Thorn shook her head. "A breeding programme, like the Scots have with the neckers, but with tricorns instead. Aaron wanted to capture tricorn babies and raise them in the Graveyard, and when they grew we could control them."

"For what?"

Quartz smiled. "What do you think the Navvies would do if they saw us charging toward them riding an army of steel-plated tricorns?"

Thorn smiled at that.

"But Oswald won't hear of it. Thinks it unnatural. And of course there's only you and Aaron with the skill to train them ... so now we're back to the bloody *Williams*—"

A bell rang.

Quartz leapt at the window, knocking over his flask. Mecks mixed with the soot and mud on the table, and splattered Thorn's tunic.

"What is it?"

Quartz fiddled with the lenses on his monocle, and squinted into the night.

"A stranger" —his frown turned up in a smile that was more like a sneer— "who is not a stranger at all."

He threw up the lever, and Thorn leaned out the window as the light ceased its rotation, pausing on the hunched figure that wandered so boldly into Stoker territory...

A stranger...who is not a stranger at all...

Thorn bolted down the steps, her muscles screaming. Coatless, the rain pelted her shoulders as she stumbled over the uneven track, gluing her clothes to her body and pulling her hair into a matted clump. When she was a few feet away the stranger lifted his hood and droplets cascaded off his steep nose and high cheeks as his face broke into a smile.

He looked a mess. Long cuts ran across his cheeks and forehead, some opened by the force of the downpour and dribbling rivers of blood over his face. He stooped so far forward she thought he must surely fall over, and his clothes hung in tatters from his sallow, emaciated limbs. A filthy rucksack – matted with rain and nearly empty – hung from his shoulder. Though his lips smiled, his eyes betrayed horror.

Thorn stood before him and he lurched forward and embraced her. She sobbed into his greatcoat, knitting her fingers into his back, where she felt only bone. He seemed awkward, as if he suddenly didn't know what to do with his hands.

"You're alive," she whispered, her words lost in the howl of the wind. "Alive, alive, alive…"

I knew it. I knew he would come back for me.

The wind tore at their skin and pressed soot and grit between their bones. Rex cupped her face in his rough hands and kissed her forehead, a burst of warmth in a forest of pain.

"Little Thorn," he shouted over the rain, his words almost lost in her hair. "You've grown."

"I'm a hunter now. Although so is Lurgo. They let anyone hunt these days, although I probably won't be allowed for much longer. I broke a Gast engine today."

"Oh."

They stared at each other for several moments. Lightning arched across the sky.

"I bring news. I must speak to Quartz and Father immediately."

"Rex … Aaron is sick. We don't know what's wrong. Oswald is in charge now."

Pain flicked across his sunken eyes, and his fingers dug into her shoulder. "When did he—"

"Two months ago. There was an outbreak of some sort of malady. It got Icabod, Frederick and nine others. Aaron's fever's gone now but he's still sick. Oswald is Chancellor now." Thorn shivered. Rain dribbled down her spine.

"I—" He pulled her to him, his embrace fierce.

"We've missed you," she whispered. The wind whipped her words away. *Now I can marry you, and I'll never be cursed again.*

"Don't just stand out there canoodling!"

They both jumped, their heads banging together. Rex stumbled and fell to his hands in a puddle.

"Inside, now!" The door swung open. Thorn helped Rex stand and he leaned on her shoulder as they ascended the steps.

Blood dripped from his wounds and mixed with the filth in the grating. Quartz threw a rag at Thorn and pushed a flagon of mecks into Rex's hand. "Blacken your tongue on that."

"I don't want—"

Quartz glowered. Rex slumped against the wall, and drowned the foul drink in one gulp. Thorn wiped his face and hands with the rag.

"Nine months, boy." Quartz adjusted his finest lens. "How's school?"

"I dropped out."

Thorn's head snapped up. *He didn't ... did he?* Rex – along with another boy they all called Sooty – had been singled out from all the youth in Graveyard. They had the cleverest minds and the most persuasive personalities: the boys most likely to make it in the city. The Stokers had pooled all the money they had to send the two boys to school in London under false identities. It was their only chance at a life outside Graveyard, and the Stokers' only opportunity to place agents in the outside world who might one day be able to end their banishment. Rex knew how much had been sacrificed to give him this chance. He knew what his schooling meant to the Stokers, and especially to his father, Aaron. *He would never quit. Would he?*

Thorn glanced over at Quartz, who was staring at Rex with a stony expression. "I think you'd better explain," he said.

"I had no choice. There are much more important matters at stake. I've been living with ... with the London Stokers." Rex stared at Thorn as he spoke. He looked a bit sheepish.

Thorn reeled. *That doesn't make any sense.* There were no Stokers left in London, save Rex and Sooty. Every last one had been sent to Graveyard nineteen years ago.

Quartz looked unimpressed. "There are no London Stokers."

"Yes, there are. Not many, but we're growing in number, recruiting more people who believe in our cause, who want to be part of our way of life."

Quartz shook his head. "Who would want to become a Stoker, the most loathed people in England?"

"Oh, all sorts. The cult of Great Conductor didn't die with Brunel; it's been dwelling underground all these years. Priests conduct their sermons in secret, extolling the virtues of steam engines and spreading the gospel of broad gauge to men who believe in the superiority of Brunel's designs. Many of these followers have taken oaths and now wear the Stoker cross with pride. And they want to help us. They want to find a way to return the Stokers to Engine Ward."

"And just how do they propose to do that?"

"Queen Victoria is holding a Great Exhibition of the

most magnificent industrial works of the world. They're building a huge crystal palace in Hyde Park to house the exhibits. Sooty and I found work on the construction gang."

"Does this concern us?"

"Robert Stephenson will be the star of the English exhibitors. Navvies will flood to London to support that treacherous gammy. The Metal Messiah's great works will not even be acknowledged. The London Stokers are planning to infiltrate the Great Exhibition, and use it as a platform to showcase the innovations of Brunel and the Stokers to the world."

"You're going to infiltrate a public exhibition and swap around some of the displays? It sounds more like a childish prank than a serious plan to restore the Stokers to London."

"Don't judge me yet, for there is more news I must share." Rex lowered his voice. "We hold our secret meetings in one of the old tunnels beneath Engine Ward. It seems most fitting. Well, recently, while making our way to our meeting place, we've seen lights flickering inside Engine Ward, deep in the darkest tunnels where no light is supposed to be. And just the other day I overheard two Metic priests on a street corner whispering about noises coming from the ruins of Brunel's old church. So we snuck up to the surface of the Ward itself, and I saw the outer foundation walls of the Chimney had been rebuilt."

Thorn leaned across the table, her chest tightening. "By whom?"

"We don't know. It's not us. We kept watch for three days and never saw anyone within the ruins; it's as if the walls are rebuilding themselves."

Quartz slapped his empty flagon on the table. "By

Great Conductor's festering turds, he's back. The bastard's back."

"Who's back?" Thorn asked, but both Quartz and Rex ignored her.

"That's what we think. Who would do this apart from Brunel? And with the exhibition's opening only weeks away—"

"He's returning to defeat Stephenson in the hour of his greatest triumph?"

"This is why I've returned to the swamp. It's not good just Sooty and I being at the exhibition. We need more Stokers ready and waiting for Brunel's return. We should be there – we *must*be there – when he destroys Stephenson and reclaims London." Rex's voice rose in pitch as he became excited. Quartz nodded, but far from sharing Rex's enthusiasm, his features were grave.

"Security will be tight around the city, so getting in is going to be difficult," Rex said. "I've a contact who will give us the papers we need to get through the gate. And then Sooty and I can sneak a team into the Crystal Palace."

Quartz sipped his second flagon of mecks in silence. Finally he spoke, his voice low, his scheming eyes darting to the window.

"I'm pleased you found me first. Your piss-pot uncles will not agree. They'd want us twiddling our thumbs in this hellhole, waiting for Brunel to call on us. If Brunel returns we leave Graveyard and go back to work in the factories and they can kiss their little business enterprise goodbye. It's best to keep word of his return as quiet as possible for now, lest it cause trouble. We'll have to approach Oswald first, try to convince him of this course of action."

Thorn was stunned by Quartz's words, for she knew

how much he loathed Brunel. Quartz had a long memory for the days under Brunel's reign as Lord Protector of England; he banished the Stokers to Graveyard, forced them to fight against Stephenson in the Gauge War, and turned the population of England thoroughly against them. But because many of the more powerful Stokers (especially the Williams) believed the Metal Messiah had been a champion of the Stokers, she knew Quartz had to be careful about his opinions. Quartz met Thorn's eye, and with a subtle shift of the corner of his mouth, conveyed to her that he believed it best that Rex believed Quartz agreed with him.

Rex nodded, his eyes fluttering shut. He struggled to his feet. "I must find Oswald. We should make plans immediately."

Thorn spoke. "You should rest." *Yes, rest with me, Rex.*She tried to push his shoulder back down.

Rex brushed her away. "There'll be time enough for that. This is *important*." When he spoke to her, he sounded impatient, condescending. He knew she didn't share his beliefs about Brunel. She couldn't, not after everything Quartz and Aaron had told her. But Rex had never spoken to her like that before. Thorn gulped back a lump in her throat. *What is wrong with Rex? Didn't he come back for me, so that we could be together?*

Quartz looked up. "Not so fast. You need to plan how you're going to approach him. You need to retain control. Oswald would have you take Edgar and Gabriel back to London. Edgar's fine; he's my man. Gabriel's mind is poisoned by the priests, occupied with Gods and gears and other lofty thoughts. He can't even swing a sledgehammer. He'll be naught use on the mission. You should insist on Lurgo Riley, Finnegan, your cousin Joel…and Thorn, of course. Her senses may prove useful."

Thorn's heart leapt.

Rex nodded his agreement, and moved towards the door. Thorn's body jarred as the heat of his hand left hers. She dashed down the stairs after him, not wanting him out of her sight so soon.

***

When Thorn walked into the glow of the fire drums with Rex on her arm, the destroyed Gast was instantly forgiven. Stokers tossed aside the long-handled pokers and rushed them, leaving trays of soot-cooked tricorn meat for the compies. Their hands grabbed at his tattered clothing as if he were some revered idol. Their voices spoke their surprise and delight; made gracious inquiries as to his well-being, asked anxious questions about his schooling and London, ululated prayers of thanks to Great Conductor, and mumbled musings about his mysterious return.

Every few paces Rex stopped and touched hands and cheeks. He ran his fingers along the scratched and defiled 'STEPHENSON & COMPANY' lettering on the side of the stores carriage. He rubbed his sunken cheeks as though the heat from the fire drums burnt under his skin. He moved his bloody lips, as if to speak, to offer words of consolation and hope, but it was as though his effort in Quartz's parlour had spent him. He stumbled and leaned on Thorn, and managed to croak out, "Oswald—"

Children stood to offer their seats as they passed by. Thorn pulled Rex onto an empty carriage seat – cushioned in faded leather, now cured with peat and gnawed by the compies – and rested his head on her shoulder.

The children huddled together, staring at Rex and whispering among themselves. Rex's sunken face and bloodied hands frightened them.

"Fetch Oswald," she commanded in a haughty tone – a tone she would never normally dare use in Graveyard – and they raced off. Thorn stroked Rex's hair and watched the untended fires splutter and fizz. Soot and ash billowed in the air, and she coughed into his hair.

Lurgo caught her eye from across the flames. He smiled and started toward her, but when he saw Rex his face flashed with surprise, then hurt and defeat. He turned away and disappeared into the night.

I can't worry about him now, not when Rex is here, and in such a state.

"Bring him some food," she snapped at a girl who stood under the arm of the carriage seat, regarding Rex with wide eyes and rolling her tangled hair in the collar of her filthy smock. She sucked the deplorable cigar as if she were a wealthy English gentry-man, and smirked at Thorn.

"Now!" Thorn raised her hand to slap the urchin, but the girl darted away towards the kitchen carriage. On the far side of the fire she heard a bow drawn across fiddle strings, and several youths leapt into an enthusiastic fire dance, spinning and swinging each other around the flaring drums. Thorn pushed Rex's head down as a hot coal flew over their heads.

Now that Rex has returned, maybe I'll dance again.

Oswald bolted through the crowd, pushing aside the dancers. The children slunk away from him, frightened by the chancellor's frenzy. When he saw Rex, Oswald dropped to one knee in the mud. "It *is* you." His features twitched. The gaggle of children ran off amongst the fire drums.

"I apologise for my sudden, unannounced return. The situation in London required me to come here with haste."

"Why are you not in school? What of Sooty?"

"He remains in the city. I have left the school, but it is for a good reason."

"But you have returned to us … surely it is the blessing of Great Conductor. And after the unfortunate events of recent weeks—"

"My father." Rex's voice strained, and Thorn saw the sadness creeping into his cold eyes. "Thorn told me. I want to see him."

"I'll escort you to the smokehouse, but it can wait till tomorrow. You must be weary. Tonight you should rest."

The girl returned, carrying an enamel plate piled with tricorn meat and another tankard of mecks. She did not run away like the others but stood on the edge of their conversation, staring at her feet and pretending to ignore them.

Rex glanced at the girl, and at Thorn. "Father wouldn't have me rest. Should we find somewhere private to talk?"

Oswald nodded. He pressed his cane – really a length of fine gauge filed down into a manageable shape – into Rex's trembling hand, and offered his shoulder as Rex rose. Thorn made to follow them, but Oswald shot her a look that said, *you are not welcome, child of Nicholas the traitor.*

The little girl skipped after them, but Thorn grabbed her arm. "That's none of your business, you little wretch."

She pulled against Thorn's grasp. "Leggo."

"Not until you tell me your name."

She poked her tongue out.

"Lucile! Are you bothering this lady?"

Thorn jumped at the masculine voice.

"Daddy, she's *hurting* me."

"Hush, pet. You were causing mischief, no doubt."

Thorn released the child, who scurried between her father's legs. Thorn rose, embarrassed, and stared at the face of the new administrator, his Williams coat now dark with soot. The dancing firelight caught on his tidy brown curls and strong chin, casting an aura over his broad shoulders and long neck. His folded slate rested under his arm.

"You must be older than you appear," she said, blushing. "A fine position and a family seem out of place on such a young face."

"I'm only twenty-five. Do not mistake the fruits of youthful amour for age and respectability. Lucile has mostly been raised by my mother, but she owes her impertinence to my influence." He patted his simpering urchin on her bouncing curls and extended his hand. "I'm Joel Williams. I'm Aaron's second cousin. I was impressed by your hunt today."

"Then you must be blind, Mr. Williams, for I lost one Gast, and a boot." She pointed to her mismatched footwear for emphasis.

He laughed, throwing back his head. The smooth line of his chin caught in the firelight and Thorn fought an unusual urge to run her fingers along his jaw.

Her face burnt with shame as she drew her hands behind her back. *Rex has returned, and all I can think of is this stranger?*

Joel bent down and whispered something in Lucile's ear. She darted off, unable to resist pulling one final foul face at Thorn before she disappeared into the throng.

Now free of his daughter, Joel settled himself beside her on the carriage seat, where only moments ago Rex had slumped. Thorn fingered her pin, feeling the prick of the gauge nail in her pinkie.

"You're Thorn, right? Nicholas' daughter?"

She nodded, her heart clenching. She did not want to hear anything more about her father's curse tonight, especially from a man who seemed so kindly spoken. "If you wish to have words about my father, I shall be on my way. Ill words spoken between Stokers will not improve our situation."

"I've no mind to berate you, Miss Thorn. I've been seeking you out for a month now, but you're awfully difficult to pin down. If you're not busy with the animals or training with the Gast, you're with Lurgo Riley, who shoots daggers from his eyes every time I approach. But I've found you now. I wish to ask your opinion on a matter."

Joel picked up the discarded platter of meat and offered it to her. Thorn took a piece and bit into the soft, fatty flesh. Her stomach growled and juice dribbled down her chin as she grabbed for another.

"Which matter is this?"

Joel dug a thin metal plate from his pocket and placed it on the seat beside her. Thorn wiped her hand on her lapel and picked it up, turning it over and feeling the rows of bumps.

"I found this in the Clegg carriage."

She gasped. "You went inside that?" The carriage was the one that had carried the last of the Stokers from London to Graveyard following Brunel's defeat. The children whispered that it was haunted, and hardly anyone dared approach it.

Joel's lips drew into a roguish grin. "Finnegan

O'Hagan challenged me to spend the night inside. Childish, I know, but I'm not one to back down from a dare. There was a fine bottle of whisky at stake. I found that plate wedged into the floor grate. It was probably left there by one of the Stokers when they came from London. I've cleaned it off as best I can."

"What *is* ?"

He frowned. "Did your father ever show you the original plates from Engine Ward? General Babbage's machines were controlled by means of these plates, even the highly technical movements of the Boilers were programmed on plates like these. No other engineer has ever been able to replicate this system. Did you father never show you a plate like this?"

Thorn rubbed rust from the enamelled corners. "I was only a few months old when my parents died. He never told me anything. Do you mean this is—"

"—a plate to control a machine? It could be. All the plates were supposed to have been destroyed when the Engine Ward was burned, so no one has ever seen one. Very few people in Brunel's cabinet had access to these plates – just Brunel, Babbage, and your father, Nicholas."

"You think this plate belonged to my father?"

"It might explain how it came to be on the carriage, if your father gave it to your mother before he went to kill Brunel. If this is what I think it is, it could be the key to recreating some of Brunel's technology. That would be invaluable to the Stokers. It might be the thing we need to restore ourselves in the eyes of the country. But first I must figure out what it does, what its purpose is."

Thorn ran her fingers over the rows of bumps, her chest heavy as she thought of her father holding this same plate. "If it is instructions for a machine, shouldn't you just be able to read it?"

"But these symbols are not letters. Thorn, I'm wondering if Brunel and your father used a code."

"Why would the Metal Messiah want instructions to the machines recorded in code? His machines were designed for people to use, and many people cannot even read simple letters. How would they know which instructions were which?"

"That is what has me so perplexed. I think there's something on this plate Brunel wanted kept secret. I thought perhaps your father might have left something behind, some other information—"

"All his effects were either burnt in London or confiscated by your uncles." She placed the plate back into his palm, and he quickly pushed it down in his pocket again. "Have you talked to Oswald or Gabriel about it?"

Joel leaned forward, casting her in shadow, so his silhouette was ringed with fire. "I don't think you understand. No one must know about this code yet."

"Why not? It's ours, part of Stoker history, right?"

"Because..." and here his voice dropped so low she leaned right over and his whiskers brushed her cheek. The sensation sent jolts of electricity down her spine. "...it could be dangerous in the wrong hands, and I have to be sure what it does before I hand it over to the likes of Oswald. The Stokers already hate your father for killing Brunel. If they found out he had a code, that he kept secrets from them, can you imagine their reaction?"

She nodded. "They'd kill me."

"And worse. They'd string your body from the gate. They'd take your hands and your heart so you could never enter the Station of Life. Their hatred runs deep, Thorn, and now that you're a woman, you walk a knife edge."

She shuddered, thinking of what Rex had revealed back at the Turret. *You don't know how true that is, Joel Williams.* "Why would Father have kept secrets? Aren't we all in the same graveyard here, so to speak?"

"I don't know. But I'm not about to get either of us killed for my curiosity. Now I trust you not to tell either." Joel's eyes penetrated hers.

He left then, and in the abrupt shift between surprise and loneliness Thorn caught a whiff of him. He smelt ... pleasant. Deep and somehow spiced, a taste on the tip of her tongue that had nothing to do with the usual smells of Graveyard. It reminded her of something she'd smelt or eaten in her childhood in London.

Oswald and Rex would likely be scheming all night. She grabbed up the platter and stepped through the crowd. *Might as well take Aaron some of the tricorn meat I shot, seems as it'll be the last time I do. If Rex finishes before dawn he'll know where to find me.*

***

On her way to visit Aaron, Thorn went to check on the animals.

The southern corner of Graveyard rose a short distance above the fenland, and the ground here was more solid and less prone to flooding. Thorn and Aaron had constructed pens and fenced off sections of the hillock, and the Stokers raised their own chickens, pheasants, deer and dogs. To many in Graveyard it seemed a fruitless task; the tiny birds were labour intensive to rear and scarcely fed six souls apiece, though the eggs were always welcome at the men's breakfast.

The noise of revelry rose from the cooking fires,

wafting over the silent city. Thorn caught snorts of laughter, snippets of conversation, the familiar smash of tankards against each other. Inside her head she heard different voices – shivering chickens, longing for a dry bed of hay; worried dogs, not knowing what had become of their master.

From her perch on the gatepost Thorn gazed beyond the city of scraps, where the luminescent orbs of the will o' the wisp danced over the stagnant waters. Across the fenland she heard the distinct warble of a male tricorn. From up here the wasteland seemed almost tranquil.

Wind, Aaron's favourite greyhound, nudged her boot with his nose. She tossed him a scrap of tricorn meat, which he swallowed in one gulp. He nudged her again, begging for more.

She sighed. "They'll be naught for you anymore, my friend. My hunting days are over."

It wasn't *fair*. But the Stokers didn't believe in fair. They believed in omens and curses, and most of them still believed in Brunel, whom Thorn's father had killed. No one knew why Nicholas Thorne had turned on his master, not even Thorn, because he too had died in the blaze that toppled the Engine Ward. But the Stokers would sooner assume her father's death a punishment for treachery than contemplate that maybe, just *maybe*, Nicholas Thorne had a good reason for what he'd done. Maybe he wasn't a traitor. Maybe they were wrong about him, and wrong about Thorn.

Quartz believed that. And so did Aaron, and a few others. But they were the minority, especially now that Aaron was ill and Oswald had control over Graveyard again. And now that Rex had returned with his wild plans to restore the Stokers, and Joel's secret plate lay ready to threaten her life, Thorn wondered how safe she was amongst her own people.

Thorn sighed. Her greatest hope – to prove her father's innocence – slipped ever further away. If she couldn't control her sense, couldn't learn to channel the connections between her mind and others, she would never find a way to learn the truth about her father.

Joel Williams' plate could hold the answer, or it could damn Father and me forever.

Wind nudged her leg again. At least he understood. Aaron had sensed Wind's mind so often that man and dog worked as one, and Thorn could connect to him without even thinking about it. Wind's mind reached out to her, and she entered it, feeling his memories, his concerns, and his hunger. She threw him another chunk of meat.

"If only every mind was as simple as yours, Wind." She scratched him behind the ears. His wide eyes regarded her drawn face. He barked once, and she stood up. The string between their minds snapped away, and Thorn was once again alone inside her head.

"Try not to worry – Aaron is strong. He won't leave you, and nor will I. I'll be back tomorrow, I promise." She waved to the animals and jogged off towards the smokehouse.

A small Rothwell carriage outside the western boundary was used as the smokehouse. Medicinal care was in the claws of Old Hatchie, a toothless crone with a hunched back and a distasteful odour whose solution to most ailments consisted of a draught of mecks and a night in the smokehouse.

Old Hatchie stood guard outside, hunched over an overturned barrel puffing on a pipe. A mountain of peat cuttings leaned against the side of the carriage, ready to stoke the smoking fires. She set down the pipe and grinned her toothless smile as Thorn approached.

"He's been expecting you," she croaked. "Try to get him to drink something. He's refusing his medicine again, the poxy bastard."

Thorn smiled. Aaron was always a sensible man.

She ducked inside and approached Aaron's bed at the far end of the smokehouse, under a grimy window so he could look at the stars. His once broad frame shivered under the threadbare blankets, and his dry, ashy skin crackled as he turned to face her. Thorn set the platter at the foot of his bed and knelt beside him, holding his matted hair back from his face as he coughed and spluttered.

"How was the hunt?" he croaked.

"Terrible, but that's not important now. Aaron, Rex has returned."

The old man's eyes grew wide, and the corners of his mouth stretched into a smile, the effort splitting his parched lips. "My son? Is he well?"

Thorn nodded. "Well enough. He'll come see you as soon as he's finished business with Oswald."

"As right he should." Aaron coughed again, cloaking the sound with his sleeve. "Why does he have business with Oswald? What news does he bring from London? How does he seem?"

"Like he's walked through the fires of hell. He's says the Engine Ward is being rebuilt. He thinks Brunel might have returned, although how that is possible I don't know."

Aaron's eyes fluttered shut. He said nothing for a long time. A friend of her father's since long before her birth, Aaron had been gravely mistreated by Brunel and was the only Stoker who openly denounced the Metal Messiah's godhood. Aaron and Thorn's father had been close friends, and had worked together to stop Brunel's most insidious plans. When the Stokers were banished to the swamps, Aaron became their leader, and his family the most important one in all of Graveyard. Aaron had always looked after Thorn, trying to change the minds of the Stokers about her. He'd encouraged her and Rex's relationship, and Thorn knew he hoped that together they would one day lead the Stokers together. But now that he had taken ill, his brother Oswald was in charge, and if what Rex was saying was true, Aaron's hopes for the future of the Stokers grew dimmer.

Finally, Aaron opened his eyes again. "Rex will inform me in his own time, I assume. Meanwhile, he is not by my side, and you are. Tell me about the hunt. Were you able to sense the beast?"

"I think I caught one tricorn, but the second fell through my senses. We lost a Gast-Engine because of my foolishness."

His bright eyes bore into hers. "You need to concentrate more. You can't expect to control the power overnight, little Thorn. It took me years to master it enough to control large beasts."

"I don't *have* years. They'll find any excuse to be rid of me. They've already thrown me off the hunt. If I make one more mistake…" *Or if anyone discovers that plate…*

"Nonsense. My son has returned to marry you, so you've no reason to worry."

Thorn said nothing. She had hoped, of course. But Rex had barely looked at her all evening. He hadn't mentioned the marriage. And he was talking about returning to London.

Aaron's eyes twinkled. "Don't look at me like that. It will happen. I know my son, and he loves you."

Thorn nodded, her heart fluttering. *He's right. Rex*

promised, and he would never go back on a promise. He did come home. He came home to me.

"I'm placing you on dragon watch every morning from now on. You begin at seventh bell."

"What? I can't—"

"You *can.*" Aaron coughed again, gesturing at his convulsing belly. "Look at me, Thorn. I can barely stand anymore. I can't keep guard over this place forever, you know." He lowered his voice, and Thorn could barely hear his words over the crackling furnace and the moans of the other patients. "I'm weak inside these iron walls, Thorn. I can feel myself fading, my power slipping. If I have a few hours respite every day, perhaps I'll grow strong again."

She stared at her feet, frightened that her very presence might be drawing his power away. "Wind misses you, and so do I."

"Tell Wind I miss him too," he replied, patting her hand. "And that he's to stay strong, and concentration is the key to his success. And that he's not to frighten those chickens, otherwise their meat will go tough."

She smiled, standing up and letting go of his hand. "I will. Goodnight Aaron."

"Goodnight, little Thorn."

***

Either Rex had forgotten where Thorn's room was, or he had indeed stayed up past dawn, for Thorn rolled over at the sixth bell and discovered she was alone. A memory tugged at her brain, an image of a shadowed face, and the smell of spice against her skin. Perhaps Rex had not been the man in her dreams last night?

She pulled her damp coat over her tunic, and wrapped

a threadbare wool blanket around her legs, securing the ends with her pin. She pulled her tangled hair from under the net and stared at her crumbled, soot-smeared face in the scrap of brass leaning against the wall. She wouldn't be allowed to bathe again until next month, and could hardly remember what she looked like underneath the grime. *Maybe Rex remembers*, she thought and she rubbed at the soot on her cheeks.

The night before he left for London they'd crawled into this same room – not really a room at all, but a low space between the third storey and the lighting rig in the Turret. Oswald had given Thorn watch duty, and Rex snuck away from the Williams' carriages – as he usually did – to keep her company.

"It will be alright, you'll see. I'll come back to visit after exams."

"No you won't. You can't risk being discovered. Once you're inside the city, you have to stay there. This is goodbye, Rex."

He sighed. "I made you something."

She set down the candle and he pressed a cold object into her hand.

"It's a pin. I figured you'd snag a necklace."

Thorn brought the pin into the candlelight. She sucked in her breath as she traced her fingers over the intricate moulded cross and engine mount, made from sharp-ended gauge nails and delicate clockwork gears. She squealed in delight as her finger hit the tiny gauge lever and it moved.

She threw her arms around him, knocking the candle sconce. The candle rolled and flickered, but didn't go out.

"I love it. I shall wear it always."

He took the pin from her and fastened it inside her

lapel, over her heart.

"Watch you don't stab yourself when you sleep, eh?" he said as he righted the candle.

Thorn started to sob.

"Why must you go?"

"You know why." He stroked her cheek. "We can't sit around this scrap heap our entire lives, waiting for England to forgive us so we can have lives again. We have no future in the swamp, Thorn. But if I go to school, I can find work in one of the engineering sects. I can work my way up. I can have influence. Maybe that will be enough to bring us out of the shadows. Even Quartz says an education is the best weapon I have now the Navvies control the railway contracts."

"So Quartz says."

"Hey...hey, I trust the old gammy. And so did you, until they chose me. You...oh Thorn..." He wrapped both arms around her, pulling her back onto the rough blankets. Something sharp pricked her heart.

"You won't come back. No one else would come back."

"*I'll* come back." His hands stroked her hair, ran along her back, over her shoulder, clutching at her hips, grasping at her chest, searching to fill that ache in her heart.

Somehow his lips found hers, and she was no longer sobbing but moaning softly, and that pain swelled and flooded her body, weighting her limbs and slacking her muscles. She was drowning into him.

"Thorn?" His breath came out in short rasps.

"Mmm-hmm?"

"That pin ... it's an engagement present."

"You mean ..."

"I've already talked to Quartz. When I return we shall

have the ceremony."

That night they spoke no more goodbyes, but fought away their sorrow with touch and breath and kiss. Quartz had known, of course, for he didn't relieve Thorn's duty till tenth bell, when Rex had already clambered away.

Quartz regarded her sleep-ringed eyes with a knowing smile, and poured himself another tankard of mecks.

For weeks afterwards Thorn felt Rex's fingers in her hair, his breath on her neck, the taste of him on her tongue. But weeks turned into months and the sensations faded. The date of his exams passed by, and weeks, and months, and the heavy pin over her heart seemed to drag her down into the mud. She donned the mourning cloak, the black of the fabric cloaking her in shadow, impermeable to touch. She feared she'd never feel again.

And just as her heart had begun to heal, he came back. Last night. And his skin felt so different and his eyes looked so hollow. *And he hasn't mentioned the engagement, has he?*

Thorn tugged on the rats' nest in her hair. It was early yet, and he'd only just found out about Aaron's illness. Rex had a lot on his mind, and he'd likely be returning to London within the month. And he wanted her there too. The thought both excited and terrified her. On the one hand, it was a chance to see England beyond the Graveyard, to feel stone beneath her feet, to smell and touch the threads of her early memories.

On the other, if what Rex said was true and Brunel had truly returned ... what would the Messiah make of her, the daughter of his murderer?

Maybe he'd explain why Father betrayed him, and what's written on that coded plate? Then everyone would discover it was all part of his master plan all along, and that my father is no turncoat, and there'd be no more mutterings about curses. Maybe it will be the best thing that's ever happened to me. If *Oswald allows me to go.*

Her heart sank. Of course it was folly to even imagine it. They'd never allow her on such an important mission.

Thorn slunk out of the Turret, anxious to find something to eat before her first dragon watch. Quartz spat from the crow's nest and waved at her. "Bring me some porridge and two pints of mecks!" he yelled over the howling wind.

A thin mist cloaked the surrounding fenland, almost ethereal if not for the sinister way it inched forward, icy fingers twisting through the carriages. Thorn shuffled through the crumbling carriages, her mind on London.

Please, Great Conductor, let me go with them. Please. I never ask for anything...just this one thing. Let me go to London with Rex.

A small group of men gathered around the fire drums, clutching their enamel tableware and rubbing sleepy eyes. Only fifty or so were awake already, but Thorn saw more shadows moving over the scrap heaps.

Usually, Thorn ate with the women and children at seventh bell, when the compies had caught the scent of food and drove down on the fires in force. The compies were a new pest, brought to England at the turn of the century from Germany by an English explorer who'd noted their lithe, reptilian bodies, delicate tapered skulls and clawed forelimbs and decided they must be *Attorcroppes*– snakelike fairies in the English legends who walked upright on hind legs and guarded bogs and waterways. His pet Attorcroppe caused such a stir in London he was soon importing the animals for other wealthy families. By the time anyone realised that the tiny dragons bred like wildfire and gnawed through wood and metal with alarming efficiency, they'd engulfed the rat population and taken up residence as England's primary disease-carrying vermin.

Compies thrived in the fenland, feasting on the bugs and small rodents. They were similar in size to the common rats and twice as nimble. They would push off with their strong hind legs and leap at the women, tiny reptilian jaws snapping for a morsel of food, their clawed hands scrabbling for a hold. The women always carried brooms and walking canes to beat away the tiny sprites.

Thorn saw their curious yellow eyes peeking between the gauge tracks, but knew they wouldn't approach the fires while the men ate. Even the vermin obeyed the Stoker laws.

Thorn crouched behind an old trolley and peeked around the corner of the ROTHWELL & CO. 4-2-4T engine, a monster locomotive and carriage that rose twelve feet above those around it, forming the central focus of the Graveyard. The heavy carriage buckled in the centre and rust widened the gash through her belly, but still she looked magnificent. Hung all around with paraffin lamps and riveted with silver pins, she housed the Chancellor and his family. If Aaron was still Chancellor Thorn would live there with Rex, instead of in the Turret with Quartz.

Bill Riley – Aaron's brother-in-law by marriage and Lurgo's father – jogged past her hiding-place and glared at the threadbare curtains covering the gash. He'd been quick to put his name forward for the Chancellorship after Aaron stepped down. When the position had passed to Oswald – Aaron's elder brother – the Rileys had been forced to give up their finer carriages and take up more modest lodgings on the outskirts of the

Williams territory. *Are you and Lurgo enjoying your new accommodation, Mr. Riley? Where are your clean clothes and rust-free platters now?*

Thorn couldn't stand the majority of Aaron's family, who came from the old priesthood of the Engine Ward and spoke of Brunel with more reverence even than Great Conductor himself. It was the Williams who stirred up the Stokers to hate Nicholas Thorne and bestowed upon his descendents the blood curse that Thorn now carried. Their continued meddling had become too much for Aaron, who'd resigned his position as Chancellor in the wake of his illness rather then face their farcical claims that his sickness was a punishment from Great Conductor for his continued heresy against the Metal Messiah.

Thorn leaned out further, trying to see what was happening at the fires. A brave compie scurried from a rusted pressure valve by her head, hurtling down the scrap pile in a suicide mission towards the vat of porridge boiling over the fire.

Thorn shifted so it wouldn't scratch her. When it noticed her, the compie squeaked in protest and tried to back up the pile towards his hiding place.

With a snap, her mind connected with the rodent. Suddenly, her head exploded with porridge – every sense, every pore focused on that bubbling vat of deliciousness. The compie let out a frightened squeak – he'd found Thorn's dark thoughts.

"Sssh." Thorn raised her finger to her lips, trying to will the compie to obey her. Unheeding, the compie's yellow eyes grew wide and it let out a gulping cry, scrambling towards the fire drums with its tiny arms grasping at midair and its tail slapping in the mud.

The connection tore, but it was too late. Several of

the men looked up and frowned at her. Thorn saw Rex in discussion with Oswald and Finnegan. He inclined his head in her direction, then returned to his conversation.

Thorn jumped down from the scraps and folded herself amongst the men. She heard a few grumbles, but mostly they ignored her. Rex's return was of more interest than the cursed girl.

Joel and another man stirred the giant vat of porridge. His face lit into a smile as he saw her, and she grabbed a long-handled shovel and went to help him.

"I hope our next shipment arrives in time," he said as he pressed his shoulder into the handle and dug through the sludgy mess. "We'll be on rations soon if the stores aren't replenished."

"A fine morning to you too, Mr. Williams."

"Forgive me, Thorn. We're all a little on edge this morning."

The porridge began to sputter and bubble. Spoons clanged on enamel bowls as Stokers clamoured around, ready for first served breakfast. Thorn gritted her teeth and lifted her shovel, and spoons and hands scraped it clean of porridge.

When all present chatter had descended into impolite chewing, Oswald stood up. A hundred pairs of eyes drew up his body as he cleared his throat and gave a succinct attempt at a rousing speech.

"Brothers, Great Conductor saw fit to return Rex to us. As we welcome him back into Graveyard with open hearts, we also welcome his news and his challenge. In a few weeks time, Queen Victoria unveils the Great Exhibition, a grand spectacle of engineering wonders from around the world, the likes of which has never before been seen. Engineers and their followers are flocking to London from all corners of the earth, and the city bursts at her britches with filthy Navvies. Wretched Stephenson will be the star of London's exhibitors. It is believed he will be revealing some kind of new technology."

The men banged their spoons against their enamel plates and hissed their disapproval.

"Rex has secured work for a small party within the Exhibition Hall. We will send our best men to infiltrate the Navvy camp and discover the nature of Stephenson's latest mechanical monstrosity."

Murmurs passed between men. They hadn't expected to be reopening the Gauge War with covert investigating. "Don't we have more pressing issues than Stephenson?" mumbled Bill Riley. His friends shushed him.

"Why must we lose more good men to that cursed city?"

"What will this achieve? The Navvies *won* the Gauge War. Technologically, they're decades in front of us now that Brunel's machines have been destroyed. How will learning about their new technology be of benefit to us?" Edgar called out.

"You want five men with no military training to infiltrate Stephenson's camp? If they are caught we cannot expect the Navvies to show any mercy. The last I heard they caught poor Davey after Oswald sent him up to spy on Forth Street Works, and they skinned him alive and hung him outside the gates for a week."

"Who will be chosen for this suicide party?" Joel asked in a clear voice.

Oswald held up his hands. "Rex has requested these men especially." He squinted into the sea of faces. "Gabriel. Finnegan, Joel," Thorn heard a sharp intake of breath, "Lurgo, Edgar and ..." He stared at the clouds and rolled his eyes. "That is all."

Thorn's heart stopped. She knew he was supposed to say her name, but he didn't. She wouldn't be going to London. She wouldn't go anywhere, ever again. Her one chance to clear her father's name, to investigate that strange plate, snapped away like a fresh sapling under the stomp of a tricorn.

I have to do something.

"I should go too!" she called, louder than she'd intended.

Heads turned to stare at her, frowning and muttering in angry tones. Joel's hand rested on her shoulder.

"I can operate a Gast as good as any man, and use my sense," she mumbled, staring at her mismatched boots. "And if the Navvies catch me, there's no one to mourn my death."

"This isn't your business," Oswald snapped. "We don't send a woman to do a soldier's job."

Thorn looked around at the filthy men. "Soldiers? I see no soldiers here."

"You'll hold your tongue, cursed one."

Thorn bristled at the insult. "Quartz said I was to go to London. Rex heard him say it, didn't you Rex?"

Rex's stone face flickered with emotion - sadness, or was it annoyance? He stepped back and shook his head, slowly. His eyes – once bright, now cold and grey – never left Thorn's face.

Why is he staring at me with such hatred... Thorn didn't understand, *couldn't* understand how the man she was meant to marry would not allow her to accompany him, how he could return and not even *speak* to her, save his friendly greeting at the gate?

What did I do wrong? What has happened to change his love so?

Thorn stepped back, her face stinging as though she'd been slapped. She tripped on her boot and collapsed against Joel, who lifted her under the arms and steadied her. She slumped against him, the fight gone from her body. The men turned away, satisfied the matter had been taken care of.

"Thorn?" Joel whispered.

"I...I..." She wanted to run, to collapse into Wind's soft fur and release her tears. But her legs felt leaden, clamping her in place.

Rex nodded to Oswald, silently asking for permission to speak. He stepped forward and pulled his heavy cloak further on his shoulders. His skin had regained some of its colour, and the wounds on his face no longer wept blood. He'd trimmed his hair since yesterday, and it framed his face in dark, matted strands.

He looked down at his feet as he spoke. "I know you'd all gladly follow me to London, brothers, but your hands are needed here, to keep our people alive and fed. We have many secret weapons that cannot be revealed for risk of destroying our entire operation. I promise I will not lose another party. You've been waiting nineteen years to return to London. I ask only that you sharpen your stakes and wait another few months."

Heads bobbed, and there was a smattering of applause. Thorn regained feeling in her legs, and she stepped forward, wanting to talk to Rex, but he and Oswald disappeared into the Rothwell. Sighing, she picked up the shovel again. *I might as well make myself useful.*

As men jostled her and drew their spoons and bowls through the congealing sludge, Thorn listened carefully to their conversation. Amongst general grumblings at her presence and her uncouth outburst, she heard other resentments and rumours. The men ignored her, the way they normally did their women.

"Bloody London's turned his balls soft. We need to escape this cursed swamp, not indulge in more skulking in corners and spying on the Navvies."

"He's not telling Oswald everything. There'll be a bloodbath by the end of this, guaranteed, lads. Or else Rex isn't of Aaron's blood."

"Pity he didn't return two months earlier. He could've been Chancellor instead of Oswald."

"Not if I had anything to say about it." That was Bill Riley. "You know he was engaged to Nicholas' spawn—argh!"

Thorn apologised profusely, making a candid attempt to wipe the hot porridge off Bill Riley's balding head. Joel smiled at her.

"Your own son wants to marry me also," she said. "Or have you forgotten?"

"You stupid girl! What are you doing here? Your time for breakfast isn't until seventh bell!"

"I have every right to be here," Thorn shot back. "You don't own this peat."

Joel shot her a pained glance. She'd given great insult by insinuating Bill Riley thought of ownership.

Bill raised his hand, drawing his face into a scowl. Thorn braced herself for reprimand, but it never came.

"Back off, dad." Lurgo glared at his father.

Bill spat at Thorn. His spittle rolled down her coat, leaving a trail of half-chewed oat husks. Her cheeks burned at the insult, but the warmth of Joel's hand in the small of her back and the fire in Lurgo's eyes reassured her. The men looked to Bill Riley, wondering if he would break protocol and admonish his son in front of them.

"There'll be words later, boy." Bill snatched his bowl

from Joel and stomped off. Some of the men chuckled as they held out their plates. Thorn's face still burned, so she handed her shovel to Joel.

"I've a job to attend. See you later."

"Thorn, wait—"

She dodged under Joel's grasp, but Lurgo wrapped his arms around her middle.

"Don't you want to sit with us?" Lurgo dropped his voice. "I wanted to talk to you."

"Later." Thorn dashed off towards the animal pens, the warmth of Joel's hand still clinging to her back.

***

JAMES HOLMAN'S MEMOIRS, FIRST EDITION

While Rex made his plans and Thorn tended her duties in Graveyard, I was a world away, sailing along the coast of Africa, a distinguished guest on board a trading vessel bound for London.

Like so many other maimed soldiers, I had no fixed abode and no regular job. I had given up a pension and apartments with the Naval Knights of Windsor to pursue a life of carefree vagabonding. I took work where and when it came to me, provided it contained an element of extreme danger and carried me off to undiscovered lands. On this particular mission I was under contract to George Wombwell, proprietor of Wombwell's Travelling Menagerie – the finest collection of wild bestiary and freakish curios in all of England. After I'd successfully trapped two juvenile tricorns from the southwest fens and brought him a shipment of neckers from the Ukraine, Wombwell declared me the perfect candidate to travel to Africa to secure a rhinoceros.

I failed miserably in my task, for trade riches had corrupted the villages along the Nile, and no native hunter would capture a live beast for the paltry sum Wombwell offered. They found it more lucrative to slaughter the beasts in a most brutal fashion, keep the meat for themselves and sell the ivory horns to the trade ships.

I considered funding a hunt from my own pocket, but two hijackings while en route through Ethiopia made short work of my savings. I knew Wombwell would not begrudge me this defeat, owing to the number of strange and wonderful specimens I'd brought back for him. Among my belongings were stashed several multi-coloured snakes, a crate of marmosets, and an African spurred tortoise inside an empty wine barrel.

The thought of returning to London greatly excited me. News of the Great Exhibition of the Works of Industry of All Continents had reached me, even in the darkest recess of Africa. Letters from my London colleagues arrived in the port city of Lagos months after they were dispatched; the embossed letters bent and misshapen and gritty with salt.

They told of the excitement in London, of the newly opened ports overflowing with rich tourists, of the hundreds of men camped in Hyde Park, working around the clock to erect the Crystal Palace, and the Palace's mysterious designer and foreman, known only by his title – the Royal Engineer. My good friend Charles Darwin (a man of such unquestionable brilliance, I'm certain one day he'll be a God) had already secured me a ticket for the opening ceremony.

England had been closed off to the world for so long.

Even though the French blockade had broken down, relationships between Industrian England and Christian Europe were still strained. With this new venture, Queen Victoria hoped to once again establish England as a nation of brilliant minds and world leaders. And judging by the popularity of advanced ticket sales, the rest of the world was listening.

The letters weren't all positive. My more conservative acquaintances worried about peace in the city with the massive influx of visitors – especially as each engineer would bring a contingent of ambitious priests and fanatical followers. The Queen had already recalled four regiments from France to keep the swell of religion under control.

Karl Marx had even publicly denounced the Great Exhibition, citing it as "an emblem of Industrian fetishism of commodities." Loathing Marx as I did, this only spurred my enthusiasm.

My heart beat with excitement just to think of it. I had spent the last two years in the company of savages and crooked ivory dealers, and I longed to return to the world of science, however fraught with pious madmen it had now become. My curious nature simply would not allow me to miss such an important event – my observations of the engineers and their various contraptions would make a distinguished chapter in my latest book. I packed my meagre possessions, brushed the flies out of my hair one final time, and booked passage on the next ship back to London.

The vessel – a English cutter crewed by the usual sort of good-natured rogues – left Lagos in rough seas, weighed down with palm oil, spices, ivory and one blind adventurer. Despite the wretched conditions and weevil-infested cuisine, the amicable crew made for a pleasant voyage. They enlisted my help on the lanyards, despite my blindness.

We stopped in Marseilles to offload some of our pricier merchandise. Ever since the Britain had been able to trade openly once more, it was as if the whole of Europe was undergoing a renaissance. Luxury goods travelled between all the major ports, and colonists set out to reclaim some of Britain's lost empire. After years of hostilities, ports like Marseilles were beginning to welcome English trade.

It was here a young Frenchman bought passage to London. The captain berthed him in the cabin alongside mine, so I felt it only polite to invite him for a smoke. He sat on my bunk while I unwrapped the glass *nargila* from my travelling case and set it up on the floor. I instructed him to fill the water jar from the pitcher on my nightstand, while I measured the tobacco into the bowl and covered it with the metal screen, placing the coals on top.

We passed the hose between us for a time. He spoke with perfect English, though he sounded young, not a day past twenty. He wanted to know about my adventures, and I told him what I could.

"Are you to stay in London?" I asked him.

"*Oui*. I join my father in the priesthood," he said

"Ah, you are a Dirigire?"

"*Oui,* Holman, although I shall not be travelling on to Meliora for some time. I studied at the academy in Paris, and now my father wishes me to assist with his clockmaking business in London. Your Queen has requested he provide a lavish display for the Great Exhibition, and he fears he will not have the pieces ready in time. You know about the Great Exhibition?"

"Yes, I've already secured a ticket."

He seemed delighted. "Then you shall see my work displayed there. We Dirigires are to have our own exhibit in the Crystal Palace."

"Have you ever visited London before?"

"I was born there. My father had taken over the London shop from his father. When the fighting entered London and Brunel sabotaged the *Thunderer*, he sent my mother and I to Paris, ordering us to never return unless he expressly requested it. He gave us money for my schooling and even came to visit us in Paris once, but he would not allow me to return to London, until now. He told me the Queen has decided to reopen Brunel's city railways along the Wall. Did you know of this?"

I shook my head.

"Not all the lines, of course – just those running from the well-to-do neighbourhoods to the Hyde Park station, and the circle line atop the old Wall. With the thousands of visitors flocking from all over, I expect London doesn't want to be seen as behind the railway race. She's put her Royal Engineer in charge, and to save time and expense, he's keeping Brunel's broad gauge rails."

I should have read the clues right then, but I did not. I could not foresee the horror awaiting me in my beloved city. I slept well that night, dreaming of London – the London that once was, and that I hoped would be again.

***

Rex busied himself with preparations all week. During the daylight hours he sequestered himself in the Rothwell with Oswald and the other elders, and he and Quartz schemed through the nights. When Thorn returned from dragon watch and tending the animals in the evening she managed to steal only a couple of minutes with Rex, while Quartz tinkered with the lens and mixed the vat of mecks he brewed in the bowels of the Turret. He evaded her questions about London, his resolve concentrated on the mission ahead. Rex made no mention of the engagement, and his touch remained frigid.

When Rex crawled into bed in the early hours of the morning, she would press her body to his, trying to recreate that steam-engine hissing inside her. They kissed, but his lips soon grew slack and fatigue dragged his arms from her embrace. He apologised profusely, but she couldn't shake the feeling something irreplaceable had been lost.

Beside Rex, Thorn slept fitfully, the few fleeting memories of London assailing her in dreams. Shadowed figures chased her through narrow alleys, and everywhere she turned she caught the glint of metal under the moonlight. She swam through soot and steam that tugged like an ocean tide, pulling her towards the iron monstrosity that was the half-completed London Wall, surrounding her dreams with towering pylons and turning, chugging, *living* gears. When her terror reached its peak her assailant threw off his hood, and it would be Rex, smiling and beckoning her with his arms open. But when she reached up to kiss him, his face would morph into Joel's, or – worse – Lurgo's. *Bleaach.*

She gagged just thinking about it.

Her morning stints on dragon watch did nothing to relieve her worry. The dragons hunted in the surrounding swamps, stalking their prey in packs of threes and fives. They could smell the cooking fires and human meat of the Graveyard. None of the Stoker technologies could yet locate their camouflaged skin hiding in the fenland. And – though they kept the fences in good repair – the dragons were clever, and the borders of Graveyard lay vulnerable to their attack. Only Aaron's all-seeing mind stood between the dragons and their human prey.

Aaron normally performed dragon watch alone, his mind strong enough to perceive the great creatures even as he slept. If ever he sensed them closing in, he could drive them away again with a simple thought. But if he needed Thorn's weak mind to assist him, he was in worse health than anyone realised. And that meant Graveyard was in great danger.

Thorn sat on the hill with her animals, trying to cast out her thoughts to focus on the expanse before her. She bit her tongue, hoping the pain would drive her to concentrate. At midday she would end her watch, drained and frustrated and not having sensed a single dragon. She hoped that meant none were nearby.

If Aaron could sense her difficulty, he did not show it. When she visited him again he gushed over her progress and gave her a second watch, for two hours after dinner each evening.

Thorn tried a different tactic for her second watch. After tending the animals and gulping down a quick dinner she would roam over the expanse of the Stoker territory, sucking in lungfuls of the rank, thick air. She tried to cast her mind back through her dreams, but all her memories were clouded by the steam and soot, as if the dirt penetrated even her very thoughts. She let the air and the dirt and the fog lead her. Twice she caught glimmers of creatures waiting in the fog, but the thoughts flittered away as fast as they had come.

On the last such stroll before Rex's company was to depart for London, Thorn took a walk along the edge of the swamp, to try to clear her head. Lurgo trailed after her. "Why are you always wandering around? Oswald thinks you're slacking off your chores."

"I'm not slacking off, I'm thinking. Last I checked, that wasn't against Stoker rules."

"Where's your husband?"

"He's not my husband, yet. And if you're trying to sound jealous, you've succeeded."

"Hey, I can't help it that you've no idea what you missed out on. Hey—" He entered stride alongside her, and dropped his voice. "Don't you think this whole mission seems a little...strange?"

"How so?"

"Why has Rex asked for so many of our best men? If I'm gone, and you're off the hunt, that only leaves Quartz who can work the Gast-Engines. So who is going to hunt? And why is Quartz stockpiling three times his usual amount of scrap iron? Why can I see Rex's shadow moving around inside the Turret each night?"

"You've been spying on Rex?"

"Dad says he's up to something, and I agree. And if anyone knows, it's you. Go on, Thorn. Tell me. You know I'd tell you."

She knelt down, pretending to tie her bootlace. Lurgo dropped beside her, no salacious smile on his lips, no surreptitious stroking of her hand this time. *He may be annoying, but he's my only friend apart from Rex and Quartz, and I trust him.*

"I presume Rex plans to tell everyone once you're close to London, but you must swear you can't tell a soul until then." He nodded, his features drawn. "The Metal Messiah has returned."

His eyes lit up.

"But you can't say anything."

60

"Not even to your new swain?"

"*Obviously* Rex knows—"

Lurgo pointed. Joel was jogging along the fence line, his dark eyes darting between the engines as he called her name. Thorn's chest fluttered as she remembered her dreams.

She grabbed Lurgo's arm – probably the first time she'd ever initiated contact with him in recent months – and pulled him up. "Joel!"

"Thorn, I've been looking for you everywhere. Oswald wants to talk to you before supper."

Thorn's heart skipped. *He's letting me go to London!* She studied Joel's face, but his expression gave nothing away.

She glanced from one boy to the other. Lurgo stared at Joel with that same seething glare for which he always regarded Rex, and he pressed his fingers to his lips, sealing their pact. Joel's face creased with concern, and he offered Thorn his arm with such grace she could not refuse.

Lurgo shot him one final, depreciating look, and stomped off towards the Rothwell.

"What was that about?" Joel whispered, his breath brushing her neck.

I am not cold, so why am I shivering? She squeezed Joel's arm, grateful for his kindness. "Just…Lurgo being Lurgo. He's concerned about Rex."

"I see."

"Rex and I were engaged before he left for London." She sucked in a breath, nervous to voice her fears aloud. "And until last week, I thought he was dead. Now he's here, very much alive, and I should be *happy*. But he's different; uncharacteristically cold. It's as if he's forgotten everything."

"Do not think me cruel to say, but perhaps he has. It's

been nineteen years since I last saw that city, but I still have nightmares. Nine months trapped inside, it could change a man. And maybe you've changed too. You've mourned him, and now he's returned ... you're young still, Thorn. Some would say too young for marriage."

"I'm already twenty."

Joel smiled. "You are slight for your age, then. I'm sure when your time comes you will have no shortage of suitors."

Thorn snorted. "That's unlikely. Truthfully, marriage frightens me, but if I don't marry they will see no reason to keep me, especially not after I destroyed that Gast and spoke out of turn the other day. Quartz won't live forever, and he's the only one besides Lurgo who doesn't hate me."

"Not quite," Joel replied with a smile.

Her heart flipped. "What of your wife? Does she worry you'll no longer want her when you return from London?"

"Isobel and I were never wed. We were young and impulsive and very much in love. She died of cholera, two winters ago, when Lucile was just two weeks old."

Her cheeks flushed. "I'm sorry. Do you miss her?"

"Immeasurably, but one's heart cannot mourn for what has long passed into oblivion. If she returned tomorrow I would not know her, and I would be cold like Rex." He dropped her arm through his and held her hand, squeezing her cold fingers. "But enough talk of sadness and loss. We must see what Oswald wants."

***

Thorn was mistaken. What Oswald wanted was to yell at her, to threaten her with banishment if she didn't prove herself useful. He'd seen her sitting by the pens and wandering aimlessly through the Graveyard and mistook her efforts for indolence. She wanted to tell him about the dragon watch, but that would embarrass Aaron. He wouldn't want his brother to know he was weakening. It would give him the ammunition he needed to rob Aaron of even more of his power. So she stood stoic before Oswald's leather carriage seat, staring at the floorgrates and praying for the tirade to end.

She emerged an hour later to find Joel outside, still waiting for her. He must have heard every word. Her face flushed red.

Joel offered his arm, but as she took it, Thorn's exhaustion and fear overtook her and she collapsed into his chest.

"Everybody hates me," she sobbed.

"No, sssshhh, it's not true." His warm hand stroked her hair. She wrapped her arms around his chest and wept for the first time in months. She wept as though Rex had died all over again.

"I don't...want you to leave," she said, sniffling.

"I don't want to leave you like this either. But I have a duty to the Stokers, as do you."

"I should be going with you, with Rex. I'd be more use in London than here. We could figure out why Father wrote that plate."

He sighed. "I know. Thorn, I—"

Someone's throat cleared.

Thorn and Joel looked up, leaping from their embrace as though they had something to be guilty about. A stretched, tense shadow slouched against a scrapped engine chassis, his sunken face drawn into a scowl. It was Rex.

"If you're *quite* finished," he hissed at Joel. "We're

waiting for you."

Joel released Thorn's hand. "I suppose we're on our way then."

"I suppose so." Rex's voice seared the cool air.

Thorn wiped the tears from her eyes. "Goodbye."

Joel said nothing, but his eyes lingered on hers as he traipsed up the mud path, towards the Turret.

Rex held out his hand. "Come here."

Thorn obeyed, placing her hand in his. She was shaking.

He pushed her hair from her face, and his features softened. He almost, *almost* looked like the Rex of her memories.

"Thorn, I'm sorry for the way I've been acting. It's not proper of me. Much has been weighing heavy in my mind. Listen, I think it's best if we call off the engagement."

Every piece of Thorn's world stopped ticking, every bone and sinew in her body ceased to function. Her heart fell like lead into her stomach, and her hands shook with violence. Every fear she'd had, every nightmare and every insult she'd endured since he'd returned hit her body at once.

Rex kept staring at her with those cold eyes, his fingers stroking her jittering knuckles. "I'm so sorry, but I really think it's for the best. I've discussed it with Oswald, and he agrees. If Brunel has returned, my life will be in London now, but your duties will always be here, with the animals. Father's world – *your* world – and my world…they don't mix."

"And your father? You've talked to Aaron about this?"

Rex shook his head. "Oswald is the chancellor now. He makes decisions on these matters. And he's released me of my duties to you. But I'm sure Father would approve – this is for the good of the Stokers, Thorn.'

But—"

Rex held a finger over her mouth so she couldn't speak. "I'm so sorry, Thorn. I really have to leave now."

"No," she choked out, and said more loudly, 'No, no, no, no, NO!"

The tears came now, spilling over her in waves. She jerked her hand from his and beat her fists into his shoulder, all the while sobbing and screaming. "No, *no, no!*"

He let her sob and thrash and scream. Even though she knew it was over, even when she felt the tearing in her chest as her heart shattered, even as her love and hate for him exploded in her pounding skull, she couldn't bear to part from him. Finally, he wearied of her anguish and turned away, winding his way up the path, towards his freedom. Though she screamed for him, he didn't look back.

Thorn sank to her knees in the mud, wishing the earth would rise up and swallow her forever.

***

Thorn woke the next morning, alone. The ache in her heart hadn't eased overnight, and her face felt dry and hot from crying. The Turret was silent, save the echoing rumble of Quartz's snores. She dressed quickly and fumbled her way down to the kitchen. After lighting the lamp on the table, she found a dirty tankard resting beside the sink, and poured herself a mecks. It stung her throat on the way down, but there was no way she would make it through the day without it.

She wanted to crawl back into bed and hide on the

third-floor landing forever. Everyone would know, of course. If Rex hadn't told anyone before he left, they would have heard her crying last night; they would know that he'd broken off their engagement. They'd know she was cursed, so rotten no man could want her. Even Lurgo, the one person who could have given her solace, had left her for London.

Everyone leaves me. I truly am cursed.

Like a death-knell announcing her ruin, the seventh bell chimed. Thorn drained her drink and poured another.

I have to talk to Aaron.

Rex had said Aaron would agree with him. It didn't seem right. Aaron loved her, didn't he? He wanted her to be part of his family. He must know that if Rex didn't marry her, she would be cast out of Graveyard. He wanted to keep her close, to pass down his secrets. *Didn't he?*

I'll go talk to him, no matter how much it hurts. I have to know the truth. I'll visit him today, after my dragon watch.

She skipped breakfast, downing another tank of mecks and hurrying up to the hillock to feed the animals. Wind greeted her with an excited bark as she prepared his bone. *At least he will never leave me.*

The deer pranced along the perimeter fence, unusually jittery for this time of the morning. One roe smashed her head against the iron gauge fence again and again, as if she expected a reward for her suffering. Thorn patted her sweating head through the fence. "It's okay, girl," she said, even though she knew it was a lie.

Nothing will ever be okay again.

Thorn settled herself in her usual spot – a hollow moulded in the peat, where she nestled her tiny body. She turned away from the fence line – Aaron said it was easier to concentrate when she wasn't confusing the images of her mind with those of her eyes – and focused on sending her tendrils of thought out over the expanse of swamp. The shifting winds carried her through the fenland and swept her through every dent, pool and furrow. The threads of her mind connected to birds, insects, and compies, but no dragons.

She directed her thoughts into a sparrow that fluttered around the perimeter of Graveyard. Her sense caught the scent of Rex, leading the others east, towards London. She forced the bird to follow the Narrow as it wound through the fenland. In no time at all she hovered above the party – Rex led the march, his mouth set in a thin line. Joel and Finnegan jostled behind him, laughing at each other's filthy jokes. Lurgo trudged at the rear, behind Gabriel and Edgar. He complained loudly about the pain in his feet.

Thorn's chest clenched at the sight of them. She steered the bird closer.

I wonder if I could push my thoughts into Rex. I wonder if I could force a connection...

She knew it was impossible; the sense only worked with animals, never humans. Aaron said that was a blessing, for being privy to all the dark and secret thoughts of men would drive him to madness. But just this once she wished...Thorn crouched lower in her hollow, pulling her hood tight around her face to keep out the rain.

If I could see his mind, if I could know what he really thought of me...then what? It won't change anything – he'll still be gone and I'll be alone. What if I found things I couldn't bear?

What about Joel...what if I found his thoughts instead?

She stifled a giggle. *What a strange thought. Stop it, Thorn, the mecks has gone to your head. Concentrate.*

Thorn released the bird, and it fluttered away in a daze. She tried to wind out her thoughts again, concentrating on Rex's trudging figure. But this time, Joel's face floated under her eyelids. She remembered his smile, and how he'd embraced her and wiped away her tears. *He's so different from Rex...*

Now Joel's kind features morphed into Rex's emaciated scowl, his sad eyes replaced by the cold stare Rex had worn ever since he returned from London. His expression burned in her sockets, so real that Thorn gulped back tears as she reached out to touch it ...

No. Not Rex. He's not real anymore. Concentrate. Aaron's counting on you.

Her thoughts plummeted back into her own head. She squeezed her eyes shut, trying to force all distractions from her mind. All she could see were Rex's cruel eyes, boring fissures in her skull.

Behind her, the deer slammed their bodies against the fence. Wind growled, joined by the other dogs, all biting and snapping.

I wish they'd be quiet, I can't think with all this...wait, something's wrong.

Thorn jerked her head around. Wind and the other dogs pawed at the outer fence, snarling into the fog-shrouded marsh. Inside their pen the chickens ran in wild circles, squawking in alarm.

She heard the crunch of metal bending.

Without warning, a stray thought connected to her mind, a thought that didn't belong in her own head. She raised her hand and sniffed it, and her immediate instinct was to bite down on her own flesh. She could practically *taste* the succulent meat...

"Oh no." she breathed.

Thorn's gaze fell on a stretch of fence, barely twenty

feet from the snarling dogs. The struts buckled, the wire fencing snapping away as one by one the spiked gauge rails slapped against the mud.

Inside her skull, she *felt* the serrated teeth scraping against the metal. She could smell the fresh prey wafting on the breeze.

Oh no, oh no, oh no.

The entire stretch of fence-line toppled with a crash. The ground shook with a rumble that jarred her bones and crumbled the earth beneath her. That powerful war cry was joined by another, and another.

Thorn scrambled from her burrow just as the first snout poked through the fog and bared its shiny teeth.

She fled back toward the fires, the cry straining her voice.

"We're under attack!"

***

Thorn rapped her fists on the Rothwell's steel frame. "Oswald. I know you're in there!"

His red face appeared behind the curtain. "Thorn? I thought I told you—"

"There's no time! There's a pack of dragons attacking the Southern boundary. You have to raise the alarm!"

Oswald snorted. "Nonsense. If dragons got within ten miles of Graveyard, Aaron would drive them away."

"Aaron is weak from his illness. He can't sense like he used to, but he didn't want you to know. I've been watching the dragons twice a day for the last month. And I'm telling you there is a pack attacking the Southern Boundary!"

"Then drive them away, you useless child!"

"I can't—" She was cut off by a shrill scream,

followed by a roar that trembled in the air itself.

No, please don't let it be true.

Oswald's eyes bore in Thorn's skull. He raised a hand as though he would hit her. She backed away, her heart seized in fear.

He snapped his hand away and bolted for the boundary, hobbling through the mud in his nightgown and slippers. Thorn followed on his heels.

Another roar tore through her belly. Several women bolted past them towards the fires, screaming and scattering supply crates as they fled. One crashed into Thorn, toppling both of them into the mud.

"What's happening?" Thorn shook the woman's shoulders. "How many are there?"

The woman screeched, clawing at Thorn's skin. Her nails raked thin wounds along Thorn's forearms, which quickly welled with blood. She wrenched and tore at Thorn's clothes, all the while screaming a long, unending syllable of distress. Thorn gave up and let her go, and the woman fled, stomping on Thorn's hand in her haste. She picked herself up and followed after Oswald.

Emerging at the foot of the hillock, Thorn froze. Four adult swamp dragons raced down the slope, hungry eyes focused on Graveyard.

Thorn had never seen their like before, though she'd witnessed the damage they inflicted on the tricorn herds. Each dragon stood eight feet tall, prancing over the soft ground on powerful hind legs. Thick claws curled from each toe, gripping the mud with ease. They stretched their spindly forearms from their scaled bodies, their razor-sharp claws readying for action. Every bone and muscle in their thick necks and elongated snouts stood taut, their jaws snapping in anticipation of the feast. Unlike the dragons of legend they didn't have wings, but they closed the distance over the hillock with such grace and speed flight would have been unnecessary.

As they dived into the panicked crowd, their thoughts drove into Thorn's skull. All her visions clouded with red. She watched, frozen, as the first dragon leapt at a fleeing woman, whose shrieks turned into curdling screams. Thorn *felt*, rather than saw, the dragon's teeth sink into the woman's torso.

Two more bent over the still-living woman, tearing at the tender flesh of her exposed belly. Her scream cut Thorn's skin, tearing her soul.

The creatures' thoughts pummelled Thorn's head. The air sizzled with fragrance; the delicious smell of taut human flesh threatened to overwhelm her. She stared at the eviscerated woman with a mixture of revulsion and hunger, feeling herself tearing at the meat, gulping down the pulpy insides.

The woman screamed once more, then fell silent.

The dragons spread out, moving to surround the stampeding village. Thorn sensed their plan as soon as they thought it, and she knew what they had to do.

"Stop running!" she cried. "Bring fire!"

Oswald's pale nightgown flapped over his white legs, shining like a lamplight inviting the monsters to supper. He clambered atop a pile of debris and echoed her cry. "Bring pitch and wood and weapons, lads!"

Someone finally had the sense to ring the bells, and the distress signal chimed over the Graveyard. While most scattered throughout the city, cowering under the carriages and praying to Great Conductor, Thorn could see the shadows of several men emerging from their workshops, their shaking hands clutching shovels and axes.

She pulled her legs from the mud and raced towards

the towering Rothwell. The abandoned cooking fires still smouldered, the dense smoke shrouding the centre of Graveyard with a protective shield.

Thorn's sides ached from the running and the fear, and her head pounded with the intensity of the dragons' hunger. She tore at her woollen skirt till she'd exposed most of her white legs, wrapping the scraps of wool around a beam she pulled from a carriage seat. She dumped the end into the drum of pitch and let the sparks of the cooking fire catch the cloth. It sprung to life.

She heard the roars outside her head and inside her skull, as if she herself made those inhuman sounds. More hunger, more death. She held the torch above her head and sprinted toward the Turret, her mind fixed on the nearest growls. She wouldn't let them get Quartz.

The dragon darted between the upturned engines; tendrils of gore dripping from its teeth. The air smelled sickly, like sweetened honey and offal.

"Quartz, where are you?" she yelled, but her voice trailed away amongst the screams and growls. She bolted down the gore-strewn road, heading for the Turret door. The green Fresnel lens swung back and forth haphazardly. She hammered on the door, but no one answered.

"Quartz, you deaf old gammy, answer me!"

Inside her head she heard the dragon register her voice, and his attention drew from the gnawed carcass at his feet toward the Turret, toward her. She glanced around her, frantically searching for a hiding place, but there was none. The beast thundered towards her, jaws slapping together. Inside her head she felt her own hunger, ready to devour herself...

"Quartz!"

Finally, she saw him. Quartz had manoeuvred the one remaining Gast-Engine onto the roof of a nearby carriage. He was fumbling with the clip rotation when he looked up and grinned at her.

"Thorn," he yelled. "Send him down this path, atta girl!"

Seizing her courage, Thorn bolted toward the beast and dived for a gap between the engines. Her heart leapt against her ribs. The dragon whipped around, using its long tail for balance, and pushed off with its hind legs, clearing the engine with a graceful bound and landing within a few feet of her. She took off toward Quartz, ducking as the heavy jaws clamped shut only inches behind her shoulder.

"Thorn!"

She dived for a row of toppled drums and the dragon barrelled ahead, right where Quartz wanted him.

"Eat this, you poxy bastard!" Quartz cried gleefully as he pumped bolts into the torso of the confused dragon. The red flared inside Thorn's head, pounding against her skull. She held herself, riding through the pain, until the dragon's thoughts faded and fell away. She looked up – the creature lay dead, its dark blood leeching into the boggy ground.

Thorn helped Quartz clamber down from the carriage. He poked the carcass with his cane, watching the beast's giant eyes lolling in its skull. "That'll roast well for dinner tomorrow," he said finally.

"There are three more. I don't know where they are now."

"Aaron will have a lot to answer for, slacking off like this."

She gasped. "Omigod, *Aaron!*"

Quartz called after her, but Thorn didn't hear a word

as she sprinted toward the smokehouse. She skirted along the western edge, keeping low to the ground and listening inside her head for the dragons' thoughts. All she could see was red, red, red.

In the minutes that had passed since the dragons broke the fence, the Stokers had organised a haggard defence. Behind a gutted Stevenson carriage, Bill Riley and William Stone led a sortie, which advanced – shovels at the ready – toward a feasting dragon. More men waited on the opposite end of the hillock, crouched behind debris, antiquated muskets poised at their shoulders. The weapons had been dug from the abandoned carriages over the years, and kept hidden from the rain and mud under beds and between wall fittings – squirreled away for a day such as this.

The dragon lifted its head and saw the men rushing them. It whipped its tail around and about-turned, snapping at its mate as they barrelled toward the defensive line.

Thorn shoved her fingers in her ears, and kept running. Behind her, explosions ripped through the smoky haze, scarring the wreckage of Graveyard with more wounds and fissures. The dragons howled, and the pain inside her skull intensified, threatening to explode from her head. She gritted her teeth to keep from screaming, and drove her legs into the soft earth, driving herself the final distance.

Great Conductor, please let Aaron be okay. I promise I'll do anything. *I'll even marry Lurgo if you just let Aaron be okay.*

The black outline of the smokehouse appeared through the red. The usually tame fire had flared up and flames encircled the mounts and casing, flicking around the wheels like some hellish coach. Screams issued from within. Old Hatchie was nowhere in sight.

Oh no, Aaron!

Thorn pressed her hand against the door, but the metal singed her fingers. She cried out and staggered back.

"Aaron, *Aaron!*" Thorn screamed his name, but she heard no reply.

She circled the burning smokehouse, desperate to get inside. In the rear corner she saw her chance. Part of the mainframe had rusted away, and someone had repaired the hole with wooden beams – which the fire curled to soot at her feet. Thorn kicked away the remaining wood, forming a gap large enough for her body. Black smoke belched from within.

Careful not to touch the glowing metal, she hoisted herself onto the ledge and called for Aaron once more. She choked on the vile smoke and coughed violently.

"Thorn?" a familiar voice croaked.

"Aar—" She broke into another coughing fit. Her eyes welled with tears. She couldn't see anything inside the black smokehouse.

"Thorn, go back. I'm not ... tell Rex ... you can't ..."

Suddenly, a strut crashed from the roof, showering sparks into the interior. Aaron screamed – a long, excruciating scream that crushed Thorn's soul – then fell silent. She choked out his name again and again, but he didn't reply.

Her head swimming from the smoke and the pain, Thorn fell away from the smokehouse and collapsed into the peat. Red flooded her vision, and the pain in her head was so great that she could no longer abide it. Her body grew slack and she relaxed into oblivion.

***

JAMES HOLMAN'S MEMOIRS, FIRST EDITION

Forgive me, for I have been tardy in my duties as narrator, and have not yet told of what I found upon disembarking in London. I'm afraid you must wait a little longer still. The additional strain of writing by lamplight caused my eyes to wind down faster than usual. The process of maintaining the mechanism myself is excruciating, especially with the pains in my old fingers, but I have only myself to blame.

At Joel's insistence, I visited with the local clockmaker. He probed my abhorrence with a look of professional curiosity. "Remarkable," he murmured as he worked. While I writhed in his chair, he tinkered and tightened and wound and greased and it seems to be in good order again.

Wisps of laudanum trail under my nose. Without the drug I wouldn't be fit to complete the task I have set myself. It used to be that when the pain gripped my limbs I'd take off; to Germany, to Russia, to Africa. By ship or by horseback, fresh air can heal nearly all wounds.

I said *nearly* all, friends. Some wounds never heal.

***

They buried Aaron alongside the other dead, as soon as the moon rose in the east. The men dug shallow graves into the hillock, to the left of the main cemetery area where the victims of fever and old age awaited their carriage to the Station of Life. Quartz and Oswald said a few words, though the cold wind whipped them away. Every man wore a solemn expression, and the women sobbed and dabbed their eyes with bloodstained rags. Aaron had been a great leader, and he would be missed.

Thorn watched the burial from the animal pens, her arms wrapped around Wind's torso. Her eyes were dry – she had no tears left inside her. The dog stood rigid, his eyes drooping: he knew his master had passed on.

After the burial, Aaron's family hosted a great funeral feast, where the remaining tricorn meat was roasted on the cooking fires and the Stokers drained Quartz's mecks tank dry. Bill Riley took great delight in telling Thorn that on no uncertain terms was she to show herself during the feast, but she wouldn't have attended anyway. The last thing she wanted to do was dance and feast and drink. She didn't think she'd ever eat or drink again.

Instead, she watched from the animal pens as the fires faded into thin tendrils that streaked across the dawn and the last of the drunken Stokers fell asleep against the drums, basking in their own silent liturgy.

Of all the Stokers, Thorn had lost the most upon Aaron's death; it pressed more ferociously on her heart than it did even on Oswald, his own brother. But then, she and Aaron had always shared a bond. He was the only person who spoke about her father. He told her stories of Nicholas Thorne's deeds, of his brilliant mind, of the friendship they had shared. But most of all, Aaron was the only other person she'd ever met who had this *sense* ... he called it power, though she didn't believe that. Yet he could talk to animals, could reach for them and direct them, using only touch and thought and love. And Thorn could too, if she believed Aaron, though she certainly didn't *feel* powerful, and the sense worked so erratically she often doubted its existence at all.

And now he's dead, and I'll never know what he and Rex spoke about me, and it's all my fault.

Later that morning, Thorn tried to sleep, but found she could not do that, either. Instead, she stared at the damp ceiling for hours, her fingers stroking Rex's pin. She noticed Quartz had left a thimble of laudanum next to her bed. She tipped the pungent drug out the window, and downed another quart of mecks.

The day after the funeral, life returned to a normal, though sombre, pace. Chores had to be done, food collected, fences rebuilt. The hunt left for the swamps without Thorn; instead, one of Oswald's untrained grandsons peeked out from behind the Gast. The four dragon carcasses were plucked clean of musket balls and Gast bolts and boiled in a salty broth. The sweet, tender meat would feed the Stokers for several weeks, though they'd paid too high a price. It had been the greatest loss of life in Graveyard since the cholera outbreak two winters ago, the one that had taken Joel's girl. Thorn worked with a sinking heart: she knew her punishment would be severe.

But what punishment could be more severe than Aaron's death? I've already lost everything – what more could they take from me?

On the afternoon following Aaron's death, Thorn perched on the deer fence, her eyes drifting over the damp wasteland that was her only home. Her whole body broken and weary with pain, she pushed away the reaching thoughts of the nearby animals. She didn't want to know what they thought of her, the killer of their master.

"Thorn."

She lifted her head at the sound of her name. The voice that spoke it dripped with hatred.

The harsh voice belonged to Oswald. The chancellor stooped against the mended fence, his cane sinking in the soft ground. She hadn't even heard him approach. His eyes met hers, and she flinched at his loathing stare.

"Are you listening to me, child?"

She nodded, unable to speak.

"The council has met to discuss your future. We can no longer abide your presence here. You are to be gone from Graveyard by sundown tonight."

"Where will I go?" she whispered.

"That is no longer my concern." Oswald scowled at her one final time, then turned his back and walked away.

Thorn returned to the Turret, her whole body numb. Quartz greeted her at the window, as he always did.

"What are you so grumpy about?" he asked as he leaned over the sill and flipped the lens on his monocle, all the better to gaze at her distraught features.

She didn't reply.

Upstairs, in her room, she packed a small sack of possessions: a comb, compass, a can of tuna hoarded from one of the stately carriages, blanket, knife, handkerchief, goggles, spare tunic and breeches. Her hands only shook a little as she tied the drawstring tight. The whole process felt surreal, as though she observed herself pack her life away over her own shoulder, removed from her body as she was now removed from her home.

Quartz surveyed her from the doorway, and though neither spoke Thorn knew he understood what had happened. He disappeared for a moment and returned, handing her a parcel of salted tricorn meat, oat cakes and a flask of his strongest mecks.

"You're better off without this rotten place, anyway," he muttered as he wrapped Thorn's scarf tight around her neck.

Thorn pulled on her warmest gloves and tied her bootlaces extra tight. Quartz helped her struggle into a thick coat and pull on her rucksack. Clasping Rex's pin over her heart, she was ready to meet whatever awaited her.

He patted her on the shoulders, and mumbled a few words of encouragement. Never one for affection, was Quartz. Thorn nodded, hearing nothing.

When she exited the Turret, the sun inched below the bloodied sky, marking her final night in Graveyard. Thorn went to say goodbye to her animals.

The dogs crowded around her feet, their high-pitched whines disclosing their distress. *They've had Aaron and me their entire lives*, she realised, *and now we're both gone.*

Thorn allowed Wind to rest his head on her knees, and she scratched his ears the way he liked. Silently they traded memories; Thorn saw Aaron as Wind did – his eyes sparkling as he readied the dogs for a hunt. She watched the threads of gossamer magic connecting man and dog as they skulked silently across the moor, returning triumphant with pelts of hare and roe. The first disastrous tricorn-hunting experiment that nearly had them all killed. The triumphant day they first brought down an immature swamp dragon. Only she and Wind knew these things, only they wept for Aaron the hunter, Aaron the mentor, and Aaron the friend.

How happy he had been to hear about our engagement. Thorn remembered how he'd embraced her, his knotted muscles pressing her skin, how he'd called her his daughter. How his smile glowed like an argand lamp as he presented Rex with an heirloom pin that had belonged to his mother. A wedding pin; she never got to wear it. *And now I never will. What would he think of me now? Abandoned by Rex, forsaken by my people; the harbinger of all death. The cursed one. Not even Aaron could argue the truth of that statement.*

"It doesn't matter what he'd think, does it Wind? He's dead now." The word *dead* swirled like a maelstrom over Graveyard, darting from carriage to tower, tearing at the forest of gauge rails, slipping cruel fingers through the peat. Wind lifted his head and howled.

"I'll be okay out there, you'll see," she whispered. The deer bounded along the fence line, their hooves clapping on the hard ground. Wind glanced at her with incredulous eyes. The animals didn't believe her. She couldn't blame them; she didn't believe herself.

***

JAMES HOLMAN'S MEMOIRS, FIRST EDITION

I'd no sooner disembarked in London and unpacked my rucksack when the invitation came to attend a Royal Society meeting. I had written to the Council earlier regarding my return and they were eager for me to speak about my travels. Anxious to meet with my peers and discuss some of my more interesting specimens, I agreed.

Although Queen Victoria had reinstated many of the traditional governmental policies that had been in place before the Vampire King's adoption of the Industrian religion, she had decided to keep the Council of the Royal Society as the governing body and ultimate arbiters of the country. Her belief was that with proper stewardship, a country was in the best hands when learned men of science were at its helm. Had she known the great quantities of brandy required to grease this great engine of the empire, I think she might have considered a dictatorship.

A carriage arrived at my apartments to escort me to Somerset House. The driver seemed in a chatty mood, and nattered all the way about the Great Exhibition and the tourists and the Royal Engineer and the reinstatement of the city trains. I ignored him, going over my findings in my head, clutching the box of insect casings I'd collected for Charles.

In hindsight, perhaps listening to this driver might have offered me another clue that all was not well in my beloved city. Blind as I was, I did not notice the half-rebuilt foundations of the Chimney as we passed by the abandoned Engine Ward, or the ominous tendrils of smoke that snaked from the supposedly derelict Wall.

We rode through Hyde Park, and the driver pointed to the near-complete Crystal Palace. I could not see it, of course, but I felt our carriage slow as we navigated crowds of tourists and revellers. Voices called and sang in a myriad of languages, and delightful smells of roasting chestnuts and hot pies wafted from busy street vendors. Hyde Park had been transformed into a true street party, a chorus in the song of the world. I felt a surge of pride for my city.

We stopped outside the Royal Society buildings on the Strand. I tipped the driver and made my way inside the building. The meeting had not officially started, and the society fellows and their amateur patrons gathered in groups to discuss news and papers and research while sipping glasses of brandy that freely flowed from the Society's copious supplies. I poured myself a glass and went in search of a familiar voice.

I did not have to search long. "James Holman, you old scallywag!" A hand clamped down on my shoulder. I recognised the deep, clipped tone of my long-time friend, Charles Darwin.

"Ah, Charles! Returned from your voyages so soon? Have you evolved swimming gills and a tail yet?'

"Gills, yes. I'm still working on the tail." We chuckled at our ridiculous joke. I held out the package.

"I've brought you a little gift from my travels. I've labelled each insect with its location and measurements. Hopefully my penmanship is readable."

The hinges creaked as he opened the box and inspected the contents. "These are remarkable. Thank you, my friend. Although next time, you must have someone else write the labels. I shall add these to my research collection. I've amassed an impressive assortment of specimens, James, and all my research supports my theories about the true origins of species."

"You must tell me all about it."

"You shall have to wait for my papers to be published, like every other scientist. Right now I'm working on a fascinating essay on the formation of vegetable mould, which I hope to present at the Great Exhibition, if I can ever get the damn thing finished on time. And I have taken a wife, who occupies far more of my time than I'd like to admit. Come, I'd like to introduce you to someone."

His hand pressed against my back and I turned with him, and walked a few steps back toward the entrance, where I recognised the voice of another fellow, William Hallowes Miller, loudly explaining, *again,*in case anyone had missed it, his notation system for crystal planes.

"—and it's really very simple. A family of lattice planes is determined by three integers, and each index denotes an intersection of a plane with a direction in the basis of the reciprocal lattice vectors—"

"William, look who's back!" Charles pushed me forward. I extended my hand a few inches in front of my body, and felt Miller's clammy paw reach out and shake it.

"James Holman, what a pleasant surprise. I was just explaining to Mr. Williams, here—"

"Perhaps Mr. Williams and Mr. Holman would like to be introduced," Charles prompted, breaking the mineralogist off before he could return to his diatribe.

"Ah, yes of course. James, meet Nicholas Williams. Queen Victoria recently appointed him to the position of Royal Engineer. Nicholas has done a splendid job designing the Crystal Palace and getting the old train lines up and running. Nicholas, this is James Holman, explorer, exotic specimen collector—"

"—and convicted English spy," Charles interrupted.

"Don't tease me so, Charles. You'll give this fine fellow a false impression of me." I grinned, and extended my hand out from my side as a gesture of friendship. "The Russians invented those charges. I had no intention of reporting their ties with North America to the King. I was merely after a crate of inexpensive vodka to ease my passage across Siberia, and happened to be in the wrong place at the wrong time. I'm pleased to meet you, Mr. Williams."

"A pleasure to make your acquaintance, Mr. Holman," Nicholas Williams said, as he clasped my hand and shook it firmly.

My blood turned cold. *I know that voice.* Although I had not heard it for over nineteen years, it still haunts my dreams. I thought I would never hear it again.

How can it be so? How is it that he is here? He is supposed to be dead? Why does no one else recognise him?

"Please, Mr Williams...do tell us about your work." I

struggled to keep my voice even. I brought my glass to my mouth and drained all the liquid, hoping for the courage only alcohol brings.

"I have been...detained, for several years, kept from this city which I love so much. But I've managed to return, and Her Majesty has granted me a generous contract. The Crystal Palace is one of my greatest achievements – over ten million feet of glass encapsulated in a skeleton of steel and iron. She stands over 108 feet high at her highest transept, and occupies over 19 acres of exhibition space. I've already re-instated sections of railway for the transportation of the tools and materials required to build her, and the rest of the London rail network will be up and running in time for the Opening Ceremony."

William and Charles chatted away, but I drummed my fingers on my empty glass, and listened. The more I heard him speak – his tone unchanging as he discussed the reinstatement of the Great Western circle line atop the old Wall – the more my bones turned ice with fear.

How could a man return from the dead? How could he defeat the laws of nature? How could he walk into a meeting of the Royal Society and have no one recognise his face? I had no answers for these questions, but I knew one thing for a fact:

Nicholas Williams – the Royal Engineer – was Isambard Kingdom Brunel.

***

Thorn knew she'd have to hike through the night without sleeping if she wanted to catch Rex's company. Even then she didn't have much hope. He knew the way to London – she did not. He had five strong men to defend against threats. She had a comb and a can of tuna.

Her decision to follow Rex had been made as soon as she'd exited the outer fence. Thorn told herself it wasn't to convince him to take her back, but she was alone with nowhere else to go, and he at least might have some sympathy. Joel was there, and Lurgo, and they'd protect her even if Rex hated her. When they reached London she would leave them, and he need never be troubled with her again.

The gutted, rusting Clegg carriage loomed on the horizon. Thorn placed her hand on the slick face of the Narrow and shut her eyes, picking up her pace as she ran past without looking at it. *Don't think about it. Not tonight, when you have so very far to go.*

She followed the length of the Narrow towards Swindon, breaking off several miles before the city and following a tricorn path through the marshes, bending low to examine with her fingers the fresh boot prints in the mud.

The moon still hid behind the cloak of fog, and she crashed through the sedge with the grace of a blind tricorn. Every few paces she stopped walking and drew her thoughts from her head, attempting to cast her mind out for anything that might be stalking her. She felt nothing, save the flock of carrion birds in pursuit of her doomed soul, and a nearby herd of tricorns wallowing in the mud.

Hours passed as Thorn navigated the trampled path, picking her way around the bracken and searching the mind of every creature she passed for some clue to Rex's whereabouts. She tried to use her power to send birds along the path, searching for the men, but in her exhaustion she couldn't make the connections stick. She gulped at the mecks – it warmed her veins and lent her the courage her heart couldn't muster.

Just as the faint glimmer of sunlight cast itself upon the damp earth, Thorn's mind attached to a lone compie, nursing a broken leg and lamenting the loss of its mate from a hunter's snare. The compie's memory of the hunter looked suspiciously like Lurgo.

They're close! Thorn urged her aching legs onward. The mecks had long ago ceased to sustain her, but she dared not touch any of her precious food. *Just a little further.*

As the sun rose the thick clouds swallowed what little warmth it gave, and rain began to fall in thick sheets. Thorn wrapped her wool scarf over her head, and continued her hunt. She waded into knee-deep water, choked with fen ragwort and dead, waterlogged branches. The rain washed away any evidence of their passing. Now she was truly lost.

Her head swam from exhaustion and pain. Every step pitched her weak body off balance, threatening to spill her into the deep marsh. Thorn knew if she fell down, she might not be able to pull herself up.

Through the fog of her pain, she felt something stir the animals. The birds twittered uneasily, and their thoughts told Thorn they'd seen an unwelcome presence in the swamp. Two of their kind had been caught in snares already.

Thorn threw her mind out again, listening for any further clues. A painful convulsion shot down the length of her body, and she grabbed a slimy tree trunk to keep from falling. *I can't go on much longer,* she realised, unslinging her rucksack and pawing at the oat cakes. She gulped down two, washing them down with another mouthful of mecks. She leaned against the tree and waited, hoping the pain would subside and her legs would once again support her weight.

She heard a voice. *Outside* her head.

Thorn froze, her weakened senses on full alert. Someone thumped towards her, heavy boots splashing in the water. She heard the grasses rustle as the figure bent over, and the scrape of a metal clamp as it freed something from a bird snare.

"Not much of a feast," the familiar voice mused to his supper, "but you'll do."

"Joel," she croaked, her voice fading with her strength. "Is that you?"

"Is someone there?" The figure stood up, and she heard the snap of a barker being cocked. "I'm armed. I advise you to show yourself, before I'm forced to shoot."

"Joel, it's me." Thorn staggered to her feet and stepped out from behind the trunk. His features flashed with recognition. He dropped the tiny woodcock he'd snared and waded towards her.

"Thorn? By Great Conductor's steaming testicles, you frightened me. What are you doing out here?"

She stepped towards him, toppling forward as blood rushed from her head and her legs buckled from under her.

The last thing she felt before losing consciousness was Joel's strong arms wrapping around her waist, and a rush of filthy peat-laced water pouring down her throat.

***

"What's she *doing* here?"

Thorn lay on her back on warm earth. Thick coats and blankets weighted her chest, and her head throbbed with pain. Fiery tongues licked her aching throat. Gingerly, she tested her fingers. They still worked.

Thorn opened one blurry eye, and could just make out five figures standing in a circle a few feet from her. They appeared to be in the midst of an argument. *They're talking about me*, she realised.

She tried to get up, to go to them, but her limbs were so tired, so sore, they refused to comply. Instead, she strained her eyes to hear their conversation.

"I've looked in her rucksack. She's hardly prepared for the journey." That was Joel. He spoke evenly, keeping his tone light. "She's not even carrying a weapon. If I hadn't found her, she wouldn't have survived the night."

"That's all very well," said Rex sharply. "But we don't want her."

"Perhaps if you hadn't been so cruel to her upon our departure, she wouldn't have felt compelled to follow us," Joel snapped.

Thorn blinked slowly, trying to wave herself. When she opened her eyes again, Lurgo's face loomed closer as he pressed his hot, sticky lips on hers. He grabbed Thorn's hair and pulled her against him, his wet tongue attempting to force its way into her mouth. She screamed and tried to wriggle away, but he held her fast. Instead, she reached up, clenched his matted hair where it had grown longer in the back, and managed to pull him free.

"Ick." Thorn spat on the ground, trying to rid her mouth of the taste of him. "What did you do that for?"

He smirked. "You looked as though you were dying. I thought I'd try to give you the breath of life."

"I told him you'd simply passed out," Joel remarked. "He wanted to be certain."

Thorn reached up to slap Lurgo on the cheek, but he ducked out of her range. Her feeble retort swiped only air.

S.C. GREEN

"Why did you follow us, Thorn?" Rex folded his arms across his willowy chest. His expression soured.

The pain in her chest seared. "I...I didn't have a choice. I can't go back to Graveyard. Swamp dragons attacked...I was supposed to hold them back but I couldn't...and Oswald, he...he sent me away."

"What about my father? Why didn't he drive the dragons away?"

"He's dead. I'm sorry, Rex. He's dead." Fresh tears fell down her face.

Rex whirled around and stomped away. Thorn squeezed her eyes shut.

Joel and Lurgo knelt at her side. "Save your strength, Thorn," Joel said. "You swallowed a bit of water."

"Joel...I..."

He pulled the blanket under her chin. "You're exhausted, you silly woman. You nearly killed yourself, running all night with no food or water. *Sleep*. That's an order."

But Thorn couldn't sleep. She lay with her eyes closed and listened to the men arguing about her.

"I will *not* have her with us," Rex snarled. "She killed my father. She's cursed."

"You honestly believe in that nonsense about curses, Rex?" Joel's voice was equally sharp. "I thought you had more sense."

"The dragons attack wasn't her fault," Lurgo added. "Thorn adored Aaron. She'd die before letting him come to harm."

I should have died.

"Cursed or not, she's no food, no weapons and no bloody sense," Finnegan's kindly voice added. "We canna leave her here to die. What would Great Conductor think of us then?"

"She's *not* coming to London," Rex said.

Thorn slipped out of consciousness, and the rest of the conversation was lost to her dreams. Joel and Lurgo must have worn Rex down for when she opened her eyes again the men were still there, and Joel even brought her warm broth. As she sipped the soup he looped the strap of a barker holster over her arm.

"You can't be defenceless out here," he said with a smile, patting her shoulder.

She nodded her thanks.

"The dragon attack, how bad was it?"

She squeezed her eyes shut, hoping she wouldn't begin crying again. "Bad."

"You don't want to talk about it, do you?"

Thorn shook her head. "Lucile is fine, though. She was poking tongues at me from across the funeral fires."

Joel's shoulders relaxed. Someone rustled through the sedge. Lurgo appeared, his features drawn.

"Rex wants us to move on. Are you okay to walk?"

Thorn gulped. "I'll manage."

Joel helped her to her feet and wrapped her thick coat over her shoulders. He and Lurgo flanked her as she stumbled through the trees to join Rex and the others.

Finnegan greeted her with a smile, but Edgar and Gabriel exchanged dubious glances. Rex turned his back to her, and he looked off into the horizon as he spoke, in his quiet, stern voice. "We continue on to London. Thorn may come with us, if she can keep up. The Great Exhibition opens in eight days' time. We cannot afford to tarry on the road."

His coat flapped against his knees as he whirled around and pitched himself forward, splashing through the reeds with surprising speed. One by one, the company fell in step behind him.

For two days they trudged through the wasted fenland. Rex stomped along in front, followed closely by Finnegan who kept the group entertained with Irish potato jokes. Gabriel and Edgar were next and Joel followed them, although he spent a great portion of the journey turned around towards Thorn, offering his hand when she stepped over fallen sedge, and talking to her in a low voice. If Rex noticed Joel's attention, he ignored it, the way he'd taken to ignoring Thorn.

Lurgo, however, divided his scowls evenly between Joel and Rex. He shadowed Thorn so close he was forever stepping on her ankles, and when she removed her boots to inspect her blisters she found her heels swollen and bloody. His face flushed when he saw them, but he didn't let up.

On the second night they made camp inside an ancient stone circle, leaning up against the tall dolmens as they pulled off their boots. Rex shared around a package of salted tricorn meat. As the group chewed in silence, he spoke in a low voice.

"You should all know I have not been entirely truthful about the nature of our mission."

The chewing ceased. Lurgo stared across at Thorn, and allowed his upper lip to curl into a slight smile.

"The Metal Messiah has returned. The walls of the Chimney are being rebuilt, and from the rumours we've been hearing amongst the underground sects, he is gathering engineers and acolytes for his new Engine Ward. He is planning something for the Great Exhibition, something big, and we need all our best men in the city, ready for his command."

The silence and stony eyes continued while Rex explained his explorations of the secret underground world he'd been living in. He described the hideouts on the edge of the Engine Ward – crowded tunnels and abandoned furnace rooms that now housed men and women of outlawed sects who had been driven into hiding. He spoke with wonder of an exploration he and Sooty had made of the gutted Chimney, the very place from which Brunel had administered his empire. As they had walked through the nave of the old church, they'd heard the familiar whirring of engines working beneath their feet. Deep underground, some machine had been brought to life once more. He described the magnificent Crystal Palace that was being constructed and their discovery that underground tunnels connected Hyde Park to the Engine Ward. *Is this what he's been doing for the last nine months?* Thorn wondered. *Chasing shadows and skulking in old, haunted places? Brunel was supposed to be part of the Stokers' past. Why had Rex not stayed in school, where he had a future?*

"So there has been a message from Brunel?" Joel asked. Thorn noticed that his eyes blazed with excitement. All of the boys leaned forward, hooked by Rex's stories of the city and the Metal Messiah. Only Thorn didn't share their enthusiasm, she'd heard too many stories from Quartz of what Brunel was capable of.

"No message. But that is not surprising. After all, Brunel would not know that there are any Stokers in the city—"

Because he banished them all to the swamps, Thorn thought.

"—and we don't yet know how strong he is or what he is planning to do. But we know that with Stephenson coming to the city of the exhibition, it is the perfect time for him to make his presence known. So that is when we must strike."

"What do you plan to do?"

"Destroy Stephenson's exhibit, of course. That is the way we will show our loyalty to him. Joel, since you're the only one who can read, you'll assist me with interpretation of the schematics. The Crystal Palace is enormous, and we'll need to be able to move quickly to the right locations. Finnegan, we need your skills with explosives. Thorn and Lurgo, we have portable Gast Engines waiting in a workshop in Shadwell. You'll provide our cover."

Thorn blanched. "I don't want to kill people."

"I'd hardly call them *people*, Thorn. The Engineering Hall of the Palace will be filled with our enemies: Stephenson and his hordes of Navvy engineers, the priesthood of the Metics and the other engineers who've entrenched their own workshops in our sacred Engine Ward. They won't take too kindly to the Messiah's return. As for the Scotland Yard boys..." Gabriel grinned wildly.

Rex looked from face to face, his own features blossoming with excitement as he saw his enthusiasm reflected back at him. "I am sorry about deceiving you all, but we'd never get this plot past Oswald if it were known."

With his stick, Rex nudged his satchel to the centre of the circle. Thorn saw the sparkle of gold. "This money will keep us while we're inside the city, and buy the equipment we need. I have a place we can stay, and we've much to prepare. London is nothing like we remember, friends. This deception of mine...it pales in comparison to that unholy place." Rex crossed himself furiously.

"But how can he bring himself back from the dead?" Joel asked. "Surely such a feat is...unnatural?"

"You speak blasphemy of the Metal Messiah." Gabriel

dived at Joel. Finnegan caught his shoulders and pulled him back.

Rex shook his head. "Ours is not to question Brunel's great power. Perhaps he never really died." His eyes clouded over. Thorn wondered what he *really* thought – she knew him well enough to sense he wasn't telling them the whole story.

"Get some sleep, everyone. We leave at dawn. If any of you wish to return to Graveyard, we'll part ways after breakfast."

Thorn had hoped to pull Rex aside after they'd eaten, and ask him about what was really going on, and about his sudden shift in character. He seemed to barely acknowledge her presence, and he hardly seemed to care about his father's death. But Rex lay back against one of the cold stones and began to snore before she'd even pulled her boots off. Thorn didn't want to disturb his peaceful sleep with her suspicions.

She leaned up against the nearest sacred stone and pulled her coat over her sodden knees. Here the rain fell in fat blobs, splashing mud in every direction. Thorn rested her loaded barker on her shoulder, and fingered the trigger every time she heard a tricorn growl or another unknown sound echo across the marsh.

While she watched and thought, Rex's head flopped against the stone. He snorted and moaned. "...Lydia..." he called, and again "Lydia, I'll come back. I promise..."

Thorn pulled her coat over her ears and fell into a fitful sleep, her eyes and nose clogged with tears. *Lydia*...that one word could explain his coldness, his reluctance to let her continue with them to London.

There is no woman named Lydia in Graveyard. He met someone in London, someone who occupies his very dreams. Someone unforgettable, unlike me...

Thorn slept fitfully, haunted by dreams of Rex and this mystery girl named Lydia. Hours later, her eyes shuddered open. She saw flickers of light and heard scuffling to her left.

She reached for the barker, but as her eyes adjusted she realised it was only Rex, cursing under his breath as he struggled to light a candle in the damp. Finally, the flame caught, and he held the flame between his knees as he dug something from his knapsack. Holding the object and candle in his arms, he rose and disappeared behind the stones.

What is going on?

As silently as she could, Thorn unrolled herself and stood up, pressing her body against the cold dolmen and inching around it, attempting to stay within the shadows. She heard Rex muttering to himself, off to her right, and the click of some kind of metal contraption. Crouching low, she crawled toward the sound and strained for any clue to Rex's odd behaviour.

The candle flared as the flame caught on another object. She leaned closer, trying to see what he was doing. A blue-white glow emanated from the flame, and she heard drops of molten metal collecting into an enamel mug. A familiar smell – almost sulphuric – wafted towards her.

Why is Rex heating lead, at this hour, in the middle of a swamp?

The lead fumes grew more potent, and Thorn inched forward, toward the glowing lump of lead. She was just building up the courage to speak out, when she heard rustling in the swamp.

Something dashed through the fens at great speed, crushing bracken and cracking the dead and rotting branches. The rustling and crackling drew closer, obviously drawn by the molten beacon Rex held. She slammed her body to the soggy ground as whatever it was sprung from the bracken beside her and broke through again. A faint wheezing, like steam snuffed in a pipe, passed by her ear. She kept her face pressed into the peat – she hadn't seen it, but she knew it wasn't friendly.

Thorn lay still, and listened. The creature circled Rex, uttering a low, menacing purr as it slipped through the bracken. It greatly desired what Rex had, but it was also wary, keeping its distance in case of a trap.

The silent night pressed against her, threatening to give her up at the slightest movement. Her pulse pounded in her ears, so loud she was certain the creature must have heard it. Suddenly, Rex spoke.

"He must know I'm nearing the city."

The creature snorted in reply, and circled again. Thorn remained still, not daring to breathe, lest it sense her presence.

"He must know that things have changed. Someone I...wanted to keep away is with us. I shall be rid of her before I reach the Wall, but I don't want her to come to harm."

A chortle, like laughter funnelled through a chimney, sounded to Thorn's right. Closer than she'd feared. *Great Conductor, preserve me.*

She lifted her head an inch, and saw through the mud that caked her eyelids two legs, puckered with black boils, standing barely four feet from her face. Between the creature's knees, Rex's face glowed in the dim light of the lead. He looked terrified.

"You bear a message from London?" Rex asked, his voice catching.

The creature merely spat in reply. A metallic object

sailed through the air, catching the light of the moon before falling at Rex's feet. He picked up the object and slipped it into his coat.

"For your efforts." Rex held the mug into the bracken. The creature snarled and snatched it up, throwing back its head and swallowing the molten lead in one gulp.

She turned her attentions back to Rex, who held his head in his hands. "I...I..." Rex's voice broke off, and his head snapped back. He crashed onto the ground, wrapping his arms around his ears and crying "MAKE IT STOP!"

His cries were terrifying. Thorn stepped forward, ready to go to his aid. But then, as quickly as his madness started, Rex seemed to collect himself, sitting up again and rubbing his head. "Tell him I will send word at the village. Tell him..." Rex's sentence trailed off, as though he fought for the right words. He seemed so unsure of himself, so unlike the Rex she knew. "Tell him I love him."

With a final grunt, the creature darted away. Thorn let out the breath she held, slowly, not wanting Rex to hear her.

She watched him for many moments, rocking back and forth in the mud, staring at the tiny flame he still held in his hand. His eyes betrayed his distress – he knew much he hadn't spoken of. Finally, he blew out the flame, and stood up. Thorn waited until he had returned to the dolmen, then she crawled back to her resting place.

Rex was already snoring when she returned to her sleeping spot. *Good.* He hadn't noticed her absence. Out of the corner of her eye she watched him slump lower against the stone. He threw his head back and forth, moaning with distress. He was having a nightmare.

***

Rustling and mutterings awoke Thorn, and she opened one cautious eye to the early morning sun, certain the creature from the night had returned.

But it was only Joel, boiling water over his argand. Rex sat next to him, sipping tea from an enamel cup, Brunel's 'GWR' crest emblazoned on the handle. Edgar and Finnegan cleaned their rifles. Lurgo still snored away in the corner. Gabriel was nowhere to be seen.

"He left," Joel said as he handed her a cup of lukewarm tea.

"He's a coward," mumbled Rex. "He doesn't have what it takes to be a hero for our people."

Thorn sipped her tea in silence. She didn't know what to say to Rex anymore. She remembered the strange encounter with the creature from the night before, and the way Rex had cried out in pain, only to quickly recover. The cold pin dug into her chest as she pulled on her rucksack.

Rex was anxious to continue, so they packed away the breakfast things and set off. As they penetrated deeper into the marshes, the tricorn grunts were replaced with deep rumbles that shook the ground. Lurgo proclaimed they must be entering Great Dragon territory. And although they knew he was teasing – for the Great Dragons were merely legend, and, even if they were real, haunted the forests far to the north, not the southern swamps – everyone in the party walked with their barkers poised, eyes darting nervously between the rushes. They slept in watches, lest some predator come upon them in the night.

On the fourth day they emerged onto a paved road. Ahead of them over the crest of the hill loomed the peaked roofs and low stone battlements of a farming hamlet. Beyond this, a black cloud stretched along the horizon, blocking all the sunlight and masking the outline of London beyond the spires of the Wall.

"Is it meant to be doing that?" Joel asked as he wiped his weeping eyes.

"I *told* you he's returned." Rex pushed his weapon up on his shoulder and started down the road.

They reached the outskirts of the hamlet before nightfall. Lights twinkled through gaps in the grout, and the smell of warm food and tobacco wafted over the wall. Thorn couldn't remember ever seeing a real town before, and wanted nothing more than to drink mecks at a pub and sleep on an actual mattress, but Stokers couldn't enter that place.

Apparently, that rule no longer applied to Rex, who assured them he had friends in the hamlet who would forge them the necessary papers to enter London. "Wait for me here," he said, gesturing to the thicket. "I shall return within the hour. Don't let anyone see you."

They crouched in the shade of the giant trunks, readied their weapons and tried to catch a few more moments of sleep. Joel kept edging towards her, words forming on his lips. But every time he started to say something, the trees rustled and animals stirred, and they were forced to sit rigid for several minutes, hands poised on weapons, listening for the sound of footsteps approaching.

Rex was gone much longer than an hour. Thorn's legs tingled with cramp. She shot worried glances at Joel, but he shook his head. He seemed more annoyed than concerned.

An animal skittered past them. Thorn froze, listening. Footsteps crunched towards them, quick and urgent. Someone was running. She pulled her barker across her lap and waited for them to run past the tree.

A figure shoved its way through the thicket and stopped, panting. Thorn lowered her barker. It was only Rex. Joel called out to him, and he jogged over, shaking his head.

"It's not good," he said. "She won't give us the papers."

"What? Why not?"

He shrugged. "I don't know. It seems there have been inquiries lately. They've increased security because of the Great Exhibition. She doesn't think it's safe to give us the documents."

I wonder if this she *goes by the name of Lydia,* thought, but didn't ask.

Joel set down his barker and stared at Rex with hard eyes. "How are we going to get into London?"

"We go through the Wall. I know of a passage."

"By Great Conductor's gurgling boiler!" Finn swore. "I didn't sign on for this. Have you *heard* the stories they tell about that Wall?"

Thorn had heard many, for the Wall was a favourite topic of the Stokers, and those few people who managed to escape the swamp for important missions would bring back much gossip about the city. After Brunel's cult had been demolished, the Wall had fallen into disuse. It was said that some of Brunel's machines still worked inside, unable to be shut down or to cease their duties. Criminals used the spaces inside the Wall for their nefarious deeds, and there were other, far more unsavoury tales told...tales of loud, wild roaring echoing through the empty structure, or footprints from animals that could not be identified, of people who went in and never came out...

The other Stokers were remembering these tales, too, for they all exchanged worried glances.

"Relax," Rex said, "I've done it before. It's perfectly safe."

Joel mumbled something unsavoury under his breath. Thorn nodded her agreement.

They made camp on the outskirts of the forest, under the shade of a walnut tree. Thorn made a hollow for herself in the crook of the trunk. She'd barely closed her eyes and relaxed her aching limbs when a voice broke into her thoughts.

"Thorn, I'm sorry."

She'd wanted to hear those words ever since he'd returned. Her eyes flew open, and she watched Rex kneel over her, his face arranged in a picture of concern. Her heart skipped in her chest. He reached out with tentative fingers and wiped her matted hair from her face.

Thorn's heart soared. This was what she'd wanted, more than anything. She wanted him to return to her, to tell her he'd made a mistake, and that they would be married after all. But after what she'd seen the other night, and the way he'd given the creature that message, *tell him I love him*, in that hushed, awe-filled tone, Thorn knew that whatever had happened in London had changed Rex forever. He wasn't coming back to her, and that made his words right now very, very dangerous.

"Rex—"

"No, you have to listen. I'm different now, Thorn. London changed me, and I can never go back to the way things were. But I've been wrong to treat you with such reproach – seeing you again unnerved me, it knocked me off balance. And now with Father dead...I feel so confused. But I can't let that ruin this mission – the fate of the Stokers rests with us. I need you to promise that you'll listen to me, that you'll do everything I ask, no matter how dangerous or repulsive it is. And when all this is over, I'll return to you, and I'll be yours. Do you understand? Do you promise?"

"Rex—" Tears rolled down her cheeks. She wanted so badly to believe him, to accept his apology and wrap herself in his warmth again, but the scene in the swamp nagged at her. She wanted to ask him about the creature, and the plate he'd exchanged for the lead, but she didn't want to drive him away again.

"Promise me, Thorn."

"I promise." Thorn heard the words fly from her mouth, as though she no longer controlled them. *No, I take it back!* She wanted to scream, but she bit her tongue. Her stomach churned.

Rex settled next to her, running his fingers over her face, along the line of her jaw. His touch – which used to bring such comfort – made her feel ill. "There's so much I want to tell you, but...I can't."

"I know. It's okay."

It wasn't okay, but she had to pretend she didn't care. She huddled under Rex's arm as he pulled his coat over their heads to fend off some of the rain. Beside them, Joel leaned against an uprooted branch, grimacing at her as he pulled the brim of his sodden cap over his concerned eyes.

I know this doesn't fix anything, Joel. But it's too painful being alone.

"Tomorrow, we shall sleep in London city," Rex whispered as he brushed his warm fingers over her cheek. His touch seared her inside, and the pin under her lapel scraped her skin. She lay awake for hours, not knowing if she shivered from fear of the iron-ringed city on the horizon, or for want of Rex's love.

***

Thorn awoke with a jolt. Someone gripped her throat. The pain stoppered her breath. Her chest heaved; sweat and tears dripped down her face.

I'm going to die. She raised her hands and clawed at her throat, trying to dislodge whoever assailed her. Her hands scraped her own skin. On the edge of consciousness, she heard the hoot of a whistle.

A train?

Surely there can't be a train nearby? There were hardly any trains in the South. Not many people trusted them after Brunel's reign, and Stephenson had concentrated his networks in the North. Thorn crawled forward, desperate to hear. *It is a train! I hear an engine puffing and wheels and pistons turning over the rails.* She coughed up air and dry phlegm. Her vision blurred as she doubled over. Pain stretched across her chest, as if invisible hands tore her open.

Beside her, the blurred silhouette of Rex coughed. He pressed something over her mouth. A damp cloth. Thorn breathed into it, and eventually her stomach unclenched and her chest rose and fell.

She could barely see two feet in front of her. The trees, the meadows, the walled hamlet, the dark Wall of London on the horizon existed only as hazy memories in a cloud of black soot. Her eyes and nose wept.

Joel crawled into view. He too, had a kerchief over his mouth. "What is this?" he croaked.

"Discharge from the Wall. The wind has turned toward us. C'mon, we'll have to change direction.

Quickly, gather the equipment!" Rex crawled off under the canopy of trees.

"But, the *train*—"

Pain spasmed along her arms. She collapsed over her rucksack, fumbling for the strap. With intense effort she pulled that and the barker over her shoulder. Her stomach heaved and she tasted bile. Her shoulders crackled like the drum fires when she pushed herself forward.

Her nose scraped the dirt. The cloth fell from her face and she froze, spluttering. The cough came from so low in her chest she felt her stomach rise, and last night's dinner of dried meat and acorns tumbled onto the dirt, black with soot.

Thorn's throat buckled of its own accord, intent on squeezing everything from her body. She ignored the searing in her chest and pulled herself forward, inching closer to the forest.

Something fell on her. She froze. There was nothing in her to scream. *I'm dead...*

The something wriggled under her arms and pulled her forward. The barker fell from her shoulder and dragged along her side. The roots and walnut shells scraped the skin from her chest.

It pulled her to her knees, but her limbs flopped about like dead weight. *I'm dead, I'm dead...*

"Cooperate a little, Thorn." *Rex? No, Joel...it's Joel.*

She dug her heels in the soft earth, and did everything she could to hold her breath and keep the coughing at bay. Something warm slid beneath her, and her feet left the ground and she floated, half-dreaming. Shapes and bubbles drifted across her vision.

Joel collapsed, and Thorn rolled off. She coughed again, and her stomach emptied its foul contents over him. She gasped; the air that filled her lungs seemed to stay in her chest.

She opened her eyes. They lay in a clearing, where a wall of heather formed a pocket in the forest and the soot-clouds seemed to pass over. Blood-red flowers dotted the strange spindly plants on the forest floor, and branches reached like fingers towards the edges, never quite touching.

"A...fairy...circle," Joel choked out. His eyes lit up at his own feeble joke.

Rex wiped his mouth with his sleeve. Rivers of sweat ran down his soot-blackened cheeks, and his eyes seemed sunken and inhuman. "This is...the Wall..."

Joel glared at him. "We know. We must press on, before it catches us again."

They dragged goggles and scarves from their rucksacks, and as Thorn fastened hers over her eyes she felt the stinging subside, a welcome relief even as the leather straps pinched her skin. They unshouldered their weapons, shaking the soot from the barrels and checking the mechanisms were still well-oiled. Edgar and Lurgo emptied out their munitions and threw away two cases of powder that were soaked through. Thorn stood on shaking legs and followed Rex from the clearing.

Joel tried to ask about the train, but Rex barked at him to be quiet. They tramped six miles in stony silence, skirting through the cracking forest and alongside rivers of black sludge. They gave wide berth to several blackened, deserted towns and hamlets. The black cloud chased them, stretching sooty tendrils through the dry air. Thorn pressed her handkerchief over her face, but every breath still sent fire through her chest.

And through the hours they walked the Wall beckoned them. The clank and churn of invisible mechanisms thumped inside Thorn's head. Whenever she passed a gap in the trees she saw it, and her chest tightened in fear. The slick iron face rose at least a hundred feet high, punctured at regular intervals with thick wrought-iron funnels pouring their black miasma into the sky. She heard many more trains go by, though she could not see them. The path they took became littered with debris, and as Thorn stepped over a tree root, her boot sank with a loud crack through the tree. She gasped; the giant oak tree was dead.

All the trees were dead.

In fact, if Thorn cast her mind back, aside from the red flowers in the clearing, she hadn't seen a speck of colour – not a green leaf nor yellowed wood – all day. The trees leaned inward, their own weight holding them upright. Thorn's boots crunched on brittle twigs. She heard no other sound; no birds, no scurrying beasts, no wind-whipped leaves brushing each other.

The tree cover grew sparse, and the stumps of oak and ash they passed were in even worse condition. Like skeletons picked clean by carrion birds they clung tenaciously to their last breath. Twigs that looked like stakes stood sentinel while their flesh and organs rotted away. As the party passed through in horrified silence, their movements shifted the air. All around them, branches folded, roots crumbled and snapped, and once-proud giants crumbled and sank to dust.

Unlike the Graveyard, the death here was palpable – sticking to Thorn's tongue like wood-chip porridge – and hopelessly sad. The machines created their own memorial, churning their death-knell behind their steel Wall. Here, what was once living crumbled to dust, with no one to mourn their passing, and what should never have lived churned forever on.

They passed into a dead field, devoid even of the sensation of air. Black dust sifted through a cold grey fog, its icy fingers anaesthetizing their senses. Only half a mile ahead loomed the Wall, invisible now, but no less frightening for its cloistering presence.

Thorn fumbled for her goggles. She wiped in vain at the grime on the inner lens, and pulled them back over her stinging eyes. She tugged her scarf across her nose and mouth as another violent cough rent her throat.

Rex thumped her on the back. "If you'd rather stay here..." The scarf muffled his voice, but he sounded annoyed.

"I'll be okay." She swallowed, trying to lubricate her dry throat.

"Then we're off." He turned into the field.

"Won't someone see us?"

"They don't need to." He did not look at her. "No talking, any of you. Use the whistle code – we don't want them to mistake us for Londoners."

We don't? And who are "they"?

Rex was already jogging across the field. Thorn followed Rex into the dust cloud, her feet crunching on dead, soot-covered ground. Her heart thumped in her ears. She heard the faint crunch of Joel and Lurgo's boots.

Within seconds she lost sight of Rex, and soot and dust curled around her. She hawked into her scarf, tasting blood on her tongue. She stopped, listening, but she could no longer hear footsteps.

A hand clenched her shoulder.

She screamed, but the only sound that escaped her dry throat was a strangled croak. Behind her, she heard Lurgo laugh, and he let go of her shoulder as he jogged past her and disappeared into the fog.

Fury boiled in her stomach. *How dare he? This is frightening enough without Lurgo playing the fool.*

A dark shadow rolled out of the mist towards her. At about ninety degrees she heard Rex's whistle. It blew three times. *Danger. Something's wrong.*

Lurgo cried out. Rex's whistle blew again. Thorn dropped to her knees. She heard the crunch of wheels against soot-dead earth churn past on her right, and sucked in her breath. Her throat seared, and she cupped her hands over her mouth and gritted her teeth to keep from coughing.

To her left, only fifteen feet away, something passed by. She heard the wheels turn again, and the scrape of metal against leather.

The whistle again, two short blasts, three long. *Run.*

Thorn heard shots; sharp bangs from behind her, a hissing that told her they were using Clegg steam-guns.

The wheels creaked towards Rex's whistle, picking up speed. Thorn pushed herself up and ran.

Something whizzed by her shoulders. She poured on the speed. *They can't see me. Remember, if I can't see them, they can't see—*

A trail of steam snaked across her face. She whirled to the right and ran on. Whatever it was, they could see her.

Something barrelled into her, sending her sailing to the ground. She gasped for air, and her shoulder wrenched. *I'm dead, they've got me—*

"This way," Lurgo said as he tugged her up. He had unslung his barker. Thorn held her tongue as pain screamed up her arm.

The whistle blew again, closer this time. They were nearly at the Wall.

Lurgo jerked left, and her hip crushed against something hard and cold and pulsing. The Wall. They ran alongside, listening for the whistle over the crunching of the wheels. Every time her foot fell on the dry soil with a snap, Thorn winced and ducked lower, certain they'd take her head off at any moment.

Something dark rose up in front of her. She froze, petrified. Lurgo pulled her shoulders, shoving her into the Wall. She expected to hit cold steel, but instead she fell into somewhere dark.

"Twice this month I've rescued you." Lurgo's breath touched her cheek.

A biting wind thrust from within, tearing through her ears, screeching along the iron depths.

"I got her." Lurgo ducked inside the recess. Thorn slumped against the wall, struggling for breath. She jumped back as the iron panel throbbed beneath her, like a pulse pumping life through the walls themselves. Finn, Joel and Rex crouched in the entrance to a dark tunnel, half the height of a man and littered with slivers of scrap metal and broken saw-teeth. Above their heads, frigid smoke gusted from a pressure valve, spewing fresh carbonic wastes across the dust field. All around them echoed the clanks and ticks of the monstrous working machine.

"We've lost Edgar," Joel said, his voice hoarse.

Rex clutched his abdomen, and Thorn saw something dark seep between his fingers. She reached a feeble hand to him, but he shook his head.

"We can't go back for him. We're inside." Rex heaved himself upright. Thorn saw him stumble. "We have to move, *now*, or they'll find us. Everyone, load your guns."

"Are they Brunel's men? Why are they attacking *us?*"

"They're not men, and they don't know we're Stokers. They don't *care*, and they're hungry. *Quickly!*"

Vibrations shot through Thorn's back and the wall

behind her clanked and ground. The Wall, dormant now for fifteen years, clanked and turned again. There could be no doubt – Rex was right: Brunel had returned.

Pulling off her goggles, Thorn bent over her barker and tipped a measure of powder into the barrel, adding a small amount to the pan and clicking the frizzen shut. She wrapped the lead ball in a scrap of cloth and rammed that on top. Outside, a dark shape slunk past. The crunch of the wheels on dry earth chilled her more than the wind. She tugged her scarf over her face again, not wanting to cough and give away their position.

After the shadow passed, Rex led the way down the narrow shaft. Finnegan and Joel lit their lamps and followed. Thorn and Lurgo skulked at the rear, their feet crunching on the metal shards. The clanking throbbed inside Thorn's skull, and she flinched every time a footstep fell heavy, certain their clumsy movements would be detected over the laboured tick and clank of the machine.

The shaft tapered downward. Rex stopped, gasping and pinching his wound. Thorn peeked around him as Joel shone the argand lamp into the gloom. The light became lost in a chasm of nothingness. In the distance pistons slammed, the force sending shudders through the metal grate they stood on.

Hundreds of lead pipes – some as thin as a penny, some as thick as the spread of Thorn's arms – ran above their heads, held in place with industrial gauge pins. Rex yanked the argand from Joel's grasp and directed it at the far wall, at least forty feet away.

"The bridge." Rex pointed to a rickety mesh platform twenty feet away. Finn and Joel darted across, with Lurgo at their heels. Thorn stepped onto the swinging mesh, but Rex grabbed her shoulders and dragged her back.

"You have to stay here, Thorn." He pointed to a rusted lever resting against the railing. "The one on the other side is broken off. All you need to do is pull it up after we're across. We have to retract the bridge so they won't follow us."

"But how will I get across?"

The answer hung in the air for a few excruciating moments, broken by the scratching and yelping of their pursuers.

Finally, Rex pointed to the ceiling. "Climb across on the pipes. You're light and nimble – it shouldn't be a problem."

Thorn's arm twinged. "I can't—"

"You *have* to. You're the only one who can." He pushed her off the bridge, grabbing her rucksack from her shoulder and tucking it under his arm. "Now, go. We don't have much time!"

She gasped as a blast of cold air from the void below screamed past her face. Rex disappeared from her view. She realised why Rex wanted her to do it. She was expendable; Rex was the only one who knew London, Joel was needed for translation, Finnegan for explosives, Lurgo could hunt better than she, and Edgar was already dead.

Every word he spoke the night before echoed in her mind. *Is this why Rex won't touch me, will hardly look at me? Is this why he sought out another to claim his heart? Has he planned this all along?*

A thread of pain arced across her face, a sting as though he'd slapped her for real. Her ears rang. Inside her heaving chest her heart quietly broke.

Thorn reached across and pulled up the lever, leaning all her weight into the mechanism. With a creak the bridge lurched away from the edge and disappeared into the darkness.

On the other side of the chasm, someone swore. Voices broke into a heated argument. But their words were drowned out by the clanking and hissing from the tunnels behind her, growing closer and more ferocious. Thorn gulped down the terror, reached up with her good hand and clasped a pipe.

I'll show you, Rex Williams. I'll show you what it is to be left behind.

Thorn swung herself up and grabbed another pipe. Her shoulder screamed in protest. She grunted and heaved her good hand forward, then her right arm, then her left. Her coat – heavy with water and accumulated filth – dragged her down, the clasps cutting across her throat. Her eyes watered as she strained to hold her body weight while she swung herself forward.

She heard a creak, too close by. Thorn looked across at her left hand. The pipe she was holding juddered, and a pin bent under her weight. She swung her body and grabbed at the next section of pipe. Missed.

Rex wants me dead. I wanted to marry him and he wants me dead.

Her stomach clenched with fear. The pin slid further and the pipe cracked. She pumped her legs, grabbing for the next section. Her fingers clasped around it, but the force of her grip yanked the pin from the brace.

The pipe buckled and dislodged, and she fell.

Sparks flew past her eyes. She had no time to scream before she hit a metal grate and wind fled her chest. Pain cascaded up her right leg. She lay on her back, gasping for air, willing herself to snap out of it, to concentrate, to ride out the pain.

The light above her head was faint. Thorn guessed

she'd fallen thirty feet or so. It was difficult to tell; the bent pipes and hazy shadows distorted her senses.

She heard voices. Rex called her name. She didn't want to speak to him ever again.

"I'm okay," she called up, as loud as she dared.

Voices answered her, speaking in harsh tones. They were still arguing. Something hit the ground beside her, and bounced against her leg. She bent down and felt it. Her rucksack? No, Joel's rucksack.

"Do your job and distract ... Sinkers. We've found ... way," Rex called. "Meet us ... Highgate ..."

"... be careful." Joel sounded worried. Panic rose up within Thorn. They were leaving her here to fend for herself. She'd never find her way in the darkness without them, not with those strange creatures prowling around.

"But how—" The light disappeared. *But how will I find you? How will I get out? What is a Sinker?*

Fingering the drawstring on the rucksack, Thorn felt hot anger flood her. She'd waited for Rex for nine long months, hoping against all the odds that he might one day return for her. She'd mourned him as a husband; night after night she cried for him, flailing her hands for his warmth and grasping only air.

She had endured the taunts and insults of the other Stokers, their constant mumblings about curses and her father's supposed betrayal. She'd ignored their gossip about Rex's real intentions, their scoffs at his declaration of love. *And for what?*

Thorn hugged the rucksack to her chest. *They expect me to die. Rex thinks he's rid of me, and earned his safe passage into London as his reward. But why should I help him — has he given me even a single thought in all his months away? Why should I not leave them all to die?*

Because Joel and Lurgo are with him, and I don't want their deaths on my conscience. They have been so kind to me. But I can still show Rex that I have worth he doesn't realise. If I can escape the Wall and survive, and help with the plot that would see the Stokers return to Engine Ward, won't Rex want me then? Won't all the Stokers have to take back the words they say against my family? Won't they finally admit Father was not a turncoat?

A new resolve settled in Thorn's stomach. She knew what she had to do.

Thorn tried to stand. Her leg wouldn't support her weight, so she strapped the sack over her shoulder, jamming it under her barker, and crawled on hands and knees along the trench. The grating swayed as she shifted her weight, and she heard the clank of machinery far below. Frigid air enveloped her from under the grate, and steam rushed from valves at either side. Her forearms bristled with goosebumps and burns.

She sensed the wall seconds before she hit it. Her head stung. *What's one more injury?*

Thorn felt out the dimensions of the wall. With no light, and only the acrid smell of iron in every direction, she relied on her hands and her God to guide her.

Great Conductor, please let there be a way ... please don't let the evil things find me.

The wall seemed solid, and blocked the breadth of the iron trench. She heard a clang as footsteps fell on the grating behind her. She turned but could see no light.

The erratic footsteps in the dark could only come from a creature that had no use for eyes. Not human then, but human enough that her sense found nothing. She unslung the barker and aimed as best she could at the advancing threat. Her arm trembled under the weight as she pulled the hammer back.

Click.

The footsteps stopped. Thorn held her breath.

Moments passed in unbearable silence. Her stomach heaved. A cramp rose in her one good leg. Her fingers shivered around the trigger.

Move dammit, so I can shoot you.

Thorn's silent threat irked no response. Another minute passed. She almost believed it was safe to move again, but she knew better. It was out there, maybe twenty feet away, waiting for her to reveal herself.

She tried again to cast her mind out, to latch onto it with her sense. She was too frightened to concentrate.

Something clattered on the grating. *Oh god.* The sack had fallen off her shoulder.

The explosion hit the wall behind her, but the jet of steam seared her arm. She rolled out of the way, lifted her pistol, and shot blindly into the darkness.

Another hiss from its Clegg, and she twisted away as the steam jet shot past, narrowly missing her head. Heat exploded around her. Thorn reached out her hand and felt something wet. *His blood, or mine? Maybe I did hit the brute?* If so, it hadn't cried out.

Its feet clanked on the grate. It was moving forward. It was coming for her.

Thorn hugged the sack to her chest. Tossing the barker back over her shoulder, she gripped the lead pipe at the edge of the steel grate and swung herself down into the void, praying she could hang on long enough for it to lose interest.

To her great surprise, her feet hit a solid surface.

Wasting no time, she dropped to her feet. She heard a sound like a low purr, heard the hiss and felt the hot rush as it let off the Clegg at the wall again. It hadn't seen her move. *I have you now...whatever you are.*

She felt around her perch, trying to figure out her surroundings. Suddenly she was bathed in light.

Sparks flew down the passage, fizzing and erupting into orange flames. A grenade. Footsteps clanged down the passage, followed by shots from a barker that wasn't hers.

"Thorn!" she heard Joel cry from deep in the darkness, his voice high with terror. "They got Rex. Move down! They're coming for us!"

Thorn started to sprint toward Joel's voice, but the grating beneath her buckled, and she fell again. As she struggled to her feet, a bright orange light rushed from the passage toward her. She leapt back as flames engulfed the passage.

She turned and half-ran, half-stumbled into the darkness as the fire raced toward her. As Thorn glanced over her shoulder, she saw a dark shadow emerge from the flames. Her heart soared as she recognised a human shape, but as it moved toward her Thorn saw that it was not Rex or Joel or Lurgo, but the creature that hunted her. A new terror burned in her belly as she gazed upon its horrid form.

It seemed human at first, but it couldn't be. What she first mistook as lead armour were metal appendages that grew from its actual skin. It seemed to feel no pain as it stood in the flames watching her, while the fire engulfed its body. Its eyes sunk so far back in its skull they rolled forward as they melted into the flames. As the fire tore away its flesh it fell on the grate, and Thorn saw the last vestiges of life fall from that monstrous face – and its greenish lips curled back and revealed fanged teeth beneath rotting gums. Silent screams escaped its mouth like hissing steam.

Then it was no more.

Thorn turned away, her mind reeling. She'd heard stories of the Sunken, the army of the Vampire King –

mostly from Quartz, who'd encountered them firsthand when he fought in the Battle of London in 1831. The Vampire King kept them in Windsor Castle until they grew to such numbers he could no longer contain them, so he set them loose on the people of London. The streets ran red with blood until Brunel murdered the King and sent his Boilers after the unfortunate creatures.

Quartz's gnarled face lit up as he described how the first Sunken were made: babies fed from birth on a diet of molten lead. Those that didn't die became twisted from within, taking on the properties of the metal they devoured. They shuffled about in a daze, baring flapping skin and long, rotting fangs, jittering mockeries of their royal master. If they caught you they would tear your flesh from your bones, or worse. They could bite you with lead-soaked fangs and turn you into one of their own.

The stories had frightened Thorn as a child and now, seeing that distorted face crackle under the flame made her realise she hadn't been nearly frightened enough.

From somewhere in the depths of the Wall, beyond the sound of bubbling lead and the smell of burning flesh, Thorn heard more gunshots. And far above, the clanks turned into pounding. A rising hiss – not steam this time – told her more of the Sunken were on their way.

She ran away from the fire until she reached the end of the gangway. She crouched on a wide lead pipe, feeling the surge of gas whooshing inside it. More pipes crisscrossed the chasm that opened out below her, descending into nothing. About twenty feet below she saw the gleam of another steel grating that might be maintenance deck.

There was nowhere else to go but down. Thorn

lowered herself on to the next pipe, her leg flaring with pain as she rested her weight on it. Her boots made a dull thump as they landed against the rusty pipe.

As Thorn crouched and prepared to move again, a fire flared out of the corner of her eye. Something was standing at the end of the pipe, flames leaping from its belly.

A Boiler.

If the Sunken were the Vampire King's offspring, then the Boilers were the beloved children of Brunel. He'd created the Boilers as mechanical workers – steam-powered mobile machines that could be programmed to perform simple tasks. Brunel had made hundreds of Boilers, using them for every project, and rendering the Stokers – his previous workforce – obsolete. The Boilers were the foremen of Brunel's great engineering projects, the generals in his army during the Gauge War, and the keepers of his Wall. When Thorn's father killed Brunel after the wreck of the *Thunderer*, the Londoners destroyed every last Boiler in their quest to purge Brunel's presence from the city.

Evidently, they had missed one.

The Boiler stood seven feet high, with a bulbous furnace belly and two skinny chimneys protruding from its shoulders like a misshapen, two-headed idol. Snapping, whirring, clanking appendages extended from every direction, framing the boiler grill that grinned at her with flaming teeth. Its body was badly damaged – mangled strips of metal hung from its body, and flames darted out through the gaps. The hulking machine trundled forward on two whirring belts, seemingly of its own accord.

Thorn froze. If it saw her, there would be no mercy from a machine.

It lowered its pressure valve and aimed for Thorn.

Pain crushed against her skull, sharper than any she'd experienced before. Waves of emotion flooded her – pain, hopelessness and sheer, paralysing terror. At first she thought the machine had hit her with a stream of boiling water, but with a shock she realised the pain did not come from her body, but from the thoughts of another creature inside her head.

The rogue emotions pushed her own thoughts away – she'd never sensed feelings so strong or so frightening before. *This can't be happening; there are no animals for miles around...*

Help me, the Boiler screamed inside her head, *help me!*

Thorn screamed as well, too shocked to restrain herself. She let go of the pipe and fell, just as the thick jet of steam and boiling water flew past her.

She landed on all fours this time. Nothing broken, though her already-beaten body sagged under the pain. Above her she heard valves clang and gears turn.

Help me, help me! The boiler's thoughts had faded, but they still pressed against her skull. Thorn trembled, paralysed by the memories that weren't her own – bounding free through a wheat-chaffed field, garrotted and captured and tortured and eviscerated while still alive. Torn limb from limb and rebuilt with iron and rivets. Thorn pounded her temples with closed fists. *Go away, go away. I don't want to know any more!*

Footsteps raced along the gangway towards her.

She darted away, following the pipes until they disappeared into the wall. She crossed the gangplank along a dark tunnel.

Several Sinkers charged across the gangway overhead. The air grew heavy and hot, as if their very breath produced molten lead. Thorn held her breath and waited.

The Boiler spat a shower of sparks, and a serious of low, inhuman growls filled the room.

It's giving them instructions. It's telling them to kill me. It shouldn't be able to do that.

The tunnel fed into two passages. Thorn raced down the left, hands held in front of her, heart scraping against her ribs. Wooden planks ran under her feet, almost like railway sleepers. Her foot clipped against something on the ground, and she fell on her knees. Her hand scraped against a metal rail. She felt the nails where the sleepers met the rail. A railway. She was running inside a railway tunnel.

Somewhere amongst the terror, she heard Lurgo shout.

"Down here!" she screamed.

*Rex is dead...*Joel's words pounded her brain. *Rex is dead...is dead...*

Another junction. Thorn dived into the left tunnel, listening for another shout. She could hardly concentrate over the clang of her boots and the pounding of her heart.

Behind her she heard a scream. Jibbers and discordant sounds bounced from the tunnel walls. They were gaining on her.

Thorn poured on speed, ducking right, then left, then left again. Her shoulder scraped on something jagged and red welts appeared in her vision. In the darkness she couldn't tell if she headed toward the city. She prayed so.

Great Conductor, grant me passage through this Wall, and save Joel and the others. Yes, even Lurgo. And Rex...

She heard another scream, further away now. She couldn't distinguish the voice.

Where are they? Why haven't they come?

Her hand hit iron, and it jangled. A crack of light appeared, brighter than the gold frame of Quartz's monocle. *Escape?*

Thorn leaned her shoulder on the panel and pushed. No luck. She tried to squeeze her fingers under the gap and pull. Another inch gave way. She heard sounds in the tunnel behind her, the squirt of Clegg guns, the stomp of feet, the laughter of the damned.

With a sob, she pulled again. There was a three-inch gap on the lower edge now, pouring in a square of light that filled her with hope. She could see buildings, a cobbled road outside. She wept with fear and relief as she tugged harder. The footsteps were right behind her.

The panel clattered away, and Thorn heaved herself through and ran. She was outside, running down a wide, cobbled street. There were a huge group of people gathered just up ahead – she could lose herself in the crowd. Steam issued from the hole in the Wall, and a great cloud of dust and soot obscured the street. People mumbled and gasped and stepped away in disgust.

Covering her face with her coat, Thorn turned toward the billowing stream. She heard a hiss and pop as the Boiler gave another command, and a dry, emaciated hand thrust itself through the hole and groped for a hold.

A woman stomped on it. A man drew a Derringer from his coat and fired it into the hole. The hand withdrew and the crowd cheered. Thorn slipped away, but her sooty clothes and unkempt hair drew stares from the enraged mob.

"Who is that?" Someone shouted. "She came from the Wall!"

"She's raised something unholy!"

"After her!"

The crowd surged forward, and Thorn hurried down the cobbled alley, ducking around the packing crates. She exited on another street and turned right, diving first one way, then another, losing herself in the throng of bodies. In no time at all, the mob that pursued her was swallowed by the anonymous masses, and she let the crowd carry her, unnoticed.

She shoved her hands in her coat pockets, trying to stop shaking. *London,* she realised. *I'm in London.*

Smells assailed her. The fresh, slightly pungent scent of horses, the harsh tang of millet and faeces stomped between the cobbles. Cloying food, rich with spices that made her mouth water and her throat burn. A sweet smell erupted from a nearby building – alcoholic, but not like the cruel mecks Quartz loved so much.

Short for her age, Thorn stumbled between coats and purses, under parasols and binoculars. Her raw skin grazed the fabrics: soft silks, scratchy brocade and rows of jewels and beads, wool that felt warm to the touch, and clean, unlike her own clothes. Cottons and linen so featherfine they seemed to float over their occupant's bodies, shifting and billowing wholly to their own design.

She touched the trim on one man's coat and felt the familiar sensation of metal. *Actual gold, on clothing?* It seemed like a dream.

The material was snatched from her fingers.

"This coat was made for me by Louis-Philippe of France. If you wish to steal it, you fear the sting of my cane knife."

She stepped back. "I'm sorry sir, I wasn't stealing, just admiring."

"Well, if that is the case." He extended his free hand a little way from his body, waving it in front of her abdomen. "It is always my pleasure to make the acquaintance of someone who appreciates the finery of a Parisian coat. I am James Holman."

She stared at the hand, horrified.

"You offer your hand sir? Do you not see the state of me?"

"I see nothing at all, but I hear a friendly voice. Please, take my hand before it drops off."

For the first time Thorn noticed the long cane resting against the man's left wrist, and the way he would not look directly at her. Instead, he angled his face upward, staring at something over her shoulder.

She thought of deceiving him, but that didn't seem fair. "I have come through the Wall. Mr. Holman."

"Really?" He lowered his hand. "If you forgive my impertinence, Miss—"

"My name is Thorn."

"Miss Thorn." He lowered his voice, and inclined his head towards her. He wore a strange hat – a cloth of fine stitching wrapped several times around his head – and she noticed for the first time his eyes were sewn shut with threads of gold. Thorn had never met a blind man before. Quartz had told her they were usually beggars, but this man looked too well accoutered to be a beggar. Fascinated, she stood up straighter to better hear him. "If you came through the wall, and you have the smell of the swamps still on your flesh, my guess is that you are a Stoker. With all due respect, you should not be so bold with your identity. Your kind are not welcome within the city, especially not with the Great Exhibition beginning in two days. Tell me, why are Stokers trying to rebuild his Engine Ward when London only wants to forget? I have heard talk of the fires burning within that cursed place. If the construction continues, the Queen will simply send in some soldiers to tear it down."

"I know nothing about the Engine Ward. I've come from the Graveyard looking for honest work. I have some important business to attend to."

His mouth twitched. "The business of a Stoker girl in London? Why, I can only imagine."

"I wish to clear the name of a man who's been wrongly convicted of a horrible crime." Thorn patted the reassuring lump slung over her shoulder. "But don't worry, I wish no harm to you or your city, Mr. Holman. If you can ask about my business, may I inquire after yours?"

"I'm here to see the parade and the Great Exhibition, of course."

"But how can you—"

Holman laughed. "But how can I enjoy the parade when I cannot see at all? The true parade experience surpasses that which the eyes take in, Miss Thorn. Why, here I can drink in the stench of London. I can lose myself amongst her citizens, I can listen to her gossip and her music, and can partake of her delicacies."

She nodded in agreement, then realised that was silly. "How do you walk so freely on the streets? Won't you lose your way?"

"Magic." His mouth twitched again. "Would you like to join me for dinner?"

Thorn's stomach grumbled, but the weight of Joel's rucksack on her shoulder reminded her of her task. "I need to find someone, in Highgate cemetery. But I wouldn't suppose you knew where that—"

"I shall show you. If you'll wait with me for the parade to finish and allow me to buy you a pie."

***

Mr. Holman explained that the streets weren't usually so crowded, but Prince Albert had organised a marvellous parade to celebrate the opening of the Crystal Palace and the first journey of the newly reinstated London rail network. Everybody wanted to see Queen Victoria ride past in her carriage. Holman said rumours had been flying for weeks about the extravagance of the affair; the exotic flowers flown from France; the building of a hundred great arches for the parade route; the chainmail parasol Her Majesty had the new Royal Engineer construct to protect her from would-be assassins.

It sounded amazing, like something from Quartz's tales. Thorn felt strings inside her clench and tug. *Rex would have loved to see this parade—*

At the thought of Rex, a single tear fell from Thorn's eye. She wiped it away, forgetting that Holman wouldn't notice. But that one tear only brought a mate, and soon her whole face was awash with salt, and the runoff dribbled down the front of her tunic, settling beneath her breasts.

They can't be dead...Rex knew the way...and Joel and Lurgo are clever. But if they survived, why didn't they follow me? Where are they now?

"She should be coming any moment now." Holman grabbed her tearstained hand. "What's this?" He sniffed. "You're crying? We can't have that."

They could already be at Highgate, waiting for me... Oh, Joel, Rex, Lurgo...please don't be dead.

"There's no hope left." Thorn sobbed into Holman's beautiful coat.

"Sssssh." He stroked her hair, his fingers catching in the tangles. His touch stirred a memory from her childhood, and she cried harder.

"I'm sorry," Thorn sobbed. "You've been so kind to

me, but I really need to find my friends. I need to know if they are alive."

"C'mon, Miss Thorn, I best take you to Highgate immediately. I'll catch the parade from another street corner."

Holman tapped his cane on the pavement. Thorn settled her arm – still shooting with pain – inside his, and they walked on. Many people stepped out of their way, tipping their hats to an unseeing Holman. Thorn gazed at her escort in awe. He tapped his cane constantly, occasionally whacking the heel of a pedestrian in his way. He never stumbled, and seemed instinctively to dodge around lamp posts and street vendors. They wound their way through alleys and over bridges, in an impossibly twisted route Thorn could never hope to retrace. She began to wonder if it really was magic.

Suddenly, Holman stopped. He pointed to the sky with his cane. "What does that sign say?"

"I'm sorry, I can't read."

"Oh…" He squeezed her hand. "Don't worry then, we should be nearly there." He walked again, slower this time, sniffing the air. Thorn sniffed too, and noticed another smell beneath the offal and spice she was coming to recognise as London, the light perfume of flowers.

"That beguiling scent is the hyacinth. There are also calla lilies in the gardens, but they do not have a scent," Holman explained. "We're on Swains Lane. Around this corner we should see the gates."

And sure enough, two pillars of stone rose from the roadside like sacred dolmens. Gates of wrought iron the breadth of her arms swung back on gilded hinges. A high fence stood on either side, its apex affixed with sharp iron spikes. Men and women flocked through the gates, calling to each other in amiable voices.

Mr. Holman wanted to escort her through the cemetery, but as they passed under the west gate Thorn gave him the slip, darting under his arm and behind the gatehouse. He called her name, but she didn't answer, and of course he couldn't look for her. Thorn watched him standing on the path while others bustled around him; he looked forlorn as he wandered a little along the main square, tapping his stick on the ground and continuing to call her name. Finally he left, and she ducked down the path in search of the hideout.

Far from a quiet abode for the dead, the cemetery bustled with life. Women in swamp-dragon corsetry and skirts like ship sails wandered past, their flimsy bodies carried by winds of exotic perfume. Men in dark suits doffed their hats and handed around cigars. Someone walked past with a tray of hot pies, the smell of the hot meat making Thorn's stomach rumble. Around every corner Thorn bumped and crashed into more people. She kept her head low and tucked her barker and pin further under her tunic, hoping no one would recognise her for a Stoker.

Halfway there she felt the tears welling up inside her once more. She gulped them back. It wouldn't do any good to cry. It wouldn't bring Rex back, and it would only draw attention to her. Thorn went to pull her scarf up over her nose and mouth, but the pie-man rushed past her. The corner of his pie tray caught her on her cheek and knocked her aside. Her scarf landed in a puddle. The pie-man rushed on, oblivious.

The cold ball in her throat grew. Thorn bit her lip, jamming her knuckles in her eyes. *He came back. He came back to me, and everything should have been perfect. Why did he hate me so much? Why did my very touch repulse him? What did*

I do to make him hate me so, except wait and mourn him! Well, now he's really dead, and I...hate...him...

It was a lie. She still loved Rex, and she wanted to go back and cast herself to the Sunken, anything to undo the pain and anger she felt at his loss, and at the loss of Joel and Lurgo. *Let them kill me too, now that everyone I've ever loved is dead. I really am cursed; those who I love betray me, and my only true friends die at my expense. I should have died there instead, and Lurgo and Joel should be in London, savouring this paradise for their kindness.*

Thorn shook her head. *Stop this. Lurgo and Joel could have survived. After all, you did. They're probably waiting for you at the grave. Calm down and keep looking. Soon you'll find it and know for sure.*

Her scarf smelt awful, so she balled it up and shoved it in her coat pocket. She sucked in a deep breath, and wiped her tears with her palm. The air smelt so fresh it tickled her nose and seemed to fill her whole head, making her feel light, like her head might float off her shoulders. A pleasure that was like pain erupted in her temples.

London.

There were birds in the trees. Their twitters accompanied the lively conversation occurring around her. There had been birds in the marshes too, once, but the explosion of the compie population all but cleared them out. Only a few woodcocks and the carrion birds remained, prowling the western edge of the estuary where the Stokers buried the dead, digging with their beaks in the soft earth and tugging unmercifully at the burial shrouds.

But not in London. Here, even the cemetery was alive with song and laughter.

Thorn wandered amongst the living and the dead,

delighting in the sights and the smell and the feel of the place, keeping her eyes peeled for Joel and Lurgo and Rex. Her heart rose and plummeted, soaring with excitement one moment and aching with sorrow or anger the next. Her eyes searched the tombs for her father's crest, browsing the graffiti for the shovel, but she saw nothing. Summoning her courage, she asked a grey-haired lady where she might find Nicholas Thorne's crypt.

"That the man who killed Brunel? He's on the eastern side." The lady had a kind voice, and pointed with her lily-white fingers towards the gate. "Just o'er the road, miss. Take care now. The cabs exit the corner with rather too much speed."

Thorn jogged across Swains Lane. *Please let them be here, please let them still be waiting.*

The east side was less crowded, and the graves here were plainer, devoid of opulent decoration. The sounds of merriment flew overhead, lost in the brambles and the branches of the oaks. She passed only a handful of people on the path.

Thorn's eye caught the familiar insignia of Brunel, scratched into a tree trunk beside a crumbling crypt. Someone had attacked it recently, and the pictogram now sported lewd appendages. She smiled, thinking it was just Rex's sense of humour.

Rex who will never laugh again.

The door hung loose on its hinges, the iron pegs scraping in the dirt. She stepped over a fallen facing stone and ducked inside the crypt. It stank of rust and stale urine. Water dripped from a lead drainpipe. She heard something scurry in the corner. There was no one there.

No one except Father.

Thorn stared at the low lead coffin on its stone plinth. Rust had attacked the seal, and someone had used a nail or flick knife to scratch symbols on the lid. Thorn couldn't be sure, but the loops and points might have been writing.

I'm too late. I could've missed them. They're probably in a pub down the road. Lurgo would have left something to let me know they're okay.

Or, they never made it. She forced the thought away.

As she stepped from the doorway the light illuminated the far wall, which was piled with empty tin cans. A lone compie emerged from the corner and twittered at her, a lump of something's flesh clamped between its front claws.

Behind the compie Thorn saw more graffiti. Someone had scratched two stick figures – one labelled with Rex's family crest, the other with an unfamiliar scrawl. The woman's bulbous breasts were twice the size of her head. There was a name, but Thorn couldn't read it. They were copulating.

"No more, you bastard. Sod off," she said to the wall, her chest tightening. was no sign of recent occupation in the room. They hadn't been here.

Thorn picked a lump of soot from her pocket and, using her finger as a brush, scrawled a giant, jagged X right through the drawing.

***

Thorn slept that night in her father's crypt, huddled in the comer closest to the door, the reassuring weight of her barker resting against her shoulder. During the night the compie was joined by two friends, and the three chattered away like gossiping ladies, their chittering voices keeping her awake for hours.

Thorn, however, remained all alone. Her nightmare ran red with blood, and the images of the Boiler's memories burned inside her.

She awoke when two shafts of light entered the leaky ceiling and passed over her face. Her neck ached from the awkward angle, and her stomach rumbled. Something tickled her neck.

"Argh," she slapped at the tickle. Her hand connected with a protruding snout. The compie darted into the gloom, chattering to its friends who were attacking the rust seal on the coffin. She shooed the rodents off her father's coffin, and leaned against its base.

"You've messed things up awfully, you know," she said to him. Her voice sounded hollow, tinny, as it bounced off the stone and lead.

"No one believes Brunel sabotaged his own train anymore. They think you framed him and led us all to ruin. I know you believed you were doing the right thing, but you had something wrong, you must have. Quartz told me about a story in the papers from some years ago about a man who thought the god Morpheus manifested in his beer tank? Is this any different, Father? Why did you have to kill Brunel? I know you must have had your reasons, but knowing doesn't make you less dead or the Stokers less hateful. I wish you were here, to teach me about the sense and how to control it, and to explain to me why you did what you did."

Thorn thought of everything she'd seen and heard so far, and how it all fitted together. *Rex said Brunel had returned, and that seems true enough, judging by the activity in the Wall and what Rex said of the Engine Ward being rebuilt. But why are there Sunken within the Wall? Why can I sense the Boilers? How has Brunel done so much work within the Wall without recalling the Stokers from Graveyard?*

She stroked the barker as she continued to talk. "I'm alone again, but I guess you know what that feels like. You've been all alone here for so many years, until Rex and Sooty and their fellow revolutionaries began to keep your company. Did they destroy your final resting place? Dammit, Pappa, I..." The tears welled in her eyes again. *No,* she wouldn't cry. Thorn blinked them away.

"I'm sorry. I'll leave you alone now." Thorn brushed the dust off her clothing. She fumbled for the rucksack. *Perhaps Joel had some food in here.* She tipped it onto her lap.

It contained two tins of beans, a flick knife, a compass, a small tin of powder, a few lead balls and scraps of cloth, three teabags, a comb, and something hard and shiny. The plate Joel had shown her back in Graveyard. Thorn wrapped her fingers around it, feeling the strange bumps.

"Why were you keeping secrets, Pappa? What does this plate mean?"

Of course there was no answer except the drip of water in the corner of the crypt. Thorn prised the lid off the beans with Joel's knife. She had no flint to make a fire, and it wouldn't have lasted long in the damp, anyway. She tipped the entire can into her mouth, juice from the cold, slimy beans dribbling down her chin as she chewed and swallowed. Cupping her hands under the dripping pipe, Thorn washed down the beans with metallic-tasting water.

"I won't quit, you know. I won't give up on the Stokers like Brunel did." She hitched the rucksack onto her shoulder, tucked the barker under her coat, and the munitions into her inner pocket. "I'll search this city until I find every last Stoker. Someone will decipher this plate and help me figure out what's going on. I'll find a way for us to return here, Father, and clear your name. You'll see."

***

Her plan came to pieces just outside the cemetery gates. The Great Exhibition would begin tomorrow, and the streets were even more crowded than yesterday. Thorn learned from the gossip in the mob that tickets for the first day ran a high price, but the celebrations were not limited to the patrons entering the Crystal Palace, and those left out in the streets could expect dancing and music and free sugared almonds. She had no hope of finding her way to the Engine Ward in the crowds.

Reluctantly, she returned to the crypt, and spent the remainder of the daylight hours fingering her father's plate and playing with the compies. Every time a twig broke or footsteps scuffled outside, she leapt to her feet and peered through the rusted grating, certain it was the boys arriving at last. But no one approached.

When the light faded, Thorn left again, ducking through the overhanging trees till she emerged on the far-east end of the cemetery. Like a giant clock the city was winding down for the day, and far in the distance she heard a train whistle. Twilight was descending. An officer waved his torch under the streetlamps, lighting the street in a faerie glow. Her eyes stung, drained of tears and burning from all she'd seen.

A light rain began to fall. Thorn heard the train whistle again and started off in that direction. Wherever there were trains, there were bound to be Stokers.

She stuck to the main streets, safe in her anonymity. She simply swept along with the people, allowing their footsteps to carry her through the unfamiliar labyrinth.

She overheard two men talking about cargo arriving on "the *Goes When Ready* line" and followed them along the waterfront. If she followed the tracks, she would eventually end up inside the Engine Ward.

For the first time she saw a river that wasn't encrusted with peat mounds and slick with engine oil, not that the Thames looked any more inviting. Raindrops dribbled down her cheeks, washing away the dirt and soot of her home. Breezes wafted by; fresh meat cooked to perfection and the salt and brine drifting off the water.

The train whistled again, closer now. Her ears pricked at the conversation of the men. When she heard the word "tricorn", her eyes drew away from the Thames and toward her targets, and she picked up her pace. Like Mr. Holman the shorter of the men wore a bright-coloured coat of exquisite detail, embroidered with meandering monkeys and galloping dragons. The other man reminded her of the fever victims in the Graveyard with his sagging, emaciated features and bony, wringing fingers – though his eyes shone with life and he walked with dignified ease. He puffed tobacco from a comically large pipe while the other gesticulated, his voice rising and falling with great distress and excitement.

They're not Stokers; maybe they're ivory dealers. They'd recognise Oswald's name and they could help me.

She shuffled closer to hear what they discussed.

"But you did receive my message?"

The fat man nodded. "I had hoped Christolf was only slightly dead."

"There's no such thing as *slightly* dead, I'm afraid, George."

"Nonsense. I won't give Atkins the pleasure, and the night before the exhibition begins, too!"

Thorn skidded to a halt as the fat man stopped. He

yanked a poster from a streetlamp, and tore it in half. The men continued their conversation.

Unnoticed, Thorn bent over and picked up the poster. She couldn't read the words, but the bright picture depicted a tall man with an impeccably-curled moustache gesturing with a short cane at a tricorn, its hide covered in a red blanket emblazoned with jewels. Bells hung from its triple horns and other bestiary – compies and horses and other creatures she'd never seen before – marched around its feet, decked out in tiny silver jackets and hats.

Thorn turned it this way and that, but still it made no sense. *Tricorns behind the Wall? But the Wall was built to keep the beasts out. Nothing in London makes any sense.*

The men had disappeared. She dropped the poster and raced around the corner, but she couldn't see them through the bobbing coats and bright-coloured scarves.

What she *could* see was a train station.

From what little Quartz had told her about the first stations the Boilers built in London, they looked nothing like this. A curved metal superstructure – like a gabled church nave in steel and glass – floated over the platform, resting on steel arches. Everything gleamed as it caught the light from the streetlamps. A crowd gathered outside the ticket booth, jostling each other as they crowded onto the platform. Ornate iron benches lined the street, and people stood on them in an attempt to see the approaching train. The whistle blew and a faint line of steam appeared in the distance.

Thorn pushed her way past the ticket office and onto the platform. She stood on tiptoe and, peering between the heads of two impeccably-dressed London ladies, could just make out the pennants of the Queen's carriage as it trundled into the station. The people around her pushed with greater urgency, surging towards the monarch.

With a great puff and wheeze, the engine ground to a halt, and the Queen leaned over the railing and waved to the people. She wore a fine dress and mantle made of white and purple silks, shot with silver embroidery and clasped down her chest with pearl buttons. Beside her, the gaunt features of Prince Albert surveyed the crowd, basking in the shouts of praise issuing from the people. His hand clasped protectively around her elbow.

The crowd surged forward and carried Thorn with it. She craned her neck and saw a dark, mechanical shape standing beside the Queen.

Above the excitement of the crowd, she heard the sound she would never forget from her nightmare in the Wall: the terrifying puff of a Boiler's valves. As the steam rose from the carriage footplate, she took stock of her enemy; its protruding belly, its pressure valves like rising, gnashing teeth, and its iron grate – the gleaming mockery of a face – grinning back at her. Steam issued from its not-human mouth and ears. Unlike the Boiler inside the Wall, this specimen did not possess tracks, but was welded to the carriage itself, its gushing steam powering the pistons that opened and shut the doors and worked the couplers.

Amidst the applause and the shouting, Thorn heard the screams that no one else heard. *Help me, help me!* clapped her hands over her ears in a desperate attempt to shut out the sense.

A man sat behind the Boiler, shrouded in a thick black cloak. He lifted one hand to his cheek, waving at the crowd. The right hand – hidden in the folds of his bell sleeves – he pressed against the iron skin of the Boiler. Though the metal must burn his skin, he remained still and did not cry out.

It could only be one man.

The Metal Messiah. Overcome with a strange mixture of fear and reverence, Thorn dropped to her knees. Filthy water seeped through her trousers and chilled her legs.

Elbows and boots landed on her back as those behind swerved to avoid her. Thorn dug her pin from her lapel and clasped it in her hand.

He's a man, how can a man come back from the dead? What will he do when he discovers me, the daughter of the man who killed him? Will he embrace me as a Stoker, or hate me because of my curse? There's little use hiding here in the crowd, if what Quartz says about him is true than he probably already senses I am nearby. He's probably looking for the Stokers now he's rebuilt this grand railway. Maybe he'll stop the carriage and scoop me into his arms, and everything will be okay again—

The engine gave another puff, and the train pulled away from the station. Brunel didn't even glance her way.

Someone tripped over her. "Get up! Bloody street urchins. Anyone would think you a Stoker, huddled down there like your god just passed by."

Thorn's face burned. She scrambled to her feet. At the mention of Stoker, people turned to look.

"Off with you now."The man waved his hand. "You're Messiah's dead an' buried."

"But—"

A woman snorted. "It's as if she thinks The Royal Engineer is her precious Messiah. Have you ever heard of something so ridiculous? As if a man could somehow come back from the dead?"

"Get *along*, child. We nae bother with the likes of you."

Thorn opened her mouth to speak, but caught herself.

Oswald had taught her well. Her face burned with shame and anger. *Don't they realise? Even with the Wall discharging its poisons and the Chimney rebuilding itself and the Boiler on the train, don't they realise who walks in their midst?*

Too much, this is too much. She pushed back through the crowd. Laughter caught her ears and spread through the gathering crowd. She listened to jeers and taunts as word of her reaction spread from ear to ear.

"Those pox-ridden Great Conductor worshippers think any fool with a spanner and jack be their Messiah!"

"Why, they'd worship a *candlestick* if it promised them a ticket to the Station of Life!"

Thorn pounded through the streets, her boots slamming on the cobbles. She ran left, then right, not knowing where she was going. The Boiler's thoughts overwhelmed her own. Thorn gritted her teeth, forcing the terrible memories down.

Nothing makes sense. Brunel is one of us. He was born a Stoker and he rose to become the most powerful man in Britain. If he truly has returned, what is he doing working for the monarchy, building trains and stations and Crystal Palaces without even contacting his own people? Why does he not come for us? Why does he stay in London?

Thorn knew the answer. London was paradise – with its clean air and fine clothing and jolly cemetery and sweet drinks and pies. *And we live in a swamp; drowning in our own filth and praying for salvation.*

No wonder they laugh. Our Messiah abandoned us.

Thorn stopped, her chest heaving. It couldn't be true. And yet—

How many have died in the swamps? For nineteen years we've lived on those squalid lands, hunting the tricorns in some vain hope we'll one day worm our way back into favour, and all the while he's been creating this paradise ... for who? Not for us. For his

Boilers?

Thorn shuddered, thinking of the horrid memories that bristled on the surface of her conscience. But now that she had seen Brunel, what should she do next?

I have to see the Chimney – I have to see for myself. But first, I need to find the Stokers Rex was working with in London. I have to know if Brunel has sought them out.

Thorn jogged back along the alley. Another tricorn poster fluttered from a nearby streetlamp. She ripped it down.

Footsteps echoed down the alley as a man hurried past her. Thorn summoned her courage. "Excuse me, sir … sir!" She jogged back after the man, holding up the crumpled poster. "Can you tell me where this is?"

A face like boiled cabbage leered over her. He breathed a wall of faeces as he smiled, and while she reeled he grabbed her arm and twisted it behind her back. She gulped back a scream as the paper fluttered from her hand.

"Hey, Dorry, 'ere's a pretty one!"

Another man stepped from the shadows. He carried a small Derringer in his thick fingers – its barrel burnished with silver – and held out a large sack.

"Aye, she's a lively tail. I might 'ave some fun wi' her before the Sinkers get her." He pointed the Derringer at Thorn's face. "In yer go, lassie."

Thorn brought her leg up to her chest and kicked him in the stomach. He bent double, dropping the gun to his side.

"Knock her out!" he wheezed.

A fist swung at her face. Luckily, her Scottish captor smelt as though he bathed in London's sweet alcohol, and his punch grazed her cheek, powerless. She kicked again, her foot connecting with something soft.

A shot rang out. Sparks flew along the alley. Thorn shut her eyes. No pain; she wasn't hit. She struggled against the man, but he held tight.

Thorn heard a sound like lightning, and her bones jangled inside her skin. The man yelped with surprise and the grip on her shoulder relaxed. She squirmed harder.

She heard the crack again, and the man dropped her and screamed so horribly she felt he must be possessed. She scrambled into the gutter.

"Girl, behind me!" A silhouette blocked her exit. Thorn squinted as the figure brought forward a lantern. She recognised the features of the man she'd followed earlier that day, the fat one talking about tricorns. In his free hand he held a long, tapered leather whip, which he bent over his head, preparing to strike.

The man with the sack took a step towards him. "Not yer business, Mister. Move along!"

The whip parted the air. The man leapt back, holding up his hands.

"Ach, Messer Wombwell, forgive me. I nae recognise ye."

"As right you shouldn't, for I don't associate with the likes of you." The whip snapped again, scoring a red welt across the man's outstretched palm. His face crumbled as he clutched his spasming hand and howled.

"I said get!"

Thorn watched her assailant turn and scamper into the darkness. She let out her breath, relief washing over her.

"Thank you, sir."

He held out a hand, and she gratefully took it. His skin was smooth, a nobleman no doubt.

"I noticed you following us earlier, lass, so I did a little following of my own. What are you doing, approaching strangers like that? You'd have been dead before the coronation was over." He flexed the whip between his fingers.

He sounded like Quartz. Thorn's face flushed. She didn't want to let on how foolish she felt. She pointed after her fleeing assailants. "Who are they?"

"Hunters."

The answer surprised her. "I'm a hunter. I don't chase young girls through London streets."

"You would if you were a hunter of girls. They work for someone evil, someone who's snatching young-uns like yourself off the streets and imprisoning them in that cursed Wall everyone is ignoring. Someone who is, I think, remaking the army of the Vampire King, but keep that to yourself for the moment. You're lucky I found you, lass. Now, what is it you hunt?"

"Tricorns. Although I'm not very good at it."

He laughed. "It seems I am also lucky to have found you. My name is George Wombwell. Might I buy you a meal?"

Thorn thought for a second, then nodded. Her instincts told her to trust this man. He folded the whip and tucked it into a deep pocket, then placed both fingers in his mouth and let out a piercing whistle. A long face appeared in the alley, kind eyes like pools of crystal sparkled in the lamplight. Thorn had never seen an animal like it before; it was similar to the wild cats that hunted snipe and grouse in the marshes, but nearly three times the size of Thorn. He lifted a regal head, framed by a mane of smooth hair – brown and wavy like Joel's – and regarded Thorn with a wary stare.

Thorn felt the threads of his mind tugging at hers. The beast's thoughts entered her head, and she felt his softness wash over her. She relaxed. He harboured no ill thought, no hunger for blood, no lust for killing.

"Come out Nero, she won't bite you."

The creature yawned, baring yellow fangs. He was a killing beast, without the killer instinct.

"You have tamed this creature?" Thorn felt insignificant. Wombwell must have amazing powers. Not even Aaron could achieve such docility from a creature built to hunt.

"There is no taming involved. Nero is my friend, aren't you, boy?" Wombwell scratched the giant cat behind its flattened ears. Nero let out a purr like the world erupting, and nuzzled into Wombwell's coat. "Nero is a lion. He was rescued from a trap by one of my men in Africa, and delivered to me. Now, he looks out for me, and I for him. We have a mutual understanding." Wombwell held out his hand to her. "Shall we?"

Does he have the sense? He must, to befriend such a fierce creature. Perhaps I have found another ally, another person who can teach me now that my father and Aaron have gone.

Thorn placed her hand in his. His warm smile and bright coat calmed her beating heart.

They walked on in silence, the timid lion falling behind. Wombwell ducked down a dark alley, and led her inside a small shop, barely fifteen feet across to either wall, packed with men and women sitting and standing around two tables, laughing and sloshing drinks from lead tankards.

She squeezed into a seat at the end of the bar. Wombwell called over a barmaid and whispered something in her ear, pressing a silver coin into her palm. She giggled and rushed off.

Thorn leaned forward and lowered her voice. "You

said those men would take me into the Wall?"

Wombwell spoke in a low whisper. "Aye, child, and be thankful I rescued ye."

"I am, immensely so. You see, I've come through the Wall. I've seen the horror within for myself, and I've no desire to return there. But isn't the Wall supposed to be ... dead?"

Wombwell's eyes lit up. "You're a bold girl, sneaking into the city by yourself. Your kind must hate us Londoners for banishing you from the city, and for our continued ignorance of your plight in the swamps. We hate ourselves too, for in losing the Stokers we gained one of the most hellish tyrants this country had ever known. Even after all these years, Brunel's evil haunts this city still, so much so that no one even seems to notice that something is going on inside Engine Ward."

Thorn's chest tightened. "So you have noticed it, too?"

"That sections of the Chimney seem to be rising from the ashes of Engine Ward like some hideous phoenix? Yes, I have noticed, and I'm not the only one. But what hasn't been decided is what to do about it. The army refuses to grant anyone access. They want to keep it under lock and key. People are afraid to speak up against the Royal Society, who have claimed they're conducting some experiments in Engine Ward. And the Queen has made it so difficult to obtain permits that few people travel outside the city nowadays, so they do not see the destruction on the other side of the Wall."

"But London is so ... *happy*."

"Aye, child, to you she must seem so. As is true of ancient cities, tyrants build the prettiest infrastructure and keep the public houses well stocked. Brunel – or the Royal Engineer, as he's calling himself now – holds this city by the throat, and the populace is too distracted with exhibitions and jugglers and parades and drink to realise it. He guards every corner, and his spies and monsters lurk in every shadow. Each night more people disappear – as you nearly did – to feed the army he grows inside that cursed Wall. London became a Venice of blood the first time the Sunken walked these streets, and you can bet your breeches Brunel is planning to open those floodgates once more."

"But why doesn't anyone *see* him?"

"Why would they want to? It's far easier to believe Brunel is dead and buried than to accept the possibility that he might have brought himself a reprieve from mortality. His curtain of smoke smothers the outer hamlets, but while it doesn't disturb the city, they do not care."

"Can't the Queen do something?"

"The Royal Engineer holds sway over her Council, manipulating it to his will. Those that speak against him disappear into the Wall. As for the Queen, she is smitten with him. She sees no threat to London from the Royal Engineer, her trusted advisor. She is useless, and that Albert of hers is not much better."

"But why do you understand these things, when everyone else remains blind?"

"I've seen too much of the world to be blind to a false Messiah, Miss Thorn. You also, don't seem to share this blindness."

"My father killed Brunel," said Thorn. "I do not believe he would do so without just reason."

"Nicholas Thorne? You're his daughter?"

She nodded.

Wombwell bowed deeply. "I'm doubly honoured to make your acquaintance, Miss Thorn. Your father did a great justice to this country, and it's a pity he wasn't honoured for his actions in the proper manner."

The barmaid returned, banging down two mugs of something sweet and a plate of something hot.

"What's this?"

"Honeyed beer." Wombwell pushed a mug and the plate towards her. "That's a mutton pie. Warm yer cockles, it will."

Not wanting to ask what a cockle was, Thorn devoured the meal in silence. Wombwell sipped his dark ale. Beside them, Nero lapped cream from a bowl. None of the other patrons seemed to consider the giant cat out of the ordinary. One drunk even patted him affectionately on the head as he stumbled past.

When she finished he reached over and wiped her mouth with his kerchief.

"Ne'er talk business on an empty stomach, I say."

"I thank you sir, for your generosity, but I'd be dishonouring my father's good name if I did any business with an ivory dealer."

"On account of?"

"On account of you're all scab-ridden, pox-infested, dishonest, money-grubbing scoundrels. His words, not mine, sir."

Wombwell knitted his hands together. "And what makes you so certain I'm an ivory dealer?"

"I can tell; your swagger, your expensive coat and all your talk of tricorns."

His laughter boomed from deep in his belly. "You certainly are a resourceful lass, Miss Thorn. No, I'm not an ivory dealer, but a proprietor of a certain travelling menagerie, and I have a mind to employ you in my troupe."

"What is this menagerie? You…keep tricorns?"

He nodded, loose hairs falling over his forehead. "We exhibit strange and magnificent beasts to the populace of fair England, and tricorns most certainly qualify."

"What do I have to do?"

"You are a tricorn hunter, yes? My tricorn – the star of my show – has just died. My other has been decommissioned for acting in a most strange manner. There is no expert that can tell me what is the matter with him. I paid a hundred and fifty quid for the animal, and I don't intend to lose him. In return I offer food and board. As you'll be living in the wagons your duties will also include feeding and cleaning the tricorns and helping with the other animals. Will you join me, Miss Thorn?"

"Does this food you speak of include more of these mutton pies?"

Wombwell nodded.

"Then I'm in."

***

Thorn saw the bright canvas fluttering before they even entered Smithfield district. The breeze rolled off the Thames and stretched the guide ropes taunt, blowing the acrid smell of the slaughterhouses over the city. The green rolled onward, stretching from the water like a green triangular sail, disappearing between the warehouses and crumbling tenements. Along the eastern fence line, gallows platforms encroached upon each other, each new structure leaning against the rotting timbers of the last. The breeze swung the nooses and slammed the flapping trapdoors against the sagging frames.

The tent itself was surrounded on all sides by covered

wagons, pointing inwards to form a semi-circle. Temporary fences stretched between the wagons, and beasts of all shapes and sizes roamed and stomped behind the flimsy bonds.

Wombwell led Thorn towards the tent, through a city of wooden stalls. From every direction proprietors leered over her, shouting "Fly the Mags! Win a kettle!", "Have a naff at Under and Over!" and "Pie on a stick! Yew know yew wants a pie on a stick!" Smells and sounds assailed her, oils and sweets, dings and snaps and gongs. And over it all pitched the smell of the menagerie – blood and faeces and fresh hay. Thorn huddled behind Wombwell, wishing they'd leave her alone.

As she neared the entrance Thorn saw the tent was not one giant complex but two separate enclosures. People milled between them, many wearing brightly-coloured costumes.

Wombwell pushed her under the edge of the left tent, and she crawled into a high ante-chamber. Painted blankets in garish colours draped either side of a dramatic red curtain, depicting herds of tricorns stampeding across a yellow desert. Other creatures – furry beasts with lithe bodies and tails like coiled snakes leapt from branch to branch over the lintel of the tent flap. Birds stretched their wings – shot with purples and oranges and tangerines – across the turquoise sky, and lines of dancing compies wearing top hats and jackets jaunted by the pegs.

The wave of thoughts slammed Thorn with such force she stumbled backward. Her skull pounded as each separate mind crashed over the others like a maelstrom. She'd never sensed so many animals, felt so many conflicting emotions. Hunger, contentment, rage, complacency, joy, hope. *This must be what it feels like to be a god, trying to pull meaning from a cacophony of prayers.* Steadying herself against a tent pole, she sucked in a deep breath, and tried to force the voices from her head.

"Are you alright, Miss Thorn?"

"I'm fine," she replied. "Just ... catching my breath."

Wombwell didn't seem at all perturbed. *He must be used to the voices."* This way." He dragged her through the other curtain, and she gasped at the sight that greeted her.

Wagons and trolleys raced from one side of the tent to the other, pulled by creatures she'd heard of only in myth. Neckers – their skin dry and scaly, and their impossibly-long necks and tails stretched like wool skeins over a wet rack. Men and women in tight pantaloons and tailored jackets led the neckers around a semi-circular area of beaten earth, attaching strings of jangling bells to their harnesses.

Something flapped past her face. She screamed, throwing her hands up, but the bird glided on regardless, executing a graceful arc before settling in the rafters with several friends. Their rainbow plumage hung down like streamers.

Chitters, screeches, growls, yips, howls and grunts assailed her from all sides. The whole tent stank of faeces. Inside her head, the world exploded in a cacophony of smell, taste and noise. She sucked in the sensation, filling herself with the new world.

Pinching her fingers over her nose, Thorn indicated a lumpy object sitting on a dais and covered with a cloth. Wombwell frowned. He lifted the corner of the cloth away, and Thorn stared into the glazed, beady eyes of a dead tricorn.

She backed away, Her chest felt tight. Images flashed before her; those lamplight eyes glaring from the gloom, the gleam of ivory tusks lowered to kill, the surge of peat as the dark shape rose up, the crash of her Gast engine crumpling under its weight, the arc of the carvers' blades, the youths stamping their frenzied dance around the fire, the slabs of meat hanging in the salting room. *Rex… Joel…Lurgo,* their faces folding and contorting in a Boiler's fire, never seen again.

Thorn choked, grabbing her head in her hands. "Where…where did you find him?"

"Never you mind my secrets." Wombwell smiled. "Suffice it to say he narrowly escaped a Stoker banquet."

Thorn shrunk away from the carcass.

"Christolf used to be the star of my menagerie. Unfortunately, in our rush to reach London from Birmingham in time for the exhibition I'm afraid he caught a nipper of a cold and now I've lost our main attraction and hordes of business to bloody *Atkins…*"

With reverence and a little trepidation, Thorn ran her hand along the rough skin of Christolf's jawline.

"You can poke him all you like, he's not gonna—" Wombwell's voice trailed off, and he slapped his forehead.

"Are you ill, sir?"

Wombwell's laugh started deep in his belly, bubbling and issuing from his mouth in an outpour of rumbles. He chortled so hard he choked on his own tongue, and coughed into his lapels.

"Sir? Mr. Wombwell?"

"Thorn, oh…you brilliant girl!" He ran off towards the entrance.

"What…what did I do?"

She pushed through the curtain. Outside, people forced themselves between the two tents, pressing against the canvas paintings in a desperate attempt to squeeze closer to the dais on which a thin man stood, donned in an impeccably tailored jacket and curled jug loops at his temples. The man gesticulated towards the other tent, adjusting his curious hat – a miniature train powered by a minute locomotive engine chugged around the brim of his oversized sky-blue bowler.

"At Atkins' Amazing Extravaganza we have monkeys who bicycle. Compies who walk the tightrope and—" he cast a gleaming eye over the audience, "—the only *live* tricorn of the Great Exhibition!"

His hat whistled. The audience clapped and cheered.

Wombwell stuck out his elbows and wobbled through the crowd. The wiry man saw him and frowned. Wombwell heaved his meaty frame onto the dais and rose up beside his rival. He stood a head shorter than Atkins (two heads if you counted the ridiculous hat) but his protruding belly and thundering voice overpowered the other man's protests.

"How splendid." He turned to his rival and applauded. "Ladies and Gentlemen, that Mr. Atkins has brought you a live tricorn. It is true that I myself do not possess such a creature, although I know you've all seen one before on many of my previous visits. What I have tonight however, for your viewing and groping pleasure, is the only *dead*tricorn at the Great Exhibition, and that's a sight you don't see every day!"

The crowd hooted, and Wombwell drew his long whip from his pocket and pointed it in the direction of his tent. "Tonight ladies and gentlemen, you'll have the pleasure of touching a once-living tricorn. Stoke its razor-sharp horns, pet its rough skin, kiss its soft beak if you wish, but only at Wombwell's Travelling Menagerie!"

Atkins scowled. "That's highly improper!"

His words were lost in the cacophony of the crowd.

Thorn cheered too, following Wombwell as he squeezed back through the throng and disappeared behind the curtain.

Wombwell's smile enveloped his entire face. "I can see you'll get along perfectly well here, young Miss Thorn. Come." He held out his hand. "I'll introduce you to Igor."

Wombwell lit an argand and led her into one of the adjoining wagons. A two-ply canvas awning hung over the iron frame, and the air inside was damp. The juvenile tricorn huddled in a dark corner, moaning into its hay bedding and lolling its head from side to side. Thorn took three cautious steps and sat down beside the animal, resting a shaking hand on his brow. His skin was slick with sweat, and the thoughts that filled Thorn's head spoke of pain and confusion.

"He's really sick."

"Well observed, Copernicus. I know he's sick. What I want to know is how he can be cured."

"What's a Copernicus?"

Wombwell sighed.

"I'm not a doctor but…" Thorn tested the hay with her boot, "perhaps if I slept here for the next few nights, I could observe his behaviour and…report to you."

She bit her tongue. The hay felt so soft. Could Wombwell see through her? *Does he really believe I know how to treat a sick tricorn?*

"You want to sleep in here with the animals?" Wombwell l looked aghast…*it's over, he's going to kick me to the street—*

She nodded, her heart in her throat.

"I would have prepared you quarters with the other trainers, but if this is what you think is best, I am happy to grant you the right of sleeping out here." Thorn gave a faint smile. Inside, her stomach relaxed. *Three nights of warm hay ...*

"Thank you."

He held out his hand. "Don't thank me, just do a good job and I'll keep you here forever if you should wish. Welcome to Wombwell's Travelling Menagerie, Miss Thorn. Now, if you'll excuse me, I really must find an embalmer." He hurried away, leaving her to her charge.

The tricorn regarded her with wide, pain-soaked eyes. Thorn crouched beside him and stroked his sweat-sodden crest, searching with her hands for signs of disease or boils. Her touch calmed the beast, as it did with most animals. She probed his memories, trying to sense if he'd eaten anything odd, but her thoughts were muddled by the other animals, and the threads snapped away.

Someone rustled the awning. Thorn looked up, expecting to see Wombwell. Instead, a petite girl – around Thorn's age, with fire-red features and translucent skin – pushed open the flap and proffered a bowl of soup.

"I'm Julianne." She jiggled the bowl a little, but didn't move from the entrance. "Is it okay to come closer?"

"I don't think he's catching." Thorn patted the straw beside her. Julianne stepped forward cautiously, pointing her toes in an odd manner as she moved. She handed Thorn the soup and sat down beside her, curling her graceful legs underneath her like a swan retiring from the water.

"I didn't believe George when he said there was a Stoker in." Julianne watched intently while Thorn guzzled the hot soup. "Its true though, isn't it? You really live in that filthy train graveyard?"

Thorn shrugged. "I did once. Now I live here, at least till Wombwell's good graces run dry, or my curse catches up to me."

Julianne's wide eyes widened further, and her face broke into an exaggerated gasp. "You don't have a curse! There's no such thing."

"There is, and I do. Because of me swamp dragons broke into Graveyard and killed several people. My whole family is cursed. Everyone thinks my father murdered our Messiah. My mother dashed herself to dust jumping from a train. My fiancé and my only friends died trying to sneak into London. I'm the only survivor, the last bloody hope of my people."

"Your father killed Brunel? That must mean you're Nicholas Thorne's daughter! Oh, they must give you no end of grief! In London your father is a hero." Julianne pulled her arms behind her back and crossed them, bending her graceful hands around her head and slapping her tiny cheeks. Thorn laughed.

"If I weren't all alone in the middle of London trying to nurse a sick tricorn, I'd think your manner ridiculous."

"I'm a contortionist, Miss Thorn, see?" Without moving from the hay, Julianne bent her left leg around the back of her head and grazed her right ear with her ankle. "And I intend to be a famous actress. I'm always studying emotions."

"Please don't study me; I'm rather a mess right now." Thorn stared at her empty bowl.

"And with good reason."

"And please don't tell anyone about my father."

"You're not to worry, Miss Thorn, I'll be your friend, and I won't tell. I don't believe in curses. Now." She reached across and placed warm fingers on Thorn's rough palm. "We can't have you slouching here all gloomy on St. Bartholomew's Eve. Come, the show's about to start."

Thorn and Julianne hid under the flap of the awning and watched Wombwell direct his workers to set up rows of wooden benches, rig streamers and swags of filmy fabric and light the argand lamps that reflected all the colours of the rainbow. Nearby a rotund man painted a sign. Julianne whispered; "it reads 'The only DEAD Tricorn at Bartholomew Fair' and he's sent the boys out into the city to spread the word. He really is a genius!"

Thorn smiled. Julianne snuggled into her shoulder. "We'll be friends, right?"

"Um..." *After what I do to my friends?* Julianne's weight on her shoulder suddenly seemed insupportable.

After an hour or so the light outside faded and the tent grew dim. Thorn pulled her coattails over her knees, shivering. People began to file inside, scrambling for the flimsy seats. When these were all taken they pushed into the spaces, crowding the aisle and the area around the dais, jostling and pushing to get closer. Suddenly, a giant lens, twice the size of Quartz's Frensel, blinked to life above the stage. A man stood behind it, swinging the bowl to direct the light over the audience. From somewhere behind the curtains dozens of drums thundered.

Suddenly, the man let go of the bowl and threw his hands above his head. Several birds fluttered from the rafters and perched on his outstretched arms. One by one he kissed the birds and sent them off, gliding through the audience and dropping bags of sugared almonds into the hands of eager children.

The man directed the lamp to the centre stage. The drumming grew louder as a line of tiny impish creatures

– a third of Thorn's height, with intelligent faces and soft brown fur – strutted across the stage, each banging a different drum. A piercing tune permeated the air as one blew into a pipe. Another hooted as it slapped a pair of maracas against the stage. The sigh of joy from the audience sent shivers of a different sort down Thorn's arms.

As the drums and piping reached a crescendo, Wombwell emerged, dressed in his spangly jacket and a top hat three feet high and adorned with raptor feathers. The audience cheered; a sound that rolled toward the stage like a hurricane, sweeping Thorn along with its force.

Without further ado, and with no unnecessary speechmaking, Wombwell lifted the cloth covering the dais and the crowd surged forward, eager to peek at the spectacle.

Thorn could not tear her eyes away from the men, women and children who climbed, punched, kicked and *snarled* each other in the frenzy to reach the carcass and run their hands along its skin, grasp and rub its deadly horns, tug its thick tail, kick its stocky limbs.

For her entire life she'd seen the creatures as majestic, fearful swamp dwellers. Now, under the artificial moon she saw them for the first time as curios; a creature to be wondered at, prodded, studied, understood.

Whip in hand, Wombwell drove them back to their seats, promising more to come. And there was more: cats the size of Igor with jet-black fur peddling tricycles in complex patterns, more of the imps – she heard someone call them monkeys – tossing coloured wool balls to each other and causing all manner of mischief. A chilling creature Wombwell called "the learned pig", a rotund porker with a long gash down his side, his rolls of skin and fat pinned back to reveal a belly made entirely of clanking clockwork notions, no doubt the work of the Dirigires. Wombwell had audience members call out their birthdates, and he pressed and prodded at the pig's ribs till it blurted out which day of the week they were born on. For the grand finale Wombwell led two neckers on stage, where they proceeded to play a jaunty tune on a miniature pipe organ while Wombwell and Nero danced to the excited clapping of the audience. After the spectacle was over the argands turned to bright, and Wombwell allowed the audience to return to groping the dead tricorn.

Thorn didn't know what to make of it. Julianne wanted her to join the other menagerie workers for their late-night revels, but the thought of that soft hay made her realise the weariness creeping over her body. She crawled back inside the wagon. Igor curled in the far corner, his body shaking with erratic snores. She piled hay around her like a cocoon, draped her coat over herself as a blanket, and lay down. Her eyes fluttered shut and she felt herself drifting off on an ocean of applause that rolled through London like a tidal wave.

***

JAMES HOLMAN'S MEMOIRS, FIRST EDITION

Charles arrived at my residence at the stroke of ten, just as I sat down to enjoy my morning tea and cake. He did not wish to join me for a leisurely snack, but tapped his cane against the footplate of the carriage while he waited for me to gather my things.

"I told you I would arrive at ten precisely, since you were so insistent we didn't take the train. Traffic is already abysmal." He grumbled as I scrambled aboard. While I settled myself he wiped cake crumbs from my chin and attempted to smooth my rumpled coat.

"And I have spent the last year living with people who believe pocket watches are fashioned by demonic fairies from the savannah. I was really looking forward to that cake."

Charles laughed. "Your hat's askew."

We drove on toward Hyde Park. I had never known London in such a state of cosmopolitan liveliness – on every corner I heard a new foreign tongue. Industrious printers hawked street maps in every language, and polyglot policemen roamed through the streets, offering assistance to every foreigner they met. Children laughed, women chattered, and men greeted strangers in the streets as though they were old friends.

After waiting for nearly an hour in a tremendous traffic jam of hundreds of cabs, omnibuses, carriages, broughams and flies, we finally passed under the gates of Hyde Park and the driver stopped the carriage so we could disembark. A light shower of rain pattered against my shoulders, but this would not deter the thousands upon thousands of people who pushed and jostled to attain the best view of the opening ceremony. Many had waited in the park for days to secure their ideal viewpoint. In the trees above I heard the rustling of young boys, scrambling like monkeys along the branches for a birds-eye view of the proceedings.

Charles and I pushed our way through the onlookers and passed through an external iron gate, showed our tickets to the officer on duty, and took our place in a fenced-off section of the crowd. Every space that wasn't filled with excited ticket-holders was crammed with wooden carts selling all manner of English delicacies, and the air sung with the smells of sweet ginger beer, fatty cakes, brandy balls, gingerbread, mutton pies, fresh oranges, ham sandwiches, trotters and roasting nuts.

By midday the carriages of state – at least a thousand of them, Charles informed me – entered the gates and the tens of thousands of privileged visitors and Royal Society Council members swarmed past us into the grand atrium. Charles stood by my side and described the scene; the gold-embroidered bosoms of the officers-of-state, the ambassadors of all nations resplendent in their national dress, the gentlemen-at-arms with their golden helmets and ribbon-like feathers steaming behind, the priests of the different Industrian sects in their silk robes, and the Queen with her retinue, wearing a dress of the finest pink satin studded with diamonds and her tiara set with diamonds and feathers. At her arm, Prince Albert, wearing his impeccably tailored field-marshal's uniform, followed by the Royal Engineer, a shadowy figure dressed all in black. Charles described the reflections of these myriad colours twinkling from the crystalline roof of the palace above, sending prisms of radiant light dancing over the crowds. How I ached to see it with my own eyes.

Every church bell in the city began to chime, joined by blasts from Henry Willie's Grand Organ, which struck the chords of the national anthem, and a great chorus of voices joined in song. Trumpets sounded and the Prince Albert declared the Great Exhibition of the Works of Industry of All Continents open.

Everything around me tingled with excitement. This was a great day for London, whose great history has been marred with blood these past two decades. I could not help but find myself smiling at her marvellous achievement. But then I remembered the voice I heard at the Royal Society, and my excitement faded away. I shivered.

I wanted so badly to be wrong, so I decided I should try and confide my fears in my good friend, in the hopes he might have already investigated the Royal Engineer and found him innocent of all witchcraft. As we shuffled towards the entrance, I mustered the courage to broach the question. "Charles, don't you think the new Royal Engineer—"

"Mr. Williams?" Charles interrupted.

"Right, Mr Williams. Does he not remind you of a certain someone?"

"No one I can think of. What are you getting at, James?"

"Brunel." I lowered my voice. "Doesn't he remind you of Brunel?"

"You'd best hold your tongue, friend. That talk could have you answering charges of treachery. What gave you such a ludicrous idea?"

"Think about it, Charles. This Royal Engineer shows up in London with no history, no lineage and no traceable fortune, bearing a name that sounds remarkably like a combination of the two men who combined forces to destroy him. Suddenly, he's secured the most prestigious engineering post in the kingdom, and has reopened the London railway on *broad gauge rails*. Do you not find this an awfully big coincidence?"

"I do, but coincidence it is. Both Nicholas and Williams are common names, and not unique among Stokers. All this is beside the point, as Brunel is dead and – last I checked – one cannot bring the dead back to life. Now, shall we talk no more of this and try to enjoy the exhibition?"

I saw no sense in trying to convince him, so I

changed the subject, and we shared other Royal Society gossip until the crowd swept us through the gates. I felt the glass walls close around us, and voices rose through the Grand Transept, rising and falling through the echoes of the magnificent building.

First, we explored the Eastern halls of the palace, where the international exhibits were housed. Charles did his best to describe the exhibits, but there was so much to see, he quickly grew short of breath. The courts burst with exotic treasures: Silks from the east, Pharaonic statues and mummies from Egypt, spices and inlaid cabinets from India, primitive weaponry from Africa and the Pacific. We passed through a room of ticking clocks fashioned by the Dirigire sect, and I remembered the young man I had met on the journey home from France. I listened for his voice, but could not hear it.

The usual polite London crowd raced about, elbowing each other aside in their impatience to examine each wonder. I grew restless and irritated as yet another careless foot tripped over my cane. I was surrounded by an orgy of history and innovation and I could not experience it. Charles had to drag me from room to room, and I met his every exclamation with a monosyllabic grunt.

Finally, even he tired of my rudeness. "You're not enjoying yourself, are you, my friend?"

I sighed. "I am sorry, Charles. I've been ill company today. This splendour makes me keenly aware of my own shortcomings."

"I can't say I blame you. I just want to view one more hall, and then we can retire to your apartments for some cigars and brandy."

The prospect of brandy perked me up a little. "If we must. Lead the way."

We walked across the Grand Transept and into the Engineering Hall – the largest and most crowded of all the halls.

Charles resumed his description as we turned about the room. "...and Stephenson's display features a machine to shift carriages from one rail to another. And there's the great hydraulic press with which he built the Tubular Bridge. Incredible, it's operated by only one man! And there's a machine for making envelopes, and one to supply the rooms in a house with pure warm air, and a carriage that lays its own rails ahead of itself as it trundles along! And there's a soda water machine that's making hundreds of glasses of soda water at a time using gas...oh and there's...there's..."

Charles stopped dead. I stumbled over his feet and fell into his shoulder.

"What's wrong Charles?"

"It's...a Boiler." Charles whispered, digging his fingers into my arm. "But it's larger, and more sinister looking than any Boiler I remember. A crowd has gathered about Mr. Williams, who is demonstrating its traction system."

"You are certain it is a Boiler?"

"I could never forget the machines that nearly destroyed London. Perhaps you were right about the Royal Engineer, James. I cannot think why any man would want to resurrect those beastly machines unless he were their inventor."

"I tire of this exhibition," I said. "George Wombwell is in town, and I heard he's concocted a genius plan to override his lack of a living tricorn. Let's go to the menagerie."

***

Thorn's proximity to the animals comforted her, and she used her time to practise the exercises Aaron taught her. Casting her mind out like twine on a fishing line, she concentrated on tugging thoughts and feelings back to herself. For once, her head filled with happiness. With the exception of the Learned Pig, Wombwell's animals were content; well-fed and kindly treated, and her senses tingled with their joy.

When she wasn't practising for her act, Julianne showed Thorn the intricacies of menagerie life. She taught Thorn how to muck out the wagon, replacing the soiled hay and laying out the oats and apples in an aesthetically pleasing arrangement. Despite his sickness, Igor gobbled up his three breakfasts, nudging her hands with his bony beak as if to ask "More?"

"If you haven't lost your appetite, what is the matter, boy?"

During the daytime Thorn remained in the wagon, sponging the sweat pooling under Igor's crest and singing him Stoker ballads under her breath. Julianne brought her the evening meal: mutton pie and a hot tankard of broth. "You're on ticket duty tonight," she announced.

Thorn glanced up in concern. Julianne's sweet smile grew wider. "Don't worry, I'll show you how it works. It should be a crowded show, being the first eve of the Great Exhibition and all. You'll have to wear something more appropriate." She flounced away, returning a few minutes later with an armful of clothes. "Take off those filthy rags. There's water in the corner to wash your skin."

Thorn obeyed, and stood starkers in the hay while Julianne held exquisite jackets and silk pantaloons against her pale skin, muttering comments about jewel tones and kohl brushes.

When she was finished, Thorn stood aghast at the transformation; she wore a crimson jacket shot with jets of silver, buttoned at her waist. It fell nearly to her skinned knees, which were covered in soot-black trousers made of a filmy fabric that flowed over her skin like water. Julianne placed a tiny cap made of the same filmy fabric over her tangled hair, set it at a jaunty angle, and stood back to admire her work.

"I can't wear these." What if she damaged them? She didn't have money to pay for clothes like these.

"No time to protest." Julianne grabbed her hand. "We should already be at our post."

She led Thorn outside, on top of the round dais inlaid with dancing tricorns. Julianne pulled a sign from under the dais and leaned it against a tent pole. She handed Thorn a bucket, and threaded a roll of paper stubs over her arm. "You collect the money," she explained, "and watch for greedy blaggers."

"Step right up, laydeeeees and gentlemen." Julianne's sweet tone turned into a thundering roar, rising over the crowd, carrying across the fairground, back towards the slaughterhouses. "See the only dead tricorn at the fair! Thruppence for the show, and a penny for a feel." Heads turned towards her, and the man standing with a bucket outside Atkin's deserted tent scowled and made a rude gesture.

"Thruppence!" Thorn rattled the bucket under a man's nose. "See the amazing dead Tricorn!"

"I'll have two tickets, Miss Thorn."

She stared up in shock. It was James Holman: the same blind man who'd shown her the way to Highgate. He wore another fine coat; this one longer and more elaborate than the last; the embroidery was of saddled elephants laden with bright squares of fabric prancing around the border, their bodies stitched with intricate flowers of gold. He rapped his stick near her feet and waited for her to reply.

"I, er...I'm awful sorry for running away, sir—"

"I understand." Holman held out his hand, keeping his elbow rigid at his side and extending his arm just enough that she had to reach to clasp it. His shake was uncertain, inviting. A second gentleman – wearing fine clothes and an expression of utter confusion – flicked his gaze between Holman and Thorn. Thorn handed him both tickets and he tucked them into the front pocket of his coat, then tapped Holman lightly on the arm.

"No, you don't. I had to find my people ... I was afraid of your kindness. I still am. People aren't usually kind to me."

"If the rumours of tonight's show are anything to go by, you've fallen in with a tough crowd for one so fearful."

"Hurry on, you blind coot!" Patrons jostled behind him, waving their coins in the air. A look of irritation passed over Holman's face.

Thorn shoved her pail into Julianne's hand and jumped down beside Holman. "I'll escort you to your seats."

"I thank you, Miss Thorn."

"Hey!" Julianne struggled forward as patrons crowded through the gate. "I need you!"

Thorn smiled an apology, looped her arm under Mr. Holman's and led him and his friend through the entrance of the tent. His friend leaned over and clasped her spare hand in his. "Pleased to make your acquaintance, Miss. You must forgive James for his bad manners. He's been in a miserable mood all day."

"Oh, yes, of course. Charles, this is Thorn. I met her two days ago, outside Highgate. Thorn, you're shaking the hand of Charles Darwin, an eminent scholar of natural science."

Thorn led the men down the path to the rows of benches. "Where would you like to sit?" She felt awkward, knowing full well Holman wouldn't see anything of the spectacle.

"Somewhere near the front, if I can. I should like to feel the lion's breath on my face."

Thorn pulled aside the gold "reserved" tape, and led the men to two empty seats near the aisle. "You're royalty tonight, sirs."

Holman set down his cane and stretched out his legs. "This will do nicely, don't you think, Charles? Will you sit with us, Miss Thorn? I should like someone to describe the show. I've worn Charles' tongue enough for today."

"I should really go back to work. I don't want to disappoint Mr. Wombwell. I will come and see you after the show."

"I should like that, Miss Thorn." He doffed his hat in her general direction. "I smell peanuts. Charles, don't you think we need some peanuts?"

What a remarkably odd man.

Wombwell wanted Thorn to help with Nero's act, up second tonight, after the birdman. At his instructions she tethered the lion and walked him once around the semi-circular stage, the way she'd seen Julianne do the night before. Wombwell called instructions from his pedestal and without a glance at his trainer, Nero threw himself up on his hind legs – standing twice the height of Thorn – and placed one paw on each of her shoulders and squeezed. She choked under the weight of fur and the sheer terror crushing her stomach. Wombwell laughed, and the audience clapped. Nero dropped down to earth, leaving Thorn gasping for air.

Next, Thorn and Julianne held hoops for Nero to jump through, directed the monkeys to play a waltz for Nero and Wombwell to dance, and placed a slumbering compie into a cradle for Nero to rock. The audience loved every minute of it and Thorn found herself enjoying it as well.

Wombwell handed her the lead, turning to the crowd and shouting. "Nero loves to be petted. Would anyone like to pet him?"

The pack of children kneeling in the earth leapt to their feet. Thorn led Nero onto a podium set in front of them and they crowded around, running their grubby hands along his spine, down his legs and through his thick mane. Nero remained stoically silent as eager hands tugged on his fur, and Thorn cooed to him to keep calm. When she sensed his agitation mounting, she pushed the enthusiastic children away.

The delight in their voices as they cooed and whispered to Nero filled the audience with gaiety. As she led Nero down the aisle parents leaned over, seeking to press their hands on the lion's warm skin. Thorn kept one hand firm around the bridle, the other stroking the soft patch under Nero's chin.

As she walked back towards the stage she paused before Holman. "Hold out your hand," she whispered. "Towards me, by your hip."

He did as commanded, and his breath came out in short, excited gasps as he stroked Nero's mane, feeling the lion's breath on his fingers. The creature gave a low purr.

"He likes you," she said, and tugged the bridle.

"He remembers me. Nero and I are old friends." Holman grinned.

Thorn was surprised. "I didn't know that. I'll be back later and you can tell me more."

Thorn replaced Nero in his cage and resumed duties with Julianne tugging animals on and off stage. Throughout the night she caught glimpses of Holman as he watched without seeing the various feats of Wombwell's menagerie. His face lit into a smile as he heard the monkey's chitters, and the squeak of the bicycle tires, the hoots of the neckers.

The argands flared to life, and the patrons pushed toward the dais upon which Christolf lay, awaiting their probing hands. Thorn ran out to rescue Holman, who was alone now and tapping his cane impatiently against the heels of an obese women struggling towards the dead tricorn.

"Do you want to touch the...Christolf?"

"I've no need for such vulgarities, Miss Thorn." Holman extended his arm toward her. "I've had more than sufficient close encounters with tricorns in my short life. Charles sends his apologises – it's late and his wife will be worrying after him."

"That's fine. It's you I wanted to talk to, anyway. I really am sorry about running away before." Thorn looped her arm in his. "I wondered if you'd like to stay with us a little longer? There's a bonfire to celebrate the end of the fair. Julianne tells me it's really an excuse for Wombwell to drink more ale than usual and drag out his hammer dulcimer, but I'm sure it will be splendid. And you can tell me more about your adventures with tricorns and lions."

"I'd be delighted. Lead the way, Miss Thorn."

She found Wombwell counting his earnings inside Nero's cage. "Mr. Wombwell, may I invite a friend to the revels?"

Wombwell smiled when he saw Holman. "James, you old rogue! I thought I recognised your face in the crowd. Do join us; you will be our guest of honour."

Thorn stared in surprise. "You know each other?"

"Mr. Holman supplied me with Igor and Christolf, along with some of my more exotic animals. Don't let his stoic demeanour fool you, he's quite the scallywag."

Thorn gazed at the blind man in surprise, but he merely smiled modestly and patted her hand.

Wombwell unclipped Nero's lead, and man and lion led girl and blind man to the bonfire smoking at the edge of the field, near the river. Wombwell's workers tipped coal and wood pilings from the fairground stalls onto the spitting bonfire, and Julianne pranced around with platters of meats and sweetbreads for everyone.

Thorn found an overturned barrel for Holman to sit on. He slid off his jacket and stretched out his hands towards the fire. Julianne appeared at his side and offered him a platter.

"I've got here mutton and fresh kippers. They're not cooked, but they do well after a few minutes on the fire." To Thorn's delight she bent her leg up and over her right shoulder, and Thorn accepted a skewer from between her dainty toes.

Holman unclipped the end of his cane, revealing a gleaming blade. He slid cuts of meat onto the knife and turned it in the fire, sharing the morsels with Thorn and Julianne. She wanted to ask him about his tricorn hunts but he brushed her questions aside. He sat for an hour listening with rapt attention while she described her life in Graveyard, interrupted at intervals by Wombwell with punctuated questions about the animals she kept and the recipe for Quartz's mecks.

Tankards of honey beer made the rounds, and soon everyone was merrily linking arms and skipping round the fire to the tune of the dulcimer. Wombwell was joined by others – three fiddle-players and a rogue monkey on the drums. Thorn clapped in time to the beat, a smile creeping over her face.

She slapped it away, guilt flooding her. *Your friends might be dead, or roaming the streets of London lost and helpless, and you've failed your mission to find the London Stokers. How you smile?*

Thorn lowered her arms, and she didn't dance or clap after that.

When the makeshift band broke down into a heated argument about augmented fifths, Holman clapped his hands. "Shall I tell a story now?"

The workers nodded, pulling their overturned drums and hay bales close to better hear over the crackling fire. Thorn leaned back against the drum, wondering what tale the blind man could possibly tell to entertain the bawdy crowd.

"Tell us something scary," said Julianne. The other children cried their assent.

"Very well," said Holman. "But you may regret it. I've survived some pretty terrifying experiences." The children cheered, and Holman grinned. Thorn could see that he loved the attention.

"Not many of you are old enough to remember," he began, "but, nineteen years ago when the Gauge War ended, the Stokers were exiled from London. There are perhaps some here who do not even know what a Stoker is."

Thorn shrunk further into the shadows. *Why did he*

choose to talk about the Stokers? I hope he doesn't expose me, or even these kind people will force me back into the wilderness. She crouched low, intending to escape into the night if the story turned ugly, but Holman clenched his spider fingers over her knee. Thorn froze, her heart pounding.

Holman continued. "In the early days of the great engineers, a man from the swamps realised money could be made in the city, working in the furnace rooms of the Engine Ward. That man – Aaron Williams Senior – brought his people to London, and he became their foreman and leader. They called themselves Stokers, for they had one job, and one job only; to shovel coal into the furnaces, to keep the Engine Ward working, so that the engineers in their lofty churches could continue the serious business of innovating. A humble purpose perhaps, but the Stokers were proud of their work, and deeply religious, devoted to their god, the Great Conductor."

"As thick as broad gauge rail, more like!" an acrobat said, laughing.

"Not necessarily." Holman squeezed Thorn's knee. "They have nothing on the Metics. Simple folk need someone to believe in, and Great Conductor spoke to the Stokers as no other god could. And it wasn't just Stokers who found solace in the god of steam – many men of science, such as Nicholas Thorne, whom my story is about, also aligned themselves with the Great Conductor's church."

Thorn's heart pounded. She couldn't run now. *I know that name, and what's more, Holman I know that name. He wants me to hear this.*

"Nicholas Thorne was born to a wealthy family with impressive lands. He was sent to the finest schools, and trained with great minds to become an architect.

Unfortunately, his elder brother was a brute. Robert terrorised Nicholas, so much so that he drove the boy to hate his family. One day, there was a terrible accident, and Robert was killed. Their father blamed Nicholas, and sent him away forever. Alone, and with nowhere else to go, Nicholas came to London and lived in the Engine Ward alongside the Stokers. He was educated in a Stoker school, and it was here under the tutelage of Marc Brunel, that Nicholas and I become schoolyard friends. There was another boy at the school, too – a boy by the name of Isambard Kingdom Brunel."

Thorn gasped, and stuffed her sleeve in her mouth. *He knows my father, and the Messiah? How is Holman so entwined in these affairs?*

"The Stokers lived in hovels on the outskirts of the Engine Ward in makeshift sheds and lean-tos. It was not always thus, for before they moved into London, they hunted tricorns in the swamps, supplying the booming ivory trade. For all the squalor they lived in beside the Thames, their life in the swamps far surpassed it in filth and stench. For a Stoker, industrial London was a paradise of fresh air and riches. But London did not see them that way. They shunned the Stokers, and forbade them from innovating.

"But Isambard Brunel was not happy with his place. He wanted more. He wanted to innovate. Even though it was forbidden for the Stokers to practice engineering, this boy took apart the engines and put them back together again, learning how each mechanism worked, how the gears and cogs and levers fitted together in perfect harmony."

"Nicholas and I could see Brunel's mind turning with ideas above his station, but we thought he would never be able to realise his grand schemes. And so the two of us went off to war. My mother was able to purchase me a commission, but Nicholas had to work his way up through the ranks. We lost contact for a couple of years, until I was given a new commission as Third Lieutenant on board the *Cleopatra*, and who was the Second, but my good friend Nicholas?"

Holman continued his story, recounting their adventures at sea, and how he was struck down with the strange affliction that cost him his sight. How Nicholas had tried in vain to help him, and how in the end, he had failed and the Captain dumped him back in England to continue on without him. Nicholas Thorne had gone on to France, where he'd escaped the Navy and got caught up in a radical Morphean sect who hid out high in the Alps. With tears brimming in his eyes, Holman recounted how Nicholas had fallen out with the cult leader, Jacques, and had to return to London under a cloud of shadow to seek out employment with the only engineer who would take him – Brunel.

"Nicholas directed the Boiler workforce; he oversaw the transportation of materials and the erection of the Wall's scaffold. He worked side-by-side with Aaron Williams, the grandson of that enterprising foreman who first brought the Stokers to London, on the early construction phases, until Aaron went into the swamps after a falling out with Brunel. Nicholas greatly admired Brunel, and spent many years defending him against accusations. Nicholas was always the first to believe the best in someone. For that reason, he was the last person to see Brunel's evil, until it was too late."

"And how did you come to be so close to Brunel, Mr. Holman?" Julianne clicked her knees backward and threaded her arms through and over her legs, thrusting her body upward on the weight of her arms.

Wombwell reached out his boot and tapped her arms. She wobbled precariously before finally toppling over in a heap atop her tankard, spilling sticky honey beer all down her sparkling costume.

Laughter erupted around the campfire. Wombwell's hearty bellow boomed loudest of all. Even Holman, who had no inkling of what had gone on, let out a chuckle. Julianne poked her tongue out at Wombwell. "I meant no disrespect!" she wailed, wringing out her dress.

"Likely not, child," Holman answered, "and so I shall answer. Brunel became aware of my unique abilities after he discovered an embossed code system Nicholas and I had developed, so we could communicate via letters. Brunel had us show him the code and henceforth hired me for some of his biological work. While Nicholas worked on the Wall and then fought as the Captain of Brunel's ironclad, *Great Britain*, I worked on another project for Brunel. I travelled across the inhospitable lands of Russia and Siberia to bring back specimens of large beasts – *Dinosauria*, the men of science like to call them, although you probably know them as dragons and neckers and other such species. Brunel studied the movements of these beasts and used that information to improve his Boiler designs. At least, that was my understanding of the assignment. When one is being handed a free ticket to explore the world, one does not ask all the right questions. And now I must ask you not to interrupt further, as I have reached the most crucial and interesting part of the story."

Thorn desperately wanted to ask Holman about the code, but she held her tongue.

"As all gods eventually do, Brunel forsook his people. He grew more reclusive and erratic with each passing month, becoming so engrossed in his creations and so apart from the chaos on the London streets he no longer conceived nor cared for the consequences he had wrought. With his Boilers able to shovel coal and keep the fires of Engine Ward stoked long after the Stokers collapsed from exhaustion, Brunel declared an entire race of people became defunct."

"Boilers?" asked Julianne.

"The very same. At first, these Boilers worked only below the Engine Ward, but then Brunel began to conceive of other uses for them. He put them to work crafting and crewing his great machines of war – the ironclad ships he used to subdue the French. And eventually, he turned the Boilers into an army – an unstoppable force that could not be killed. Brunel used them first in the Gauge War against Stephenson, and then, in the hours leading to his death, he turned them loose upon London. The Boilers were Brunel's ultimate abhorrence – demons of iron that only he controlled. Legend tells Brunel worked some dark and ancient magic to create them – a type of alchemy so pure it could imbue life itself. *Living* machines at Brunel's beck and call. Imagine it!"

Thorn frowned as she remembered the thoughts she'd heard in the Wall. *Help me,* the Boiler had screamed, even as it rolled forth to destroy her. *Help me,* a dark magic had been wrought inside that iron beast.

"As the French blockade began to crumble, Brunel's ire turned from the French threat to Robert Stephenson and the Navvies. And so the Gauge War began. Brunel marched his army of Boilers and Stokers out to meet Stephenson, who had amassed a large militia from the local populace willing to stand against the Metal Messiah. The battle had been won before first blood have even been shed, for who can stand against an army of machines? But stand the Navvies did and, just as the battle began, the Boilers stopped dead. They would not move forward. They would not budge. Seizing his chance, Stephenson surged forward and quickly took the day.

"Back in London, Nicholas Thorne had finally started to see what Brunel truly had planned for the country. He snuck into the secret control room beneath Engine Ward and pulled out the plate. The one master plate that controlled all the Boilers." Holman's sightless lids turned to Thorn as he said, "Nicholas Thorne was a hero. His actions stopped the Gauge War from becoming a bloodbath."

He faced the crowd again.

"Brunel and Stephenson declared a truce. But Brunel didn't quit. He knew what Nicholas had done, and he intended to emerge the winner of the Gauge War, while destroying Nicholas, all in one go. And so Brunel got diplomatic; he opened his circle line around the entire city, operating on top of his impressive Wall. The *Thunderer*– the first engine built entirely by the Boiler workforce and considered the finest passenger train ever constructed – was to make its maiden voyage around that circuit. The finest of London society snapped up the tickets. To demonstrate his commitment to ending the Gauge War, Brunel gave a heartfelt speech at the opening ceremony and even allowed Stephenson to cut the ribbon. He also sent a team of Boilers ahead, to set a trap.

"To accommodate the train through the more well-to-do areas, namely Mayfair and Belgravia, the citizens had paid Brunel handsomely to build the track on a tight curve through a tunnel within the Wall itself. As the *Thunderer* entered this tunnel and rounded the first sharp curve, it met with the tampered track. The driver couldn't see the damage in the dark and had no chance of stopping the train in time."

Julianne gasped, and put her hands over her mouth. Thorn didn't react – she knew this story well, though the Stokers told it very differently.

"It was a terrible accident. The engine, tender and postal van derailed, skidding along the track for some two hundred feet, their bellies torn open by the force of their journey. The first three carriages telescoped into each other. The second carriage mounted the first, completely destroying the first car as it rammed its body through the interior. The third carriage drove itself under the wreckage, obliterating everything except its underframe. The impact welded everything together, and the upturned oil lamps caused a fire to break out – those who weren't maimed or crushed in the collision burnt to death inside the wreckage.

"Meanwhile, Boilers poured from within the Wall. Their instructions: leave no soul left alive. The people called out to them, thinking they were saved, but instead, the machines went mad. One wrenched off the engine's firebox, spewing hot coals and sparks over the injured crew. Another snapped an exhaust-steam injector, giving the fireman trapped in his seat a shower of scalding steam and water. The driver managed to pull the screaming man from the cab, and the pair, badly scalded, crawled away from the wreckage. A Boiler chased over them, and ran them under its treads until their bodies were merely gory puddles on the mangled track.

"Nicholas Thorne was on that train. And although he tried valiantly to help the passengers, he was the only man who made it from the Wreck of the *Thunderer* alive."

Thorn gasped again, too stunned to speak.

"Brunel nearly got away with it, too. No one had lived who saw the Boilers' madness, and certainly no one suspected Brunel of sabotaging his own train. But Nicholas Thorne knew the truth, and he could no longer abide it. He went to the Engine Ward with blood on his hands and rage in his stomach."

"And what of you, Mr Holman?"

"Before the train was set to leave the station, Nicholas hid me in an attic with his wife Brigitte and their daughter, then only a few months old. For hours we three huddled between crates of fishing tackle and sail sheets, squirreled away like a dangerous secret with no knowledge of the situation outside. His young wife fought through isolation while the battle raged outside; a remarkable woman with the heart of a lion." He patted Nero's mane. Thorn noticed how Holman's face had changed, his usually jovial mouth was turned down at the sides, as if something were deeply troubling him. *Is it something to do with my mother?*

Her mother. Thorn couldn't believe what she was hearing. All her life she'd wondered about the woman who'd given birth to her and then abandoned her. The Stokers didn't know her, and so of course they had nothing good to say. But here was a man who Thorn was certain had not only met her mother, but who actually loved her as a friend. Could Holman shed light on the mystery of Thorn's past?

"The situation grew increasingly desperate. Brunel locked himself inside his Chimney with his Boiler guard. The terrorised populace – their eyes opened to Brunel's treachery – flooded the Engine Ward and destroyed everything mechanical they could lay their hands on. Then, they attacked the Wall itself. When Brunel saw them tearing at his greatest creations, he sent the Boilers after them. But he couldn't hold out forever. Reinforcements came from all over the country, and even the French contingent nearby stormed in to lend their guns. Eventually, they broke down the Boiler defences, and they came for him in his steel palace.

"Brunel knew they would, of course, and he had prepared. He shut himself in his workshop, bolted every door, set every trap, and oiled every remaining Boiler. He was ready for a fight."

"And what happened to you and Brigitte and the child?"

"You're interrupting again. When I told Brigitte that Nicholas had sent me in order to keep her safe while he went after Brunel, she grew angry at him. She felt, and rightly so, that he had abandoned her. Brigitte refused to leave on the boat to France, as Nicholas had wanted, but took Ophelia and went instead to the last train leaving London – the train carrying Aaron Williams and the brave few Stokers who'd followed him through the Wall in order to stand against Brunel. I found Brigitte on the platform and tried to convince her to change her mind, to remain with me. But she refused, and she boarded the train with the child in her arms. I never saw her again."

"What was the child's name?" Thorn whispered, her nails digging into his trouser leg.

"I can't recall." Though he squeezed her hand, his voice breezed over the question. *He won't tell them who I am.*

He knew my father, he knew my father as a soldier and a scientist. He knew my mother, and he was with us...he helped her to look after me. He knew...as soon as I said my name, he knew me.

He knew me before the curse.

Holman continued. "Not knowing what else to do, I

took my one remaining ticket to the docks and boarded the ship to France. Many others milled around, anxious to leave the bloodied city. I sold the other two tickets and pocketed the money to cover my bills while away, and I waited on decks for the ship to set sail. Suddenly, I heard a loud *BOOM*, and everyone around shrieked and gasped. 'What is going on?' I asked a man standing beside me, clutching his little girl to his chest while she sobbed.

"'The Engine Ward is on fire'," he replied. 'A great plume of flame has shot up into the heavens'."

"As the boat pulled away from the docks, taking me away to my new life, my heart was heavy, for I knew then that Nicholas had succeeded where so many before him had failed. He had stopped Isambard Kingdom Brunel once and for all, but in doing so, he had sacrificed himself.

"I heard later his body was discovered deep in the burnt shell of the Chimney, and The Queen herself paid to give him a proper burial and a tomb at Highgate cemetery, as deserving a hero of the people. And that, my friends, is the story of Nicholas Thorne, and how he saved us all from many years of unspeakable terror."

Thorn wrenched her knee from Holman's grasp and stood up. That hard lump rose in her throat again.

She opened and shut her mouth, but no sound came out. There were no words to express her feelings. To Holman, her father had been more than a cursed Stoker who betrayed his people for London. He understood something of the faceless man from her shadowed memories, who now seemed glaringly, frightfully alive. And her mother...she couldn't face *that,* not now. She turned on her heel and climbed the rise, bolting back towards the tents.

"Thorn!" called Wombwell, a sharp tone in his voice.

"Thorn?" Holman sounded concerned, lost. She ignored them both, stormed back to her wagon, collapsed in the crook of Igor's shoulder, and started to cry.

***

In the early hours of the morning Thorn awoke from a nightmare, her skin dripping with sweat and tears. In the dream she'd been on the train again; that stout Clegg carriage screeching along the tracks. She was not a baby this time but in her adolescent body, and she choked in the black air as hundreds of bodies pressed her in. Thorn looked up at her mother, but the shape that towered over her wasn't her mother anymore. It was Rex, scowling as he tore gears from her wedding pin.

"You're cursed, Thorn," he said, grabbing her roughly and pulling her through the crowd, toward a large, jagged hole at the back of the carriage. "I don't want you. *No one wants you*. Not even your own mother."

Thorn stood on the edge of that hole, looking out into nothingness, a great black chasm. Rex planted his hands on her shoulders. She opened her mouth to scream, but the wind streaming past her face tore away her cries.

Rex shoved her, and she fell backwards, flailing and screaming as she tumbled from the carriage into the deep, bleak abyss...

Thorn woke, panting. Her body was slick with sweat. It took her a few moments to realise where she was. She lay awake, waiting for her heart to return to its normal rhythm, and noticed Igor moaning above her, thrashing his head from side to side.

"I'm coming, poor boy." Thorn wrapped her arms around his stiff neck, an act that calmed him, as it seemed to do for all animals. She still had no clue what was wrong with him, and with every day that passed she grew closer to being forced onto the streets. When Igor inched forward to nibble his oats, she saw the underside of his belly scrape on the wood floor.

Perhaps it's an allergy? Sometimes the deer at Graveyard accidentally ate the blackthorn berries that encroached upon their fence line, and their stomachs would bloat and squirm until they purged the poisonous fruit. "Can you roll over for me, boy?" Thorn nudged Igor and – with a groan of protest – he dutifully collapsed onto his side. His skin stretched and tugged with the weight of the lump. His eyes fluttered shut, and he moaned.

Thorn ran her hand over the lump, feeling for pustules and sores. Her mind reached out, but instead of seeking Igor, it attached to another animal. A tricorn, warm and cosy and blind to the world. She stroked the lump of Igor's belly.

The lump kicked back.

"Oh," she breathed, suddenly understanding.

"Wombwell?" Thorn leaned out the door of the wagon and yelled "Mr. Wombwell, sir!"

A minute later the proprietor popped his head through the flap, a long pink nightcap dangling from his ear. "It's very early, child. What is the matter?"

"Igor's pregnant."

"Igor…what?"

"Either that, or he's digesting a monkey."

Wombwell set down his lantern and rushed to her side. Thorn placed Wombwell's hand over Igor's swelling belly. When he felt the movement, his eyes widened. He left his hand there for a long while; stroking the tricorn's drawn, sweating face with the other. Then, slowly, carefully, he turned Igor over, and inspected the area between his hind legs.

Finally he said; "I'll murder Holman, that blind old coot. Imagine not knowing a cock from a cunny! Our Igor is indeed a *she*. How far along is she?"

"It won't be long now. A week, I'd guess."

"This changes everything." Wombwell's eyes sparkled with that same mischievous wit she'd seen when he'd one-upped Atkins with the dead tricorn. "We're going to have baby tricorns. I don't think this has ever been seen before! We'll make hundreds! Thousands!"

Igor opened one eye, moaned, and flopped back onto her belly. She sniffed her dwindling food pile, and snorted in disdain, dribbling sweat and mucus over Wombwell's pink sleeping bloomers.

"I'll get some water." Thorn avoided Wombwell's eyes. Although she was elated that Igor wasn't sick, she knew that she was no longer needed. Wombwell would send her away, and she'd be alone once more.

He wiped mucus from his trouser leg and sniffed it. "Yes, you had better. She'll need to keep her fluids up. Of course you will stay with the menagerie now; Igor needs someone to watch over her until the brood is born."

Thorn nodded, barely able to suppress her glee. She darted from the wagon and skipped to the water pumps. *I'm safe here, for a while longer at least.*

Light poured through the flaps in the wagon while Thorn watched over Igor, and like a locomotive thundering into the station the menagerie rumbled to life. The birds received the rising sun with a high-pitched song. The monkeys responded in choruses of hoots, while the neckers bellowed of their hunger to all who would listen (and many who would rather not have heard). Workers scrambled this way and that, fetching food and water, brushes and clothes, tools and ladders for packing down the tent.

Wombwell had already dispatched a hurried letter to the Royal Society, inviting any interested fellows to view the rare spectacle. "I'll charge sixpence for a gander," he exclaimed over breakfast, "and two quid to examine one of the babes. We'll be rich, Thorn m'dear!"

But Holman called him away for a private talk, and when Wombwell returned to the table, his features seemed more taut and serious than usual. "I'm afraid there's been a small change of plans. We will be leaving London. Today, in fact, just as soon as I finish my sausages. I need you all to wake the rest of the crew and get these wagons packed up."

Julianne opened her mouth, but he shushed her with a wave of his hand. "We have tarried too long in the city," he explained. "We should be bringing Wombwell's Travelling Menagerie to the people who can't afford to come to the Great Exhibition."

The menagerie workers exchanged worried glances. Thorn understood their concern. *Why are they giving up one of the prime events of the season? What does Wombwell hope to gain? What did Holman say to him?*

Wombwell wanted to leave the fairgrounds before lunch, just as soon as they'd bathed the animals and packed away the equipment. He had already plotted a grand tour, beginning in Oxfordshire and travelling along the east coast all the way to Scotland. He spent the morning sending dispatches ahead to his contacts throughout the country, informing them the menagerie would be arriving in their towns in a matter of weeks. He then drafted another letter to the Royal Society, apologising for the confusion and explaining his schedule for the next month, should any member wish to meet him on the road to examine the tricorns.

Thorn didn't want to leave London without ridding herself of Joel's rucksack and the mysterious plate, so she offered to deliver the letter to the Royal Society. She left Igor in the care of Julianne and went to seek out Rex's London Stokers. Once she fulfilled this final duty she would be free from the Stokers and her curse forever.

Maybe I'll stay with the menagerie forever, if Wombwell could offer me permanent employment.

Thorn's first stop was Somerset House, just east of Waterloo Bridge on the southern side of the Strand. The ornate building – rebuilt after a fire on the final night of the Vampire King's reign burned it to the ground – housed the rooms of the Royal Society, and Thorn knocked on the door with some trepidation, feeling the looming façade tower over her like one of Wombwell's monstrous neckers. Its outer brickwork was stained black with the fire damage it had suffered.

She was greeted by a russet-haired pageboy, not two years older than herself, who took her letter and promised to deliver it to the Fellows as soon as possible. Thorn thanked him and asked the way to the Engine Ward.

He stiffened at the question, his shoulders hunching into his neck. "You'll pass by it on the way to Paddington Station," he mumbled, his eyes on his shoes. "Just on this side of Bishop's Bridge. But you shouldn't go there – it's not safe."

Thorn thanked him, and he looked up at her with wide, frightened eyes and slammed the door in her face.

After twenty minutes of brisk walking she could see the smoke billowing over the tenements. Buildings on these streets did not look like the rest of London – every window boarded up, and the only sound of life came from a screaming child corralled somewhere within. The few men on the streets rushed past at great speed, their heads bent down and their eyes shifting nervously, as if they expected her to draw a knife on them at any moment. In the distance, machines clanked and steam hissed.

She followed the disused railway lines running along the centre of the debris-strewn street, until the road came to an abrupt halt, and she peered up at a steep metal barricade. Sulfurous gasses poured over the side, shrouding the height of the wall in a grey-black mist. She placed her hand on the surface. It whirred and vibrated under her hand, just like the metal in the Wall. *I've found the Engine Ward.*

Her eyes stinging, Thorn followed the wall across the street, around the corner, and over the bridge. The whirring noises grew louder, as though they followed her movements, gaining momentum as they sought her out. She stared down the expanse – she could see no gatehouse, no entrance. The fear crept into her chest again, and she decided to give up.

She trudged along Bishop's Bridge Road until she could see the gas lamps of the ramshackle railway station on the outer edge of the Wall. As she passed by on the east side of the road, the semaphore signal flickered to red, and gears clanked and drove the swinging arms into the air, halting the foot traffic. In the distance, a train's whistle screeched.

The station consisted of abandoned foundations and splatterings of lewd graffiti. It was created to serve the needs of the engineering sects within Engine Ward, but now that the Ward was deserted, the station was no longer in use. Although Thorn could see the railway itself had been repaired recently and trains obviously ran through the station, the station itself still remained derelict. Abandoned coal stores and piles of rusted rails leaned against the empty carriage sheds. A statue of Brunel – the head cloven off – lay on its side under a crumbled stone plinth, coloured grey with compie droppings.

This was where she'd find them. Stokers always stayed close to the trains.

Sure enough, as soon as Thorn entered the precinct of the coal factories, she noticed a cross formed of two gauge nails – the Stoker symbol – scrawled on the wall in soot, hiding amidst the amorous stick figures. She tapped on the adjacent door. No one answered. She rapped harder, and tested the door with her boot. It swung inward on one rusted hinge.

"Hello?" Thorn took a step inside, her heart pounding. They wouldn't be expecting her. *Please let them hear me out before they start shooting.*

A compie scrabbled across the floor. Thorn heard the clank of other rodents skittering across the ceiling beams.

"Wassssit?" Something wriggled in the corner. A man tugged a filthy blanket off his head, rubbed his eyes, and stared at her in disdain. He might have been young, not much older than Thorn, but his face was so blackened with soot and his eyes were so filled with hatred, it was impossible to tell. Thorn's pulse quickened as she took another step towards the slumped figure.

"Excuse me, sir. I've come from the Graveyard, part of Rex Williams' crew. I have a package to deliver to the London Stokers—"

The man spat at her feet, and grabbed for a bottle on

the windowsill. His fingers clasped at the neck, but his twitching caused the bottle to crash to the ground. Thorn winced and jumped back.

"Buggerit," he said, glowering at her. "See what you did? Coming in here with talk of Stokers. There are no Stokers, girlie."

"Please, you can trust me. I'm a Stoker. Rex told me there were others in London, that Brunel had returned —"

He threw off the blanket, and the naked, hairy, grizzled body barrelled towards her, its shaking hands grabbing for her throat.

"Don't *say* that." He grabbed handfuls of her hair and yanked it back. Her scalp exploded with pain. "Don't say *his* name around here."

"Who? Brunel?"

The man yanked Thorn's head back so she stared into his wild eyes. "*Fuck* Brunel. He can return all he wants, but no one 'ere wants him. Some idiot calling himself Aaron Williams' son came in here a couple of months back and tried to convince us to march into those Walls and beg for mercy at his feet. What a load of codswallop. The Sunken are chomping at the bit for fresh blood. Where's the Royal Engineer's bloody apprentice Rex at, anyhow? I haven't seen him skulking around for a few weeks."

Thorn was still reeling at his words. *He's a Stoker, but he doesn't agree with Rex. That's not what Rex said. What happened to the network of believers who were going to exalt the Metal Messiah's return? And what is this about the Sunken?*

"He's...dead...I think."

"He's dead to us, alright, him an' his Whitechapel harlot. You'll nae find your precious Stokers here. And as for *that*—" releasing her hair, he ripped the pin off her coat lapel and threw it to the floor. "Why would you wear that in the streets? You askin' for the noose?"

Thorn bent over and retrieved her pin from the pile of compie faeces. One of the silver-plated gauge nails had snapped off. She couldn't see it anywhere. She bit back the urge to cry.

The man sneered. "We don't need your Messiah in this town, lass. We've gods aplenty already."

Sobbing, Thorn threw the pin at him and raced into the street.

I hope it stabs him through the eye.

All the people who were supposed to care, the close network of spies and comrades, the rising movement Rex had sworn was ready for action...it didn't exist. It was a lie. It was all a lie.

Thorn rubbed the torn fabric of her coat in her trembling fingers. *Don't let me descend into this madness, father. Don't let me become like Rex. Let me be brave like you.*

PART II:
WALL

1851

JAMES HOLMAN'S MEMOIRS, FIRST EDITION

Of course when my good acquaintance Mr. Wombwell suggested I remain with the menagerie, I could not refuse. My decision was partly based on my observations of Miss Thorn, a lady of remarkable mystery whom my inquiring mind could not seem to dislodge. I had already ascertained her relationship to Nicholas, given her name and circumstances, as well as her reaction to my story.

Notwithstanding, since my return from Africa, the pain had crept into my joints again. Worse this time, and with the fires from the Engine Ward spewing filth over the city, I knew it prudent to leave London as soon as I was able. I explained my fears to Wombwell, and he – being the only man sensible enough to see the Royal Engineer for who he truly was – reluctantly agreed it was imprudent to remain inside the Wall, baby tricorns or nay. Brunel did so love a huge public spectacle as the backdrop for his crimes, and the Great Exhibition seemed tailor-made for this purpose. And so, Wombwell had the menagerie on the move before lunchtime, in his usual efficient fashion.

I could barely contain my joy. With all the excitement over the Great Exhibition, my Royal Society stipend was late. A jaunt in the country seemed just the thing I needed to replenish my spirits and my forlorn finances.

Famed as Wombwell was, they gave us no trouble at the city gates. Thorn had returned from wherever she'd visited that morning, and went straight to her chamber. She did not emerge, and when I inquired within she simply pretended to be asleep. Julianne sat with her while we drove under the Wall, and said that although she trembled, she remained composed.

Imagine, nineteen years on, the child of Nicholas returning to the city, and how remarkable that she was so much like her father. Thorn possessed more than just Nicholas' powers – she had his kindness, his easily trusting nature, and above all else, his courage. I was pleased that we were taking her far away from the returning Metal Messiah, for should Brunel learn of her, he would take a great interest in the daughter of his killer.

But I knew we could not hide in the countryside forever. London had not seen the last of the spirited Miss Thorn, of that I was most certain.

***

Only days after she first set foot on London cobbles, Thorn found herself settled within a hamlet outside the horrible Wall, less one fiancé and two friends, less her precious pin, and still clutching Joel's satchel containing her father's embossed plate. The weather had been appalling – rushes of filthy sleet that crashed like pistons over the meek stone wall surrounding the hamlet, pummelling the flimsy wagons and frightening the animals. Fog and soot hung so thick she could no longer tell night from day, and all the while the Wall chugged away in the distance, spewing forth more of the noxious misery.

Exhausted by the events of the last few days, Thorn slept through the crossing of the Wall and the three occasions Holman stopped by to apologise for upsetting her. He wanted to talk further but she wasn't yet ready to redress the painful memories of her parents.

When she woke again, they had already pulled in at their evening's camp, and the menagerie was a hive of activity as workers rushed about, setting up the tent and seats and preparing the animals for the night's entertainment. Julianne put Thorn to work mending the leaks torn in the canvas by the force of the rain, and fetching food and water for Igor, who was doing very well.

Thorn and Igor were interrupted every half hour by Wombwell, entertaining yet another troupe of well-dressed men from the Royal Society, who had come out in cabs or on horseback just to see the pregnant tricorn. Their cigar smoke stank out Thorn's wagon, and made Igor cranky. Wombwell slipped her a few coins, so she couldn't stay annoyed long.

Thorn wanted to give the tricorn a more feminine name, but none she thought of sounded right. She settled finally on *Igoria*. The pregnant tricorn curled up in the straw beside her, burrowing down into it and using her thick skull to push aside the straw to make herself a nest. When she had finished, Igoria's speckled head with its collar of bone and juvenile horns – the ivory still brittle and no good for trade – was the only part of her visible under the straw. Outside, rain patted gently on the canvas and formed large puddles on the flagstones. But for once in her life, the rain didn't bother her. Thorn was dry.

Compared to the third storey landing in the Turret – only half as tall as a full-grown man, with barely enough room to lie out straight – Igoria's wagon, despite reeking of cigar smoke, was a palace. When Thorn was much younger, and visions of her mother throwing herself from the Clegg carriage rather than look after a child haunted her sleep, Quartz would sit with her and tell stories about a princess and her pet serpent who lived in a castle made of silk in a vast, jewelled desert where it never rained. Thorn would eventually fall asleep with the sensation of gritty sand behind her eyes and a cosy feeling that the dribbling rain over her head could never quite destroy.

But though she felt like a princess and the soft hay and clean blankets cradled her like a baby, Thorn couldn't sleep. Now her nightmares were of a different sort, and though she tried to picture the castle in the desert, all she could see was the shadowy figure of her father, hunched over a big, heavy desk across from Holman. He was drinking sherry and smoking a fat cigar with nary a thought for his daughter lost in the swamp. In another dream, Thorn ran from the Sunken in the Wall, its flesh burning and peeling away as it drew closer, closer...and then the dream changed and it was not a Sinker at all, but the glowing smile of the Boiler as it advanced upon her, its screams echoing inside her skull.

But most of all, Thorn dreamed of Rex. At first the nightmare started as her favourite dream; a fine day, a Stoker wedding, her wearing a long blue dress, him in pressed leggings and doublet – with a silver gauge nail cross pinned through the lapel – waiting to take her hand. Over and over the image played in front of her eyes, each excruciating detail – the songs they danced to, the bitter taste of the wedding toast, the way his head inclined as he bent down towards her for the kiss…and then his face changed. His expression darkened, twisting with malice as he spoke his last words to her – how he had dismissed her as expendable. The world opened up around her and everything gay and happy sank into a deep pool of black nothingness. And she was falling, toppling into that bleak chasm.

And yet I survived and he—

There was no solace in that thought, no sense of justice. And that haunted Thorn most of all. *I still love him. I still wish he was here.* She cried so long she thought she'd broken her eyes; *why else do they continue to leak so?*

Beside her, Igoria pawed the ground and whimpered. Thorn stroked her hide, just behind the collar of bone on her neck. She seemed to like that; snorting and curling her legs and tail around her nest of eggs. Igoria's thoughts were inquisitive; she had heard Thorn sobbing, and wanted to know what the problem was.

"I'm sorry to have woken you, little one." Thorn squeezed Igoria's paw. "Boilers took my husband away. I guess…you probably know a little how that feels—"

Thorn heard a rustle on the tent flap. "Who is it?"

No one answered. Thorn held her breath, her pulse quickening. *Why would someone creep silently into my caravan?* felt foolish for her fear, knowing there was probably a sensible explanation. *Maybe it's Wombwell, telling me to get up. Or Julianne, playing some sort of game. Maybe one of the animals got loose?*

A human figure – too lanky to be Wombwell, too broad-shouldered to by Julianne, too bipedal to be an animal – stepped into the moonlight and cast his shadow over her bed. She screamed.

"Thorn? Bloody hell!"

"*Lurgo?* You're alive?" Relief washed over her. She reached up and grabbed his wrist – rejoicing at the familiar solidness of it – and pulled him down into the straw.

"Yeeeooof! What are you doing?" he hissed.

"I'm asking you the same question?"

"Sssssh, not so loud," Lurgo crouched down even lower. "And I asked you first."

"I work for Mr. Wombwell. He's the man who owns the menagerie."

"You've been loose in London less than a week and you got a job?"

"It's a long story. But I want to hear about you. How did you escape? And why are you here? Why aren't you in London?"

"I heard there was a tricorn in the menagerie. I thought I'd capture it and take it back home. For Quartz." He held up his barker. "At least then I could return with some good fortune."

Thorn leapt to her feet, standing in front of Igoria with her arms folded. "You're not taking Igoria."

"Igoria? That's a weird name for a tricorn—"

"Could we focus on more important matter, Lurgo, *please?*Where are Rex and Joel?"

He recoiled at the mention of Rex's name. "We got separated. I tried to go back for them, but it was so dark in the Wall—"

"I know." Thorn remembered how afraid she was lost in those tunnels. "So they're—"

"Rex had taken that bullet outside the Wall, remember? They must have smelt the blood. Those *things*…" He gulped.

"The Sunken."

"They *tore* at Rex with their lead claws. He could not have survived. Joel…I didn't see. I just ran." Lurgo stared at his feet. They both knew the answer. Tears welled in Thorn's eyes again.

"Thorn," Lurgo said, dropping his voice, "Rex set us up. I think he intended us to die in that Wall."

"That's not true." But as she said it, she knew he spoke the truth. She told Lurgo about the creature Rex had called in the night, the one who came for the lead and delivered a message on a metal plate. "I wasn't sure at the time, because it was so hard to see, but I'm certain now the creature was a Sinker."

"It all fits. Maybe Rex didn't mean for everyone to die, but he certainly had it in his head that some of us were expendable. It explains his erratic behaviour and his sudden indifference toward you. Something in that *city* —" Lurgo spat in the direction of London, "—corrupted him good and proper. After we left you behind – which Joel and I fought him hard on, by the way – he led us through a dark passage he said would take us outside, but the Sunken were right there waiting for us – Rex spoke to them. He marched up to one and told it they could have Joel and Finnegan and me, but they were to take him to the 'Royal Engineer'. But they didn't listen, they just gobbled him right up. And then they came after us—"

A light flickered outside. "Thorn, is everything all right?."

It was Holman. The tent flap fluttered. Lurgo dived for the straw.

"Is someone else in here? I heard voices. I may be blind but I am armed and deadly." Holman pulled his cane to chest height, and unscrewed the handle.

Moonlight glinted off the hidden blade.

Lurgo shuffled into the corner, accidentally stomping on Igoria's tail. The tricorn sprung up and let off a low growl.

"Aieeeee!" Holman pounced, waving his cane around. Thorn screamed, and ducked to avoid a premature decapitation.

"James, put the knife down. It's okay, really. This is Lurgo. I know him from the swamps."

Lurgo smirked, throwing his arm around her shoulder. Thorn shrugged it off.

Wombwell chose that moment to poke his head around the door. "What's going on? I heard some commotion and ... Thorn, who's your gentlemen caller? My, you move fast, lass."

Holman lowered his sword. "Oh dear. Thorn has a gentleman? And here I am interrupting them. Are they in the middle of—"

"No!" Thorn's face flushed red. Lurgo looked pleased with himself.

Igoria shovelled her head into the straw and butted it everywhere. Thorn tugged pieces from her hair.

"James Holman, and George Wombwell, may I introduce Lurgo Riley, of Graveyard." She mumbled, staring at her boots. Grinning, Lurgo took a deep bow.

Holman extended his hand. "Pleased to make your acquaintance, good sir. Will you and Miss Thorn be marrying this year?"

Wombwell shook his finger. "Look at Igoria, she's all fussed and bothered. You should know better than this, Thorn. Keep your amorous affairs well away from my tricorn."

" I *tried* to stop her," Lurgo added, "but she was all over me. Thorn can be a real wanton harlot when the mood strikes her."

Her cheeks burning with embarrassment, Thorn held her hands over her ears and flashed demon eyes at them all.

"Get out, all of you!"

***

Thorn slept deeply that night. No dreams haunted her. A bell sounded the following morning. Thorn's eyes fluttered open, and came into focus on Lurgo's leering face, inches from hers.

She screamed. He laughed and shook her shoulders.

"Time to rise, sleepy Thorn. Wombwell says we have baby tricorns to deliver."

"This is *my* job." She pulled the blanket over her bare shoulders.

"Not if you sleep through it." He ducked as her boot sailed past his ear. "Tsk, that's no way to treat your lover. Were you always this rough on ole Rex?"

Thorn pulled the blanket over her head so Lurgo couldn't watch while she put on her tunic and coat. When she peeked through the blanket again, he was gone.

"Some midwife he makes, eh girl?"

Igoria moaned in reply. She had rolled onto her side, and her swollen belly rose and fell with every breath. Sweat poured from the folds of her skin, drenching her body in sticky slime. Her eyes rolled around the room, searching for Thorn.

"I'm here, girl." Thorn sponged her forehead with the sodden towel and tried to cast her mind back to her half-day of midwife training.

At a certain age all the young women were forced to

sit through midwifery lessons with Old Hatchie, who smelt so heavily of cabbages and birthing fluid that even the other girls with their Stoker noses complained of the reek. Thorn found Hatchie's lectures about poultices and birthing stool construction excruciatingly boring, and spent her morning directing spiders to shift the teacups around, until Hatchie sent her back to Quartz. All she remembered was something about pushing and using salt or natron to soak up the residue.

Residue? Oh dear.

"Well, I'm not much help, am I?" Thorn gave Igoria's belly a light press with her palm. The tricorn puffed her cheeks, her face contorted in pain. She bucked her hind legs back, arched her back, and let out a bellow that shook the axletree of the wagon.

Lurgo returned with more towels. "I thought we might—"

Thorn waved her arms for him to be quiet. Igoria rose up again, heaving her belly back and moaning. Blood and goo splattered over Lurgo.

Thorn snorted a laugh. He spat a mouthful of birthing fluid into the hay, dropped the towels, and stormed off. Igoria groaned her pleasure, and the first wriggling infant rolled onto the hay.

He, or she, was beautiful. Each tiny limb perfectly formed – a miniature, goo-covered mirror of its mother. The ivory horns that would be so deadly in its adulthood were only white smudges across its nose and eyebrows. It flared its tiny frill and let out a piercing wail.

Thorn wrapped it in a cloth and brought it close to her chest. Rocking back and forth the way Hatchie had showed her, she used a corner of the cloth to wipe blood from its tiny face. The creature croaked and wailed, its voice high-pitched and piercing compared to its mother.

Thorn wiped the congealed mess from behind its bone frill – barely the size of her palm – and inspected its screwed up face and flailing limbs.

"Water," Thorn thought aloud frantically. "You'll need water." But before she could react further, another wail – like steam issuing from a smoke stack – bellowed from Igoria, and the second tricorn slid into the world. Thorn set the blanket down in the hollow she'd fashioned herself to sleep in, and set off after the other.

"Send for Wombwell," she snapped to Lurgo while she worked. "He'll want to be here for this."

"No way." Lurgo backed up, holding his hands in front of himself in mock surrender. "I'm not going out there. I'm still a stowaway, remember?"

Within the hour she had eight whining parcels lined up along her hollow, each with eyes jammed shut and faces like wrinkled sackcloth. Igoria collapsed, her breathing slow and heavy. Thorn cupped water in her hands and tried to dribble it into the babies' mouths.

Despite Lurgo's cooperation it wasn't long before word spread through the menagerie that Igoria's babies had arrived. Julianne stopped by to let Thorn know Wombwell was on his way, and a few minutes later, the awning rustled again. Wombwell rushed towards her. "Are they—"

She smiled, and handed him a blanket. "All eight of them."

He cradled the tiny tricorn, his eyes alight with joy. "We shall call you...Igor the Second."

"I named this one Bridget." Thorn handed him another. "And that tiny angel over there is Lurgette."

"Hey!" Lurgo stepped from the doorway.

"And here are Verne, Bernard, Nicholas, Rose and Isobella."

Wombwell moved beside Igoria, who dragged her swollen belly forward, ready to do her duty by her children. Wombwell unwrapped Igor and placed him by her teat, where he suckled happily. Soon his seven siblings clambered over each other for a turn at the milk.

The show was cancelled that night, for the winds whipped up worse than before, blowing clouds of soot over the town and draping their convoy in a blanket of black dust. Even the Royal Society men stayed away, preferring the comfort of their lodgings to the sodden wagons. Thorn stayed with Igoria, sending Lurgo out for food and water and fresh hay. He always returned coughing, and hawked black spitballs into the corner.

"This weather is so bad it makes the Graveyard seem cheerful." Lurgo slumped against the limbers and took a bite from a loaf of bread, mulched to sodden dough by the rain.

"You never made it inside London, did you?"

Lurgo shook his head. "I ran back the way I had come."

"The air in the city is so fresh, it gave me headaches. I never imagined such a place was possible – the sky arches over the city like a citadel, and nothing within is disturbed. Even the rain feels fresh and cleansing. But for Brunel and his evil machines, I would mistake it for the Station of Life."

"You're too young to remember much, but it never used to be like that. Father would come home from the trains reeking of sweat and grease, and the coal dust would leak from his skin. Everything in our house was stained black, even my mother's skin where he touched her. I remember..." He closed his eyes. "Mother took me to the station when the first run on the *Goes When Ready* went out, to take the first batch of Stokers back to their homeland. I sat on Mother's shoulders and peered into the engine room. Father's shovel made this sound... as it scraped and scratched across the coals, as it swung and scraped and scuffed and chaffed off that coal. It was the soul of London, bit by bit being worn away. On dark nights, I dream that noise, over and over again..." He bit his lip. "Sorry, I shouldn't talk like this."

Thorn leaned closer. "What else do you remember?"

"The Wall. I remember Father saying it was our saviour, it would keep us safe from the Great Dragons, and he could work on it each day for a decent wage, building the railroad tracks and doing all the jobs the Boilers couldn't touch. That was before the Gauge War really took off, before that Wall became a symbol of everything we had lost. All day and night those gears turned, and the clangs and clanks rattle inside Father's head even now. London was not kind to us. For all the others say about your father, Thorn, I always agreed... we couldn't have stayed in London. They didn't want us."

"Lurgo...I'm sorry."

"Don't be. You've less to do with it than everyone thinks. And you saved Igoria's babies." He sighed. "I couldn't even save Rex or Joel."

"It's been a long day. We should sleep." For the first time in the eighteen years she'd known him, Thorn allowed Lurgo to curl up beside her, his arms entwined in hers, soot-caked dreams swelling behind their eyes.

***

The weather hadn't much improved by the morning, so the menagerie departed without a performance, rising with the dim pallor of light that signalled the sun's ascent through the soot, and packing down the seating and decorations ready for the next town. Thorn and Lurgo helped Julianne tidy away the stores, but Thorn fretted being away from Igoria and returned to her charge. With the storm damage to one wagon irreparable for the time being, Wombwell had to pack other animals into Igoria's wagon – two monkeys, six ostriches and one misbehaving compie – and the new mother wasn't overjoyed about sharing. She snorted and stomped and fussed till Thorn strapped the bridle on and forced her to sit in the corner and feed her babies.

The compie was a different story. It stirred up the straw searching for insects, and soon hay and oats were flying everywhere. The babies – still with their eyes tight shut – couldn't figure out what was going on, and became quite alarmed. The monkeys – Bella and Alberto – thought it a marvellous lark, and soon the limbers rocked under the weight of swinging monkeys.

Thorn was trying to disentangle Bella's claws from her scalp when Lurgo banged on the canvas.

"We're hitching this now. Hold on, Thorn."

"I can't!" The compie chose that moment to chomp down on her hand. She gritted her teeth and tore Bella out of her hair. Pain seared through her scalp as monkey claws scraped along her hairline.

Thorn fell forward as the ground rolled beneath her. She heard the men grunting as they lifted the brakes and pushed the heavy carriage. She landed on her knees, cuddling Bella under her arm and watching the compie chasing its tail in a haphazard circle. The carriage jerked as they heaved it backward. She heard the slide of the pins into the yoke, and the men struggling to untangle the traces.

Lurgo appeared at the doorway, his tunic soaked with

sweat. "You could stand to lose a few pounds," he said.

"You're funny." Thorn shot back as she unwrapped Bella and plonked the scrabbling monkey into his arms. "By that I mean, funny-looking."

"Hey!"

Lurgo lunged for her, but Bella caught a tendril of his hair and pulled, swinging her tiny body into midair. Lurgo yelped and fought to disentangle her. Thorn broke down into giggles.

The carriage began to move. They settled the animals, and sat side by side just inside the canvas flap to watch the journey.

Instead of horses Wombwell relied on teams of neckers, which weren't as fast but were much sturdier and could cross longer distances without need of rest. He'd had Holman procure the beasts from the dispossessed Scottish clans occupying the North and East forests. For fat-bellied creatures with legs like smoke stacks, they glided on the road with an amazing grace. Their flat tails whipped through the air and their tiny heads bobbed low on their elongated necks as they stretched themselves parallel to the ground.

"I'm surprised people still use horses," Thorn remarked. "Neckers seem so much more efficient."

"Is that an actual attempt at civilised conversation?" Lurgo grinned. "Why, I'm shocked."

She blanched. "Can't you be pleasant?"

"Can't you be—"

His words died. Lurgo's face had turned bone white, and he opened and shut his mouth as if he spoke prayers she wasn't meant to hear. She thought Bella had bitten him, but she lay curled in his lap, sound asleep.

Thorn looked to where his eyes fixated, and saw what frightened him; a wall ran down the outskirts of the village. That in itself was no strange sight – many villages still retained their ancient fortifications. But this was no ordinary wall. It was steep-sided and made entirely of metal, smaller in scale than London's, but still wide and black and deadly. Thorn's heart clenched as smoke billowed from a chimney stack protruding from the structure and blew black smoke across the village. The wagon rounded a corner and drove alongside, and they shuddered at the sound of the gears and clanks from within.

"That wasn't there when we drove in to the village yesterday."

"Nor when I snuck in," Lurgo muttered, his eyes wide. "I scaled a stone wall. It's appeared overnight, like magic."

Thorn pulled her blanket over her shoulders. Suddenly she felt a chill that had nothing to do with the cold.

"It's a *wall*," she said to no one in particular. "It shouldn't be growing."

A high metal arch rose in front of them, barred with iron grates. The road sloped upward as it curved through the arch and off to the side. Thorn guessed this ramp led onto the parapet. A black locomotive waited on the Wall above, the eight-foot driver wheels oiled and ready. She was a 4-2-2 named *Emperor* with passenger carriages and open-topped goods-wagons coupled and waiting for cargo. Steam hissed from the gleaming black boiler, curling over the buttress and simpering through the air. *What is going on? Why is that train stopped here as if it were waiting to commence its journey? Its journey to where?*

Up ahead Wombwell's wagon slowed, and she saw the jolly man rise from the footplate and disappear into the shadow of the Wall. Their neckers halted, and Thorn felt their fears sliding inside her head.

Holman poked his head from the back of the wagon in front. "Kids?"

"We're behind you." Thorn called back.

"I smell something unsavoury." He sniffed the air, wrinkling his nose. "Something is different."

"There's a Wall here, like the one in London. There's —"

The wagons jerked forward. Thorn saw the grate creak open, and Wombwell directed his neckers through.

They wouldn't go. They stopped short and bucked their heads in defiance. Wombwell yanked on the reins and they reared up, again refusing the door. As the confusion and panic spread along the column of wagons, emotions flooded inside Thorn, and she pressed her fingers to her temples, trying to block out the animals' distress.

"Even the Neckers don't like it," Lurgo observed.

"*I* don't like it."

Wombwell was yelling. Thorn had never seen him raise his voice before. Seizing her courage, she leapt from the wagon and sprinted towards the front of the convoy.

She halted so suddenly she tripped over her bootlace and scraped her arm on a wheel arch.

A Boiler emerged from a dark doorway in the Wall and rolled towards Wombwell. But this wasn't a normal Boiler, not anything like the one that chased her inside the London Wall.

For one thing, this Boiler was twice the height of a man. Steam hissed through two vertical pistons underneath its belly, and it sunk onto itself, stooping to pass under the gate of the Wall. Black smoke poured from the funnelled blastpipes that protruded from its steel-plated shoulders. Its armoured body gleamed in the daylight like a freshly-polished suit of armour.

Thorn braced herself, waiting for the onslaught of horrible thoughts that accompanied her first encounter with a Boiler. But nothing came. Her sense could not find the Boiler, not like the Boilers in London. *That doesn't make any sense. They should all be the same, shouldn't they?* Thorn relaxed her mind and searched the surrounding area. She could feel the fear of the other animals pressing against her own mind, but she couldn't sense the machine like she could the London Boilers.

What's going on?

Unfazed by the machine's advance, Wombwell stepped forward to address it. He pointed at the wagon, then at the gate, speaking slowly and carefully as he requested the right to pass. In response, the Boiler opened its belly-plate and spewed orange flames in the air.

Thorn yelled at Wombwell to get back, but all that exited her mouth was a dry croak, which the wind soon carried away. She dragged her frozen legs forward, inch by inch catching up to Wombwell. Thorn tried to stand beside him, but in the presence of the Boiler that felt too open, too exposed. She hid behind Wombwell's bulk, her hand resting protectively on his shoulder, and gazed up ... and up. The Boiler's chimneys stood so tall that their true height was obscured. They appeared as squat little turrets, and not the thin, elegant chimneys of Brunel's designs. Standing this close to it, Thorn could feel the heat pouring off the Boiler as a fire raged within its furnace belly. It hissed as steam forced its way through the valves, the sound like a snake ready to strike. Her legs quivered with fear, and her mouth dried out as she stared at it, trying to comprehend why it existed, and what it was doing in this tiny village.

Wombwell reached up and grabbed her hand, pulling her trembling fingers from his shoulder. He turned to face Thorn, and she saw his usually kind eyes flashing with a combination of fear and fury. "Go back to your wagon," he barked. "I'll take care of this."

"They're not normal Boilers." Thorn managed to choke out. "I can't sense—"

"Thorn, I said *get back*." Real terror flickered across his face.

She stepped away, backing up against the first caravan. Her eyes flicked down the length of the Wall. A shadow darted between the pylons. She took a few tentative steps closer, slipping under the heavy shade of the overhanging Wall.

What is that? The shape didn't look like a Boiler. It was too small, too nimble. *Why is it watching us?*

"Hello?" Thorn called out.

Something moved out of the corner of her eye. She whirled around, casting her eyes around the gloom. From the shadow a wrinkled hand reached toward her. It was attached to the looming face of a Sinker, his rolling eyes ringed with blood. The sight of him froze Thorn with fear. She watched, stricken, as he drew his hand to his face and bit into a lump of lead like it was a delicious mutton pie. His skin glowed and stretched as the lead slid down his chin.

The flesh of the Sinker's face sagged over his cheeks and eye sockets, as if the bones were the only thing holding it on. Thorn stared at those wretched eyes, still carrying the expressions of the man it had once been. Her heart pounded against her chest. *Run. You have to run, before it bites you.* But something held her there, froze her in place like a statue. It was the eyes. There was something about them. They looked...*familiar.*

The entire world halted on its axis and the jolt of recognition hit her. Her memories, her nightmares...they all soldered together within that monstrous face.

"Rex?" she asked, breathless.

Is it truly him? Is this what he has become?

The Sinker opened its mouth, as if it were trying to speak to her, but all that came out was a human *croak.* The inside of its mouth was black from the hot metal, a gaping hole into the soul beyond.

Rex, no.

Thorn stumbled backward, desperate to get away. The Sinker lurched forward, and she pulled herself away again, this time tripping over her own feet. She crashed to the ground, smashing her knees against the cobbles. The Sinker leaned over her, dribbling hot lead onto her boots. He reached out with long, clawed fingers and grabbed for the front of her shirt. Thorn scrambled backward. A strangled sob escaped her throat.

Someone grabbed her arm.

"Thorn!"

It was Lurgo, pulling her back, pulling her away. The Sinker made one final, desperate grab for her, then retreated into the shadows, purring like a lovesick kitten as it crouched in hiding.

"What in the name of Great Conductor's engine pit did you think you were doing?" Lurgo grabbed her shoulders and shook her roughly. Thorn sobbed. She couldn't form words. Her whole body shook uncontrollably.

"Bloody hell." He wrapped her limp arms around his shoulders and lifted her from her feet. "Let's get you back to Igoria."

Lurgo carried her back to her caravan. She barely

registered the warmth of his arms around her neck, or the concerned look he gave her as he laid her down in the hay. The thoughts of the animals swam inside Thorn's head. Distress for Wombwell's safety sent shudders through the entire menagerie. Their fears weighed heavy on her bones. But from the Boilers she sensed not a peep, and that silence worried her more.

Thorn and Lurgo watched from their caravan as Wombwell argued with the Boiler. Finally, the proprietor waddled back to his caravan, and the menagerie began to move once more.

Wombwell's solution was not pleasant, but they had no choice. They couldn't continue along the road, for the road no longer existed. They couldn't turn around in the narrow street, and a scout soon informed them *every* road out of town was blocked by the Wall. Wombwell would lose too much business if they didn't make the next village before noon the following day.

As Thorn watched through tear-clouded eyes – Lurgo burying his face into her back – Wombwell tied the protesting neckers to long lengths of rope, his hands shaking as he tried to soothe the worried beasts. Two of the giant Boilers – with bellies plated in iron cages that flicked rogue sparks like blasphemous ovens – emerged from the darkness, their tracks bumping along the cobbles. Twists of iron pipe shot from their bodies and coiled around the ropes. As they pulled Wombwell's wagon under the arch, the neckers were dragged along by the force of the yoke. They howled in protest but neither the Boilers nor Wombwell paid any attention.

Thorn tried to send out calming thoughts to them, but she was too frightened herself.

The carriage rolled under the Wall, onto a ramp and disappeared from view. Two more Boilers appeared and strapped themselves to the next carriage. Holman was next. Another pair of Boilers approached his team of neckers. His head snapped back at the sudden movement.

"Its okay, James. We're watching you."

Lurgo placed his hand on Thorn's shaking shoulder. For once, she did not shrug him away.

Thorn felt the jerk of their own carriage being dragged forward, and the shriek of the neckers as they twisted in the harness to escape the Boilers. She looked up. That was a mistake. The Boilers stared back at her with their eyes-that-were-not-eyes, grinning from their twisting valves with smiles of steam and brass.

Lurgo whimpered. Beside him, Igoria growled and narrowed her eyes. The babies cowered behind their mother.

Thorn wanted to turn away, but her eyes remained glued to the monsters. Their internal gears shifted and locked as they levered the wagon along the path, a threatening sound that resonated in her stomach. Outside in the light the Boilers looked so foreign, like creatures from another time, not fashioned by man but issued forth – piece by piece, gear by gear – from the womb of a metallic mother.

But after watching them at their work, something struck her as odd. Aside from their immense size, they did not function quite as Boilers should. Thorn couldn't remember the Boiler she'd seen inside the Wall having retractable arms like these; hollow pipes stacked end on end, creating the flailing arms that easily wrapped around the harness.

In fact, in all of Quartz's descriptions, and her own encounter, Thorn was certain Boilers should have no such appendage. Nor should they be so...sentient. The

Boilers Quartz described rolled about on skids, and they worked in unison, their bodies jerking through the functions they had been set. But these Boilers moved fluidly, as if they were able to respond to their environment and adjust their actions. The fact she could no longer sense these Boilers made them even more menacing. Compared to these towering leviathans, the London Boilers seemed…tame.

Perhaps Holman can shed some light on this observation. I have much to discuss with him tonight. That is, if I can ever pry Lurgo's cold fingernails from my thigh.

Thorn didn't dare lift her gaze from the Boilers as the gateway towered overhead. Their gears ground against their iron chest-plates, and the gratings became slick with fluid. From the protection of the Wall's shadow, the Sinker hissed and chittered. *Please Great Conductor, don't let him leap on the wagon.*

The Boilers rolled them up the spiral path on a steep incline, bringing them above the fields and forest on to the top of the Wall. The runners creaked under the effort. They mounted a steel platform and rolled the wagon onto a waiting freight car, neckers and all. After securing them in place, the Boilers backed down the path to haul up the next wagon.

Thorn's knees went weak. Save the tiny wagon the Stokers used to drag the tricorn carcasses back from the swamps, she hadn't rode a working train since…since the night she came to Graveyard… *and this is no ordinary train. It's a train that runs on top of a Wall that builds itself and appears overnight like some dark magic.* She hugged her knees to her body, wondering if she would live to see the next day.

Thick smoke clouds billowed from grates in the Wall below. The plumes further spooked the neckers and obscured Thorn's view of the vehicles in front. The air felt heavy, like it sat in her chest for longer than it should. On the wagon ahead of her, Holman coughed.

The road along the Wall was buttressed on both sides by steep walls of iron plate, riveted in place and reaching as high as the wheel ridge on the wagons. Tall pennants dyed black with soot hung every few feet, jerking violently in the rough wind. The track itself was wide enough for two broad gauge trains to run alongside each other, though as far as Thorn could tell theirs was the only locomotive on the track. She could hear neither the chug of wheels nor the puff of steam approaching from the distance.

With a clank the last of the Boilers disembarked and rolled away into the fog, leaving the convoy stranded on the train, strapped two to a freight-wagon. All along the train animals yowled, growled, hissed, and cried. The air crackled with tension; the hissing and clanging as the locomotive roared to life, the nervous whinny of the neckers, the howl of the wind through the buttress. And over it all swirled the smoke, black and foul as it pressed on Thorn's skin.

The train whistle blew, and with a heave, they pulled away from the station.

Thorn thought the shock of it would kill her, but the gentle chug of the train had a calming effect – it seemed to be the only mechanical thing around doing exactly as it should. The familiar smell of steam rushed past her face, and Thorn took a deep breath and felt...almost calm.

Almost.

Lurgo buried his face into Bella's warm fur, and his fingernails still dug into Thorn's leg. She prised his hand off.

"I think we're safe now. The Boilers have gone."

"Safe? Have you looked around, Thorn? We're on a *train. broad gauge* train!"

"This isn't so bad, actually. It's just a train."

"If this is *just a bloody train*, I'm just a bloody Navvy." Lurgo's skin turned green. "How did this train get here, overnight? I've been living inside trains my entire life and I couldn't get one to do that. And where is it taking us?"

"I'm sure Wombwell will have some kind of explanation." Thorn jumped off the perch, her feet making a dull thud on the iron grate. She pressed her hands against the wagon's limbers for support.

"Thorn, wait, *please*—"

Careful not to step too near the open edge, Thorn inched along the platform and grabbed the railing over the couplers. The gap between her car and the one in front was a good four feet. Wind whipped around her, threatening to drag her over the edge. She sucked in a deep breath, climbed over the railing, threw her arms in the air and pushed herself off.

For a second Thorn seemed to hang in the air, and her stomach plummeted as she realised she wouldn't made it, and then she crashed into the opposite railing, knocking her breath away. She perched on the thin metal grate, awkwardly clutching the steel and fighting for breath, for several minutes before she could rouse her shaking legs to climb over the railing and continue her journey.

The train juddered as it rolled through a junction. She grabbed hold of the nearest wagon and looked up in time to see another Wall, crossing over this one and trailing off in both directions, like the threads of a giant mechanical spider web. *I wonder where that Wall goes...*

Thorn found Wombwell on the next car, sprawled

across the coachman's perch of his private coach. He patted a distressed Nero, scratching behind the lion's flattened ears and muttering to him in low, soothing tones.

Wombwell saw her and made to say something, but she cut him off. "We're stuck on a Wall that grows like magic. The neckers won't budge and the animals are in a state. Lurgo's shaking so bad he can't function. What do you think you're doing?"

Thorn instantly regretted her words. How dare she be so forthright with her employer? She opened her mouth to apologise, but Wombwell looked up then, and his face was drained of colour. "I had no choice, Thorn. This is the only railway through Oxfordshire."

"But it wasn't a railway yesterday!"

"No." Wombwell sighed. "It wasn't. But now it is, and it's the road we must travel, I'm afraid. We've already lost precious time at the Wall gate. And time is money in the menagerie business. Can you help me calm these animals?"

Thorn spent the next hour wandering the length of the menagerie while the train hurtled on, leaping between the carriages so she could whisper to the neckers and stroke their long necks, drumming her fingers against their tough skin. She passed calming thoughts into their minds, thoughts of food and warmth and fresh watering holes and kind masters like Wombwell. When they ceased rolling their heads around, Thorn made the leap back to her own car, and opened the flap to Holman's carriage. She wanted to talk to him. *Immediately.*

***

"Is the Wall alive?"

Holman upended the kettle and poured tea into a delicate cup, hanging the tip of his finger over the rim to judge the level of the water. Outside, the English countryside whooshed by, lost in the clanking and pounding of the steam engine.

"That is precisely my thought. Sugar?"

Thorn nodded. Holman waited, holding out her cup, until she realised her mistake. "Oh, sorry. Yes, please."

Holman dropped two cubes into the steaming cup, stirring with a silver teaspoon. "Brunel designed the original Wall to be adaptable. He thought the design should be fluid, so that future generations could use it to protect the city against threats he couldn't conceive of. The Wall is a machine, of course, and a creation of man, so all these adaptations require human interference. This is not evolution in *nature*, as my friend Darwin discusses. And yet…the Boilers are also machines, and if what you say is correct and they are indeed *evolving*—"

"All I said is that they are different to the Boilers I saw in London."

"That's called evolution, Thorn. It's a new branch of biological science – my close friend Charles Darwin is creating a new Industrian sect in order to study it. The idea has already gained popularity among eminent scientific minds. In fact, last I was in France I heard a brilliant paper by a man named Lamarck about neckers. Have you ever wondered why a necker has such a long neck?"

Thorn shook her head. "It's not my business to ask."

"Well, Lamarck has a theory that long ago neckers had short necks and they looked a little like stumpy tortoises. But they lived in the oak forests where the delicious leaves on the trees were very high, so if one of them had a longer neck he could reach higher than the others and have more food to eat. Therefore, all the neckers with the longer necks got more food, so they survived longest and had the most children, and their children would be more likely to have long necks, and so on down the generations. Until now, where it is impossible to find a necker that doesn't have a long neck."

"That sounds like a children's story. And it doesn't explain why there are Boilers outside London."

"It could. If these country Boilers have to perform different tasks, they need to adapt to those tasks. Out here the Boilers have to be more mobile, and very robust and sturdy, and they require the use of arms. So they have evolved giant bodies and legs and long arms."

Thorn shivered. "But they're machines!"

"Precisely." Holman's mouth set in a thin line. "So the question we have to answer is, *how are they doing this?*"

"There's something else..." Thorn set down her saucer. "I'll be right back."

She peeked out the tent flaps. Behind her, Lurgo remained where she'd left him; frozen to the bench, face bone white, eyes like the glazed sugar on Holman's teacakes. Three wrinkly tricorns slept in his lap. Behind him, Bella and Alberto swung gleefully from the limbers.

"Lurgo," Thorn whispered. She called louder when he refused to answer. "Lurgo!"

His mouth opened and shut again, but no sound came out. He nodded instead. He heard her.

"In the hay behind my sleeping hollow, there's a rucksack. I need you to throw it to me." He didn't move. "*Lurgo*, it's important."

Lurgo nodded again, and disappeared inside. He returned a few moments later with Joel's rucksack tucked under one arm and a playful Bella clinging tenaciously to his scalp. With a feeble swing he tossed the rucksack across the expanse between the vehicles. Thorn stretched out for it, but the wind hurled the bag away. Thorn's heart skipped as the satchel bounced off the necker's harness and the handle snagged on the buckle.

"I'm sorry," Lurgo called over.

"Ah, finally you speak! Congratulations, you foolish gammy." Grasping onto the limber, Thorn leaned over the gap and stretched her fingers out, just brushing the harness. The wind whipped her hair around her face and the axles of the train churned underneath her. *Almost... nearly got it...*

Finally, her fingers clasped around the strap and she unhooked the rucksack and pulled it in.

"Lurgo, your head's bleeding; you might want to do something about that." Thorn clutched the rucksack to her chest, waiting a few moments for her heart to return to normal. She frowned at Lurgo one final time and ducked back inside the tent.

"He's even more frightened of the train than the neckers." Thorn informed Holman as she dug through the bag. "It's strange. I've never really seen Lurgo so afraid before."

"Lurgo has his reasons, as do you."

Thorn nodded, thinking of the Sinker that had Rex's eyes. That was plenty terrifying for her. She pressed the plate into Wombwell's hand.

"What treasure do you have here?"

"My friend Joel found this in Graveyard, hidden in the Clegg carriage – the one that took us all to the swamps after the wreck of the *Thunderer*. He believes it belonged to my father. I wondered if...since you knew him..." The words caught in her throat. She stared at her boots.

"I apologise for the other night. I had wanted to tell you in private, *Ophelia,* but I wasn't sure if you'd run away again." Holman smiled then, a sheepish grin that made Thorn's heart melt.

"You know my real name?"

"Of course. But don't worry, I shan't reveal it to anyone. There's much power in a name, Miss Thorn, and that's power you best keep close to your heart." His fingers traced the patterns on the plate.

"You said you and Nicholas created an embossed code? Does that mean you can read this plate?"

"I may be able to, eventually." Holman paused. "My mind is weak and often forgets, and it has forgotten the code we created all those years ago. Besides, I never created this plate. Brunel did. This is not a coded message, but some kind of...I'm not sure, actually. I cannot translate this plate yet, but if you leave it with me, I will do all in my power to recall."

"And the Wall?"

"There's nothing we can do. Perhaps there will be more clues in the next town. In the meantime," Holman set down the plate and picked up the delicate tea kettle. "Would you like another?"

***

Thorn never imagined a convoy of exotic animals could be so quiet. The gentle heave and throb of the train seemed to rock the menagerie to sleep. Only the neckers remained awake; they cried and snorted with renewed energy, as though they realised the louder they protested, the sooner they would be free of the Wall.

She tried to cast her mind out, searching for answers

in the animals' fear. Too rattled herself to concentrate, she sensed nothing.

Around suppertime, the train screeched to a halt. Along the line of the convoy she heard neckers screaming. The other animals joined in; a wild cacophony dashing over the falling rain. Thorn peeked her head out of Holman's canvas flap, but couldn't see anything past the sheets of water.

Lurgo poked his head out, and yelled at her. His words were lost in the storm. "I don't know!" she called back, shaking her head vigorously. His head disappeared from view.

There was nothing to do but wait. Shadows lurched alongside the train, and Thorn heard the unmistakable hiss and rattle of the Boilers. Holman reached out to her, clasping her tiny hand while his other stroked the mysterious plate. A little time passed, and they heard Wombwell stomping up and down the flooded road, cracking his whip through the air and barking hoarse commands at the neckers. He peeked his head in.

"It's all rather curious, James. We're several miles from Kidlington, but we're heading off the Wall. It seems the next section is unfinished." He gave the nearest necker a sharp kick, and they were off again.

Holman sipped his tea as if nothing were amiss. Thorn rested her chin on her knees and prayed it would all be over soon.

***

JAMES HOLMAN'S MEMOIRS, FIRST EDITION

After those hours on the Wall, Thorn was too frightened to leave my carriage, even though we now drove toward Kidlington under our own power. She blew out the lamps and I tucked her into my bed, covered her with the blankets, and let the rattle of the wheels along the old road rock her to sleep.

My fingers traced the patterns on the plate. Inside, I fluttered with excitement and shame. I wanted nothing more then to reveal the truth to Thorn, but it would be too dangerous. No sense in distressing her further, when the emergence of the Boilers already caused her such pain.

That's what I told myself as I sat alone in my darkness. That's what I told myself every night when I turned the plate over and over in my hands, when I wrapped it in a silk kerchief and settled it into my deepest pocket. That's what I told myself whenever Thorn inquired after the translation and I informed her I could remember none of it.

Now, when I write these words, I regret my lies. Of course I do. I look at the person I was as I stared down at that plate and cannot imagine where I managed to dredge up such greed and selfishness. But you cannot possibly understand the allure of what was offered to me, all those years ago. And what, if all the signs spoke the truth, could be offered to me again.

The key to unlocking my future happiness had fallen into my lap. All it required was that I find the right door.

***

Kidlington was larger then the last hamlet, and considerably further out of range of the Wall's smoke. The first thing they did after erecting the tent on the town green – and 'they' encompassed every man, woman and youth in Wombwell's employ, including Nero, a cantankerous baboon, and several wayward birds of paradise – was invade the local public house. Not wanting to miss any of the fun, Thorn linked arms with Holman and led him to a table in the corner where Lurgo waited with a platter of mutton and guineas pies.

Gravy dribbled down Thorn's chin as she observed Wombwell directing Nero to dance with a giddy barmaid. "He doesn't seem so affected by what happened today."

"He is a singularly remarkable man." Holman wiped the corners of his mouth with a kerchief, and set down his fork and knife. "While he chases after profit as much as any man, Wombwell cares too much for the pleasure of others to allow himself a night brooding alone in his carriage. Never you fear, Miss Thorn. In the back of his head he's pondering these new developments, and in time his astute brain will offer an ingenious solution. Did you know how he came to be in the menagerie business?"

Thorn and Lurgo – their bellies stuffed with pie – shook their heads. Holman waited, and Thorn realised that she'd neglected once more to remember he couldn't see their action. She gulped down her mouthful of pie. "No."

"George Wombwell was born of a shoemaker in Wendon Lofts, Essex. Even from an early age he displayed a talent for showmanship and delight. Many thought he'd become an actor, but he found the theatre too self-indulgent, too oafish. Instead, he moved to London and opened a cordwainer's shop on Old Crompton Street. One day an exited dockworker arrived in the shop with a remarkable story: two boa constrictors had been found in the hold of a South American trade ship. Wombwell closed up shop and raced down to the docks as fast as he could. And sure enough, there were these two snakes, writhing and flapping about on deck, the sailors poking them with their muskets and all the people gawking and exclaiming. And right there, Wombwell had his greatest inspiration. He offered the captain seventy-five quid for the two snakes – a mighty sum for a lowly cordwainer – and the captain, who'd intended simply to kill the snakes and roast them for his supper, couldn't refuse. Wombwell placed the snakes in a small chest and took them to every pub in London, charging the sozzled patrons a penny to open the chest and take a look inside. He made back his initial investment in a week."

Thorn and Lurgo both laughed. Holman leaned forward, lowering his voice as if they three were conspiring to commit some grand crime. "Wombwell's one greatest ambition is to exhibit a Great Dragon, to be known as the tamer of the world's most frightful beast."

"But Great Dragons are just a myth, a story for children."

"Ah, but that is simply not true. In the long ago ages, before humans even walked on British soil, Great Dragons dwelt here. Scientists find their massive skeletons embedded in the cliffs, so old their bones have turned to stone. But when Man first wrote down the histories, he recorded no trace of the Great beasts, only their smaller cousins, the dragons of the swamps of which you are both well acquainted. No one knows what happened to the Great Dragons, although stories exist from modern times of hikers or pleasure seekers reporting sightings of great monsters wandering in the wild Northern Forests. Some men, like George, believe the stories. Personally, I believe it's all codswallop. But maybe one day George will prove me wrong."

Thorn watched as Wombwell spun the dizzy maid in another lopsided circle and proceeded to pull dozens of coloured ribbons from behind her ears.

"How do people laugh and cheer still, when the Wall approaches over the horizon?"

"You've lived in that wasteland too long, you two. You've forgotten the simple pleasures of being alive; laughing with friends, a full tankard of ale and a mutton pie. That is Wombwell's magic; he exudes joy like a sausage crank. How – in the face of such epicurean delights – can Brunel's Wall stand a chance?"

The dancing began, and Julianne approached their table and took Holman's arm. Thorn and Lurgo watched them shuffling together around the bar stools, knocking the patrons with their elbows and causing at least three spills. Thorn wanted to laugh, but her muscles sagged with fatigue and fear.

Lurgo's face remained equally drawn. He pushed his plate aside, leaned over the table, and whispered to her. "How can we laugh when back home they think we are joining Brunel in London?"

Thorn reached across the table and squeezed his hand. "I know. This all feels wrong, Lurgo. Why do we flee the city when we could be there, helping somehow? I don't know what Brunel plans to do, but it can't be good."

"I wish Rex had filled us in on the plan, but I guess if he had, none of us would have followed him," Lurgo said grimly.

The mention of Rex's name brought back an image of that fearsome Sinker, its eyes boring into hers. "I can't... we shouldn't be..."

"I know." Lurgo lowered his gaze. "I'm so sorry he's dead, Thorn. I know I haven't said it yet, but it's true. I am sorry. I feel as though it's all my fault."

"It's not even that…" Thorn wrung her hands. "I see his grand plan so clearly now. He's been putting the pieces of this together for years. He only wanted to marry me so he could sacrifice me in that Wall."

"That can't be true, Thorn. Rex was—"

"—my betrothed, I know."

"I was going to say 'a mad bastard', but yours works, too. But Rex loved you. It was obvious. He didn't have some grand scheme when he left Graveyard. London and the Metal Messiah changed him, corrupted him. That's what you have to blame, not Rex."

Thorn clenched her hands into tight fists. "He had someone else in London, a woman named Lydia. Did you know that? But that's beside the point now. If I had done what he wanted and let those Sinkers take me, instead of falling down that tunnel, Joel would still be alive, and maybe things would have worked out differently."

"You mean Brunel revealing his true identity to the people and returning the Stokers to the Engine Ward?" Lurgo shook his head so vigorously he flicked his hair into his tankard. "It was never going to happen. Brunel doesn't need us – this cursed Wall proves that good and proper. Rex was dreaming. All that London air addled his brain."

"If you say so." Thorn thought of the lewd pictograms of Rex and Lydia copulating in her father's tomb.

"Thorn, we don't know why Brunel is building this new Wall, or what he plans to do now he has returned. Certainly no one in London knows. I don't even think

Rex knew, although he sold his soul readily enough, so the promises must be convincing. If we'd managed to find the Metal Messiah amongst his Boilers and Sinkers and other monsters, do you think he would have allowed us to return? He deserted *us*. He betrayed *us*. He's moved on to bigger, more lofty ambitions, like twelve-foot bloody Boilers and the cursed expandable Wall we travelled over today."

"Joel…he had this little girl…"

"You know Quartz or Joel's mother will probably be looking after her." Thorn felt something warm on her hands. Lurgo pulled her fists apart, encasing her fingers in his. Staring at him, she no longer saw the irritating boy who followed her shadow with relentless ferocity while they were growing up. Instead, there was the caring, passionate face of a man who saw in his comrade something of his own fear.

"Thorn, I swear to you by our god and our friendship, that all this suffering will not be in vain." Lurgo gave her hands another squeeze, then suddenly dropped them. Thorn looked up to see what diverted his attention.

Julianne returned to their table, dragging an exhausted Holman behind her. Her skin glowed with warmth and delight. She tugged on Lurgo's sleeve. He shot Thorn one final, depreciating smile, then lifted himself from their table and followed Julianne across the room.

Thorn stared after them, listening for the swell of the music as they dipped and spun. Lurgo laughed as Julianne twisted her feet around herself as feet should never be twisted. Holman sat across from Thorn, smiling and nodding and tapping his cane on the floor. She felt empty, drained of mirth, feeling that something vitally important flitted past her nose and she couldn't even see it.

JAMES HOLMAN'S MEMOIRS, FIRST EDITION

After the Kidlington performance, Thorn came to visit me in my caravan, wanting to learn about magic.

"I've seen you do magic," she said, placing a warm crumpet in my outstretched hand. "I've known only one other man with power such as that, and he is now under the earth. Why is it the Gods and the engineers have such control over the magic of the world, and we must battle our own way through the dark?"

"Because there is no such thing," I told her. "Magic is simply unexplained science. That is why the engineers toil eternally at their instruments. They seek the ultimate understanding; when they impress upon the secret working of the earth, they can manipulate it to their own end. Come, I will teach you my magic."

I bade her to close her eyes. Slipping into my finest pair of velvet slippers, I walked silently around her. "When I tap the cane, tell me where I am standing."

When I stood facing her, I tapped my cane on the ground, several inches in front of her boots. She paused for a few moments. "You're in front of me," she said.

"Very good," I slipped around her again, standing to her side this time and tapping the cane in the same spot.

"I don't know," she said. "You have tapped in the same place, but you're not in front of me any more. I think you're on my left."

"Precisely," I tapped the cane again. "This is how I find my way. When I tap my cane on the earth, I can hear objects around me. I know what size they are, and how they encroach upon my path. It is a skill I have

227

honed over the years, for I had great need of it. But to anyone who sees me do this and doesn't understand, it's magic."

"Aaron thought I had magic. He could push animals with his mind – calm and understand them without speech or touch. It was as if threads of life entwined both of them, wrapping their dreams together. He thinks…or rather, he *thought* I could do the same."

"Can you?"

"Sometimes, but I don't understand it like Aaron did."

"Describe it to me."

"Sometimes I will be with an animal, like Igoria or the dogs back at Graveyard, and I'll just *sense* them. I can whisper and move and think, and they can think too. They can know my thoughts and I can know theirs. Inside my head, I think 'this is what you should do' and I push the thought out, and sometimes they will do."

"Wombwell has commented on your empathic connection with Igoria and the monkeys; how they defer to you for every action. Whether that is magic or science is of no consequence. No engineer has tackled thought-resonance with any authority, so until it is understood, it is magic. Likewise, do the Gods really perform miracles or are they simply the master manipulators of science? It doesn't matter. The end result is the same."

"You sound awfully well-versed on the subject."

"That is because you are not the first person I've met to describe this same special talent."

Thorn bolted forward, her hands gripping my knee like talons. "Did my father have the sense?" she demanded.

"Yes, he did. Your father heard the thoughts of animals inside his head, just as you do. He would be proud to learn you had inherited his unusual trait. You did not know this?"

"I didn't know." Thorn's voice strained. "Aaron never told me."

"Then he had good reason not to. Perhaps he did not want to make your father into any more of an outcast. Do not hold it against Aaron too harshly. He and Nicholas had a complex relationship." I heard her stifle a yawn. "The hour is late. Get some sleep, Miss. Thorn. Worry no more about sorcery and spell-casting. Not even the Gods trouble themselves with such questions right before bed."

***

Thorn rolled over. She felt pain in her side. Igoria butted her again, sniffling, and moved away, pacing in a circle around the tiny wagon.

"What's wrong?" *I hope she's not truly sick this time.* Thorn fumbled for the lamp, succeeding in lighting the argand wick just as Igoria swung round and butted her again.

"Bloody hell." Igoria's stub of a nose horn connected with Thorn's hip bone in a most unpleasant manner. There'd be a bruise the size of a swamp dragon, no doubt. She swung around to inspect the wound, and as she did she saw the blood.

It smeared across her inner thigh, and soaked the straw under her legs, staining a crimson blob in her beautiful blanket. The sight of so much blood worried her. *I'm not ill…did I fall on something? Have I cut myself? No, that can't be it…*

Oh. She had forgotten about *that.*Rex's return, the mission through the Wall, Wombwell, Holman, Lurgo, sweet Igoria…she'd forgotten the bleeding.

A high whine escaped Igoria's throat. She went to butt Thorn again. Thorn swung the lamp in Igoria's eyes and she backed off, whinnying.

She's worried about me. "Igoria, go back to sleep." Thorn used her stern trainer voice. Igoria's eyes grew into wide orbs, and she immediately plonked back down into the straw and regarded Thorn with a worried stare.

Thorn folded the blanket over itself, disguising the stains, and wrapped it around her bare legs. Trying to appear nonchalant, she ducked from the wagon and snuck around the rear of the kitchen, where they piled the scraps and other unwanted detritus.

In the rubbish pile Thorn found a threadbare wool blanket stained with grease, and one of Wombwell's linen shirts, torn across the chest by a sharp gash. Never one to waste anything on the road, Wombwell used his old clothes to clean the grease from the hotplate in the cookhouse. She slipped the latch on the props store and found sewing scissors and needle and thread. She cut the shirt and blanket into strips, and made five piles of fabric, each with a wool layer sandwiched between the linen. She was just sewing the final rectangle together when she heard the door thump open.

"I know you're in here. You'll nae trespass again, you lousy blagger!"

The whip cracked and Thorn jumped, knocking over the sewing stool and sprawling across the floor. Wombwell stood over her, confused.

"By Great Conductor's leaden faeces, what are you doing here so early in the morning? I thought you were a burglar. I might've flayed you alive!"

Thorn pulled the corners of her blanket around her as Wombwell dug his hands under her shoulders and tugged her to her feet. "What are you doing in here?" he repeated sternly.

"I have the women's disease."

"The...what?"

Her face flushing with embarrassment, Thorn let the folded flap of the blanket down. His brow creased as he stared at the red stain, but it faded after a moment, and he smiled.

"Ah, *that* women's disease. You Stokers sure have some strange ideas. You really ought to move into the nineteenth century."

Thorn stared at him with questioning eyes, and he laughed.

"Incidentally, between you and me, it's not a disease at all. Oh, the Royal Society will tell you differently of course, but they're a group of quaff-scratching Neanderthals – Holman notwithstanding, of course."

"Old Hatchie says the blood is a punishment from Great Conductor. All the women who have their blood have to sit in the smoke house until—"

"Misinformation, bandied by layabouts who'd rather keep their women for domestic servants than grant them any kind of freedom. Trust me, Thorn, I've worked around animals for long enough to understand that something that bleeds for five days and doesn't die is expelling something the body no longer needs. Bella and Myrtle have it as well, once a month unless they're pregnant. Exactly the same as a human woman, and you can't hardly accuse my monkeys of being cursed. Seems to me its just part of the reproductive cycle. Unfortunately, the smell is potent and I can't have you near the animals for a time. Can you handle kitchen duty this week?"

Thorn nodded, her knees weak.

"Good girl." Wombwell patted her shoulder,

readjusted his sleeping cap, and left her to her business.

Kitchen duty was unexpectedly pleasant, if only for the fact that Thorn faced a whole week without close proximity to Lurgo. Julianne (who unabashedly informed Thorn she had had her blood discharge, too) gave her a tour of the kitchen and the stores before running off to practice her routine, leaving Thorn alone in the sheltered kitchen.

Thorn went straight to work on breakfast; she sliced bacon with a great knife, and fried it over the tiny stove with field mushrooms and thick slices of potato. She cut some bread and placed that along with knobs of butter and honey on the table. While she waited for the staff to return from the morning feeding she ducked outside to check the stores.

Kitchen duty also included preparing two feedings a day for the animals. The menagerie had two more nights in this town, and another day on the road before resupplying. Thorn counted barrels and sacks; they were okay for straw, hay and millet, but had enough smoked meat to last Nero only one more day. They'd need another bag of apples, and the oranges had gone off. Rancid juice dribbled from the corner of the sack. Holding her nose, Thorn threw it into the refuse pile and made a mental note to purchase more oranges.

She returned to the kitchen as the others filed around the table. Wombwell poured himself a cognac and munched on his bacon. Lurgo shuffled so close to Julianne he might as well have sat in her bowl. He made faces at her and chewed with his mouth open. Thorn would've shoved his head in his porridge, but Julianne simply laughed. She had the monkeys on a lead and Wombwell kept slapping their curious hands off the table.

As she'd seen Julianne do, Thorn listed the items they needed and Wombwell emptied a heavy pile of coins into her hand.

Holman beckoned her over. "You'll need to know how to count with those. Here." He held out his hand and she tipped the coins into it. "This is thruppence. You can feel the picture of George IV? Four of these have the same value as this one, the shilling. Sometimes you'll find these with Victoria's head on them." He ran his fingers over the fine relief bust. "And twenty shillings make up a pound. See how heavy that is?" Thorn tested it in her hand. It did indeed feel heavier than the others. "These are hard to come by, so don't give them away lightly. One pound should buy us all the grain we need, and the hay besides."

Thorn nodded, tucking the coins into her coat pocket.

"I'd like fish and chips tonight," said Wombwell. "So buy fresh catch and vinegar if we're out. There's enough there for you to buy lunch also."

Thorn left for the market after breakfast, unaccompanied save a large wicker basket and her thoughts. The square reminded her of a miniature London, the press of people coming and going, the jovial conversations that blended into one harmonious gaggle of banter and gossip. The smells – both delicious and disturbing – rose from the barrels and baskets on display. Thorn walked slowly, savouring the sights.

She spent a good fifteen minutes haggling with the grain merchant before finally settling on a price. She suspected Wombwell would not send her to market again when he saw how few of his coins she returned with. She located the fishmonger and vinegar merchant with ease, and at reasonable prices too. Next to the monger was a stall of sweetbreads and biscuits, decorated with dots and swirls and smelling of honey and roasted almonds. She counted the remaining coins and brought herself a pastry.

As Thorn savoured the smell of the hot pastry through her gloved fingers, she saw a figure step off a horseless carriage along the street. The steam propulsion engine squealed to a halt as he yanked out the injection lever and settled a soot-black bowler hat atop his flame-red cowl and dusted charcoal from his immaculate morning coat.

She peered at him, curious. *Why would a man wear such a thick cowl while he travelled? Surely he would want to see the way—*

The man turned then, and she gasped in recognition. The same hunched figure, formed entirely of shadow, the left hand hidden in the folds of his cloak. The same loving reverence afforded to the machine as he stepped from the footplate and stroked the churning engine.

Brunel.

To see him again, in broad daylight, where for eighteen years he existed only as the shadow of a legend, brought Thorn's conflicted thoughts to the surface. Here was the man her father had supposedly killed, alive and walking. Her one chance at redemption strode towards her with measured steps. But he was up to something, and Thorn knew now that only evil lurked inside those piercing eyes.

Twenty years of Stoker doctrine flowed through her mind, and Thorn went to kneel. But she caught herself when she was halfway to her knees. *Why should I?* The defiant thought ran through her head. And again, *why should I?*

Thorn straightened and glanced up at the man, mouthing a silent prayer that he wouldn't smite her for her disobedience. He didn't even look up from the pie selection.

Summoning her courage, she reached over and tugged his sleeve.

"Do I know you?" From inside the hood, his deep voice tinged with impatience.

Thorn gulped. She was speaking to a God, a man who'd survived beyond the grave. All words flew from her head. She mouthed something, searching desperately for her voice. The Metal Messiah frowned. Finally, she managed to find some words. "I'm Thorn." She traced the outline of a Stoker cross in the air.

He sighed. "I thought you people were all rotting in the bogs."

The comment sounded so crass, so *common*. It confirmed everything Thorn had already known – the Metal Messiah would not be freeing his people. Thorn narrowed her eyes. "Did you know your Wall is alive? Are you here to stop it?"

"Why is it your business why I am here?"

"You are our Messiah." She meant to berate him, but the words seemed asinine, meaningless. He glowered at her as she shuffled from foot to foot, trying to articulate her thoughts. "When my…when you were killed, the Stokers were forced from London. They went, trusting that you would not desert them, and they built a life – or the shadow of a life – in the swamps, many believing that one day you would return. You hold within you all their hope for a real home. Do you not care at all about the Stokers? Without them, you would be *nothing*."

"Who are you to lecture *me?* You are nothing but a girl. You can't comprehend the torture I've been through the last nineteen years. My life was stolen from me by a petty man who was jealous of my success. I have spent two decades hovering over a great, empty abyss, clinging to life by mere threads, each fragile tick of time bringing me closer to the sweet release of death. With agonising slowness I pulled these threads together, and wove for myself a second chance. I broke the laws of science in order to return to a country that needs me, that *desperately* yearns for my innovations, for my stewardship. And after all my years of agony, you expect *me* to help *you?* Where were the Stokers when I needed them? Where were they to drag me from the precipice of death? No, girl, all the love I have left belongs to my machines."

"But your machines are *killing* people—"

"Well, fancy that." His sneer bit into Thorn's resolve, robbing her of her final comeback. The baker held out his pie. Brunel snatched it away and flung two shillings on the counter. "Do not speak to me again." He stormed down the street.

Thorn stared at his departing figure, stunned. She urged her feet forward and raced after him, her hands balled into fists. He saw her and darted through the market, losing himself in the press of people. Thorn stopped running, gasping for breath, and noticed she stood outside a stone chapel, home to the Christian engineer, one of the few banned sects Queen Victoria had allowed to return to England. Thorn set her basket down in front of the chapel, and snuck inside.

There was no service, but several people sat in the pews, chatting amongst themselves or staring at their boots in contemplative silence. The altar stretched the width of the room, piled high with set-squares and hammers, offerings from local carpenters who claimed patronage from the Christian Engineer. Thorn folded her legs under herself and stared at the kindly face staring down at her from the trusses.

"I don't understand what's happening. It's as if everything the Stokers told me about London and Brunel and my father is false. All these years I've been praying for Brunel to return and defend my father's actions, and he's..." She sniffed. "He's worse than Bill Riley, worse than...than *Rex*. He's a brute. He doesn't care how we suffer. Instead he had the horrid Sunken kill Rex, and Joel's gone too, and everyone in London is laughing, and he probably laughs with them, he laughs loudest of all! Meanwhile, all the Stokers are just waiting for him to come along and forgive them, and he won't, he won't! He doesn't care! But perhaps if he heard it from you – one Messiah to another – he would *have* to help the Stokers."

The gilded face of the Christian Engineer regarded her with cool precision.

"Well, you're no bloody good, either." She stormed from the church.

I saw a Metic shrine back in the square. Perhaps the engineers of measurement would...or Mama Helios...do they even worship her out here? Thorn looked again at that sandstone façade, where creepers shackled the gables to the earth; a fortress from the hearts of man. *It may as well be the Wall, for all it keeps out His followers. No, I'll find no answers with the other engineers.*

Old Hatchic used to say – before the plague reduced her voice to its dry hawk – that when you said your prayers and your head felt hollow and free, that your words had left the station and Great Conductor bore them on his golden railroad to the heavens, checking each for a ticket and assigning each a seat.

But she was wrong, Aaron was wrong, Father was wrong, we were all wrong. The gods don't listen, they've never listened. It's all empty, mechanical lies.

Thorn's faith shattered. The process was quick and painless, like a knife slicing through butter. Thorn picked up her basket and returned to the encampment, sure now that her entire life had been a falsehood.

***

JAMES HOLMAN'S MEMOIRS, FIRST EDITION

Thorn and I often discussed her sudden turn to godlessness. She said she hadn't realised at the time how much it was like losing her virginity, where in a pinprick of pain she entered a world so unlike the one before, that she ceased to recall a time when she ever *did* believe. It was years before she would speak in great detail of her first encounter with Brunel, but I sensed the moment she settled in my carriage after dinner that she had changed forever.

"Do you believe in the Gods?" was the question she asked me that night, and this same question she repeated every night thereafter, as the Menagerie wound its way up towards the North alongside the Wall as it twisted and snaked its way across the countryside. It was as though Thorn thought my constructed discourse would affirm her own timid realisations.

On the eve of her nineteenth birthday we rode along the banks of the river Tyne into Newcastle-upon-Tyne, passing under the Wall that had appeared there only the night before us. And the following day I led a curious party of menagerie workers along a stretch of Hadrian's Wall.

While Julianne laid out a picnic and knocked Lurgo's fingers away from her fresh-baked scones, Thorn pulled her necker alongside mine and we travelled along the crooked path accompanying the broken stretch of wall. I heard the scrape of her nails along the crumbling limestone blocks, and she sighed heavily and asked again what I thought of the Gods.

"You know my answer, child. Is this truly the time for such heavy discussion?"

"Is there ever a time for joy, I wonder? I have scraped my knees raw praying for salvation, and I have nothing. And you who believe in no God are not scarred by this hopelessness."

"Hopelessness can strike any man, God-fearing or nay. How do you think it feels to wake up one morning to find your entire world cast in eternal shadow?"

"I'm sorry. I meant no disrespect. You seem to not mind the darkness."

"Whether I mind or not is of no consequence. I have been blinded, and it's for me to live the remainder of my days as I see fit. You wonder if I would exchange my religious intolerance for the gift of sight, and the answer is yes. I would give *everything* I had to see the world again. Vision is *sublime* beyond compare. It is the epitome of loneliness to suffer this way, but it is far easier to accept and live than to hunger for what once was. If I relied on Gods to cure me, I'd be raving in an asylum by now for my impatience."

"You seem so happy in your faithlessness."

"I have faith, Thorn."

"But you don't believe—"

"—in Gods and engineers and Messiahs and all that codswallop? No, I don't. But faith can be for other things. I believe in science. I believe through exploration and experimentation and accurate plotting of the earth's curiosities, we will one day penetrate her deepest mysteries. I believe one day I will see again, and it will be not God but a man who will restore the light."

"If a God can fail me, then a man cannot hope to penetrate this darkness," Thorn declared.

I almost laughed at her word choice, but instead I touched my hand to my heart. "You are no man, Miss Thorn, and you are capable of remarkable things. When everything around you crumbles, you must be able to have faith in yourself."

I heard her sigh. "Tell me about this Hadrian."

"Hadrian was a Roman ruler, over a thousand years ago. He governed England and built many great monuments; villas and roads and garrisons and aqueducts. He built this wall to keep out tribes of raiding Picts."

"But it's only seven foot high."

"Ah, but it was accompanied by a deep ditch and bank system, and patrolled by vicious Roman soldiers. The Picts had never encountered anything like it. Imagine emerging from the gloom of those forests and encountering this gleaming wall of white polished stone, Roman sentries marching atop—why are you crying?"

"I'm not."

"Nonsense, I can smell the salt."

"How could Hadrian *do* that? I mean, he was their governor, their protector. He was meant to look after these people! How could he just say, 'go, do what you will, I don't care. Just don't come into my paradise'?'"

"They weren't his people, not really. But we're not talking about Hadrian, are we?"

"Sometimes I wish I'd never seen him."

"Surely it's better to know the truth?"

"Really? To understand that the Stokers lived for so many years in that hell, to realise how many sacrificed themselves for him in the Gauge War, to know how many days I suffered their insults and curses, all for nothing. No matter what I said they would not relent. They would never return and demand what is theirs. No James, I think knowing is utter desolation."

Thorn didn't often speak my name. When she did she transformed, becoming someone remote from the girl I adored. She rode behind me as an equal, and the finality of her words spoke of the pain and determination that marked her as a heroine entirely unique to our country.

I started to reply, but the pain seized me with fingernails of ice that sliced through my skin and slithered through my organs. I clamped my tongue between my teeth and concentrated on riding forward, on not crying out.

So, Thorn lost her Gods, and my pain had returned. Perhaps, in some inconceivable way, the two were connected.

***

Everywhere Wombwell's Travelling Menagerie travelled, the Wall followed close behind. If she craned her neck hard around, Thorn could always see the wisps of black smoke from its chimneys, puffing as it struggled to keep up.

"It's following us," Thorn told Wombwell one morning, as they attached bridles to the babies and lead them (or dragged them, in Igor's case) around the edge of the village green. The tricorns had grown steadily in the last month, the tips of their frills now reaching just below Thorn's waist. Wombwell entertained a steady stream of illustrious visitors who travelled from as far afield as Russia to examine the babies, but he wanted them ready for the public as soon as possible.

Wombwell shook his head. "The Wall is not after us. It's after England. It wants to surround the entire country."

"But how is it doing this? Where is it getting all the materials? How does it build itself?"

Wombwell rubbed his chin, as he always did when he planned some great escapade. "Perhaps we should find out."

***

"Thorn, come quick!" Lurgo banged on the tent canvas as he sprinted across the field. "We've caught one!"

Thorn dropped the rag she was using to wash under Igor's frill, and darted after Lurgo. Her heart slammed against her chest. She'd never expected Wombwell's plan to actually *work*.

She raced across the green after Lurgo. At the edge of the field a thicket of holly bushes pressed against the whirring Wall. It was here Wombwell had instructed Lurgo to set the trap.

Thorn followed Lurgo into the holly, barely feeling the thorns prick her bare arms. It was just past dusk and Lurgo carried a tiny argand lamp. The light flickered in front of her, casting eerie shadows against the bodies of the excited menagerie men who also strode toward the trap.

She heard the screech before she saw the creature; high-pitched and almost human, like a teething infant at the edge of madness. She entered a clearing in the holly and saw the Sinker. Its leg had been caught in a snare, the same kind of rope trap the Stokers used to catch *Iguanodon* and other smaller creatures in the swamps, and it now dangled upside down by one leg from a sturdy branch. Her breath caught in her throat as she watched it claw at the ground as it scrambled for purchase against the wet earth.

In the light of Lurgo's lamp, it appeared even more sinister and otherworldly than the Sunken she'd last seen beside the Wall. Glowing pustules dotted its swollen skin, some breaking apart as it strained for freedom and oozing leaden blood onto the damp ground. Two eyes bulged from red, weeping sockets, and as it screamed its lips tore open, revealing dark blood and rows of jagged, broken teeth. A rod of metal protruded from its left temple, like a waterspout carelessly left behind by some hellish godly plumber. The Sinker swung itself higher, pawing at the ground with every rock of its body in a desperate attempt to grab the glowing orbs of lead that rested in the centre of the trap. Every sinew and muscle tensed and contorted as it scrambled for the lead feast only inches from its grasp.

Proud his trapping skills had proved useful, Lurgo stomped in front of the Sinker and waved a lump of lead about its face with his tongs. "How do you like this, you gammy monster?" he roared. "If your master tries to hunt us and trap us with his Wall, he can expect the same in return!"

The Sinker howled and grabbed for the lead. Lurgo threw it to the ground in disgust. Thorn stepped back. She'd never seen him this enraged before. She could understand why. To see one of the Sunken so close up, and know that the Metal Messiah had chosen these creatures instead of his own people, filled her heart with fury.

The other men waited at the edge of the snare, unsure of what to do.

Lurgo drew his knife and for a moment Thorn

thought he would cut the creature's neck, but he slashed the rope just as two other men pounced with chains and tether. The three men dragged the screaming Sinker into an open lion cage and tried to hold it down while they shut the door. The Sinker clenched the bars with white, bleeding hands and howled as it struggled against their efforts. It managed to push the door open again, and snapped and snarled at the men as they fought to pull it off the door.

Lurgo waved her over. "Give us a hand, would you?"

Thorn didn't want to touch the cage or be near the creature, so she stood behind the men and raised her hands and pretended she was pushing the creature back inside, too. Finally, Lurgo prised the Sinker's fingers from the door and shoved it back into the cage. He slammed the door and slid the bolt across, locking the cage tight.

The Sinker cried harder now, dribbling lead down its knobbed chin. Now that it was trapped, it looked almost pitiable, slumped in the corner, its head hung in defeat.

Lurgo gestured for Thorn to hold one corner of the cage. She bit her lip, repulsed by the idea of approaching that close to the creature. But she didn't want anyone thinking she was afraid. Grabbing one corner, she helped the men lift the cage and drag it into the empty green.

Wombwell stood at the edge of the makeshift arena, tapping his cane against his boot. Beside him, Holman leaned forward, his thin fingers gripping Wombwell's wrist in his excitement. They set the cage down and Thorn slunk away and stood behind Holman, her eyes darting between the proprietor and the howling Sinker. Wombwell circled the cage, his beady eyes taking in every movement, every deformity of the creature's body.

"Now that we've caught it, what do we do with it?"

she asked.

Holman smiled. "We study it."

"And then we train it, so it can become part of the show," Wombwell added, cracking his knuckles and twirling his whip around his fingers. He prodded the creature through the bars, and it snarled and backed away, burrowing into the furthermost corner.

"Is that really a wise idea?"

"It's a brilliant idea, if it works," Wombwell replied. "Brunel expects people to be afraid of the Sunken. But if they see something as entertainment, as a spectacle, then they will no longer fear it."

"Can you sense anything?" Holman whispered to Thorn. She shook her head. That confirmed the stories that the Sinkers were once human.

Wombwell ordered the handlers to sedate the creature with a powerful drug. When it was lethargic, they set it free in an enclosed pen where it dragged itself around in slow circles and wailed pitifully. Thorn shuddered. This all seemed a little too *scientific*, as if they had themselves taken the first step on the path to Brunel's madness.

Conducting a scientific examination of an abomination was no small task, as Holman discovered after his first attempt to measure the Sinker's temperature nearly resulted in two of his fingers being removed. He had to administer more sedatives, which made the creature lie down and snore soundly. Holman poked and prodded and measured the Sinker on the grass of the arena while Thorn hid in Igoria's wagon and pretended she couldn't hear its whimpers.

When she emerged for dinner, the Sinker had been returned to its cage, where it hunched in the corner, holding its melted face in its hands. The sedatives had worn off. When it looked up at her, its eyes were wide, understanding. Thorn pushed her plate away. She had lost her appetite.

She could not explain what drew her to sit on the grass beside the pen and study the Sinker as it paced across its cage. In her mind, she saw Rex's gaunt figure, his once-strong shoulders devoid of muscle. It looked up at her, and its eyes opened and shut slowly. A gargled cry escaped from its throat. Thorn turned away, wiping a tear from her eye with the sleeve of her tunic.

That was a man once, a man with a family, a life.

They carried the cage with them to the next town. As the days progressed, the Sinker grew increasingly calm and easy to handle. They had no lead to feed it, so Wombwell set out bowls of raw meat, which it gobbled up hungrily. Thorn sat in front of the cage for hours, watching and not watching, speaking and not speaking, just being with the creature, for it had no one else. Her presence seemed to calm the Sinker, and sometimes it would even stop its pacing and thrashing and sit quietly to stare back at her. *Something inside it must still remember its human spirit.*

Each night, as she tossed and turned and waited for sleep to take her, Thorn listened to it wail and sob and beat its head against the steel bars, and the sound bore deep fissures within her, as though it latched on to long-forgotten pain.

One day, Holman and Julianne sat down beside her as she stared into the cage. Holman had Julianne read from the pages of a history book, a book about the Vampire King and the Battle for London, a book of lies and half-truths. Thorn sat at his feet and marvelled at the magic of reading, losing herself in the mythical London created by the author. When she looked up from her daydream, the Sinker sat very near her, bone-still, its face pressed against the bars as it listened to Julianne. Sometimes it seemed to react, drawing breath and exhaling, beating its fist against the steel, sometimes casting its eyes to the floor.

Julianne finished the chapter. Holman shut the book and sat for a time, his hands folded neatly in his lap. Finally he said, "I feel perhaps as though we understand each other."

The Sinker lifted his head, and Thorn could swear a look of understanding passed over its face.

Holman turned his head to stare with his unblinking eyes at a spot just over the Sinker's right shoulder. "Do you have a name?" he whispered.

The Sinker stared at the ground. It smacked its lips together, flapping its charred tongue against those razor-sharp teeth. The only sound that came out was a strangled sob.

Thorn tugged Holman's sleeve. "I don't think he can talk," she said. "All the lead he's consumed must have burnt his insides."

Holman thought for a moment. "You could be right. Run to Wombwell's office, and bring back a fountain pen and a bottle of ink, and several sheets of paper. Tell him we may have a breakthrough."

Thorn did as he instructed, and returned a few minutes later with the requested materials, a red-faced, puffing Wombwell, his knuckles white around the shaft of his cane, and a stone-faced Lurgo.

Holman pushed the pen and ink and paper through the corner of the cage, setting them in a messy pile on the steel supports. The creature shuffled towards these new objects, but didn't move to pick them up.

"Go on," Wombwell whispered. "We don't mean to hurt you. We only wish to know your name."

The five sat on the wet grass, watching. For a long time the Sinker did nothing. It did not move, just stared at the objects in the corner of its cage with a look of hunger and sadness. Then, just as Thorn had given up on the idea, the Sinker bent down and, with trembling, clumsy hands, unscrewed the bottle of ink, dunked the pen inside, and scribbled something on the paper.

Wombwell leaned forward, his bright eyes dancing. "Can we see? Can you give that to me?"

Frowning at the paper in his hand, the Sinker grabbed it between his teeth and pulled. "No!" Wombwell rapped the cage with his cane, but the creature tore half the paper away and swallowed it. He poked the rest of the page through the bars, and Thorn and Wombwell watched it flutter to the ground.

Thorn wanted to jump on the piece of paper and learn for herself whether the Sinker was Rex. But of course she couldn't read the paper. She felt that familiar flicker of remorse as Wombwell picked up the torn sheet and scanned the scrawled note. His eyes darted over the scrawl, and Thorn looked away, as though he performed some magic she had no right to witness. *How does he see the meaning of those dots and wriggles?*

Even Holman – who by all accounts shouldn't be able to see meaning in anything, wrote his notes on a machine that scored lines in paper, which he felt with his fingers. If Wombwell needed something written down Holman could do that too, although Wombwell always complained his handwriting was impossible to read back again.

"What does it say, George?" Holman asked.

"Maxwell," Wombwell said. "His name is Maxwell."

Holman's face broke into a smile. "Maxwell, how do you do?"

Maxwell leaned against the bars and rolled his eyes around his head. He picked up another sheet and scrawled a second message, which he dropped through the bars. Wombwell snatched it up and read aloud: "I do poorly, Mr Wombwell. I need lead. I will die without lead."

"We will not let you die, Maxwell. Of that you have my word. But we seek information about Brunel and the Wall. If you answer our questions, we will give you all the lead you can eat."

Wombwell read the next paper with a frown on his face. "If he finds out I have spoken, I die. He will rip my heart from my chest and give it to a Boiler."

"That's a fine death compared to what I might do." Lurgo clenched his hands into fists.

"Don't be rotten." Julianne shot him a reproachful look.

"Brunel can't touch you here, Maxwell." Wombwell patted the pistol in his pocket. "We do not wish to hurt you, and we would not return you to Brunel without ensuring your safety."

"I can tell only what I know. I remember being flesh and blood and feelings. I do not wish this life on my fellow Englishmen."

"Ask him about London," Thorn whispered. "Ask him how he came to be what he is."

Wombwell tapped his cane against his ankle, debating the right words. "Can you remember, Maxwell, how you became this creature born of lead and blood? How did you come to serve the Vampire King and the Metal Messiah?"

The Sinker scribbled away for many minutes, covering two sides of the paper, before handing it back to Wombwell.

"I was the gardener at Windsor Castle, and I did many small duties for His Royal Majesty George III. He trusted me above all other men, save his physician, the honourable Joseph Banks. It was Banks who first prescribed the lead infusion to cure His Majesty's malaise. And it did, but it also gave His Majesty a craving for lead, and for flesh. His first Children were victims of his lead-induced frenzies, but the rest of us were born of his love. Brunel would come to the castle often, to talk about the Wall. He had many secret meetings with His Majesty. Together they drank the lead, although it never turned Brunel into one of us. I was already an old man when I had my first taste of lead, and so I was responsible for the others, until the hunger took me over so completely that I knew nothing else. I lived in the castle with the other Children, and we feasted all day and night. His Majesty wanted more Children, more feasting. He broke open our chambers and we went out into the city. We found a meal sweeter than lead – human flesh. We feasted. We fought for our dinner. They beat us back, and many drowned in the river, but not all. I don't remember how I got trapped in the Wall, but sometime later I found Brunel in the shadows, and he was dead. I stayed with him for many years, until he was dead no longer. Many of us lived there, in the shadows. We brought him food. We helped him stay alive, and he promised to bring us the things we craved most."

"How did he survive?"

Maxwell scribbled a single line. "He is a God. He does not die."

"What does he have you do inside the Wall?"

"We steal children and animals from the towns to increase our number. We help him build the Wall. We obey the commands of the Furnace Masters."

"The Boilers?" This time, Maxwell nodded.

"If we let you go, would you return to him?"

"Yes. He is a God. He makes the lead."

"And you need the lead. We understand. But if you could have lead every day, all the lead you could ever want, and you didn't have to build, or murder, would you leave Brunel?"

"Yes."

Thorn sat upright, startled by his answer. She studied his face, and saw sadness in his eyes. *He is human inside, after all. He does not want to kill, not in his heart.*

Wombwell continued with the questions. "Would others leave?"

"Yes. We follow the lead. We seek no master but the feast."

"Can you tell us anything that may help us defeat him?"

The Sinker hesitated over his paper. Thorn leaned forward, watching his eyes loll back in his head. She didn't breathe for several moments. Finally, the Sinker seemed to reach a decision, and he scrawled a single line of letters.

Wombwell frowned as he read the message. "Only a God could defeat him."

"Well, that's just wonderful." Lurgo said with a snort. "We're buggered."

They had run out of paper. Wombwell ordered the handlers to bring Maxwell a dinner of lead – an old water pipe melted over the blacksmith's fire into a malleable lump. Thorn turned away as the creature pounced on the morsel, licking its parched, broken lips. She couldn't bear to see him devour the metal.

Lurgo chased after her. "Thorn, wait!"

She looked at his face, pale and drawn, and she

realised she wasn't the only person stricken by the Sinker's tale. "He was a man once, just like you," she said. Her stomach heaved at the thought. "Inside that charred skin, Maxwell is still human."

"I know. I want to hate him, but I can't. Not now."

"Do you think Rex..."

"What do you want me to say? Could the Sunken become human again? No, Thorn, I don't think so. Rex is lost to us. Even if he could return, what would he be? Would he choose us or his life in London, serving Brunel? It's best not to ponder that question."

"I wish I could forget. I want so badly to forget."

Lurgo shook his head. "No, don't forget. Don't ever forget. You are strong because you know the truth of the Metal Messiah. You know who you are and what your father sacrificed himself for. That same blood runs in your veins. When next you meet Brunel, you will be victorious, because you will not forget."

"It feels wrong to be so far from the Graveyard. What if they've gone after us? What if the Wall has found them also?"

Lurgo looked at his feet. "We have to believe they can defend themselves. We do more good here. Besides, if you returned, they would not have you."

Thorn's cheeks turned red. She'd forgotten she was no longer welcome in Graveyard. She was banished. One of the tears that had been threatening spilled over. She wiped it away with her hand.

Lurgo put his arm around her shoulders, and they walked together to Igoria's wagon. He made to leave her, but she pulled him closer, burying her face in his warm shoulder. Lurgo spread out a blanket and they slept there together, wrapped in each other's arms. The tricorns huddled beside them, their collective warmth radiating through the soft hay. Thorn knew now Lurgo no longer felt for her what he once had, for his touch was not the nervous caress of a boy, but the tender warmth of a much-needed friend.

Thorn awoke to the sound of shouting men. She rolled over. Lurgo had gone, and outside the menagerie was in uproar. She poked her head through the canvas flap. Men ran in all directions, cursing and gathering weapons. The women tossed clothing and blankets out of the laundry tent, frantically searching for something.

Julianne darted past and caught Thorn's eye. "He's escaped!"

"Who?"

"The Sinker! And he stole Holman's cane."

Thorn ran to the cage. Sure enough, Maxwell was no longer inside. The steel bars had suffered great damage, bent and mangled beyond repair.

Holman threw a steel scrap into the bushes. He seemed oddly naked without his cane between his fingers. "He's chewed them clear through, the poxy lead-sucker!"

"Will we find him?"

"Not bloody likely. That lead-stewed bastard has gone back to his master, and taken my cane with him!"

***

The summons came by gold-spangled messenger. His coat hung so heavy under the weight of its decoration that he slumped as he walked. Thorn longed to run her hands over its surface; finger the shimmering jewels and embroidered fleur-de-lys that put Holman's fine clothes to shame. Of course she did not, busying herself with untangling Igoria's bridle, watching and listening to

Wombwell's exchange.

The messenger handed Wombwell a gold-bordered envelope stamped with the royal seal. He slit the envelope open with a flick knife and scanned the letter. Bella caught the glint of gold and wriggled from Lurgo's grasp. The messenger shrieked as a tiny hand clawed at his exquisite coat. Wombwell threw the squabbling monkey onto his shoulder and folded the note into his lapel before she could nibble off the edges.

He shook the messenger's hand. "Tell her Royal Majesty we shall endeavour to arrive within the week."

The messenger bowed and left on his necker. Wombwell put both fingers in his mouth and blew. A whistle like a train screeching to a halt echoed over the circus. Of course it set the monkeys off.

"Pack in!"

Lurgo pulled Bella off Wombwell's shoulder. He struggled to tug a leash over her face. "What was that, sir?"

"Pack in, Lurgo. We're leaving in an hour."

"But tonight's show?"

"It's cancelled, I'm afraid. Queen Victoria has summoned us to court."

The Queen? Thorn couldn't believe it. *We're going to perform in front of the Queen? What an incredible honour. In just a few days, after we've returned to...*

London.

The letter was a trap. It had to be. For whatever purpose, the Royal Engineer wanted the menagerie back in London. And it was a clever trap, too, for Wombwell could not very well refuse. They had no choice but to walk headlong into Brunel's snare.

They packed the menagerie into the wagons in record time. An air of excitement fell over the crew, and even the animals seemed on edge. Wombwell and Julianne checked over the stores, and sent Lurgo and Thorn to town for extra bags of potatoes and apples.

"I'd also like some canned peaches, some *Latakia*tobacco and a liquorice twist." Wombwell counted the money into Thorn's hand.

From the town of Gilsland – on the Northumbrian side of the River Irthing – they would return to London along the Wall railway, once again meeting those fearsome giant Boilers and riding that fearsome black train. Thorn ambled towards the market, ideas and plots circling in her head. Lurgo shuffled behind her, hands in his breeches. He didn't utter a word. *Good.* needed to think.

I will not return to London. Brunel will kill me if he meets me again, of that I have no doubt. Quartz and Oswald must think the party all dead by now...what other madness are they planning? The question turned her blood cold. *I have to return to Graveyard and warn them, if only for Quartz' sake...why is Lurgo following me?*

Thorn walked on, but his presence distracted her. It was not Lurgo's nature to remain quiet. Thorn prepared herself for another fight and did not want to let her excellent insults go to waste. She turned around, and snarled, "What's the matter with you now?"

Lurgo shrugged.

"Compie got your tongue?"

Lurgo looked at her then, and she saw something she'd seen only once before, when they'd first encountered the Wall railway; his features were pinched and drawn with fear.

"Is it London?"

He nodded. "The Wall. I can't face it again. I wish—"

Thorn remembered how he clenched her hand when

first they passed through the Wall. "You're not going to cry, are you?"

He snorted.

"You haven't even been inside London. I've been inside. Do you see me sniffling at the thought of going back?" *He doesn't need to know I'm not going back.*

Lurgo kept pace with her. "What's it like inside, now?"

"It's…not what everyone describes. There's no smoke, no fires burning in the sewers, no fog hanging over the water. The air's so fresh it makes your head spin. No one is afraid. It's as if they've unmade all the madness."

"But the Sunken—" His voice choked.

"—and the Boilers, and Brunel, I know. It frightens me to think they could overrun London at any moment. I think they're waiting for something, but what I don't know. All I know is it will not be good. If we're in London perhaps we can convince someone important of Brunel's return, and save another generation from slaughter and blood. Seeing the Wall all the way out here, I don't like it. It doesn't make sense." She frowned. "Don't make that face. It's not the London you remember. It's…pleasant. You probably won't even want to leave."

"Forgive my scepticism, but I'll believe it when I see it."

Thorn smiled, linking her arm in his, and lead him down to the market and the pie shop. *He's quite sweet, actually. I feel almost sorry to leave him…*

***

Thorn didn't have much time to prepare. She wanted

desperately to retrieve the plate from Holman, but couldn't think how to do it without arousing his suspicions. So she pocketed what food she could, and added fresh flint and tinder and two candle stubs to her rucksack, along with Joel's compass, a flick knife, powder and balls for her barker, and a length of coarse rope. She filled the remaining space with oat cakes wrapped in wax paper.

The tricorns knew something was amiss. Igoria butted Thorn with his hard beak, anxious to see inside her rucksack; now that she had grown to just below Thorn's shoulder, the horn above his beak left a red welt when it grazed her skin. The others moaned and stomped the hay when she hugged them goodbye.

Thorn stroked Igoria behind her frill and wiped her down one last time with soaking rags. She checked Igoria's feet, pulling stones and dried mud from between the cracks of skin. "There you go, girl. Now you won't even miss me."

Igoria moaned in return, as if she understood. Her thoughts were uneasy. She knew Thorn was up to something, but she didn't know what. Thorn wrapped her blanket over her head like a cloak, secured it and the rucksack with another length of twine, and laced her boots extra tight. Igoria stared up at her with frightened eyes.

"I'm sorry, girl, I don't want to leave you, but you aren't rightly mine to take, and this isn't going to be a pleasant trip."

"You're leaving, aren't you?"

Thorn whirled around. Lurgo stood in the doorway, a soggy mutton pie in each hand and an expression of rage on his face.

"When did you plan on telling me about this?" He

squeezed his hand into a fist, gravy dribbling between his fingers. Igor rolled underneath him and lapped the morsels from his boot.

"Lurgo, I—"

"You were just going to run away without saying anything. What about Holman? What about Igoria? What about *me?*"

"James is fine and I've already said goodbye to Igoria – she understands. And you'll be fine too, you just need to relax."

"Where are you going?"

"I'll leave the menagerie while it is being loaded onto the train. That Wall won't stop until it's encircled the entire country, and that includes our home. It's moving towards Graveyard and bringing the Sunken with it, I just *know* it. I have to warn them. Quartz will know what to do."

Lurgo slumped in the corner. "Well, *obviously*I'm going with you."

"You can't. I need you in the city, watching over this lot. I will come to you."

"You *need* me in Graveyard! Have you forgotten that they banished you? Quartz is too old and frail to save you from Oswald's wrath. One step beyond the Clegg carriage and you're dead, Thorn."

Her face paled. "I remember well. But if you return with me, they'll kill you too. Because of our friendship, the Council already harbours mistrust for you. I must go alone to live or die by their mercy."

"So what? I'm just supposed to wait?"

"You do what you're born to do, Lurgo; hunt. Hunt for information, hunt for Brunel's weakness, and hunt out every self-respecting Stoker sympathiser or enemy of Brunel who might remain behind that Wall. Hunt for

Lydia, and punch her in the face for me."

"I *hate* you." Lurgo whirled around and stormed off into the rain.

He returned a few minutes later, hitched up the neckers and slumped down beside her on the footplate. He wouldn't meet her eyes nor respond to her questions. For perhaps the first time ever it was he that shrugged away her touch. But when the wagon wheels rolled their way along the road and the convoy juddered across the cobbles as they ascended the Wall ramp, he slowed the neckers so she could dart outside.

"Be careful, Thorn."

"You too, Lurgo."

They parted ways with a touch of the hand. Thorn clutched her rucksack to her chest and ducked under the shadow of the parapet, praying to her godless soul she wouldn't be discovered by the Boiler guard. They crowded around the first vehicles, pulling them onto the freight-cars of the black train and locking them in place.

Thorn watched the tricorns' wagon moving slowly up the ramp. The canvas flapped in the wind, and she thought she saw a dark shape fall onto the cobbles.

She squinted, wiping the rain from her eyelids. Another dark shadow rolled onto the ramp, then another. Suddenly, something barrelled towards her, a wobbling limp of brown flesh. She heard his thoughts before he reached her, excitement for adventure.

"Igor!" she hissed.

He butted her arm with his beak. Lurgette, Rose and Nicholas shuffled over, followed by the other babies. They lined their enormous hides under the parapet, as if they thought to disguise themselves as boulders.

Thorn looked back at the wagon, now nearly at the top of the ramp. Another round shape toppled from under the canvas and trudged towards her.

"Igoria...no. *Get back.*"

But all Thorn's hissing and gesturing and attempts to push Igoria's thoughts back to the wagon wouldn't make the tricorn turn around. She plodded across the cobbles and squeezed her enormous hide beside Thorn, squashing her right back against the stone. Thorn pressed her face against Igoria's warm, scaly skin, and waited.

She sent waves of calming thoughts into the tricorns' minds, trying to keep them still.

Luckily, another convoy of carriages joined the line to be loaded on the train, laden with crates of kippers. The hoots of the animals as they smelt the brined fish caused ruckus enough, and no Boiler noticed Thorn's less-than-stealthy hiding-place.

She pushed herself between Igoria and Igor, sheltering under the overhang of the buttress. Metallic rain poured down her face, stinging her eyes and skin. Beside her, Igoria moaned, pawing at the ground. Thorn rubbed her frill, trying to calm her.

The whistle blew, and the great black locomotive pulled away, carrying Wombwell and Holman and Lurgo and Julianne and everything good in her life with it. When the last carriage passed by and Thorn could no longer hear any Boilers sliding about on their mechanical treads, she rose and began the walk back down the entry ramp to Gilsland. She cradled her rucksack over her shoulder with one arm, and looped Igoria's lead rope around the other. The babies bounded around her; jostling and knocking her as they fought to stay close. The stinging rain poured down her face and soaked her clothes, scalding her skin.

After barely a hundred paces Thorn had to stop and

rest. It could take her hours to exit the road if she had to continue dragging Igoria and handling the squabbling babies, and all the while the rain burnt and tore at her skin. She wished she hadn't made Lurgo continue on to London.

It's all on you now, she reminded herself. *You have to do this.*

She picked up the rucksack again, and took a step out under the stinging rain.

A carriage rattled up the ramp, hurrying to catch the next black train. Thorn ducked back in the shadow as it clattered past, beckoning the tricorns to follow. Igoria whinnied, rearing up as the shape passed, and hit her head on the iron buttress.

"Sssssh, please girl, be quiet." Thorn glanced around. The rain smashed against the cobbles, obliterating all sounds save the clunk and churn of gears inside the Wall's iron shell.

Thorn looked left, then right. She couldn't see anything coming. Not that she could see much at all through the black rain.

You can't wait on the side of the road forever.

Sighing, Thorn picked up the rucksack and the lead and started back down the ramp. Immediately, the rain pummelled her clothes against her skin, blurring her vision so the world swum in waves of iron and stone and tricorn.

Igoria dragged on her chain, desperately blinking water from her swollen eyes. The babies butted at each other, attempting to burrow their way further under the shelter of the buttress.

Calm down, little ones. Thorn pushed out happy, pleasant thoughts, trying to get the tricorns to behave. After a few steps they stopped fighting each other, and just sat still as statues, staring out into the rain with wide, frightened eyes.

Thorn wiped her weeping eyes and pushed on, gritting her teeth against the pain in her shoulders and the pain in her skin. With every step Igoria grew more crotchety, growling and pulling on the lead. She wanted to go back.

Don't we all? Thorn's clothes – heavy with water – dragged her down. Her boots filled with water from the knee-deep puddles pooling on the road. Now her toes itched and stung.

Finally, she saw a light flicker in the distance. The reflective globe of a Fresnel lens, the signal that the ramp levelled out and the gate to the town lay just beyond. Thorn poured on speed, a new energy coursing through her blood.

Almost there, almost safe…

The light went out.

Did it? No. A dark shadow stood before it, obscuring the glow. Thorn's scream died on her lips. All she managed was a rush of air that stung her face as the wind threw it back at her.

A Boiler – of the twelve-foot high and terrifying variety – waved its iron arms at Igoria. A Sinker leapt from its mainframe and snarled, lead-crusted eyes glowing like embers. They knew the animals should have been on the last train. Thorn staggered back, pushing Lurgette back behind her.

"No," she managed. The Sinker regarded her for several moments. Her heart beat against her chest with alarming ferocity.

With a clank, the Boiler advanced. An iron pipe shot at Thorn. She threw herself down – landing in a puddle of dirty water – and it sailed over her head. She rolled toward the buttress in time to see the Boiler fire another, directly at Igoria.

The pipe hit her in the side. Igoria roared in pain and toppled forward, blood pulsing from the wound, distorted by the rain into rivers of muddy-red water. The babies cried and ran to their mother, crowding her and increasing her distress. Overhead, thunder applauded the Boiler's victory.

Thorn screamed, dropping the lead from her hand. Igoria's pain slammed into her skull. The tricorn thrashed her legs wildly, and Thorn's mind fought to maintain life. She could not go to Igoria while she was like this – one kick to the head or chest and she would be dead. All she could do was try and send calming thoughts, try to ease the pain that clouded Igoria's mind.

The Sinker leapt off the transom and dived at her. Thorn rolled again, but the Sinker grabbed her coat and pulled her down. It pinned her arms, and a face from her nightmares loomed over her, dribbling her death from his maniacal smile.

"No, no, NO!" She kicked and bucked, trying to knock the creature off, but it simply sat and stared. Thorn stared back. Something in its face jolted memories inside her, pleasant memories of hands clasping in the darkness, of a touch that lit a fire in her heart. They regarded each other in awed silence for several moments.

"Rex?" she choked out.

Rex…not Rex. It's not Rex anymore.

The Sinker removed its rough claws from her wrist and bent a finger to stroke her face. Mustering all the strength and courage she possessed, Thorn pulled her arm back and punched it in the nose.

It reeled back, clutching its face and howling in pain. With both arms now free, Thorn pummelled his neck, chest and guts, wiggling her legs free as the Sinker struggled to fend off her blows. She yanked one leg free and with a solid kick in the chest sent the Sinker sprawling back across the ramp. Igor and Lurgette bounded after it and stomped on its legs.

Igoria heaved herself upright and swung her tail at the Boiler. Though she lacked power, the blow connected with the furnace unit and knocked the cumbersome contraption over sideways, dislodging another iron projectile which missed Igoria by inches and sunk into the buttress above Thorn's head. The Sinker scrambled to right the flailing machine. Thorn rushed to Igoria's side.

"We have to get off this road!" She tugged the lead. Igoria's eyes puffed with pain, but she rose onto her front legs. The tricorn's pain tugged inside Thorn, searing her own movements.

Thorn shoved a howling Igor forward, off the road and into the wet grass. The other babies followed him, and she dragged Igoria in behind. The grass cut her raw skin, and her whole body shivered with cold and fear.

Behind her, the Sinker screeched. She looked back. It had remounted the Boiler unit, and stood behind the mainframe, tugging at the pressure gears and kicking the footplate. Gears whirred inside the Boiler, and black steam shot from its pressure valve in defiant bursts. It didn't clank after her, but groaned as it struggled to lock its safety gauge. Foggy smoke spluttered from its pipes.

It's hurt. It doesn't like the stinging rain.

Water collected in the drainage under the buttresses and cascaded off the Wall, drowning her in mud and road detritus. Thorn pulled the tricorns as fast as she could away from the road, into the scattered debris of Hadrian's Wall, her boots slipping over the wet stones.

Neither the Sinker nor the Boiler followed.

Now where do I go?

Igoria pulled at her aching arms. Thorn dodged under the crumbling foundation of an old Roman watchtower, her breath raking her raw throat. The babies tumbled over the rocks, crawling over each other in a desperate attempt to follow their mother. Thorn glanced up at the Wall, and saw the Sinker dancing across the buttress. His lead-coated skin glowed in the moonlight like an aura.

Is it Rex? She didn't want to think about it, didn't want to know the answer. Better he should have died than end up like that. *No.* She shook her head. *I won't accept it. Rex is dead. You just see his face on every one of the Sunken because of your dreams.*

Thorn looked up again. The figure had disappeared.

She did not know how long they ran. Her chest heaved and her limbs shook, and twice she toppled over into the grass, but still she ran – heaving and coughing – away from the Wall. The rains eased off and moonlight cast long shadows through the ruins.

Thorn figured the fields would be swarming with Sinkers in a few minutes, hunting for the animals that had escaped the black train. She squinted at the horizon. Across the fields she saw the outline of an outcrop of oaks – the edge of one of the northern woods. They could hide there until light.

She crashed through the blackberry, but her tricorns hesitated before the towering trees. Their thoughts pounded against her skull – they didn't want to enter the dark forest. Thorn pushed Igoria into the shadows, sending calming thoughts to erase the tricorn's panic. If she could get their mother to enter the forest, the babies would follow.

But Igoria refused to budge. She moaned, lolling her

head to the side and shooting Thorn an incredulous look. Thorn grabbed her rucksack, swung it behind over her head and brought it down with a *smack* on Igoria's rump. She howled in protest and bolted into the trees. The babies followed after her, convinced it must be a game. *One, two, three*...counted them off in her head as she glanced over her shoulder.

She glanced behind her again. Shapes on the edge of the watchtower flickered – and a long, black shadow moved between the stones. A trick of the moonlight, perhaps? Or a Sinker watching her?...*Four, five, six...*grass rustled. *Seven*...waved a squabbling Bernard from behind a pile of stones.

She scanned the vicinity for Igor. He wasn't anywhere near the treeline, nor could she see a rust-coloured lump in the long-grasses. She saw more shadows moving now – and heard the distinctive hiss of a Sinker, closer than she'd hoped.

"Igor!"

Thorn spied his giant bulk sticking out from either side of an oak tree. "Igor, come out! I see you! This isn't a game!"

He crawled out from behind the oak tree, a sheepish look on his mud-streaked face. He yelped as she grabbed his lumpy tail, and yanked him in the direction of the forest. He raced after his siblings. Thorn threw her barker and her rucksack over her shoulder and bolted into the cover of the trees.

Behind her, more Sinkers hissed and the grass crackled and squelched as several creatures raced towards the trees.

Thorn poured on speed, her body tingling with pain as branches scratched her raw skin. Her feet slipped and skidded over the damp ground. Blood pooled from shallow cuts on her arms and face, blurring her vision. *Red, red, red.* She couldn't see her tricorns anywhere, but she heard them up ahead, hurtling through the trees. Her chest heaved with the effort. Cramps shot up her swollen arm.

"No, no. no." Thorn's breath raked against her throat as she pushed through the gloomy trees, searching for a place to hide. She heard a Sinker crash through the undergrowth behind her, snarling and grabbing at her legs. Igor barrelled up behind her and knocked him into the dirt. She ran on, fear licking her heels.

Blind in the darkness, Thorn skidded on a smooth stone and stumbled off-balance. Her ankle snagged on a root and she toppled over a fallen log. Her ankle throbbed, and when she tried to stand, it buckled under her weight.

I'm doomed.

Wincing, Thorn tried to stand again, but pain shot up her leg and she stumbled over. Through her blood-soaked eyes she saw Rose and Bridget emerge from a thicket and exchange a worried gaze. She listened for the hisses of the approaching Sinkers, knowing with a sinking feeling that a lead-soaked bite would soon end her life.

Thorn heard nothing but the songs of birds and the dribble of raindrops through the leaves. Even her tricorns had gone quiet. She tried to stand again, gritting her teeth with the effort, but collapsed again. *No, that isn't possible.*

She leaned against the tree, fighting to catch her breath. Moonlight poured through a hole in the canopy above, casting the forest in eerie, glowing light. Pulling her barker off her shoulder and securing it between her legs, she stuffed powder down the barrel, filled the pan, secured the flint, and cocked the hammer. Now at least she was prepared.

She waited, focusing on the rustling in the thicket of ash trees to her left.

A short, straight branch lay at her feet. Thorn snatched it up, peeling off the protruding leaves with one hand and, using the rope in her rucksack, splinted her leg. She tested her weight – it still hurt, but she could hobble on it. Satisfied, she pulled herself close into the tree, and raised the barker to her cheek. *Come out, you filthy leaden vampires. I'm prepared for you...*

What she wasn't prepared for was the creature that burst from the thicket and bounded across her path. It stood as high as Lurgo, bounding forward on trunklike hind legs. It lowered its flat, avian head – the long snout tapering to a sturdy beak – and thumped onto all fours, its muscled fingers gripping the dirt. Instead of a thumb it had a long, sharp spike.

Thorn threw up her hands – scrambling to keep a hold on her weapon – as its stiff tail knocked against the trees. A branch as thick as Igor's belly whirled over her head and crashed just inches from her hiding place. Sharp splinters rained down around her.

The forest heaved and groaned as more of the strange creatures thundered through, leaping over the uneven ground on thick hind legs. High warbles of distress issued from their beaked mouths. Twenty...thirty of them darted past, the criss-crossed designs on their leathery skin blurring in the foliage as they churned the mud into a juicy maelstrom.

Wombwell said the northern forests were home to strange animals, worthy enough for the menagerie if he could find anyone willing to catch them. He said people didn't enter the forests because they were dangerous...

Thorn struggled to her feet, slung the barker over her shoulder, and scooped up the rucksack. The herd paid her no heed. *They're afraid of something...*

Swamp dragons wouldn't pursue a herd of this size – no, it was something bigger, more terrifying...a beast of such size and ferocity it should have existed only in legend.

Thorn heard the roar before she saw the trees buckling under the weight of two monstrous legs, their skin like burnished leather that dripped with sweat. The fresh forest scents turned to blood and hot, sickly saliva, and hunger. She could sense its hunger.

A Great Dragon.

Feelings rushed her, knocking her backwards as they slammed into her head. The fear of the herd washed over her, paralysing her with wave after wave of terror. Beyond that, she *felt* the dragon's hunger, *felt* its joy as it pursued its stampeding breakfast.

Each tree that fell snapped and crashed, tumbling through the foliage like masts falling through the decks during a naval engagement. The dragon roared again, a rumble that rattled Thorn's ribcage against her trembling chest. A clawed hand appeared below the treeline, minuscule compared to the hind legs, but with claws each the length of Thorn's body, and dyed red with death.

Those claws scooped up one of the stampeding creatures, who squealed and bucked and wriggled, but it couldn't escape the dragon's serrated teeth. The flesh tore like paper, and blood scarred red fissures across the fallen trees. The herd ignored their screeching relative and ran on, breaking into smaller bands and thundering into the valley. *They're confusing the dragon, clever creatures.*

But the dragon had lost interest. It had its kill. Its

head bent down below the foliage, teeth gleaming like tricorn ivory as they crunched and tore the carcass. Rumbles and gurgles, tearing, and screaming. Screams from Thorn's own throat.

Steam poured from its nostrils. A lolling yellow eye streaked with red, blinked and rolled, searching for her. Thorn snapped her mouth shut and ducked behind the trunk.

Oh Great Conductor oh god oh god oh god, it's going to eat me, I'm going to be eaten. I'm going to be eaten in the middle of the Northern Forest and I'll never see Quartz or Lurgo or Wombwell or Holman again…

Her tricorns were screaming. She had to move. She had to find shelter, find hiding, find a weapon, find *something*.

Has he seen us? I can't be sure. Oh bloody hell, can't they stop screaming?

Thorn *reached* her mind, reeling herself in, collecting her senses. The tricorns ceased their wailing.

The steel barrel of the barker rolled against her shoulder blade. She had that, loaded and ready. It wouldn't even prick the dragon, but she had more powder in her bag; perhaps she could set a fire of some sort…

The forest is sodden. Nothing will burn. Oh god, oh god.

No gods. Thorn reeled back her panic. *Only you. Stay alert.*

The dragon snorted. Sparks flew amongst the detritus. Igoria growled, a low, menacing sound Thorn had never heard before. Before Thorn could reach out to stop her, Igoria edged her way toward the dragon, placing herself between the beast and her babies. Blood still bubbled from the gash in her side as she lowered her horns.

Thorn's mind flooded with conflicting thoughts – the

hunger of the beast mingled with Igoria's maternal anger and the babies' fear. The intensity of feelings crippled her – she had no room inside her head to think for herself. She heard a rustle as the dragon dropped the masticated carcass into the rowan and strode toward Igoria. Thorn screamed as she felt his attack. The tricorn swung just as the beast opened its great jaws—

"No!" Thorn cried, as the teeth slashed and stung. The tricorn reeled – her hide slick with blood – but she did not lower her horns. She barrelled forward and struck again, driving her horns into the beast's flesh.

Igoria's thoughts tore from her mind. Now all Thorn felt was the beast. Igoria's horns had opened a long gash in the tough skin of his belly, but rather than slowing him, the wound made him angrier.

Thorn had no choice. She ran, as best she could with her damaged leg, throwing the rucksack over her shoulder and barrelling towards the cover of the ash thicket. Her barker thumped against her leg.

The tricorns squealed and thundered after her. Behind her, Igoria wailed – a horrible scream of pain. Thorn slid down a muddy bank and hobbled on, her boots now slick with mud and slipping on the wet ground. She stumbled again – her sore ankle twisting away from her within the rope of her splint – and tumbled down the valley, feet over bosom right down into the mud.

Her ankle screamed, her ears rang with pain, and red welts appeared before her eyes. She reached out, and grabbed the sack just as the mud threatened to devour it. She rolled over and tried to struggle back towards the trees.

The tricorns – who could see better in low light – took the more sensible path, edging their way carefully down the slip, skirting the shallow bog and hiding themselves in the thick tangles of blackberry. All except Igor, who bounded from the thicket and splashed straight through the mud.

"Igor, *no.*"

He looked indignant, stretching his legs and back and splashing across the verge. Thorn struggled forward on her elbows, trying to get him to come to her, but he remained just out of reach of her fingers, enjoying the game.

Then he heard the roar.

Igor leapt two feet in the air and landed on Thorn's hand. Howling in pain, she pushed him off and shoved him ahead of her into the blackthorn. Using her elbows and stomach to pull herself forward through the mud, she crouched under the cluster of blackthorn bushes. Behind her, she heard the dragon approach the edge of the slip.

Thorn rolled deeper into the bushes, dragging her rucksack behind her. Her arm disappeared into the ground. With great effort she tugged it free. It was coated with sticky peat.

She looked around. The blackthorn hid what appeared to be a small bog, about forty feet across, perhaps more. A desperate idea flashed in her mind.

Thorn pushed Igor down into the mud. "Stay there." He made to protest, but she silenced him with a single authoritative thought.

Igor looked up at the dragon placing step after careful step, manoeuvring itself down the slippery ridge. Igor began to shake. He whimpered and began to slide back under the blackthorn. Thorn shook her head. "Stay, Igor."

She dragged herself further under the blackthorn, cringing as the thorns pricked her raw arms. *A Thorn* *amongst thorns, the perfect hiding place. I should blend in well here.*She hoped it was true.

The dragon slid closer, flailing its tiny forelimbs for balance. As it lifted its feet droplets of mud the size of potatoes rained down on poor screaming Igor. *Stay Igor, stay, stay…*

If there was ever a time Thorn needed her sense to work, it was now. She focused on Igor, drawing her mind away from the danger, away from the mud and the pain and the gnashing teeth dribbling with blood, toward her frightened charge, abandoned and alone and about to be dragon dinner—

Thorn *felt* rather than saw the dragon pounce. The forest seemed to groan with relief as the dragon launched its heavy frame through the air towards Igor.

"To me!" she yelled, but she didn't have to. The frightened lump executed a perfect summersault into the blackthorn. The dragon reeled in surprise, lost its footing and sailed past, skidding in the mud and toppling into the peat. The bog closed over his thighs, and when he struggled to lift them out he pushed himself deeper into the sticky peat. He snapped his jaws at the wych elm branches that clustered overhead, in a furious attempt to get free.

Igor burrowed into Thorn's back, not wanting to look. She crawled from the shrubs and started her slow ascent of the ridge, clutching the wild cheery stalks for handholds.

The dragon whirled its head around and snapped its massive jaws.

Thorn froze, her fear clutching her chest, but though the Great Dragon roared and thrashed about, he couldn't reach her. She struggled on, his roars growing distant and more distressed as he sank deeper into the bog.

Finally, he ceased to roar at all.

Thorn scanned the forest, searching for Igoria. She heard a faint moan from a amongst the birch trees – near the unfortunate corpse of the dragon's last meal.

Igor found his mother lying under a downy birch. She'd collapsed on her right side, leaving her gaping wounds exposed to the rain. The dragon had torn open the gash left from the Boiler, and it leaked bloody water over the babies, who crowded around, moaning for her to stand up. She lifted her head to greet Thorn, her eyes wide with pain.

Thorn didn't have any material long enough to wrap around the tricorn's stomach as a tourniquet. She removed her sodden blanket, wrung out what water she could, and placed it over the gash in an attempt to keep out the rain. Igoria moaned again, low and painful. With each intake of breath her thoughts left Thorn, until they were only a whisper; muddy and unclear. Tears mingled with the mud and blood on Thorn's face.

She cursed herself for not thinking to bring along medical supplies, for she had nothing to stitch the wound or stop the bleeding. She couldn't move Igoria, and she wouldn't leave her here alone. She could do nothing except wait with her tricorns while their mother died.

Fatigue and hunger overwhelmed Thorn. She remembered the pie Lurgo had brought her earlier; the one he'd crushed through his fingers. She wished she'd thought to eat before she left.

She pulled herself down behind Igoria's neck, where the stiff bone frill created a hollow. The babies curled up around her, wrapping their tails around their mother. Igor crawled under his mother's arms and snuggled close to her belly, crying in fear and sadness. Thorn didn't blame him; she wanted to cry, too.

Thorn hugged her knees to her chest, pulled the corners of her coat around her, and fell into a restless, uneasy sleep.

***

Thorn awoke to a rough tongue flogging her cheek. She pushed Bridget away and lifted herself onto her knees. Her whole body ached, and when she raised her hands, she saw the skin on her arms was blistered and peeled over red welts. Running her hands over her cheeks, she felt the same welts and blisters.

Bridget nudged her again. The first morning light fought through the canopy and spread smudges of light over Bridget's hide. Birdsong mingled with the chitters of insects and far off rumbles of enormous beasts. Thorn rubbed her eyes, trying to focus her groggy mind.

She checked her other wounds. Her ankle throbbed. Her wrists ached where the Sinker had held her, and blood poured from a shallow gash on her knee, probably sustained when she fell down the bank. The rain had torn her skin raw, and thin cuts crisscrossed her arms and ankles from the blackthorn. Apart from her sore ankle, nothing else seemed broken or missing.

The stinging rain had come and gone all night, but had now subsided, existing now only as giant drops burning through the overhanging leaves. Although the birch had shaded her from the worst of the weather, the rain had seeped in and soaked every layer of her clothing, staining the wool with brownish streaks.

During the night, the babies had covered their mother with the warmth of their bodies, wrapping themselves around her torso like scarves. Thorn shook Rose and

Nicholas awake, pushing them away so she could check the wound.

They moved behind her, their unease slipping into her mind and filling her with dread. Igor glared at her with accusing eyes.

"I'm sorry, boy. I don't know what else to do."

He snapped his sharp beak, burrowing deeper into Igoria's arms. She pulled her coat off the wound. Black tar and pus oozed from the cut, and the air smelt like rotting meat.

It was then she realised she could no longer sense Igoria's thoughts.

Thorn held her hand under Igoria's nostrils, but could feel no breath. She poked the tricorn's cheeks, pulled at her eyelids, kicked her ribcage, but could elicit no sign of life.

"No, no, no, *no.*"

The babies tugged at her dry teats, their cries mingling with her sobs.

Not Igoria too. Everyone I touch dies.

"Please, no." Thorn gasped for air. The forest spun, shades of green and brown fading before her eyes, everything around her becoming red, red, red. Tendrils of fog reached in like children's fingers in a candy box, wrapping her heart in ice.

The babies cried harder, stamping their huge hooves in the soft earth. Soon their wails would draw the attention of other creatures lurking in the forest. Thorn looked around, panicked.

We must keep going, and find a way through this forest, before we all become dragon food. But where could she go? She'd never had to navigate her way back to Graveyard from so far away before. Thorn found a sharp twig and drew what she remembered of Holman's map in the mud.

If the wagons were travelling behind her and they headed to London, then South was that way. If she was in Northumbria, and Graveyard was inland from the Southern coast, west of London…she needed to travel…sort of south-west.

Thorn took out the compass and twirled it through her fingers. Quartz had taught her to read one – the wavy line pointed South, and the pointy squiggle was West. South-West. That seemed simple enough.

Leaning on her good leg, she broke off a section of birch and peeled off the grey bark. Now she had a cane, just like Holman. She tested its weight – it seemed to support her if she balanced herself with her free arm. She turned to the tricorns. "We're not in the menagerie anymore; I can't lead you around the green. You'll have to walk yourselves."

They wailed in reply.

If Aaron were here he would calm them with a single thought, but Thorn didn't have the skill to harness that power. She pushed with her mind, sending calming thoughts she did not feel toward the babies. They ignored her, their cries bouncing through the forest and cascading into the valley below.

Thorn leaned against the nearest trunk and swung herself forward. Her ankle throbbed, but she started walking. *This will be a long day.*

She turned and waved goodbye. Realising she intended to leave them, Igor gave a disgruntled snort and barrelled after her. The others followed behind, their wails subsiding as they concentrated on navigating the muddy valley.

After many hours of walking the canopy thinned a little, and shafts of daylight penetrated the trees. With each hour that passed without another Great Dragon, her spirits soared. Her ankle still throbbed, but she found she could rest weight on it for a few moments. She picked up her pace, cajoling the babies onward with handfuls of oats.

The oak and walnut trees gave way to hawthorn and spindle. Blackberry bushes dotted here and there, but when Thorn stopped to collect berries she found the fruit dribbling off the cracking branches in rotting, brownish lumps. The grass and twigs she pushed through – taller than her height – were all dead and crackling.

Igor ran ahead. He yelped in fright. *What now?* dropped to her knees and inched forward, unshouldering her mud-crusted Barker.

Only a few feet in front of her, Igor whimpered. Thorn pushed her hand through the grass. Her fingers grazed cold iron.

No, oh no.

She stood up, felt along the surface in front of her, hoping it wasn't true. But Great Conductor had a sadistic sense of humour.

She pressed her head to the warm metal. She heard the Wall purring – that familiar churning of gears and levers…and something else underneath. A low rumble. A growl…almost…she snapped her head back. The rumbling wasn't coming from inside the Wall.

Igor whimpered again, and buried his head in the grass.

Thorn turned her attention back to the Wall. Obviously, she couldn't scale it. The sides were far too slick and steep. She would have to follow the Wall until it reached a town or ramp, or head back into the forest to face the dragon. She counted her babies, finding all eight present and accounted for – including the irrepressible Igor, once again trying to hide his impressive bulk behind a thin wych elm.

Inside the Wall, footsteps clanged along a metal grate, moving west. It was an army manoeuvring through dark tunnels. Thorn hobbled after the sound, the tricorns trudging after her. Igor lumbered so close, he stomped on her heels.

"You're just like Lurgo, you know that?" Thorn snapped at him. Igor gave her a wide-eyed look. He seemed to take that as a compliment.

Brambles and branches scratched her face, but she hardly felt the pain. *I'm so close to finding out what's really going on, and why the Wall spreads so fast—*

Suddenly, the footsteps stopped. Thorn stopped also, panting. She jammed her ear against the iron. Nothing.

She waited for several minutes, but the footsteps had vanished. Overhead, a crow circled, admiring her with bloodshot eyes. In the distance the dragon roared again, the deep growl soon joined by another.

Heart pounding, Thorn picked up her barker and hobbled on.

The Wall ended abruptly three miles or so from where she left the forest. There was no town, just a mangled heap of twisted iron in the middle of a derelict and untended field. She crouched behind a cairn and watched from the crest of the hill as Boilers crawled from the mangled scaffold, using their mechanical arms to bend and twist and hammer the metal into the existing Wall. An army of Sunken marched through the structure, passing out lumps of lead and rolling a great gear cog into position. An overwhelming smell of sulphur and burning birch and aspen permeated the air.

That explains the footsteps I heard. There's a whole army of Sinkers in there. Now I know how the Wall is spreading – they're building it, like slaves. But it doesn't tell me why. *It doesn't make any sense.*

The tricorns tumbled over the ridge, chasing the flies that buzzed between the charred wheat husks. Their game disturbed a warren of compies, who skittered down the ridge and across the field, squawking at a piercing volume only a compie could accomplish. A Boiler on the periphery, nearest to her hiding spot, fired his steam valve at the scampering brood, and several Boilers pointed their periscopes towards the tree line.

Thorn ducked further behind the cairn, pulling Igor and Bridget down with her. After a few moments of frantic breathing, she dared another peek into the valley. The Boilers gesticulated with their pipe-arms, the flames in their bulbous furnace bellies licking through the grates. Three Sinkers leaned the giant cog against the scaffold and scrambled for the hillock.

She scampered backward, connecting her mind with as many tricorns as she could sense and urging them to follow her into the hawthorn. Suddenly, the ground bucked and tore itself from under her. Thorn skidded into an uplifted root, its tangled appendages scraping the skin from her flailing arms.

Tricorns bounced around her. Thorn tried to pull herself to her feet, but the earth had become unsteady. She looked back to the Wall, and choked back a scream.

The dragon crashed from the forest, thick oaks snapping over its flanks like twigs. It bounded across the field with surprising speed, whipping its long tail through the air. Sections of the hillside broke away and rolled down into the field below. Another beast thundered after it, a smaller version of the larger one, standing a little over twice the height of Thorn. They swept through the Sinkers and scattered them like children's knucklebones.

The Sunken screeched like a swarm of frightened monkeys, and clambered back underneath the scaffold. Steam spewed from the Boilers, obscuring Thorn's view. The dragons roared, the machines hissed, the Sunken shrieked and jittered, there was a sound like the earth being torn asunder on the eve of the Great Forging, and the smoke cleared to reveal a smoking pile of debris and twitching limbs. The dragons rested at the other end of the field, the smaller one licking clean a long gash in the other's side.

Thorn leaned as far over the cairn as she dared, watching the detritus for any sign of life-that-was-not-life. A Sinker pulled its mangled legs from the wreckage and dragged the bloody stumps towards the trees. Another wailed as it inspected the remains of its severed arm. Yet another flailed in desperation, pushing its spilling viscera back inside its open ribcage. Thorn looked away. She had seen enough.

She gazed into eight pairs of intelligent, frightened eyes, and she smiled. *Now I know. I know how to defeat the Wall.*

***

JAMES HOLMAN'S MEMOIRS, FIRST EDITION

Of course, Lurgo and I knew nothing of Thorn's encounter in the forest. While she battled against the Great Dragons of legend, the black train carried us uncomfortably on the Wall railroad back to London.

Lurgo performed a marvellous acrobatic feat clambering along the open wagon and leaping onto the backplate of my carriage. Unfortunately for him no one witnessed his exploit (myself included, for obvious reasons) and cannot validate his claim of a perfectly executed triple somersault.

All I know was one moment I was absorbed in my reading, when suddenly the canvas flapped and something barrelled inside my carriage and crashed into my writing desk.

I cast my hands out to save my Turkish glass paperweight, but it clattered to the floor and smashed. Instead, I reached out to the trembling boy, and, clasping his arm, I forced him to sit on my bed. "Lurgo, you frightened me."

"She's gone. Thorn's gone back to Graveyard, and the tricorns followed her."

"What, all of them?"

"Even Igoria. She didn't take them on purpose – Igor went after her when she snuck away, and once he'd gone, the others had to follow. I couldn't stop them. I hope Wombwell won't think too ill of me."

"George will understand." I wasn't really so sure he would, but Lurgo sounded distressed. "Why has she done this? I thought she was happy here."

"I think it's a misguided sense of loyalty. Thorn wants to warn the Stokers about the Wall. She thinks Quartz – that's the old man who looks after her – will know how to stop it." Lurgo sniffed. "If something should happen to her – I'd never live with myself. I never should have listened to her and stayed behind. I should have followed her, too. At least then I could stop her being killed, like all the others."

I pulled a handkerchief from my sleeve and handed it to him. I bumbled my way through some words of encouragement and instructed him to remove the *nargila*smoking pipe from the shelf above the bed.

"Holman, this is—"

"Trust me boy, a smoke will calm your fears."

I schooled him in the method of filling the water jar, tightening the grommets, placing the tobacco in the bowl and laying the coals on top, and attaching the *amjïd*–the mouthpiece – to the smoking pipe.

"It is customary for each person to have his own personal *amjïd*," I explained. "Some are highly decorated, jewelled or enamelled, or made of tricorn ivory."

I heard the water bubbling through the bowl as Lurgo took a drag. "Thorn would hate this," he said, coughing as the smoke entered his lungs for the first time.

"Thorn isn't here, now is she?"

Together we sat and puffed away, and as the sweet smoke filled the cabin Lurgo calmed and ceased his rambling, and instead we chatted of his own life. He told me much of their childhood in Graveyard. How, as a boy of three he and his father had fled London on the Clegg train, crammed into the carriage with a hundred others. How Brigitte Thorne handed him a tiny baby, then fell from the carriage as she attempted to fight off a Boiler. How that little girl hadn't cried or cooed once during the journey, but tugged his fingers and regarded him with wide intelligent eyes. How he'd loved her. How as they'd grown he'd chased her over the fens and through the mud and fire, only to see her run to Rex. How he'd chased her still.

The catharsis of the tobacco worked its magic, and though Lurgo spoke words of great sadness, he did not cry. He slept the night in the upper bed of my bunk, snoring his way under the iron gates of the Wall.

A while later, the train entered a long tunnel, and when we exited the other end, I realised we'd entered

London. Even on a moving train, I recognised the sound and smell of my city.

The train slowed, and rolled past a platform on Fleet Street. On the other side of the platform, I heard hundreds of people shouting and cursing. Their yelling woke Lurgo, and he peeked from the canvas and told me what he saw.

"There's at least a hundred of them, and they're crowding the platform – I think they're trying to leave the city," he said. "Boilers have blocked the ticket office and are trying to sweep them back off the platform, and no one wants to approach them. But they're still shouting, and I heard someone say no one has been allowed to leave for several days. But that doesn't make sense. How would that messenger have found us, then?"

"If these Boilers act on orders from the 'Royal Engineer', it's likely he lets the Queen's men through, at least for now. We shall have to investigate further."

We disembarked at the next station – on Holloway Road – and the Boilers dragged our vehicles out onto the cobbled street. People shouted at us as we rode by.

"Hey, those country toffs must know why we can't go nowhere!"

"Mister, mister, stop! You have to help us! We're trapped in the city!"

Our carriage shuddered as people crowded around us, pushing against the body in a desperate attempt to gain our attention. A woman threw herself at the footplate, but her dress caught in the wheel and she couldn't scramble aboard. She screamed and screamed as she fell off the side and was dragged along the cobbled street. Lurgo went to see to it, and after a few moments of pulling at her skirts, they tore free and she rolled to safety. The screaming stopped, but not the angry shouts or the jostling.

Wombwell retired the menagerie to the Queen's private gardens, and finally discovered his tricorns had disappeared. He seemed oddly calm about losing his major attraction – almost as if he'd expected it to happen. "I knew that Thorn was trouble, even when I hired her," he growled.

Wombwell and Lurgo joined me in the cramped – soon to become unbearably so – apartment I kept in the city, not far from the palace. No one had visited the rooms for some weeks, so the air smelled musty and there were no supplies for making tea. But at least we had room to move, unlike the cramped carriages of the menagerie. No one spoke of the events at the station, but as we dressed and shaved and combed our hair we all worried privately about the state of affairs. Finally, Wombwell was satisfied we all looked presentable, and we left for the Palace – Wombwell was to take summons with the Queen, with Lurgo and myself invited to high tea as his guests.

In the short distance from my apartments to the palace, we passed seven buildings on fire. The smell of blazing wood and brick reminded me of the last time I was trapped inside London, when Thorn's mother Brigitte and I were desperately trying to find a way out of the city before the Sunken could find us. Lurgo said he thought he could see flames licking from the sewer gratings. I wondered how London could have allowed itself to fall into this trap again.

Then I remembered the plate I still kept hidden in my trunk, and how I still wished for what I should not, and I remembered how easy it is to throw others to the fire to save your own soul.

We parked within the palace gates and an armoured

guard escorted us to the banquet hall. All about us, we noticed signs of the Royal Engineer's increasing power. A Boiler guarded the reception hall, its sputtering furnace spewing soot into the scented air. Lurgo said the tapestries were stained black from its emissions. People pushed past us without a word, as if strangers arriving at the palace were an occurrence to fear, and not to celebrate.

Her Majesty Queen Victoria, however, at least made a show of light-hearted pageantry. At this most lavish reception with more forks than a blind man knew how to eat with; she sat at the head of the table and led the guests in conversation, avoiding any mention of the Royal Engineer or the Great Exhibition. Instead of addressing what was foremost in all our minds, we discussed the arts and the illegal Dirigire immigrants and continuing troubles with France.

Wombwell and Nero performed a few perfunctory tricks; dancing together, tossing a cricket ball between them, and removing small, humorous items from under the banquet table. As Nero removed a tiny statue of a well-endowed Greek Titan from under her throne and set it upon her lap, Her Majesty snorted with laughter. Unfortunately for her she was lifting a scone towards her mouth at the time, and accidentally sniffed a raisin up her nostril. Several courtiers shuffled forward with silver-edged spoons to remove it, but Wombwell simply slapped her on the back until she spluttered it out again.

I thought Prince Albert would surely have him jailed for Royal assault, but I clearly misunderstood the man's stern voice and quick temperament. He congratulated Wombwell with gushing praise and offered to purchase him a lavish present.

"I am deeply humbled by your generosity, good

Prince." Wombwell slurped on his wine. "But I have everything on the Conductor's good carriage that I desire. There is nothing you could procure for me that would bring any greater pleasure than good food, good drink and fine company."

"I take that as a challenge, George. But for now, let us rejoice." The prince clapped his hands. "Music!"

After dinner Lurgo and I snuck away from the ballroom and wandered the halls of the palace. Without my cane I relied on Lurgo to guide me through the cavernous halls. Lurgo would stop often to describe objects to me.

"There's a portrait on the wall encasing the staircase," he said, "at least twenty feet high. It is of a man with sunken cheeks and pallid skin. His expression is serene, out-of-place. It's as if the artist..." I waited for him to collect his thoughts. "...doesn't want to paint what he really sees. The canvas shimmers, as though it's sewn from threads of gold."

"As indeed it probably is. That portrait is of the Vampire King. You should consider yourself lucky that you never encountered the man. When his hand clenched mine it was as if fingers of ice encircled my heart. All that was good within me shrivelled to dust."

"When did you meet him?"

"In his formative years, before his madness took full force. He presided over meetings at the Royal Society. He even presented papers on several occasions – tracts he'd written himself on the old literature; dragons and bestiary and the demons of Scandinavia and the Baltics. Most of the scholars scoffed at his rantings behind his back, but Brunel found him fascinating. We were all too blind to see, of course, what the two of them were plotting together. And when the Wall went up and the fog of London turned as black as the Vampire King's heart, it was too late."

"Did Brunel really kill the Vampire King? Why would he do that, when they seemed to be working toward the same goal?"

"I couldn't say. It seems most likely to me that Brunel did it so he could be seen as the hero and the people would raise him up to the position of ultimate power. Or it could be that they quarrelled over some aspect of their plan and his death was an accident. Perhaps his Royal Highness tripped and fell on the knife. Only Brunel and the king and Thorn's father know what went on inside that room. Certainly I don't believe Brunel was in the palace to look out for the public good."

"To think this king was so powerful, and yet Brunel could sneak right inside his very bedchamber. His hands…" Again Lurgo shuddered. "They seem to reach out across the stairwell, grasping at me. Was he really a vampire?"

"He believed so. And when a man has his teeth filed into fearsome fangs and drinks the blood of his courtiers, and transforms other souls into creatures such as he, does it matter if his vampirism is real or imagined?"

"It is hard to believe Queen Victoria is of the same blood."

"Her Majesty seems a sensible lass, despite her unwise choice of Royal Engineer. If she does not now know his true nature, she certainly suspects. She is fearful for her subjects, yet she must hide behind a brave face until she figures out how to save them. She fears she is responsible for the miseries to come. She knows naught of matters beyond the Wall, but Thorn will soon change that."

"Holman ... will Thorn ever love me?"

"Well, you certainly like to bounce around all manner of conversational subjects! Thorn already does love you, lad, but not the way you wish. You are her oldest and most trusted friend. The bond you two share was forged in that Clegg carriage, forged in fire and soot. For the remainder of your days on earth you will count her among your closest friends, and you will be among hers. But her heart belongs to another."

"But he's dead."

"Her whole world is death, lad. Her parents reside there, her spurning lover and her doomed prince; they taunt her from the depths of that abyss. Death is in her past, her present and her future. In your fingers is life; you have no part of that world, and you cannot follow her to that dark ravine."

"What will I do, then?"

"A blind man cannot see the future, Lurgo. You can't have all the answers so easily. Fear thee not; we're not leaving this city any time soon, and I have much to occupy your time in London. How are you at croquet?"

***

For many days, Thorn and her charges marched through the soot-caked moors and across charred wheat-fields – all that remained of the once-fertile English countryside. Hundreds of acres of farmland – once rich fields of wheat and produce – were burned and trodden to dust by the march of the Wall. She ate burnt, blistered potatoes, and stole milk and oats from untended barns to feed the babies.

A stiff wind threw up the blackened chaff, whipping and scratching Thorn's already torn skin. She had never been so miserable, sore, or tired in her life. She pulled her mud-caked blanket over her head, its weight bending her further towards the ground. *Just keep putting one foot in front of the next,* she reminded herself. *And you'll get to Graveyard eventually.*

They clambered over a rotting fence, forded a blackened creek, and passed through a prickly hedgerow. Still the scenery remained unchanged. The wind picked up, swirling the shifting chaff in dusty plumes around Thorn and the babies and carrying the sound of the Wall, constantly moving across the countryside, destroying everything it touched. She coughed as she swallowed a mouthful of ash. Igor whined. Thorn stopped, resting her wooden cane in the wheat, and stroked the edge of his frill. He pawed at her arm, wanting her to wrap her arms around him, but he was too big for that now. His eyes wept, and dried blood from his various wounds mingled with the mud to form a scabrous shell. She tried to wipe the grit from his eyes but her hands were too dirty. He yelped and squirmed away.

"I'm sorry, boy." The other tricorns cried too. Bridget and Nicholas bounded back towards the hedgerow.

"Not that way—" Thorn started to yell after them, but then she heard something that made her stop short. She strained to listen. The wind blew another sound to her ears.

Chanting. At least three voices chanting in the middle of the chaff-storm. Thorn squinted at the horizon. *Dirigires.* Through the gusts of ash and chaff she saw the bulbous outline of a balloon rising over the wheat, puffs of smoke swirling from the funnel as the propeller tossed them into the dusty air.

We will hike around them. It will be okay. But she knew it wouldn't. She slipped her loaded pistol from the sling on Igor's back.

"Sic itur ad astra. Ad astra! Ad astra!" The chanting grew closer, the foreign words sounding malicious and threatening.

Igor spied the Dirigires and let out a wail. Surprised by his vocal prowess, Thorn cried out. The chanting stopped.

Oh bloody hell. They've seen us.

Thorn knew they had to run for cover, but by the time she'd rounded up her scattering tricorns, two figures were running towards her from the mist, trailing clouds of soot and chaff like ribbon-tails. She pulled out her barker and fired at one, but missed.

Quartz had told her stories of the Dirigire sect, for their occasional visits to London before the Wall was built brought much fanfare. Worshippers of the French engineer Blanchard, they fled persecution in France across the channel (many illegally) in contemptible flying balloons and built isolated cities high above the ground, striving for communion with Mama Helios, the sun goddess and Blanchard's supposed lover.

If the Stokers imbued the powers of soot and coal, and Brunel commanded his empire of iron, then the Dirigires were masters of the mechanism. The sect produced the finest clockwork devices in the world; complex engines that fit into the palm of the hand and wound and unwound the corners of the universe. Precise and intricate beyond comprehension, their magic swirled in every turning gear and swinging pendulum. It was said that in the hands of a skilled Dirigire priest, time and space became as loose and malleable as soft clay.

When he talked about his part in the Gauge War, Quartz would describe with awe their sky balloons –

fearful bulbous creations of smoke and steel, like the one rising before her this very moment – and their disdain for those who dwelt in the earth and mud. Stokers and Dirigires had long despised each other. Thorn assumed that the two men advancing toward her were not intending to inquire about the weather.

"*Arretez-vous!* Whoever you are!" The tallest one – clad in the jet-and-crimson robes of a Dirigire priest – pulled ahead of the other. He was gaining on her, vaulting through the wheat with unnatural speed.

Thorn gritted her teeth and drove after her tricorns, leaning as much weight on her cane and her sore ankle as she dared. Behind her the wheat cracked and rustled, and someone puffed and wheezed through unhealthy lungs.

But even those unhealthy lungs easily overcame Thorn's exhaustion. It wasn't long before she heard his footsteps right behind her. A hand clamped on her shoulder. Thorn screamed as the Dirigire pulled her down. She tried to swing her arm up to hit him with her pistol, but he pinned her arm behind her back. The sharp bone of a knee dug into her chest, and he yelled something foreign into her ear. Thorn reached for her barker, but another hand clamped her down. Someone threw a charcoal wool cloak over her face, stuffing the material in her mouth. She gagged and spluttered.

"How dare you trespass on my land and interrupt our ritual?" It was the voice of the priest, coarse and smoky and dripping with malice.

"Hey, Pierre, *regarde ça!*"

Igor barked and the other man – younger, with a soft, careful tone – yelped and jumped away as Bridget swung at him with her sharp horns.

"Those...they're from the swamps. You a Stoker?" Thorn remained silent. "*Je l'ai dit*, are you a Stoker?"

Pierre's rough hands shook her, jolting pain through her leg. She choked out an inaudible reply.

"Imagine, a Stoker, all the way out here. What shall we do with her, Frederique?"

"That's up to you, sir." The other voice sounded nervous.

The wool was yanked from her face. "Call your heathen beasts," the priest snarled in her ear.

"They're not hunting dogs. They aren't bound to my service." Thorn spat on his coat. Over his shoulder she saw Frederique attempting to approach Lurgette, arms raised in a gesture of surrender. The tricorn hissed and lowered her horns. The boy named Frederique stepped back, cautiously circling the tricorn.

The priest grabbed Thorn under the shoulders and hoisted her up. She winced as her ankle buckled beneath her, and sagged into his chest. Affronted, he yanked her hair, dragging her towards the bobbing iron monstrosity.

"Stop...hurting...argh!" Thorn's ankle snagged in the dead husks and she crumpled to the ground. Her scalp singed. When she opened one swollen eye she saw the Dirigire drop a clump of her hair, wiping his bloody hands across his robe.

Another pair of feet appeared. "What's a Stoker doing out here?"

Move voices, talking a mix of French and English. Thorn's head began to swim. "*Qu'allons-nous faire?* We can't leave her here."

"Barnaby, remove her iron and her satchel. She's clearly entered my property with ill intent."

"She's deranged," said another, sniffing. "And smelly."

"She's hurt." That was the voice of Frederique. The priest hushed him.

"*Oui*," said another, "and when she recovers? Don't

forget her demonic minions."

Thorn opened her mouth to protest, pushing and hawking at her throat, but all that emitted was an inhuman croak. She felt rough hands on her right shoulder, jerking her up to remove her pistol before pounding her face into the dirt.

"Take up a limb, gentlemen. We shall take her to Meliora. The Council will deal to her."

As the hands grabbed and tugged and twisted, and her babies bellowed in the background while the Dirigires clobbered them with their staffs, Thorn's mind swam with terror, and she passed out.

***

JAMES HOLMAN'S MEMOIRS, FIRST EDITION

"I've found one!"

Startled, I jerked backward and banged my knee against the underside of my desk. The correspondence I'd been writing on my noctograph soared from my hand and scattered across the floor. I felt Lurgo's frame lean on the arm of my leather chair, breathing heavy, excited gasps.

"By Galileo's tides, boy, can't you learn to knock?" I rubbed the offending knee.

"I've found a Stoker!" Lurgo cried, his tone both reverent and smug. "His name was Sooty, although he has a ponsy London name now. He left Graveyard over a year ago with Rex, only Rex claimed that Sooty was part of the underground Stoker network, and it doesn't look like that's true. He's a publican now at one of the dockside taverns. Julianne and I sat down for a pint, and I recognised him, completely by chance—"

"What do you want me to do about this?"

"I've asked him to meet us when he closes the pub. He shall arrive at three."

"You can't ask every scoundrel you find in the gutters over for supper, Lurgo. I did wish to go to bed at an early hour tonight."

"I need you to sit with me, Holman. I'm not certain how this meeting will proceed. It is strange that Sooty left the school, and he has changed since last I spoke to him. I fear he may not be sympathetic to our cause."

I sighed. My work would have to wait for another day. "Of course."

I had Lurgo help me retrieve my scattered papers, and I did a little work while he paced the room and mumbled about the Stokers under his breath.

At precisely three in the morning, the doorbell rang. Lurgo ran to answer it while I moved to the drawing room and set the kettle on the fire. I pulled my case of cigars from the box on the mantelpiece and set this beside the tea set on the table.

The lad who followed Lurgo into the room smelt of smoke and stale beer. He greeted me with a voice like leather, introducing himself as John Cromwell, and gave my hand a firm shake. We sat down around the empty fireplace and I proffered tea and cigars, which both Lurgo and John Cromwell accepted with grace.

"Lurgo says you're a publican?" My hands fumbled with the teapot. I hooked the tip of my index finger over the rim of the cup while I poured. When the scalding water bit my finger, I knew the cup was full, and I stirred in the sugar.

"That's correct. After my contract at the Crystal Palace finished, I was working as a kitchen boy when the previous publican disappeared with naught but a word,"

John Cromwell explained, "I've been fortunate to keep the patrons in good spirits, lest he should return."

"Any idea where he went?"

"None whatsoever." If he knew something, he hid it from his voice.

I shuffled forward in my seat. "I visited the Great Exhibition on the opening day. It is an astounding undertaking, one of the greatest collections of wonders in all the world. Tell me, what work did you do there?"

"I worked alongside the Royal Engineer," John's voice rose a little, his pitch revealing his pride. "I oversaw one of the work crews who erected the Crystal Palace, and when it opened, I ushered guests through the Engineering Hall. What news do you bring from Graveyard?"

John's words struck me as very odd. Lurgo and I figured that Rex had lied about the underground network of Stokers. And yet here was this boy, who was a Stoker through-and-through, and it looked as if Brunel was looking after him just fine.

"The situation is as dire as always. There was another dragon attack," Lurgo said. It sounded as if he was choosing his words carefully. "Several were killed, including Aaron Williams. Oswald is now in charge."

John Cromwell coughed violently. I could tell he was using the cough to mask his real reaction. After he cleared his throat, he said. "That is ill news. Oswald is not the right leader for the Stokers."

We puffed our cigars in silence, letting the thought of who the right leader is hang in the air.

Finally, Lurgo cleared his throat, and continued.

"I was sent to London with Rex Williams. We were supposed to join other Stokers that have been hiding underground in London—"

John shifted in his seat. "Where is Rex?"

"He is dead. And he acted very strangely up until his death. In fact, ever since his return from London he'd been plagued with ill thoughts. What happened here to haunt him so?"

"We passed into the city, no problems, and enrolled in the school. At first, everything was fine. I was excelling at my studies and had even made a few good friends. But Rex wasn't doing so well. He was obsessed with the Engine Ward. As soon as school finished he would run down to the abandoned district and clamber through the burned out ruins of the Chimney. It was as if he was searching for something. I didn't realise what, until the students started talking about smoke and lights coming from the Wall. The next day, I followed Rex to the Engine Ward, and saw with my own eyes that the Chimney was being rebuilt."

"What happened then?" Lurgo asked, his voice tight. I heard the chair creak as he leaned forward.

"I pressed Rex for information, and reluctantly he revealed to me that he had joined others in the tunnels beneath the Ward. He brought me there, and I found the people Rex called the London Stokers. But they were not of sound mind. They were homeless, desperate men and women, and they had been plied with booze and opium and Great Conductor knows what else, until they did not know their own minds any longer. They gnawed on lumps of lead and scratched at each other's skin. When I looked into Rex's eyes I realised that he had been indulging in the same vices, and that his mind was no longer his own. I told Rex that I wanted no part in his plans, and left him with his new people.

"Rex never came back to the school after that. I did not return to the Ward to look for him, but I kept an ear out for news of the Chimney. More walls had gone up, and steam poured from the vents leading to the underground tunnels. A fellow student, Samuel, lived in a house not far from the edge of the Ward, and he said that at night he could hear screaming coming from the vents. Something was *definitely* going on in Engine Ward, and Rex was mixed up in it.

"A few weeks after my visit, a man came to visit me at the school. The headmaster called me into his office, and then left me alone with a tall, willowy man with the most intelligent, penetrating eyes I'd ever seen. He was dressed in a smart suit and stovepipe hat, which he took from his head and placed on the table in front of me with his right hand. His left hand he kept tucked into his jacket.

"'The headmaster tells me you're the most intelligent boy in your year,' he said. His voice was like honey. I nodded, too nervous to speak. 'And you have a keen interest in engineering,' he continued. I nodded again.

"'That is interesting, for a Stoker such as yourself could find themselves in grave danger if it was discovered he were studying engineering within the city walls.' The stranger leaned back in his chair, and the smile he gave me was casual. My blood froze. How did he know I was a Stoker? So of course, I had to listen to what he said next.

"'Don't look so worried. I have a job for you.' He explained that he was the Royal Engineer, and that if I went with him, I would be a member of his elite engineering team. And that he would look after me and ensure I found suitable employment after the job was finished. It was too good an opportunity to pass up, so I left the school and went with him."

"What did you do on the Great Exhibition?"

"Oh, this and that." I waited for John to elaborate,

but he did not. "I only worked with him for a couple of months. After that, he didn't require my services any longer, but he was good to his word. He helped me find work on the docks, and now I have my pub. It's a good life, better than I could have hoped for in Graveyard."

I bit down on my tongue, struggling to hold back the urge to strike the man. The tone in Lurgo's voice changed, and I could tell he chose his words carefully before he spoke.

"Do you know the Wall now stalks across the countryside, like a living thing?"

"I know the Messiah has new plans, and he requires the network of Walls running across England to bring them to fruition." John, too, phrased his words with care.

"Do you not feel this is...unnecessary?"

John laughed. "Of course it's necessary. The Metal Messiah is the Great Conductor's stationmaster on earth. Surely he too must have a transportation network worthy of a God?"

"I don't understand."

"The Messiah sees beyond railways, beyond machines that must be powered by steam and coal. His world is one of symbiosis between man and machine, where each feeds off the other, part of a great system of life."

"Do you not think this symbiosis...frightening?" Lurgo pressed.

"In the hands of the Metal Messiah? Oh, no. It's just what the Stokers have wanted for so many years, don't you think?" The chair crinkled as John rose. "Thank you for the brandy, and the cigars. But I must be getting back to my establishment. I shall inform him of your arrival. He will be grateful for new acolytes."

"I wouldn't worry," Lurgo said hastily. "We won't be

in London long."

John was silent for a few moments. "Surely you're not leaving the city?"

"We have no more business here."

"I don't think you understand, Lurgo. There are Boilers guarding every exit from the city. Brunel does not wish anyone to leave London; he wants the whole city to be present for his first great miracle."

"Then if the Messiah wishes us to stay, I'm sure our business will wait." Lurgo rose too, his voice calm. "Would you like me to show you the door?"

"No, I will see myself out. Goodnight, gentlemen."

John disappeared into the hall, and a few moments later, we heard the front door creak open and shut again. It was only then I let out the breath I had been holding.

I heard the fabric tense as Lurgo slumped into the armchair. "Well," he said, "that was illuminating."

"It appears your mission to recruit the London Stokers is doomed before it even began."

"Sooty always craved power," Lurgo said. "I can see now that he would be an excellent choice for Brunel. Rex, on the other hand, was so easily swayed by his emotions. Do you think Brunel somehow plied him and the others with some substance to turn them into Sinkers?"

"I think that very likely. John was lucky to have escaped that fate."

"But do you think the Sunken could be convinced to turn against Brunel?"

"No, Lurgo, I do not. The Sunken have had their minds stripped away. They are no longer human, but have been stripped back to base instincts. They have only two desires – to feed, and to kill."

"But if I can find the Sunken he has made…" Lurgo

talked excitedly. He didn't seem to have noticed I had spoken. "I can make them understand. They would join me."

"Do you really believe that?"

"I have no choice. I *have* to believe something."

***

Hours later, or days, or weeks, Thorn awoke. Warmth surrounded her, and familiar smells; the acrid tang of smoke churning through dirty stacks, and juicy meat burning on the fire. In the distance, the chugs and puffs of a steam engine, straining to power something or other.

She sat up, expecting the low roof of the Turret landing to close over her head. Instead, cogs spun over her, folding back in on themselves in a complex mechanism that gently rocked her platform like a mechanical wet-nurse. She gazed in wonder at the hissing contraption, following the filigree of gears with her eyes, expecting to find some kind of engine, remarkable or whimsical or deadly.

Instead, she faced a vast cloud, a splatter of grey and blue that seemed at once diaphanous and solid, creeping towards her with villainous certainty.

She screamed.

Her head felt light. *I'm falling.* The cloud loomed in front of her. She waited for her brain to explode from her body.

Nothing happened, save the coruscating waves of blue-grey mist circling and diving betwixt the spinning gears. Thorn shrieked and stumbled back, further into the unfamiliar darkness.

A hand clamped across her face. She swung to hit her

assailant, but whoever it was grabbed her arm and bent it around her back.

"Stop squirming," a strong male voice commanded, his French accent dripping with malice. "You nearly killed yourself."

"I'll kill *you* if you don't tell me where I am, and how I get out. And where are my tricorns?"

The voice tsked. "You're in no position to threaten me."

"Think of it more as a spurious boast."

"*Oui*, you're a clever girl. Which of your questions do you wish me to answer first?"

"Where am I?"

"We call this place Meliora, the Land of the Better."

"Oh gee," Thorn said, her voice dripping with sarcasm. "That's cleared all the confusion right up."

"You're in the city of the Dirigires, high above the Duffield Frith. We command excellent views over Yorkshire, if you can see that far down."

"Does the Queen know of this city?"

"She knows of a French lord who owns many acres of forest in the Yorkshire Dales. What he does with that forest is his own business."

"Where are my tricorns?"

"Can't you smell that fire?"

Thorn's heart slammed against her chest. Her fist shot up and launched at his face. Because of the awkward angle, the blow glanced off his cheek, and he laughed. She wrestled with renewed vigour, but he merely drew her arms up higher. She had no hope of escape. *They're hurting my babies...my sweet little ones...*

"Cease your movements, you'll upset the mechanisms."

"You...idiots!" she sobbed. "Those babies were our

only hope."

"Are you speaking in riddles again, Stoker?"

"Surely you've noticed it…the Wall, the charred fields, the frightening figures wandering across the landscape devouring lead and iron?" Out of the corner of her eye Thorn saw the barrel of her captor's barker flapping uselessly against the side of the platform, the strap looped over a delicate screw. *If only I could reach it…*

Her captor fell silent, and Thorn knew she'd struck a chord. She continued, "I know how to defeat those creatures and the Boilers that command them. I have the key to England's freedom and you…you're eating them for supper!"

"Those fat beasts of yours are the saviours of England?" He laughed again; a cruel sound. His fingernails dug into her shoulder. She searched her mind for the voices of her babies, but it was silent. Eerily, horribly silent. Thorn gritted her teeth and prepared to strike. *That is it. I'm not staying here any longer.*

With all the strength she could muster, Thorn swung out her arm at the mechanism, dislodging a drive pin. The cog spun free, upsetting the timing and causing another cog to jam. With a sound like hundreds of barkers exploding, tines snapped and ground into the cogs, the pressure belts slipped and the mechanism groaned its disapproval. Something hissed behind her and the platform juddered and tilted to the left.

"What have you done?" her captor screamed, fighting to maintain his footing.

Thorn slipped from her assailant's fingers as he leaned out to inspect the whining machinery.

She dived for his barker. He dived for her. The platform pitched forward at an alarming angle.

"You've broken it!"

Almost there, almost got it… Thorn jammed her fingers under the barrel. He kicked her swollen ankle and she cried out, jerking her arms up and knocking the pistol over the side.

"No!" She scrambled forward. The platform lurched further. Now she had a view of the ground, or what one could misconstrue as ground from her position. Through a maze of swirling, tinkling gears and mechanisms the pistol banged and clattered, upsetting the counterweights and buckling delicate tines. Finally the clatter ceased, and a flea-sized barker disappeared into the mists. She didn't hear it hit the ground.

The mechanism groaned, clanking and whirring in desperation as it tried to right itself, as it tried to set its tines and regain its meticulous task. As the platform tipped nearly vertical, Thorn grabbed the outer edge, wrapping her whole body around the steel truss the way she'd seen Bella and Alberto clamber through the trees. Beside her, the man clung with one hand to the opposite edge, his other reaching for a disengaged beam.

"I can do worse," Thorn snarled. "I will bring your floating city crashing to the earth, if you don't take me to my babies."

The man stared at her for a few moments, sweat slicking the surface of his face.

"Your hand is slipping," she reminded him.

He sighed. "Grab onto that escapement arm behind you. Swing it over here." She stretched out, wrapped her fingers around the arm, and pulled it over. The man heaved his body up onto it, then reached down to help her. Thorn shook her head.

"I'm not going to drop you."

"I'd rather not take the chance, thank you." After a couple of tries, she managed to swing herself onto the escapement.

"*Suivez-moi, s'il vous plait.*" He skirted along the thin beam. Thorn followed, taking timid steps, trying to avoid breaking anything and keep a close eye on the man at the same time.

He descended a mesh staircase. Thorn winced as she rested her weight on her bad ankle and stepped after him. As her weight shifted, the stairs moved, rocking forward on their clockwork pinions. Each minute oscillation wound her down into the heart of the mechanism.

She gazed around herself in awe. Clockwork mainsprings coiled like power-driven vines around pillars of iron, driving the movement trains that swung overhead. The entire clockwork city existed in the bowels of those movements, an endless expanse of living mechanisms bound together with infinitesimal tines and the continuous *tick-tock, tick-tock* of the turning gears.

"How does this city stay afloat?" she asked.

"Now you want to talk?" The man sneered.

Thorn said nothing. Her cheeks burned with anger.

"The engines at the centre of the city power the balloons, which hold Meliora in the sky," her captor said, pointing up into the mist. "The furnaces fill the balloons and create the mists. Everything here is perfectly balanced; even the people here exist as intricate elements of the great machine. We can't have outsiders like you stomping around and messing things up."

Foods and goods tumbled through complex conveyers, bursting forth from lead bowls that passed from pinion to pinion. Hammocks rolled away in steel cylinders, guarded by the sharpened pendulum of a giant clock. Staircases like the one Thorn stood on moved like waterfalls above and below her. As people passed by they waved at her captor; he acknowledged them with a bow of his head, but spoke not a word.

They sank deeper into the mist. Thorn sucked in her breath as the burning smell grew stronger. Her mind frozen, she could not sense the babies. She bit back the fear that threatened to overwhelm her.

I won't be afraid, I shall be angry. If they've done anything to my babies...they'll know the wrath of a Stoker, even if I die here...

The staircase clipped on its tines and stopped. Thorn's feet slid onto a steel platform. The misshapen branches of an aging oak twisted around the outer pylons; each strangled leaf curling, gasping for air.

Through the bleak mist she saw draped figures scrambling across the platform. Flames licked the gray haze; a cooking fire. Two hands appeared under her face, clutching a delicately-painted china platter heaped with meat.

"Roasted tricorn?" someone bellowed.

Thorn spat on the plate, jamming her shoulder into the exuberant chef. He buckled, crying in surprise as she dashed his culinary masterpiece on the floor. Thorn pushed through an ocean of dark-cloaked men, tears brimming in her eyes.

The flames. The fire. A carcass roasting on the spit, it's ribcage split open and slabs of fatty breast already stripped from its innards. Three white horns gleamed in the firelight. Bridget, it was Bridget.

"No, no, no..." She sank to her knees.

Laughter arose, but Thorn no longer heard anything around her. Despair rang in her ears, tunnelled through her brain, tore and gutted her heart. She clawed her hair, pounded her useless arms against the steel grate. *I thought I could save Graveyard, save England? I couldn't even save my babies...*

Over the laughter, over the echoes of her own failure, there rose a familiar whine. It was not mechanical, nor the steady click of a pendulum, but...

Thorn peered through the grating, squinting through the mist. "Igor..."

Her mind reached where her voice and vision wouldn't; down, down through the mists and machines. Down there she could hear them singing a low, whining dirge – a requiem for their departed friend.

Hope amidst my sorrows. A rose amongst all the thorns.

She reached out as if in a daze, and pushed her hands into the barrel holding the fire. The heat was so intense it was like ice – numbing her skin. She drew out an oak branch. Sap bled from the wounds dealt by the axe. Pitch dribbled down the shaft and the flames licked her makeshift torch, tugging at the flaking bark, pulling and curling to reveal the tough heart beneath. Thorn's hands stung from where the fire had touched her, but she did not care.

Hands reached for her. Thorn swung blindly with the torch, watching with satisfaction as the flailing flames caught on their flimsy robes. "Stay back, you foolish gammys! I will talk to your leader."

"Imagine, she dares to make demands of us—"

"Silence! I *will* talk to your leader." Her voice bounced from a thousand tiny mirrors, through a thousand escapements, into a thousand funnels. She spoke as a god herself, in her husky, soot-raked throat. In their city of the heavens, she spoke as the earth and the flames.

A Dirigire priest stepped forward, pulling his cloak from his face. "I shall speak to her."

Thorn squinted at his smooth cheeks and clipped blonde curls, recognising him from the fields. "Bugger off, *Frederique*. I'm not here to talk to a *boy*. I want your leader, the landowner who abducted me this morning. Where is Pierre? I would speak to him!"

A profound silence was her answer.

"No? He does not wish to join your party. Pity that, for I would have him know that he has doomed you all."

"This girl speaks riddles and falsehoods. She would seek to sully the name of our most hallowed priest!"

"He's murdered my tricorns. You're all enjoying a fine feast of the very beasts that would have saved you. Or do you all expect you are safe up here? Do you honestly believe your flimsy walls of balloons and pinions and your shroud of mist will stop them? Do you know that your fields have been burnt? Do you know Brunel's stinging rain will invade your city, and turn this ethereal mist to poison? Do you know your master and his acolytes secretly attempt to escape your clockwork prison? Ask *him*." She jabbed the torch – nicely blazing now – at the youth. "He was there today."

"It's all lies," someone spat.

"No, it isn't." Frederique's face turned red. Thorn jumped. She hadn't expected him to agree.

"*Frederique!*" a woman hissed.

"No. Miriam, this stranger speaks the truth. I've seen the fields with my own eyes. I was there today as Pierre and Barnaby attempted to set Blanchard's dirigible in flight. I have heard them talking of escaping back to France."

"Frederique!"

"No one has flown that machine since our God first crossed to our shores from England. It's blasphemy to suggest—"

"He has worked on the dirigible in secret," another acolyte insisted. "He has encased it in armour and fuelled it with the rancid soot of the earth. I have seen him—"

"Blasphemy!"

"If you'd seen what those ghoulish contraptions have done to our fields, you would not dismiss her so. This woman speaks the truth. Meliora is not safe!"

"I've been to London and travelled all over the countryside," Thorn said. "I've seen the Wall and what it can do. It murdered my betrothed and my friends. I'm going to stop it. I *know* how to stop it. If you'll just let me go, I can stop it before it gets to you."

"She speaks sense," said Frederique. "We should consider—"

Someone pushed through the crowd. Pierre's thin lips smacked with a scowl and his wild eyes flashed as he grabbed Thorn by the arm and pulled her forward.

"See this witch?" he bellowed. "See how she attempts to control you with her words? As my most gifted acolyte, I thought you, Frederique, would be able to see through her sorceress lies!"

"I don't think she's a witch, Pierre. I think she's—"

"Silence!" Pierre tossed Thorn to the man who'd guarded her before. "You've been lax in your duty, François. You should have clamped her tongue. Take her to a more secure prison. When we've eaten our meal, the Council shall decide how best to dispose of a witch."

***

François took Thorn to another prison; strapping her into a winch and lowering her down into the mists, until her feet touched a small, flimsy platform that seemed precariously balanced upon the thinnest wires. They had no need of chains; the platform seemed suspended in midair, with nothing within arms reach that could support her weight. Tendrils of willow entwined the grating, though she saw no tree through the mists.

The clicking tines and cogs suspending it creaked under her weight. If Thorn moved even a foot, she could knock the balance and fall into the mist. She could not lay down without her head and knees dangling over the edges of the platform.

Through the wisps of fog – now notably darkening in colour – she saw workmen swinging through the maze of tines, setting about righting the mess she'd made. They sang as they worked. Songs of great hope and abandon.

"*Meliora, alis volat propriis…ad astra, ad astra…*"

She closed her eyes, finding the darkness a welcome release from the grey shroud. *So this is Holman's existence behind the veil of mists.*

With nothing else to do but wait for them to kill her, Thorn cast out with her mind, trying to see without seeing, searching for her lost babies. She focused on her breathing the way Aaron had instructed, and tried to sink into herself, into the platform, into the mist. *Igor, Nicholas, Lurgette…if you can hear me, you can get out…save yourselves.*

The platform shuddered.

Thorn's hands flew to her sides. She tore at the truss on the platform. *Please hold, please hold, please hold…*

Something sharp jammed into her backside. Thorn winced, and slowly turned her head.

A metal truss swung from the mist and hit her again. Behind the truss, two orbs glowed, and blinked, accompanied by a low whine.

"Igor!"

Thorn's heart soared at the sound of his whine. He responded by butting the truss into her back again.

She had no way of knowing if it would support her weight, or if Igor even knew what he was doing. Even if she could clamber off the platform, she had no idea how to find her way to the ground again, if there even *was* a ground. But right then, she didn't care. All she wanted to do was get closer to her beloved baby.

The platform sagged, bringing Thorn's stomach with it. She snapped back to reality. Igor had dislodged one of the split pins. The others would go soon too, if she didn't do something.

She lifted her arms back over her shoulder and grasped them around the pipe. Bending herself up onto her knees, she slowly unfolded her left leg and placed it on the edge of the platform.

A tine slipped, springing into the mist.

Thorn shrieked. The platform gave another jolt. Her heart plummeted. *The other leg.* She lifted it over the other, and slowly turned her body over. The platform pitched backward. Thorn adjusted her grip on the swinging pipe and leapt off the platform, kicking her legs up and pulling herself onto the pipe in time to see the platform clatter down into the mist.

She inched backwards. Her foot hit the iron chain that held the pipe. She leaned over her shoulder, saw Igor only two feet from her, feet firmly planted on another, thicker platform. Summoning her courage, she reached up and clasped the chain, swinging her legs into midair and stretching for the edge. Her foot grazed steel and she leaned further, catching her toes in the grating and swinging herself onto the steel.

Thorn's heart thundered in her chest as she lay still on a solid surface, gathering her composure. Igor butted her face with his cold beak. She patted behind his frill, listening for signs anyone nearby had heard her escape.

But there was nothing, save the rapture of tinkers and ticks.

Thorn glanced around the platform – five foot square and wonderfully, gloriously robust. To her left she heard the click of an ascending staircase. *That's probably how he got up here.*

Relief flooded her, and Igor's thoughts suddenly entered her mind. She saw him mentally retracing his steps, readying himself to lead her back down the staircase to the others.

Igor nudged her again. Thorn followed his gaze, searching the gloom for the other tricorns. "If they're down there, then we must go there also."

Igor pushed the gear train with his beak, jamming the movement. Above them, several of the lights flickered out. He clambered onto the clockwork structure and hobbled over the gear teeth and brackets – mangling several in the process – until he reached the staircase. Stepping gingerly onto the moving platform, he sat down to wait for her, his enormous torso gradually shifting out of her vision.

Thorn followed, crawling over the mechanisms and stepping onto the stair. She ducked as a pendulum swung overhead, clicking into the verge escapement and pushing the staircase along. She tugged Igor's tail. *Down, we have to find the others.*

The oscillating platforms confused Igor. As he leapt from one to another, that jammed mechanism waited for him. He kept looking back for her, losing the ground he was making. Thorn's ankle throbbed with renewed passion. She forced herself to push harder, but she couldn't beat the staircase. She slumped onto the stair, wiping the sweat from her face. The cold fingers of the mist raked her face as she trundled by.

His confusion turned to fear. He didn't understand why she wouldn't follow.

"Carry me, Igor." She clasped his frill and pulled her aching body onto his back. He groaned under the sudden burden. As she pulled her arms around his neck, he set off, instinctively grasping what she would have him do.

Down the stairs they barrelled; an injured girl on her tiny monster, scampering for freedom like a fly from a steam room. Thorn had no time to be frightened of the blinding mist, nor worry for the eldritch blue and green lights that flickered as they passed.

As they descended further, the mist grew dense and smoky. Thorn spluttered, and Igor wheezed and slowed his gait. The lights dimmed, obscured by the profuse fog. The ticking of the gears had slowed, and now sounded inside her head as dull, rusted clunks.

Her lungs filled with foul smoke, and she broke into convulsions. Igor took one final leap and landed on something – Thorn couldn't see what – that creaked in protest and rocked dangerously.

Brass and iron buckled under his feet, and she heard tines tinkle away into the void. Igor followed the tines, plunging off the edge. Thorn screamed as she plummeted through the murk. Barbs and gears struck her back and arms.

Igor landed with a crunch. Gears screeched in protest. He whined, and his voice was joined by other whines, each a blessing that eased Thorn's fluttering heart.

"My babies, oh, we've found you!" She stumbled through the miasma, touching each in turn, stroking their frills, petting their rough skin, wiping away the fluids that wept from their wounds. She counted seven – all alive and breathing, save poor Bridget. Relief erupted in her skull as she sensed the tricorns' understanding of her return.

Thorn's hand brushed something rough, solid. Not metal nor tricorn. She investigated it with her hands, as she'd seen Holman do. A tree trunk. She found branches – ruinous twisted effigies of a nature abhorred – and crisp leaves, hardened by death. Someone had nailed thick metal grates into the surface of the branches, forming wide stairs.

Will it hold us all? There was only one way to find out. Thorn swung herself down, catching a mouthful of dust. "Can you follow?" she spluttered at the tricorns. Their heads crowded around her. She pulled herself down. "This way."

The metal staircase felt thick and satisfyingly sturdy. Chips of bark flew overhead as the tricorns stumbled down after her, their hoofed feet finding grip between the metal and the wide, wrinkled branches. On they climbed, stumbling through the underbelly of the clockwork city. With each footstep, Thorn pulled her tricorns forward with the sense inside her mind. She felt stronger, more in control of her power than usual.

No lights shone in the mists, and all the air swelled with dust and soot and black, corrupted filth.

Even the skies are not safe, for if a God commands it, men shall destroy the entire world in pursuit of relentless mechanical commandments.

To her right, something clanged. Thorn stopped, her chest tightening. She strained to see through the mist, hoping she hadn't stumbled upon a guard post—

"*Qui est là?*"

Oh, no.

Thorn remained frozen, holding in her aching lungs. *Be still,* she willed her tricorns. *There's danger ahead.*

"I said, who goes there? I can hear you breathing." The voice sounded familiar. Something metal scraped the tree, and Thorn felt air whoosh past her face.

"*Vous?*"

The voice gasped from directly in front of her, only a few feet away. Thorn fell back against the trunk. She recognised Frederique's voice.

"Please don't hurt us," she whispered into the mist. She raised her hands to her face, ready to fend off any blows that might come from the mist.

"I will not."

The metal scraped again, and she felt him inching along the branch toward her. Behind her head, Igor growled.

"Stop! I can't see you. Igor will bite if he thinks you're attacking me."

"I'm holding out my hand." He moved closer, and his fingers brushed her shoulder, warm against the cold tendrils of mist. She reached up and clasped him, and he pulled her forward gently, until she stepped onto a metal platform.

"This is a wide platform. They should all fit if they bunch together."

Its okay, babies. He's a friend. I think. Igor and the other tricorns followed behind. A sudden gust of heat shot through the platform, and a hissing sound came from above. Thorn gasped and stumbled back.

"Don't be afraid. It's the engines refilling the balloons. There's a chair behind you if you want to rest."

"You're not going to turn me in?"

Frederique snorted. "To Pierre? Hardly. You're the most exciting thing to happen up here for a long time. Do you have a name?"

"Thorn. I'm called Thorn."

A rough hand grasped hers. It reminded her of Joel's somehow, warm and friendly. She bit her lip.

"It is a pleasure to meet you, Thorn. Here, have this." He pressed an object into her hands. She sniffed. It was a bowl of something warm and delicious-smelling.

"It's *Soupe à l'Oignon* – onion soup. Nothing much, I'm afraid, but you'll need to eat something."

Thorn raised the bowl and, after a few false tries, managed to pour some onto her tongue. The strong onion soup burnt her throat, but she gulped the bowl down. Her stomach growled. Frederique refilled her bowl.

When she'd finished she set the bowl at her feet and folded her hands across her lap. "Thank you for believing me."

"Don't thank me. It's easy to believe someone who's telling the truth."

She didn't really have an answer for that. "How did you come to live with the Dirigires? Your accent sounds different."

He sighed. "I grew up in London. My father worked as a Navvy on Stephenson's railways, then as a clockmaker – the finest clockmaker in all the world. When the Gauge War entered London, he sent my mother and I to Paris, and ordered us never to return.

"I came to London several weeks ago, to help my father finish his display for the Great Exhibition. His invention – a clockwork eye that allows a blind man to see again – was to be his crowning achievement, but it was not to be."

"What happened?"

"The Royal Engineer wanted my father's exhibition space. I don't know why. At first, he offered us money, more money than we could ever dream of seeing, but my father refused. I returned from Mass one morning to find our apartments torn apart, the device stolen and my father missing. The Dirigire Elders told me it was no longer safe for me in the city, so I came here.

"I've seen the Wall moving across the countryside, and it frightens me. But no one *listens*. As far as they're concerned – even if he *has* returned – Brunel's an inferior god, incapable of world domination. In reality, they don't want to interfere with English matters in case the Queen should deport them all back to France. But I won't stand by and do nothing any longer, not if you really *can* destroy him. I've been worrying all night, trying to think of a plan to free you, but I see you've no need of my help."

Thorn smiled. "When did you notice the Wall out here?"

"A few days ago, but it could've been here for weeks beforehand. Every day it creeps closer." He shuddered. "I don't like it. I thought I'd left the suffering behind in London."

"What about Pierre?"

"He's dangerous. I think he knows something he's not telling. He used to work for Brunel, you know, back when he was the Lord Protector, Brunel gave Blanchard this land. It rightfully belongs to the Crown, but they have not tried to take it back. Pierre was the first Dirigire priest. Our God Blanchard gifted his dirigible to Pierre, and Pierre flew it all over the country, gathering followers and artisans from every corner of France, forming a cloistered community of artisans from which Meliora eventually arose."

"When Brunel comes for Meliora, on which side will Pierre fight?"

"Honestly, I do not know. Several months ago, he

took all our dirigibles away and hid them – he does not want anyone to fly away from here, but I don't know why. I know only that he's the only one with a dirigible, and he wishes to escape before the fighting even begins."

Weariness overtook Thorn, seeping into every muscle. She closed her eyes, forcing herself to stay alert. "I feel like a tiny mouse charged with a King's duty. If by some miracle the Stokers listen to me, we cannot on our own defeat Brunel's machines. I would need every man, woman and child in all of England to stand with me. With *me!*'s utterly hopeless." She buried her face in her hands.

"You underestimate your fellow countrymen, Thorn. Whatever old feuds we may have, none of us wish to be trapped between metal Walls, at the mercy of whatever monsters Brunel would throw at us. If you will fight him, Thorn, we will fight him also, with or without Pierre."

Thorn heard his knee land on the grating as he knelt beside her, and his warm hands found her and wrapped her into his arms. She buried her head in his shoulder, not crying, but letting the enormity of her task settle in her heart, binding her resolve. He smelt sweet and fresh, just like Joel. She bit back the urge to run her hands across his warm cheek, and press her lips to his—

Overhead, a bell tinkled. Frederique's head snapped up. "That's the signal for the changing of the guard. You cannot stay here."

Grateful to shake away her amorous thoughts, Thorn stood up and moved to the edge of the platform. Only the cool haze greeted her, shrouding her descent in milky blindness. She shuddered.

At her feet Igor whimpered, butting her leg with his sharp nose horn. She cried out as her knee buckled and she pitched forward, flailing into the mist.

Something clamped on her arm and yanked her back, wrenching her shoulder. She toppled over Igor and landed sprawled across the platform.

"Are you okay?" Frederique grabbed both her hands and helped her to her feet.

Thorn struggled to catch her breath. "Yes, thanks to you."

"You must keep control of those animals. They'll be the death of you."

"They'll be the saviours of all of us, provided I can return to Graveyard alive. How do I escape the city?"

"You must continue down the staircase for a good while longer," Frederique said, not moving his fingers from hers. "You'll find plenty of branches and platforms to grip. I've disabled the outer alarms, so you'll escape undetected. Once you reach the forest, move quickly, for Pierre can scour great distances with ease in the dirigibles. Oh, I almost forgot." He bent down, and pushed something into her arms. It was her rucksack. It felt heavier than she remembered, and something unfamiliar clanged inside. "I'm sorry, I cannot give your weapon back, but I've placed some food and milk inside."

"Will you be punished for my escape?" Thorn didn't think she could handle leaving knowing that Frederique would be hurt.

"I don't know. They cannot prove I helped you. But Pierre is displeased with me. The elders don't like me – I'm forever questioning their stupid rituals – but many of the other acolytes follow me. If you ever need us—"

Thorn squeezed his hand. "I'll remember that."

Frederique helped her over the edge of the platform and counted her seven tricorns as they bounded after her. She called goodbye and continued through the miasma.

Hours seemed to pass as they descended further into the gloom. As she dragged her throbbing ankle over another knotted stump, it occurred to Thorn that she might be going the wrong way.

Maybe I'm heading further within the earth, down into the furnaces that power the tides and shake the mountains. The curse...it's come full circle.

And then she *saw* her hands, wrapped in lacerations and stained with soot. The mist was thinning.

Thorn lowered herself onto the next branch. *Yes*, she could see the faint outlines of her feet, and the twisted branches and metal brackets she rested on. Far above her, the clockwork city ticked away, oblivious to her escape.

Another thirty feet and Thorn could see colours again. She appeared to be in a forest, although it was like no other forest she'd ever visited before. From her branch she saw hundreds of oaks, taller than any she could imagine. Oaks that grew from each other, roots twisting back inside themselves, drawing nutrients from their brothers like cannibal parasites. Corruptions distorted from the air and the steel.

But far below, there were patches of green, and real English fog – not these polluted miasmas – puffing through the foliage. She smiled; a weary smile, for there was still a great distance to climb, but Thorn felt like nothing was beyond her reach now.

The tricorns clomped after her, their steps careless now that they had full capacity of their vision. Thorn let them clamber ahead, enjoying the surge in her heart as she watched the sun nudging below the western canopy, a glowing beacon upon her journey, lighting her way home.

Soon, Thorn too fell below the canopy and rejoined the earth-rooted trees and the rain-cleansed air. The tricorns danced through the hawthorn, heedless of her cries to cease as they rejoiced in the triumph. Thorn laughed with them, and she set off into the west, trailing the dappled path of the setting sun.

***

The sun peeked over the Wall, sliding shafts of light across the fields of brown-grey potatoes and grain. They'd walked nonstop for three days, leaving the dale behind them as they crossed more ash-fields.

The tricorns now stood over four feet high, and Thorn could find no wall or valley or barn large enough to hide them, so she walked them boldly through villages and across farms, hoping their size and ferocious horns would deter any would-be assassins. They followed in single file behind her, nipping each other's tails and pouncing on unsuspecting foxes.

Every step tore at her swollen ankle and drove her muscles past their limit. She raked her fingernails through the mud in her hair, in her pockets, in her breeches, under her eyelids.

When the daylight passed under the horizon, and she could no longer place one foot in front of the other, Thorn dragged herself a couple of miles from the last town and collapsed by the roadside. Too exhausted to bother with the scraps of food in her rucksack, or to even set one of her empty jars down to collect rainwater to drink, Thorn tucked her legs to her chest and closed her eyes. She thought of Graveyard, so far away. *I wish I could open my eyes again and be standing in the Narrow.* The tricorns curled themselves around her, their thick skin shielding her from the incessant rain. She faded into the night, not sure whether she slept or dreamed or simply drifted.

Thorn grew cold.

Her eyes fluttered open. A light bobbed close to her head – not sunlight – darker and more cruel. Her tricorns were gone, and rain pelted her sodden clothes.

"Stoker," a voice hissed in her ear.

Thorn bolted upright, nearly piercing herself on a long dagger pointing directly at her throat. *What is going on? Who is after me now? And why do they know I am a Stoker?* She squinted into the gloom; six men, their faces stained with soot, leered over her as they brought their argand lamp. She winced away from the heat.

"I could burn those pretty cheeks right off," the man holding the knife whispered, stroking her face with a rough hand. His breath stank of alcohol and rancid meat.

"I…"

"Oh, don't be afraid. You can talk to us now. Get all your talking done before we rip your tongue right from your pretty mouth."

Thorn gulped back her terror. "What do you want? I don't have money."

"We don't want money, *Stoker.*" He pulled up the sleeve of his greatcoat and thrust his hand under the light. "Perhaps you recognise this?"

A deep scar marred the cracked shin of his palm – a crude tattoo of a railway track. A symbol Stephenson's Navvies had adopted to honour those lost in the Gauge War.

"Ah." The Navvy leaned in even closer. "You see now, dontchya? You see why we're very interested in a little Stoker girl sleeping on the road beside our territory, dontchya? You see why we'll be confiscating your weapon and hanging you as a spy, dontchya?"

"The Gauge War is over – you *won*, remember? Your rail network runs nearly the length of the countryside, while the Stokers are banished to the swamps. What would the Stokers possibly gain from spying on your pox-ridden Navvy piss-hole?'

Thorn pushed aside her fear, and cast her mind out, searching for her tricorns. She knew the men weren't any match for her beasts, if only she could locate them and get them to help her. Sure enough, her mind snapped into Igor's, and she found the other tricorns nearby. They had heard the men and had hid behind a low stone wall, just thirty feet from the road's edge. *Stay there,* she told him. *Wait for me to call you.*

Her words seemed to amuse the man. "Either you're a very convincing spy, or a very stupid girl. We've seen that cursed black train, running on broad gauge on top of that whirring Wall like some kind of locomotive for the damned, cutting through our territories without authority, pulling up our lines near as soon as we lay them. I know that's bloody Stoker work, and I know you're a Stoker, and the two things ain't no coincidence. Now get up, you're coming with us."

"No, I really don't think I am." Thorn *pushed* with her mind, sending her command out through her sense. *Now, babies, now!*

The man opened his mouth to reply, but Lurgette knocked him aside, pinning him to the ground with her thick front legs. The dagger sailed from his hand, and Thorn bent down and picked it up. Igor and Bernard barrelled toward the other men, who scattered, crying out in fear. The others stood side by side, forming a protective wall around Thorn, heads lowered and horns bared.

"What in Great Conductor's name are these?" the man under Isobella wheezed.

"They're tricorns," Thorn said. "They are creatures of the swamps, and they obey me. I am taking them to London to fight Brunel."

"Bollocks. Your wretched god died nineteen years ago, and even if he were still alive, you'd be running to him like a child to her Daddy."

"Brunel's no god of mine," Thorn spat back. "And he was dead, but now he has returned. Although they call him the Royal Engineer now, so I could understand how you might have overlooked this fact. He has infiltrated the palace and built the railway that builds itself and resurrected the Sunken and the Boilers and murdered my people and destroyed the name of my father and I *will* have justice for his crimes."

"She speaks the truth, Sam," one of the other men said. "I've seen them what builds that railway – and they are no Stokers."

"My son returned from the south just yesterday," another said. "He was going to Brighton to visit his Ma, but he couldn't travel on the train. He said a mechanical giant stood on the ramp to the black train, and hissed at him till he backed away."

Sam scowled. "We'd better take her back to Second Works. There's only one man that can tell us whether she speaks the truth or not."

"I don't see any reason to go with you, what with you threatening to hang me and all."

"If you really are intending to fight Brunel, and rid the countryside of that cursed Wall, then Mr. Stephenson would not want us to let you on your way without meeting you."

"That's fine, but he comes to me. I'm not walking into

the heart of a Navvy stronghold – I'm not stupid."

"Very well. If you and your—" Sam searched for the word, "—*creatures* would follow us, I will see you meet with Mr. Stephenson."

***

Sam led Thorn a little way down the road, and up a dirt path she would never have noticed in the early gloom of morning. The sun had began to rise – though she could never see it through the clouds – and it cast a fuzzy light on the world, blurring the edges of shapes and illuminating the green overalls worn by Sam and his friends. They rounded a bramble-thick corner, and Sam pointed to the town ahead.

Second Works – the name for this particular shanty town - stretched for a mile or more across the muddy fields, cloistered behind a high chain fence and impressive iron gates, flanked by multi-barrelled volley guns and men with stern expressions. It was modelled off the main Navvy stronghold, Forth Street Works, which was located further north. Beyond the hastily-erected lean-tos and shacks, the first rays of dull sunlight danced off machinery and iron-roofed shacks.

"You wait here," Sam pointed to a dry patch of earth five hundred yards from the gate, just out of range of the guns. "We'll return with the boss."

For all of his gruffness, Sam was as good as his word. He and his men trudged across the field, and passed through the gates with no problem. Thorn lost sight of them beyond the fence. She waited, cursing her stupidity. If she'd been able to read a map, she could have avoided Manchester and not risked her life crossing Navvy territory.

Sam returned as the dim light of day cast its full glow across the muddy field, escorting a round man wearing a deep-green frock coat – the buttons pulling across his wide stomach – and a tall top hat. A great string of men, women and children trailed behind them; they sang bawdy songs and pointed and exclaimed over the tricorns. Evidently, the arrival of a Stoker girl was big news. Thorn's stomach squirmed with nerves when she saw her audience, and she touched Igor's frill for reassurance.

The gentleman stopped a few yards from her, and held out his hand. "Robert Stephenson," he said, his voice clear and kind. His rumpled curls stuck out at odd angles under his hat, and his collar was stained with soot. Thorn, not taking her eyes off his, stepped forward and shook his hand, her other hand resting firmly on Igor.

"People call me Thorn. My father, Nicholas Thorne, killed Brunel the first time, nineteen years ago. Sam said I should talk to you about the Wall."

"He's returned, hasn't he?"

Thorn nodded. "It's him who's building the Wall and digging up your railway lines. I am taking these tricorns to London in the hope I can destroy him, for good this time. I did not mean to trespass on your land, Mr. Stephenson."

"I'm quite sure you didn't. Did you know a man named Aaron Williams, by any chance?"

"He was like a father to me," Thorn said, her body stiffening at the mention of Aaron's name. "He died."

"I am sorry for your loss. A truly great man has passed into the Station of Life. I have no more quarrels with the Stokers, Miss Thorn, especially not with friends of Aaron Williams. Although you might not believe it after speaking with my new, our old animosity long ago passed into the history books. We have done our work without hindrance these last nineteen years, and will continue to do so, after that cursed Wall comes down. My men may have been rough with you earlier, and for that I apologise, but we have not seen a Stoker in these parts since those ugly days. You can understand how they might think the two occurrences related."

"I assure you the Wall is no work of the Stokers. The Boilers build the Wall, aided by the resurrected army of the Vampire King. Brunel is in London right now, advising the Queen and overseeing the Great Exhibition. I know he plans something terrible, and I intend to stop him."

"I travelled to London recently, to unveil the construction methods for my new tubular bridges at the Great Exhibition, and I saw the giant Boilers on display and the smoke issuing from the Engine Ward. I believe you, Thorn. But I would like to know how a Stoker woman and eight swamp creatures came to be embroiled in all this madness?"

After Stephenson explained his association with Aaron, Thorn determined that she could trust him. She recounted her tale, right from the beginning; the flight from London after the Wreck of the *Thunderer*, her mother's fall from the carriage, her life as an unwanted orphan in Graveyard and her banishment. She recounted Rex's betrayal and her time with the menagerie, and all that she had seen while she trudged across the countryside. Stephenson listened, removing his hat and clasping it to his chest. His eyes regarded her with empathy and a little awe, and she could see his astute mind working away in the background, putting all the pieces together and formulating a plan.

When Thorn had finished, Stephenson spoke, his

voice dripping with sadness. "I never wanted to destroy the Stokers, Miss Thorn, only to silence Isambard after all he tried to do to my people, to this whole country. I was greatly relieved upon his death, and to learn that he was not truly dead at all fills me with a tremendous dread."

"You should stay with us a few days." Sam said, staring at his feet. "Your leg looks a bit gammy. We could fix that up."

"And we have food and drink aplenty," a woman called out. "You look as if you've been living on air and tree bark. A pretty lass like you shouldn't be travelling all this way on an empty stomach."

Stephenson smiled. "What do you say, Miss Thorn? Will you and your tricorns accept a little hospitality from your sworn enemies?"

Thorn laughed. The whole invitation was so absurd. After everything she'd been through, could she accept the hospitality of the Navvies?

"I'd be delighted."

***

Stephenson let Thorn lean on his elbow as he escorted her through the entrance of Second Works. Beyond the gate, Thorn saw her life as it should have been. The Stokers had not worked the railroads for the past nineteen years, but this Navvy city clamoured with industry: all manner of hammering, pounding, smelting, and digging echoed over the field. Lead and sulphur clung in the thick air, mixed with the fresh smell of morning and of bacon cooking over a fire. She saw pens of livestock, and long, graceful neckers pulling carts of produce and construction materials. Makeshift houses –

made brown brick and iron and stacked one on top of the other – surrounded the work areas. Women bustled from doorway to doorway, trading fresh loaves of bread for cups of milk and sugar. She shuffled out of the way as a flock of chickens scurried under her feet.

At the centre, a gleaming iron edifice bore down, casting a long shadow over the entire settlement. Thin, slotted windows gave it the appearance of an ancient fortress. Men surged through the lower entrance, carrying trolleys stacked high with supplies and barking orders left and right. Everyone had a job, a purpose.

Stephenson ordered milk and oats be fetched, and had workers empty two of the animal pens. Thorn ushered her tricorns inside. The children pushed and jostled each other to stand on the wooden fence and stroke the strange creatures. They seemed happy for the attention and Thorn felt their anxiety lifting.

Someone had taken great care in erecting a long brick building in the corner against the fence. Hundreds of men crowded outside it, passing around pints of beer and slamming their fists in the dirt as they tossed dice and bet their wages away. Stephenson gestured for her to sit at one of the low wooden tables and, almost immediately, two women appeared with trays of ale and bacon sandwiches. He passed a plate to Thorn. She stared at it, her stomach growling.

"Go on," Stephenson smiled, raising his glass. "Eat. You must be starving."

Stephenson talked while she devoured the entire stack of sandwiches, the bacon juice dribbling down her chin. He told her of the recent goings-on: the broken, uprooted tracks that greeted his men as they left for work each morning, the mysterious Wall that wove like a spiderweb across the countryside, the Sinkers who prowled near the city, snapping up what morsels of lead they could.

"I even saw one in town the other day," a jolly man piped up. "It was carrying around a fancy walking cane, all genteel-like. 'Twas quite a sight."

Thorn smiled to herself. *So Maxwell hasn't returned to Brunel after all.*

Stephenson talked of the Gauge War, his horror at Brunel's plan to blame him for the Wreck of the *Thunderer*, and his relief when his rival supposedly died in the fire that consumed the Engine Ward. He spoke with pride about the creation of Second and Third Works and his expanding engineering empire. His men crowded the table to shout their own tales of bravado and loss. Thorn found their company both uplifting and saddening, for her own people could have had such a life, if they hadn't clung to their old hatred like swaddled children.

Sam's wife – a jolly lady with a kind face named Annabel – ushered her into a cosy shack, made from mud bricks and a packed earth floor. She ran Thorn a bath of warm water – a luxury she hadn't experienced for over a year now – and washed the filth and mud from her skin and hair. As Thorn pulled on a clean Navvy tunic and dried her hair, Annabel propped her swollen ankle on the table and applied various poultices and fresh dressings.

"It's not badly hurt," she said. "Just a couple days of bed-rest and we'll have you back on your feet."

"But—"

"No buts. To bed with you, Miss Thorn."

Thorn stayed with Sam and Annabel for two nights – sleeping and eating and entertaining Navvies who "just happened to stop by." She hardly left the shack except to check on her tricorns – happy and greedy for the lumps of sugar the children kept feeding them.

As Annabel predicted, the swelling in Thorn's foot quickly subsided and she could walk near as good as new. She repaid their kindness by helping Sam and his crew transport wooden rail sleepers on the little jigger out to the track-laying team.

Stephenson invited Sam's whole work crew to dine in his iron palace. Annabel leant Thorn a simple dress – the first she'd worn since she was a little girl – and dressed Sam in smart slacks and combed the dust from his hair. They gathered in Stephenson's Great Hall – a friendly room of simple furniture, a roaring fire, and barrels of beer. Stephenson's two house maidens served steaming platefuls of sausages, potatoes and mushy green peas.

Thorn ate and drank with relish, for it would be her final night at Second Works. Stephenson wanted her to stay a few more days, but Thorn – though touched by the Navvies' kindness – felt keenly the pressing of time. She had to return to her own people. The sight of those men, so content and happy in their work, filled her with sadness. Their life might not have been easy, but at least they had something to work for, unlike the Stokers.

I will change that, she thought as she lay down to sleep, her belly full and her mind racing. *I will give the Stokers something to work for.*

***

Over breakfast the next morning, Sam offered to take Thorn as far as Bristol on the supply train, and she gratefully accepted. He even helped her push the tricorns into the open-sided wagon, where they shuffled amongst the crates of coal and gauge nails and complained loudly about their cramped conditions.

Everyone in Second Works took a break from their industry to wave her farewell. The children lined the edge of the railway, calling cheerful goodbyes to their new tricorn friends. Stephenson stepped forward and patted Thorn on the shoulder.

"I haven't seen the last of you, Miss Thorn, or your magnificent creatures." He looked up at Sam. "Give her the supplies."

Sam pulled the sack from his back and dumped it on the ground. "This is from us," he said. "We figure, if you're going to betray your own God, you should at least have some Navvy clothes with which to do it."

Cautiously, Thorn stepped forward and lifted the flap of the sack with her boot. Inside she saw green overalls and tunics and even a pair of linen bloomers. They'd stacked packages of food – oats and beans and bread and corned beef – and two canteens, which might have held water or some other, darker fluid. Annabel stepped forward and laid a rifle across the sack.

"That is for you, also." Stephenson said. "On one condition."

Thorn stared at the rifle – an 1848 Brunswick with a polished wooden butt, burnished to a high shine. The only rifles Stokers managed to salvage were the standard issue Baker guns used in the Napoleonic wars. She'd never seen a weapon so beautiful.

"You must allow the Navvies to send an army of men to help you in London."

Thorn froze. She hadn't expected him to say that.

"I…er…yes," she stammered. "Thank you! But if I send someone here to call upon your men, how will you know they come from me, and not from Brunel?"

From his pocket he drew an object, which he tipped into her hand. A small Navvy sign of a railway track dangling from a string of black pearls. He clasped her fingers over the string.

"If you need us, send this to Forth Street or Second Works, and I will trust any man who carries it."

Thorn climbed aboard the tiny shunter, standing beside Sam on the footplate. He stoked the furnace and pulled the whistle, and with a jerk they heaved away from Second Works and trundled down the narrow-gauge track towards Bristol.

The railroad ran through the centre of Manchester – a smoky, industrial city of grey factories and puffing stacks. They passed through moors, woodlands, villages and fields – and Thorn gasped at the damage Brunel had already wrought. Everywhere she looked fields lay fallow, the once-beautiful moors heaped with industrial scraps, quaint towns drenched with soot, or hidden from view behind the living Walls. Sam kept his eyes on the track, not wanting to see. He talked a little of his life, but mostly he stared at the track ahead, watching for the encroaching Wall.

Five hours later, he pulled into a supply depot on the outskirts of Bristol. "Are you sure you don't need me to come with you?" he said. "I feel awful leaving you here alone."

Thorn smiled. "I have seven mischievous tricorns. I don't know the meaning of *alone*."

Sam embraced her, and she wiped away the single tear staining his cheek. He showed her a road to take through the dead farmland, so she would pass around the outskirts of the city and avoid detection. He trudged off towards the city, and she tied the sack of supplies and her new rifle to Igor's back, and set out toward Graveyard.

***

Five days later the Dirigires caught up to her again. Thorn heard their contraption before she saw it, the unnatural hiss and *pffft* of the hydrogen engine. It bobbed along the horizon, driven by ridiculous flapping wings and emitting a plume of smoke that would have a Boiler quaking in jealousy.

Her chest closed. No tree or building nearby could hide all seven tricorns. She pulled her Brunswick from Igor's back, lined up the girdled bullet with the rifling grooves and rammed it into the muzzle. She crouched in the dirt, steadying the weapon on a gatepost. She was ready for them.

But then they crashed into a tree.

If that wasn't punishment enough, the crash mangled their funnel, causing the next puff of engine steam to spark, igniting the combustion gases. Thorn jammed her hands over her ears as the balloon exploded.

She watched, smirking, as debris tumbled to the earth, and two priests lay convulsing in the cherry bushes, their delicate robes crumbling to ashes. Beside her, Nicholas whined. He stared at the screaming figures, but his eyes did not convey triumph.

But they locked us up in that horrid place! They killed Bridget!

His eyes drooped in the corner. *Don't become one of them.* The thought, probably not her own, entered her head. *If Aaron were here now, he would help them.*

Maybe I'm not like Aaron, she thought bitterly. But she knew it wasn't true.

Thorn removed her tunic. Clad only in her light vest and new Navvy trousers she hobbled across the field and pounced on the nearest priest, smothering the flames on his back.

"Stop screaming. There's a river a mile north. You can clean your burns." He snarled at her, his face contorted in hideous pain. She pushed his face back into the dirt. *He'll survive.*

The other priest was Fronçois, and he was worse off. Flames engulfed his face, curling his skin into wafers of peeling, grisly mess. She wrapped her tunic around him, but his screams only intensified. The wrenching pain of his final moments was too much for her, and she fled from his death, the tricorns thumping at her heels.

Thorn remembered what Frederique had said, and wondered if her escape had prompted Pierre to retrieve the balloons from hiding.

Footsteps crunched across the field behind her. She turned around and saw a shadow running towards her. She pulled the rifle off her shoulder, but as he came into view she recognised his face and lowered her weapon.

"Sam!"

He slowed as he approached her, his breathing short, sharp rasps. "I saw the dirigible flying south as I crossed into Manchester, and I knew they would be after you. We came to rescue you, but I see you've done a fine job without us." Thorn gasped as more men stalked across the field – Sam's whole work crew, each carrying a Brunswick and a huge grin.

Thorn embraced him. "You pox-ridden gammy! You've done too much for me already."

"We couldn't have you come to harm on the final leg of your journey." He glanced at the sky. "We should arrive in Graveyard before midnight."

"*We?* You can't come to Graveyard, Sam. They'll kill you."

"They'll kill *you*, if what you've told us is the truth. We're not going to let that happen."

Thorn could do nothing to dissuade him, and so she had both tricorn and human company as she trudged the final miles toward her home. Farmland gave way to familiar swamps – wet and sticky and shrouded in mists – and as night fell she noticed a long shadow on the horizon. A familiar smell – iron and fire – blew on the breeze. They pressed on, eyes on that black line, an impression in the peat surface that whet Thorn's heart with hope.

She ran ahead, tumbled over the edge and landed on her hip. She rolled and clutched her side as pain shot down her leg. Her face grazed something cold and hard.

Iron.

Thorn squinted at the object. It was darkened with rust, and nestled in the peat at an odd angle. The glint of a gauge pin glimmered in the twilight.

The Narrow!

***

JAMES HOLMAN'S MEMOIRS, FIRST EDITION

I weep as I write, for though I long to gloss over the next chapter and hide forever my betrayal, I cannot.

I wish I had some excuse for my deplorable behaviour, but there is none and worse, I do not stop at cold words and empty promises. I let greed and fear rule me, when always I promised to remain a man of reason and kindness.

I *must* at least attempt an explanation. Perhaps you could then understand how I came to make this wretched decision.

I confess that my travels have been fuelled by more than a desire to "see the world" (if you will pardon my pun). For reasons that escape even the best London physicians (although London physicians seem at odds to explain anything without referencing Freud's genitalia) the fresh air and harsh conditions of solo travelling ease the pain that crushes my body. But as the years passed, I found the relief less and less noticeable. I'd thought to have one final jaunt before I sat down to write my latest memoir, and accompanying the world's foremost menagerie seemed a fine way to finish.

Unfortunately, far from easing my pain, the months I spent on the road with Wombwell aggravated the aches into shooting, searing spasms. Every step I took tore at muscle and bone and burned the flesh from my limbs. Every mouthful of food scorched my insides as it rent gaping fissures in my delicate stomach. My ears could not hear voices over the pounding in my skull.

And my eyes! It seems so cruel that two organs I no longer possess should slice and scald me still. I have always tolerated the pain, but this new torture drove me mad. I ceased to sleep, and the epicurean pleasures that sustained me for so many years – food and wine and tobacco and theatre – became abhorrent; the unmerciful harbingers of pain.

When we reached London, the madness drove me to seek what the doctors could not provide. I went instead to Engine Ward.

With the gates to the city barred and the citizens unable to escape, the Engine Ward once more teamed with life. How it had been rebuilt and repaired so quickly I didn't know, but I could guess that Boilers were involved somehow. Every corner crowded with preachers extolling this or that theorem or proclaiming the properties of a new alloy or clockwork device. The weight of the stone and iron shrines leaned over the streets, pressing in the smoky air. And above it all, Brunel's towering Chimney, casting a looming darkness upon the streets that even I could sense. I moved slowly there, the echoes lost in the smog and slurry. And everywhere I heard the clank and grind of machines, unrelenting, immutable. How I longed to be one of them!

I shuffled along with the crowd; fellow sufferers just like me, seeking machines to cure our ills, streamline our inconveniences and satisfy our whims and whimsy. I had my own mission; surely one of these illustrious engineers could furnish me a pair of mechanical eyes?

But though I searched those streets every waking hour, I could find no man, engineer or otherwise, who would dare the unthinkable...who could take upon himself the duties of a god. I found none of them could – or *would*– furnish a viable cure. And all the while the madness and the pain tore at me, until I could no longer see sense.

The day I dropped my message through the slot on the Chimney door, the sky seemed to press down on me, as if it wished to crush me against the earth. As soon as the embossed paper left my hands, the guilt I'd pushed down for so many months gripped my heart with ice. Knowing what I did about Thorn's plot to destroy him, knowing of the telltale plate burning at the bottom of my trunk, how could I continue this madness? But I could not turn away now.

A week later I received the letter at my Mayfair residence, written in that secret language of dots and flicks that allowed me to keep my correspondence private. There were only two others in the world who remembered that code, and they were both meant to be dead.

The message read:

I have not forgotten my promise to you. Bring the plate to the Chimney.

He'd detailed a time and date a week hence. I resumed my search through Engine Ward with frantic obsession, searching, hoping I could reclaim my life without resorting to his sorcery. But no engineer – no matter how clever, no matter how many worshippers flocked to his shrine – could suggest an artifice that would allow a blind man to see again.

So on the appointed date I once again shuffled through the Engine Ward. The air grew hot with the increased temperature, slicking my skin with wayward chemicals. I smelt burning all around me. The pain swelled through my chest, and I gulped back the urge to cry out.

I halted, took several shallow breaths, and only when my heart returned to a safe speed did I step back onto the street. With every pace I took the heat intensified, till sweat poured from every pore. I must be close.

The echo of the Chimney bounced inside my brain, sending a searing pain to my eyes. I clutched my head and stumbled forward, gritting my teeth and willing myself on.

You shouldn't be here, James. This is not the way to fix things.

I couldn't listen anymore. I'd lived with the pain long enough. I pushed through the Chimney entrance.

Brunel's congregation occupied the lower platform, which spread into a wide, hollow nave, complete with a steepled ceiling where smoke from the pyres could curl through the upper levels of the Chimney. From the far end of the room a priest read the liturgy on broad gauge rail in dulcet tones. Echoes of a thousand private prayers muttered from iron-shod mouths reached my ringing ears. If Lurgo wanted to find the Stokers, he need look nowhere else than the nave of this iron church. His friend Sooty probably knelt in the front row.

When I'd known him, Brunel hadn't wanted this ... godhead. He'd abhorred the religions, as all sensible men of science should. But day and night as he tinkered with his creations they built the Chimney around him, walling him up with iron and brass and filling his shrine with holy symbols and lofty, hopeful prayers. How could a man resist such adoration?

I clomped through the floor of Sinkers, feeling my way with sounds to the hidden stairwell at the far end. Everything was exactly as it had been nineteen years ago. I descended into the bowels of the Chimney. The reds I imagined pulsed in my head – red for the pain, red for the blood that lined these walls.

I was surprised I even knew what red was anymore, so long had it been since I'd seen the colour for real.

When last I'd set foot here, after the Wreck of the *Thunderer*, London lay in ruins. Every man, women and child who could wield a weapon bashed at the entrance to Engine Ward, calling for Brunel's blood. He'd barred every door and sealed every crevice in a vain attempt to keep his machines safe. But I knew the secret way.

Brunel had made a promise to me, that before I died I would see again, provided I returned to him that which was his, that which we all thought lost forever. I'd held it once, clasped my freedom in my hands, but it had disappeared again. I prayed for his kindness, but there was no kindness left within him...he told me to run, and I did. I ran like a coward while Nicholas fought on...

Not those memories, not now. I had eyes to heal. Reflections on my foolishness could come later, when I could bask in my folly with restored sight.

After descending for many minutes, I came to a sturdy platform. An investigation revealed the thick iron door, just where it had always been. I cranked the handle and it swung inward. I entered the room.

A rush of warm air greeted me, an unsolicited welcome that seized my joints and caused the air to hiss from my lungs.

"Greetings, friend."

It is *him. He truly has returned.* The emphasis on the second word was a *pffft*, as though he spoke through a ventilator. Above the doorway I heard a valve jam, and the machinery ground to a halt. I leaned on my cane — the intense heat made my head spin.

"Greetings Isambard," I managed. "It has been too long since you joined us at the Royal Society."

"Ah, yes." Steam hissed from a valve directly behind me, and the door swung shut. "But you have been absent as well, I heard."

"Recently I've spent much time on the road with Master Wombwell. I did have the chance to visit your Crystal Palace—" I shambled forward, unable to hear the echoes of my surroundings. In this vacuum of energy I lost my way.

"It is one of my most beautiful creations. And soon you shall see it with your own eyes. Here, take my hand."

I reached out with tentative fingers, and grazed something smooth and cool; it could have…should have been metal, but it pulsed under my fingers like it drew breath. As soon as I made contact, whatever it was jerked away and Brunel's fingers found mine; but despite the heat, his touch was metal-cold.

Brunel directed me to a folding chair, and I lowered myself into the coarse canvas seat.

"Speak to me of the pain, my friend."

"It burns inside me like searing embers; its cruel fingers lick at my joints and tangle through my mind. It attacks me at rest, and when I seek exercise or leisure. I find simple tasks difficult to attend, and important details slip through the agony web. I have endured too long in the dark, Isambard. I would either be cured of this godforsaken curse, or I shall endure it further with all five senses."

"I'm afraid not even I can cure the pain. We must travel a different path, James. But you knew that already."

I nodded.

"Many writings – the Torah, the Bible, the Liber Aethera, the Book of the Metics – speak of the prophets – the first engineers – who could cure the blind with a touch of their fingers." He chuckled at that, a sound that to my ears seemed more like the lid of a tea-kettle rattling over the heat. "I am no such sorcerer, but I have concocted a little magic of my own. The mechanism is made in Meliora, of course. I would trust no other with such delicate movements, but the design…that is all my own."

"When can I have it?"

"We will perform the operation right now, if you wish. Have you brought the payment?"

I drew the plate from my pocket and with trembling hands held it out to him. Something tugged it from my grasp. I felt a tug inside me as well; Thorn's knowing smile, perhaps.

She doesn't know what it says. It's of no use to her.

Of course it isn't now, scolded another voice, one I had

pushed down deep inside me. *Now you've betrayed her.*

Brunel croaked as he took the plate and I heard the scrape of his metal rings across the embossed letters. I wanted to ask for it back, but knew it was too late.

When Thorn sees me walk without the cane, when she sees me read with my hands clasped in my lap, when I gaze upon her face and call her by name, she will understand why I did this.

"Lie back, James."

I obeyed. Brunel set the machines in motion again, and life-that-was-not-life filled the room; clicking and clanking and whooshing and squealing. A roar like a swamp dragon rose from the boiler behind Brunel's seat, and I heard him laugh in delight as the temperature soared another thirty degrees. Metal scraped metal as he sharpened his knives and chisels.

Metal grabbed my hands, pulled them down, stoppered them to my sides. I wriggled to try to get comfortable, but they held tight. I tried to swing my legs up but found them glued to the spot. Something cold crept over my jugular, and I could no longer move my neck.

"Hold still." Brunel's hot breath caressed my ear. "This is going to hurt."

I felt a tremendous pressure bearing down on my skull, and then the pressure was *inside* my skull, like a compie trapped in my cranium, scrabbling for escape. I heard whirring, and felt the slice of metal through my hairline, through my skin, through bone, and deep into tissue. I screamed, oh how I screamed and howled and gibbered for it to cease. Blood poured down my face, pooling in my nostrils and cascading into my open mouth, falling down my gaping throat until I choked on my own metallic essence.

But that would not be the last of it. I felt Brunel's

fingers inside of me, shifting things around, fitting the gears and pendulum and escapement and the quartz, turning and tinkering and testing the clockwork while I soiled myself in the torturous spasms. My ears rang as the heavens raced towards me. He remained indifferent to my agony, offering no pain relief, for what is pain to a machine? And he was master of the machines, the doctor of clockwork about his daily business, fixing a faulty unit.

It was when he dug his nails into my eye sockets and removed the oozing, useless bulbs that I finally lost consciousness.

***

Thorn leapt to her feet. The Navvies ushered the tricorns into the ditch and jabbed at the iron gauge rail with raw fingers, examining the strange atmospheric rails that they had never seen up close before. The wind tore at Thorn's tear-soaked face as she sobbed with relief. She had made it.

"Come on you lot, we're so very close now." She marched down the Narrow towards home, Sam and the Navvies stalking behind, rifles loaded and ready. The tricorns bounced after them, whining about her sudden surge of energy.

Thorn saw the outline of the Clegg station, its toppled funnel like a broken arm flailing over the edge of the Narrow. On she ran, past the cairns of rust, past the Clegg carriage where her mother had left her. Fear and sadness no longer clawed her chest – her emotions were of a different breed: pride for completing her journey, anger that they'd stone her and the Navvies as soon as they laid eyes on her, awe at Sam's bravery as he walked into enemy territory out of trust for her. Behind her Thorn heard the *pat-pat* of tricorn hooves slapping against wet peat. Squinting, she could just make out the perimeter fence—

"Who goes there?"

The voice grated her conscience like steel on flesh. Memories and ghosts tugged at her mind. In her mind she saw Rex rushing towards her, a polished amulet pinned to his chest and a wedding garland in one hand...

"Thorn?"

Not Rex, *Joel!*

The colours and images of her memory swirled and formed the reality before her. He lifted the hood from his eyes, and the mattock fell from his hand and sank in the mud.

His arms folded around her, and her head sank into his shoulder as though she lacked the strength to support it. The emotions surged inside her and erupted, cascading down her face in tears of joy and sorrow; the sweetest of all bittersweet victories. Joel stroked her hair with ferocity, tugging the roots from her scalp.

"I was certain you were dead." His tears mixed with her own; the salty pools rolling off the raptor feathers that lined his hood.

"I was certain *you* were!"

"I barely escaped with my life. Lurgo had disappeared, and we were surrounded by the Sunken. I saw Rex go down—" he caught himself, "—and they kept coming. Hundreds of them, it seemed. I had the dynamite, so I laid down a trail of fizzers. That disorientated them long enough for me to escape down one of the tunnels. I found a hole in the Wall that led outside, and I scrambled out into the city, then caught a ride back out with the first cart I found, and came back here. When you didn't return, I thought..." He let her go, clasping her numb fingers in his. "You must be freezing, and hungry. Come back with me. I will make certain no one hurts you."

"No, wait—"

Joel's eyes burned in her face.

"It's okay. We don't even have to see anyone. I'll sneak you in. We'll go to the Turret. Quartz will figure out what to do."

"Joel...I...thank you."

He clasped her frozen hand to his heart. "You came home. My prayers were not in vain."

"You prayed for me?"

"Every night." He glanced down at her with a strange look in his eyes. "What *are* you wearing? That's a dangerous colour for these parts—"

The Navvies stepped forward. Joel's face turned white. Thorn grabbed his shoulders.

"This is Sam. He's a friend. A *friend*." She emphasized the word when she saw Joel's hurt expression. "He saved my life. These are his men. They're not here to hurt anyone. We need to talk to the Chancellor."

Joel's eyes flicked from the men to her, and Thorn saw the fear and bewilderment there. Igor stepped out from behind the men and let out a bellow, and Joel forgot all about the Navvies. He leapt back in terror, his eyes wide as he watched Igor bound up to Thorn and nudge her hand.

"Get away from her!" Joel bellowed, reaching for his knife.

"Joel, no! Don't be afraid. Igor is my friend. And so are the others."

"What others?"

The other six tricorns skulked out of the shadows.

Joel's hand tightened around the handle of his blade.

Thorn reached out and clasped her fingers around his wrist, enjoying the warmth of his skin against hers. "I said, *don't be afraid.* I've trained them. They listen to me."

"Where *have* you been, Miss Thorn?"

"All sorts of places." She pulled his hand down, so that he was touching Igor's frill. She showed him how to stroke it the way Igor liked, and in a few moments Joel was smiling again and Igor was nudging his hand, too.

"They're pretty neat," he said, as he ran his fingers down Igor's spine.

"And you haven't seen the half of it, yet." Thorn linked arms with him. "Take me home, Mr. Williams. I have quite a tale to tell, and only a tankard of Quartz' finest mecks would do it justice."

***

After much convincing from Thorn and Sam, Joel agreed to sneak them *all* inside the fence. They hid the tricorns behind the enormous scrap heap stretching between the Turret and the boundary, and left the Navvies to guard them. The Turret loomed ahead, shrouded in low-lying cloud, and unlit. Rust encroached in the spokes of the gear wheels that spiralled down the stack's chamber. Thorn hid amongst the scrap heap while Joel drummed his fists on the Turret door.

She heard nothing from inside. Not the clink of machinery nor Quartz's characteristic snores. Joel grabbed the crooked handle and pushed open the door.

Thorn raced from her hiding place and ducked inside, her boots clanging against the familiar metal grate. "Why isn't the door locked?"

Joel stared at a space above her head. "Thorn, I have

to warn you. He's sick. Some days he cannot get up at all."

Thorn's boot froze above the first step.

"Its okay." Joel gave her a light push. "They don't think its cholera. He's coherent."

She stomped up the stairs two at a time, the clang of her boots echoing around the silent tower. She passed the kitchen — its usually meticulous shelves lopsided, the preserves and mecks bottles stacked in lackadaisical fashion, and covered in grime. Two compies chattered in the corner, snapping at each other over scraps of tricorn bone.

She continued up the stairs. Thorn stole a glance at her quarters under the second-floor landing, biting back the urge to cry. Someone had boarded up the entrance with empty mecks crates — perhaps so Quartz didn't have to look at the empty room — but through the gaping borer holes she saw her furs and blankets rotting and soiled by vermin. Water dribbled through a leak in the corner, soaking the wooden struts and causing the charcoal and lead doodles on the walls to run.

She heard a moan from upstairs, and a dry, hawking cough. Thorn dashed up the final flight onto the observation deck. The clockworks strained through their movements, creaking and hammering in violent protest; the dulcet harmonies of a tone-deaf orchestra. The Fresnel dangled precariously from one pin; the other two had rusted away. Water dribbled on the instruments from more leaks in the ceiling, and the room stank of piss and bile. She heard another dry cough.

"Quartz?"

More coughing. Joel passed by on her left and handed her a dusty argand. She directed the lamp into the darkness.

He lay on a hammock, his face slick with sweat. He had drawn back the blanket and pressed his hands against his protruding belly, swelled with red, viscous welts. He turned toward the light and blinked. His muscles tugged a wan smile.

Oh, Quartz. What has happened to you?

Thorn knelt at his side, setting the lamp on the floor and adjusting the damp pillows behind his head. "Why aren't you in the smokehouse?"

"I don't wanna go. I've got everything I need right here." He tapped his near-empty mecks bottle. "Joel said you were dead."

She shook her head, tears brimming at the corners of her eyes. "I've brought you a present. But they won't be much use to you if you're sick."

"What kind of present?"

Thorn opened her mouth to tell him about the tricorns, but Igor's distinctive wail rose through the window. Quartz struggled to sit upright. "What was that?"

"Those poxy *friends* of yours are meant to be keeping them quiet," Joel muttered. "We'll have all of Graveyard over here any moment." Thorn ignored him.

"That's your present. Can I help you to stand?" Quartz protested weakly, but allowed her to lift him off the hammock. Resting his weight between her and Joel, he staggered to the window.

The seven tricorns paced in a circle around their tether, splashing mud all over each other and snorting and growling and making a hell of a racket. The Navvies danced around them, trying to coax them into submission without being trampled. Quartz's eyes lit up, as though the fire of his life had once again been stoked with fresh coal.

Thorn feared at any moment Oswald or Bill Riley would hear the noise and that would be the end of her. "Igor, Nicholas, Lurgette, stop that! Verne, Bernard, Rose, Isobella, sit down right now!" As she spoke, she pushed the thoughts into their minds. Immediately, the tricorns ceased their mischief and sat on their hind legs, staring up at her with expectant faces.

Thorn might have imagined it, but she thought she saw colour return to Quartz's fetid skin, and the light of plans and schemes flickered in his eyes.

"You're an angel." He squeezed Thorn's shoulder. "Welcome home."

***

"I'm sorry." Joel squeezed her hand. "I didn't want you to see."

Thorn blinked, hoping she dreamed the horror. But the sight before her was painfully real.

She'd insisted Joel sneak her up to the animal pens. Most of the Stokers were asleep or tossing dice in Bill Riley's carriage, and she wanted to hold Wind in her arms again. Joel hadn't wanted to go, and now she saw why. A fire had ripped through the stable area and animal pens, ripping apart every wooden support and mangling the carriage beyond repair. The fences she and Aaron had lovingly constructed ten summers ago lay toppled in rotting heaps, strung with the half-devoured carcasses of their beloved animals. Carrion birds circled overhead, eyeing the charred field with hungry stares.

"They torched it all after you left." Joel kicked a rotting post. "It was Bill Riley's idea."

Thorn sagged against him, resting on his chest. He stroked her hair with light fingers. She wanted to cry, to mourn her animals and her last living connections to Aaron, but she couldn't muster the sadness with his fingers in her hair.

Finally, she asked, "Wind?"

"The dogs escaped this carnage. They skulked around the outskirts of Graveyard for a while, picking for scraps and snapping at the hunters. Oswald ordered them all shot. They got a couple, but the rest – including Wind – ran off across the fenland." He pulled her closer to him, wrapping her in his coat.

She rested her cheek against his, letting his stubble rub against her skin. He felt warm – huddling so close to him made her feel warm too, inside and out. She breathed in his scent – the mud and sweat of the Graveyard, but tangier, like a spiced mutton pie – and all the sorrow and fear slipped from her body.

Thorn took another deep breath, and whispered, "I loved them, and they are gone. Such is the fate of all I love. You'd best watch your back, Mr. Williams."

Joel laughed. His breath tickled her cheek, sending a shiver of delight through her body. "Do you love me, Miss Thorn?"

"That's not what I meant, it's…I mean…I hardly know you—" Her cheeks flushed, and she buried her face into his collar, her heart fluttering.

He laughed again, but nervously. With strong fingers he lifted her chin, so she stared up into his soft brown eyes. Her heart leapt faster.

"Joel—"

He pressed his lips to hers.

Thorn's heart burst in her chest, spreading warmth throughout her body, touching every limb with fire. She pressed against him, suddenly feeling as though she weren't close enough. She wanted to fall into him.

His tongue fought for hers, searing a path from the warmth of his mouth through her body, enclosing her in flames. He clamped his hands behind her neck and forced her even closer.

Joel tore away, his eyes wild. "Thorn, I'm so sorry." He stepped back, his face drawn in fear.

Thorn blinked, her whole body aching. *What's wrong, does he not want me? Am I doing this all wrong?*

"Joel, please—" she reached out a tentative hand for his sleeve. He pulled away, and her chest clenched in fear. "I don't understand..."

"It's wrong." He stepped back. "I'm so wrong. You've been through so much, you've lost so much, and here I am, trying to...to...you must think me a monster."

"Oh, Joel..." Thorn reached out to him again, a faint smile playing on her lips. "Here with you, I will never feel sadness or fear again. Please, don't leave."

Their lips met, and Thorn lost herself to the fire inside.

***

When Thorn and Joel returned to the Turret, the found Quartz had invited the Navvies inside for a round of mecks. They crowded into the observation deck - the only space large enough to accommodate everyone, and even then she had to sit on Joel's knee. They sat up for hours drinking the scorching mecks (Thorn swore it had grown in strength and foulness since she'd last drank it) and relating the tales of the previous weeks. Together they formed a plan for attack.

Much had changed in the Graveyard since her banishment. After Joel returned with news of the failed mission and Rex's betrayal, he had risen in prominence among the community as a kind of living martyr, so far their only still-breathing soldier to return from London. The Williams, of course, rode along on Joel's impeccably folded coattails, lording their rank over the rest of the populace and generally making a nuisance of themselves.

Oswald, reported Joel, had simply stepped back and allowed his family to have the run of the place, requisitioning supplies at their fancy and trading what little ivory they'd acquired for exquisite coats and silk breeches. They had already squandered what little wealth the Graveyard had acquired, driving up debt in the nearby towns with rich food and gambling. Although Joel had the support of the majority of Graveyard, with Quartz ill he had little sway in the decision-making, and could not convince the elders that something needed to be done.

"Did you tell them of the Boilers and the Sunken inside the Wall?"

Joel shook his head. "Only you and Quartz and Oswald know. I thought if I said anything, they would run to London as quick as lightning, guns blazing, begging to join Brunel's army."

"And a fine grave he'd have dug for them, too. It's much worse than we could ever have imagined." Thorn filled them in on all she had seen since arriving in London.

"Do you still have the plate?" Joel leaned forward, his tone lowered. "Did you find out its meaning?"

Thorn shook her head. She didn't want to think of it — another mystery surrounding her father. "I gave it to… a friend, for safekeeping. He is attempting to decipher it. So far, he has been unsuccessful."

That night Joel lay with Thorn, stroking her fingers till she closed her eyes. She heard him breathe heavily beside her, his chest rising and falling with a steady rhythm. But she could not sleep. On the deck above, twenty Navvies snored and moaned, and the five outside on guard duty told bawdy jokes that made her ears turn red. Rain soaked through the rags she'd stuffed in the hole in the corner, and she counted drips till she heard sixth bell.

In the morning, Joel left her in bed to attend to his chores, and the Navvies made a stack of bacon sandwiches and went outside to watch the tricorns. Thorn shuffled down to the kitchen and found a package of salted meat. She took this and a tankard of mecks to the observation deck and waved it under Quartz' nose.

He snorted and sniffed, his hooked nose snaffling the air as it caught the scent of meat and booze. She called his name and his eyes flickered open. He grinned maniacally when he recognised her.

"So you *did* return. I thought it might have been the mecks messin' with my brain."

"It's really me." Thorn dangled a strip of meat in front of his face and he snapped it between his teeth, just like the monkeys back in the menagerie.

"Let's see these tricorns—"

He was cut off by the shrill clang of the warning bells.

They've discovered the tricorns! Thorn raced to the window, expecting to see men surrounding her babies with rifles and pitchforks. But the tricorns slept soundly in a haphazard pile: they had not been discovered. Sam gave a frantic wave, an expression of confusion on his face.

Quartz pulled himself out of his hammock and grabbed the rifle from behind the Fresnel. "The bastards are back again."

"I don't understand."

"Ever since you left, the dragons have been attacking the perimeter fences once or twice a week. Twice now they've breached the walls – they killed ten men last week."

"I can stop them, but you have to bring me closer."

Joel's head popped around the doorframe. "Hand me that gun." Quartz tossed him a rifle. Thorn grabbed his wrist and picked up her Brunswick. "I'm going too."

He looked as though he would argue, but he gritted his teeth and dragged her downstairs. Outside, they bent low and ducked behind the carriages, following the muddy path behind the old GWR engines. Men ran past them, shouting instructions at each other and loading their dusty Baker rifles. Joel fell back, leaving Thorn cowering between the rusted couplers while he shouted to William Stone.

Joel returned a few seconds later. "They're along the western fence," he whispered.

"Get me to the cemetery. I can sense them from there."

He pulled her behind another carriage, ducking and weaving as he dragged her around the stampeding men. Thorn's heart thundered as she glimpsed familiar faces, and she tugged her hood low over her face. But if anyone recognised her, they didn't cry out.

Finally they reached the cemetery dug into the side of the western edge. The bells clanged above their heads, so loud they could not hear each other shout. Joel tugged her behind Aaron's gravestone, and mimed that he would go to help the men. Thorn shook her head, forced his head against her chest, and held him tight. His warmth triggered her sense, and she flew out of her head, across the fence, and into the minds of three swamp dragons.

In her arms, Joel changed. He smelt delicious, more tasty than the first mutton pie she'd ever eaten. *I'm inside their heads now.* Thorn choked the hunger down, forcing her mind out, willing the dragons to leave the fence. *Turn back, turn back...*

She felt their minds turn, weighing up this new option. They hesitated, pausing just outside the hole they'd torn and sniffing the air. Thorn searched with the tendrils, locking herself into their thoughts. She saw though their eyes the men readying their guns, and she *pushed* with all her strength, pushing them back, away from Graveyard, away from Joel.

But they would not go. Thorn sensed something more powerful than her command. *Fear.* They did not want to turn back, for something in the swamp would devour them. And she could see into their thoughts; she knew what it was.

"That's why they're attacking Graveyard," Thorn cried. "Because the Boilers are attacking them!"

Bill Riley let off the first shot, and she dropped the threads of the dragons' minds and slipped up, up, over Graveyard, directing her thoughts down to the clearing behind the Turret where her tricorns waited. Thorn plunged into their minds, and with a cry they pulled as one and tore free of their tether. She pulled them towards her, listening as they crashed through the carriages and barrelled up the hill.

"What in Great Conductor's name—"

The men fell to the mud and covered their heads as the tricorns charged past. They crashed into the fence, tearing a wide hole as they stampeded into the swamp. Thorn leapt up and raced after them, and Joel raced after her, calling her name. He was joined by more men, and a party of Graveyard warriors followed her into the swamp.

Thorn could not see her tricorns through the thick bracken, but she could sense what they saw, and it filled her with rage. A Boiler stood on a metal platform, held above the swamp by a team of sweating Sinkers, while still more of the unholy creatures clambered over a delicate scaffolding, pinning and riveting and hammering the Wall into place. It was coming closer. It was nearly at Graveyard.

"No," Thorn screamed. "Not here! You're not welcome here!"

Her rage poured from her skull and entered the tricorns, who barrelled forward with a speed she'd never known before. As one, they crashed into the Wall's frame, buckling the scaffolding and sending Sinkers flying into the mud, where they were trampled into the peat. Their cries reached the men, who broke into the clearing and saw the grisly scene with their own eyes.

The battle between the beasts and the Sunken quickly turned into a massacre. Lurgette tore apart the Wall with her horns and hooves. A brave Sinker leapt from the debris, but she swung her head around and impaled him on her horn. He twitched a little before sinking further down the shaft, flopping about uselessly while she tore at the structure.

Bernard and Verne made great sport of squelching through the mud, stomping on every Sinker they could find. The sound of bones snapping and organs oozing into the mud forced the other Sinkers to back away, clambering over each other in their haste to retreat back into the Wall.

Igor, Nicholas, Rose and Isobella charged the Sunken who held up the platform, and they toppled over, crushed between the hooves of the tricorns and the heavy iron grate. The Boiler flailed its giant arms as it slid into the mud, rolling on its side and submerging its furnace belly into the peat. The mud began to bubble and boil.

Igor rammed his horn into the pressure valve, and steam pissed from the wound. The Boiler made a sound like air deflating from a balloon, and then its head exploded, sending shards of metal flying in all directions. The tricorns chased away the last of the Sinkers, and came to rest, panting and sweating, in front of Thorn.

The men stared at her, mouths agape, weapons hanging useless by their sides. They looked as though they'd seen a ghost. Joel took a cautious step towards her, and clasped her trembling hand.

He started to speak, but screams drowned him out. Screams from Graveyard, screams of pain and death.

Without thinking, Thorn leapt on Igor's back and kicked her ankles into his sides. He tore off toward Graveyard, his siblings galloping at his heels.

She passed through the trampled fence in time to see the massacre. Stokers ran in every direction, diving behind carriages and barrels to avoid the flames as they leapt through every structure. One look towards the fire pits told her what had happened. The Sunken had breached the fence and thrown the fire barrels into the wooden storage carriages, which had quickly caught alight. The flames leapt from carriage to carriage, devouring homes and belongings and people trapped inside. Desperate Stokers fled the blaze, running straight into the arms of the Sunken, who now tore unhindered through Graveyard, ripping heads from necks and sucking up the salty blood before it could spill in the mud. A trail of broken, bloody bodies stretched between the carriages.

The screams of her own people filled Thorn's head, pushing aside her connection with the tricorns. Terror pounded against her chest. *Not here, not now. There are too many of them, I can't stop them...*

She saw a man, bent double, crouching behind the Rothwell's drivewheel. *Sam.* He raised his rifle and fired. Thorn watched, numb, as a Sinker dropped a half-chewed child and fell, twitching, into the mud. More guns exploded, and the screaming women were joined by wailing Sunken as their own lead-soaked blood mingled with their victims in the mud.

A crowd of Stokers, led by William Stone, took the opportunity to dash across the cemetery towards the eastern gates. Three Boilers rolled through the fire pits to cut them off, crushing men under their treads. The men scattered, screaming as scalding streams of water from the Clegg guns poured over them, and their skin blistered and peeled away.

Thorn pushed her mind back into her tricorns and drove them around the back of the Rothwell, so they barrelled into the Boilers from behind and crushed the frames into the mud. Again and again she had them stomp on the machines, until the furnace units were mangled beyond repair, and the only response from the Boilers were the final hissing of expelling steam.

She slid off Igor's back, picked up the nozzle of a flailing Clegg gun and pointed the hose at the retreating Sunken. The scalding water finished off what the Navvies had started. Sam reloaded and sent his men after the straggling Sinkers, who turned on their heels and met their charge, but their snarling and lunging was no match for Sam's bullets. Many fell to the ground, their emaciated bodies dotted with dark bullet wounds, their limbs twitching as the last vestiges of life were snatched from them. The Sunken that were still standing scrambled back through the fences and headed toward the Wall.

"Joel," Thorn yelled. "Secure the fences!" Joel raced off, a half-dozen of the Navvies not far behind.

The tricorns' horns made short work of the rusted rivets that held on the Rothwell's roof, tearing off the metal in one solid sheet. Sam and his Navvies carried it across the fire pits and placed it over the breach in the fence. One of the Navvies found welding equipment behind the Turret and started to seal the breach. Thorn left three of them to guard it, and turned back toward Graveyard.

Seeing the immediate danger had passed, the remaining Stokers emerged from their hiding places, their eyes taking in the horror. Their homes were burning. of broken bodies smouldered between the ruins – some the twitching remains of Sinkers, but too many were the corpses of mothers and fathers and sons and daughters.

Sensing a rising tension, the Navvies ran ahead of them and crowded around Thorn, their rifles reloaded and ready for trouble. Joel's fingers entwined with hers, his sobbing daughter clutching his leg. But they needn't have feared for her safety – the Stokers were utterly beaten. They did not have the strength for another fight.

The Graveyard fell silent – the only sound the sobbing of women and the shuffle of boots in the mud as every remaining Stoker turned to stare at her.

"Right," Thorn said. "I'm back."

***

JAMES HOLMAN'S MEMOIRS, FIRST EDITION

I woke up to pain; searing, unending pain, leaping from my skull to my limbs, shooting through my abdomen, my pelvis, my grasping fingers. My chest gurgled as through my internal organs had liquefied. A thunderous ticking emanated from within my skull and bombarded my eardrums in a final testament to my madness.

I opened my eyes, and I screamed again.

Light poured into my skull from every side, crystalline filigree arcing across my vision. My senses were swamped, and sounds and smells and visions tumbled through my broken head.

My eyes adjusted, and I began to recognise the colours; browns and black and shiny silver and burnished bronze. Somewhere in my pummelled brain, memories surfaced, and euphoria washed over me. Flames leapt from the fire under the giant boiler, the orange soaking my vision. I felt drunk from the sensation.

I could *see* again.

"Praise be," I whispered, awestruck by the revolving machines that orbited the aging engineer. Brunel chuckled, leaning back in his winged chair and keeping his hands behind his back.

I felt my bonds slide away. I leaned forward, but as I lifted my head my body spasmed in pain, and red splotches floated over my new eyes.

"Red..."

"Slowly, James. You do not want to damage yourself."

I moved my arm to my head, running my fingers over my pallid skin, up towards my temples. In the corner of my eyes I saw my fingers dance across my features. The sensation of vision threatened to devour me.

"Lie back, James, and close your eyes. It will take time before you can move again. By the by, we must have a chat."

"Pleasant weather we've having?" I croaked, suddenly nervous about the strange tone in his voice.

"This is no joke, James. We must have no secrets between friends."

"Of course not." I thought of the metallic object I'd unwittingly touched earlier. I wondered why he concealed his hands from me now.

"I thought that plate lost forever. Where did you find it? Answer carefully now, I don't need to remind you that I shall know if you lie."

I chose my words carefully. "Nicholas placed it in the care of an acquaintance. It is from the acquaintance that I acquired it."

"Nicholas trusted no man as he trusted you and I." Brunel leaned close and the orange flames danced on his bulging, monstrous eyes. "Who is this man who gave you the plate? I must know the name. He must have some powerful magic to keep the plate secret from me for nineteen years—"

"That's not the way of it, I swear! A...Stoker gave me the plate. They could not decipher the code."

"Let us hope that you are correct." Brunel leaned back into the shadows, his silhouette framed with the fierce yellow aura. From the shadows of his darkness, his eyes smouldered. "But to make certain, I'm sending a messenger to the Graveyard. It would seem my presence there has been sorely missed."

I nodded, barely hearing him, not registering his veiled threat until much later; my senses swam in their ravenous pursuit of colours. From every corner of the dark room prisms of light glinted and teased. Suddenly, an arm reached out – an *arm-that-was-not-an-arm*. Its mechanical fingers stroked my chin, my chest, the nape of my neck. Brunel smiled. Drowning in my own horror, I fainted.

***

Hours later I awoke, wrapped in the familiar cotton blankets of my own bed. A man stood over me, his black curls slick with sweat. Worry creased his aquiline nose and furrowed his wide brow.

"Holman?"

Lurgo's voice emitted from that strange mouth. How odd it was to place a visual image to the voices I knew so well. He looked nothing like the Lurgo I had imagined, but then, I didn't know, did I?

He reached a hand toward my face.

"Don't touch it!"

Lurgo jumped back, startled. In the corner under the window, a hunched, fire-haired beauty I assumed to be Julianne started to sob. Shafts of light passed through the gossamer curtains and danced on her pale green dress, darting between the creases and hiding under the embroidery. My swollen eyes gorged themselves on the new sights, and I reeled, trying to pull myself back to face my friend.

I choked "Lurgo—"

"I'm sorry, I'll call Wombwell." Lurgo backed from the room, his eyes flashing with terror. Julianne wiped the snot from her face, regarding me with blazing eyes.

"How did I get here?"

"Lurgo found you. You were lying in the street, white as a sheet and talking in tongues. You had that contraption on your face, but we couldn't seem to get it off." She swallowed. "We've been so worried, Mr. Holman."

"I'm sorry. I didn't mean to frighten you."

"You can see me, can't you?"

I nodded. She regarded me still. "This is advanced sorcery—"

"It's *science*," I corrected her.

"What is the difference? I hope you paid a fair price for your luminosity, Mr. Holman."

I thought of Brunel's final words. "The price was blood, Julianne, and I've spilt gallons of the stuff."

I started to sob. Oil leaked from the contraption and splashed on the blanket. Julianne took my hand in hers and laid her head on my lap. "When I see these gears turning inside you, the many words you've spoken to me taste like poisonous lies. You are a fool to think this monstrosity will bring you happiness."

As the gears wound their way through my skull I lost the hold on my tongue. I screamed for mercy, bawling for the comfort of death. I blamed others. I cursed the world and everyone in it. I cursed the absent Gods; I cursed my parents, my country, my friends. And, forgive me, but I cursed Thorn.

PART III:
<u>RETURN</u>

1851

No one spoke. Hundreds of eyes darted to Thorn's face and away again, as if expecting her to hex them with her gaze. She wished she could curse them all, as they had cursed her.

She had spent weeks trying to figure out a way to save them, but now that she was back here and she could again feel their accusing eyes upon her, she wasn't certain she wanted to save them after all. In fact, she wished she'd left them to their fate.

How she *hated* them; all the lies they had told her, all the years they wanted her gone, wanted her dead, and now she'd rescued them and they *still* shied away from her as if she carried the plague?

"Now you see?" she yelled into the silence. "Now you see what your Messiah has done?"

Joel squeezed her hand. Lucile stared up at her with wide, frightened eyes.

Bill Riley lurched forward, his face twisted with rage. His fist sailed towards her face, too quick for Thorn to react. Joel stepped in front of her, and the blow glanced off his broad chest.

"Thorn saved us all from utter ruin today. You will not lay a finger on her, do you hear me, Bill Riley?"

"She *saved* us? She brought them here!" he screamed. "She's the witch who's cursed us! She killed my son—"

"No!" Thorn cried, stepping forward, the rage boiling through her veins. Joel shoved her back. "I didn't kill him. Lurgo is alive. He—"

Sam pointed his Brunswick at Bill's chest. Two Navvies grabbed him under the arms and dragged him back. He kicked his legs and flailed madly, screaming at the top of his lungs.

"My son is dead. She's lying! She's brought Navvies into Graveyard and destroyed our homes and murdered our families! See how she's warped Joel's mind with her witchcraft."

In the crowd, several voices mumbled in agreement.

Thorn glowered. "Joel is in perfect control of his wits, unlike you. And if these men hadn't been here, you all would have died tonight, on Brunel's orders. Lurgo is alive and well in London. And as for Rex the *hero*: he betrayed you all. There are no London Stokers. You're not returning to the city. Brunel has come back, but he will not be calling on you. In fact, he's sent his Wall here to destroy you. You cursed me to die in the swamps for an innocent mistake and sent our best men to their deaths, all to let Rex have his glory. *Rex* brought Brunel back from the dead. He sold his soul to the machines, and doomed you all in the process. So you can shut your mouth, Bill Riley, and *listen* for a change. Where is Oswald?"

Oswald hobbled forward. Older now, his skin dotted with liver spots, he bent over his cane and regarded Thorn with shrewd eyes. "I think we can both agree that this matter had best be sorted in the privacy of the

Rothwell, before these well-meaning folk bring out the torches and pitchforks. Shall we?"

"I'm staying right here. You can run home to your Rothwell if you wish. I think you'll find it's now an open-air carriage."

"How dare you speak to an elder like that? Despicable child—"

"I'm not a child."

Joel clenched her hand. "Sir, Thorn means no disrespect—"

"Speak for yourself, Joel. He *banished* me. I've no elders here anymore."

"—but you must appreciate what she has endured these past months, and what she has rescued us from today. Her anger is justified. You cannot deny that you condemned an innocent girl to death in the swamps for failing to use a power she could not control. And now she *can* control it, you cannot even find the words to thank her when she uses it to save your life. I have explained Rex's betrayal, over and over again, but still you would not revoke Thorn's banishment. Instead, you let Bill Riley stir them all to fury with his wild tales."

" I *saw* her," one of the men said. "She controlled those tricorns, just like Aaron could. She really did it."

"But how do we know we can trust her?" his wife shot back. "Maybe she brought them here to take revenge on us. Our sons are *dead*. Did you not see the Sunken gorging themselves on their blood? What proof can she offer that she's not behind this massacre? She could be using it as a way to get back in with us."

"She could be controlling all these demons, trying to turn us against the Metal Messiah!"

"That is ridiculous!" Joel screamed.

Thorn bristled. "I'll not take this from you, any of

you. I came back, didn't I? I didn't need to come back here. I have friends, a job, a *life,*outside of this pox-ridden swamp. But I came back for you, even after the way you treated me. I brought men and weapons and helped you destroy this threat, when you've done nothing to help yourselves for nineteen years." She pointed to the body of a Sinker, lying prone across an overturned fire barrel. "Brunel hasn't come back to return the Stokers to London. He never sent us here to save us – he cares not one whit for our people. He's built himself a better workforce – an indestructible army – and you are obsolete, cast aside and forgotten. Why else would he design and build the greatest effigy to engineering in the world, and not even invite the Stokers to exhibit there?

Oswald opened his mouth to answer, but Thorn cut him off.

"You may have lost many today, but you will lose many more when he comes back here, and he *will* be back. Brunel cannot rule England while the Stokers still live, for you are still hated enough that your presence here will cost him support. Your doom marches over the valley. I have seen it. I have fought it. I know how to stop it. If you want my help, you'd do well to remember that you were the ones who sent me to die, and nevertheless I have returned with an answer for your doom, and there be no seats in the Great Conductor's Golden Carriage for turncoats and would-be murderers." She spat in the mud, and turned her back on them all. Joel and Sam placed a hand on each of her shoulders.

"You dare speak for the Gods?" Oswald's voice thundered off the walls.

"Brunel is no god, but a man with a ridiculous notion to rule over England. And as for Great Conductor, where is he? No, Oswald, your gods don't *exist!* They don't *care!* Your ridiculous faith in them is the *real* curse!"

"Thorn, listen to me..." Oswald's voice was soft, placating. She paused, listening for the slightest nuance of insincerity.

"No. You listen to *me*. You follow my plan, you follow every word I say exactly as I say it, or I'm gone, and you're all Boiler fuel. If a single word...if even the echo of a word on the breeze...is uttered in this bloody hellhole about my father or the curse, I take my tricorns back to London and you can all die rotting, festering, well-deserved deaths, for all I bloody care. These are my terms."

"Don't listen to the witch—" yelled Bill Riley.

"Goodbye." Thorn kicked splatters of mud at Oswald's slippers as she stomped away, calling her tricorns to follow. Sod them all. She would go to London by herself.

"Wait..." Joel held her arm. She wrenched it from his grasp.

"They don't *care,* Joel. Let the Boilers boil them, let the Sunken gorge themselves on this ruined city and suck the juices from their eyeballs. That's all they wanted for me, after all."

"Thorn, please..." Oswald reached out a frail hand. "Your actions today more than revoke your banishment – everyone standing here alive is in your debt."

Thorn froze. Was he serious? Had she really heard those words come out of his mouth? But Oswald's face had softened. He was looking at Thorn with an expression she'd never seen before – awe.

Oswald continued. "And Joel has taken up your cause, which is all the proof I need." He turned to the elders behind him, who, one by one, nodded their agreement. All except Bill Riley, who regarded her with raw, fierce hatred.

Her heart pounding, Thorn reached out and shook Oswald's hand. His grip was frail and cold. He smiled at her, a wobbly, frightened smile. "What is this remarkable plan of yours?" he said.

"It has two parts. The stinging rain that falls here sometimes, after the bonfires in spring? The rain that burns our skin and reduces our iron homes to decaying crumbles of rust? The Boilers fear it also. If we use that same principle to fashion a weapon, we can overpower them. Quartz has already drawn up a blueprint."

This sent murmurs throughout the crowd.

"And the other part?"

Thorn nodded at her tricorns, dancing in the rain.

Oswald sighed. "Quartz *will* be pleased. He's rallied for this day for a long time."

Thorn smiled.

***

JAMES HOLMAN'S MEMOIRS, FIRST EDITION

As the days passed in London, we waited. Each day I rose with the sun and oiled the mechanism before taking my peregrinations about the city. Every alley I wandered, every puppeteer and hawker and pie seller I encountered provided me with new visions of wonder. The flowers in Hampton Court exploded from their beds in an orgy of sensation – sight and scent entwined together, intoxicating me so I took leave of all sense and leapt over the hedges to dance in the coloured ocean. The guards found me rolling in the hyacinth bed, oil leaking from my eyes and staining the flowers. Wombwell had to come down to Scotland Yard to bail me out. He chided me for my foolishness, but I didn't care.

I cared for nothing anymore, save the colours. My selfishness and ignorance blinded me to the escalating situation in London. I didn't notice the locked doors and empty footpaths, the hushed conversations at the public house, the sombre mood and polite applause at the Crystal Palace. I overlooked the simpering Sinkers lurking in the shadows, the terrors cloaking the eyes of every pedestrian I passed.

In my defence, Wombwell too excised a less-than-thorough observation for the worries of the *hoi polloi*. He had other concerns, enamoured as he was of his newfound wealth and reputation. Having visited the palace again for a magnificent ball, Prince Albert – convinced he had found a gift to satisfy a 'man who had everything' – presented Wombwell with a fine mahogany coffin. It was at this very ball that Nero choked on a fish-bone and passed away.

The loss hit Wombwell harder than any of us could have anticipated. He retired to his room for days on end, emerging only to refill his brandy cravat. Julianne organised a lovely funeral service and I commissioned a French sculptor to create a stone effigy to Nero before his body decayed and his noble image was lost forever. Wombwell's acknowledgement of our efforts extended to a few supercilious grunts and an inquiry about the depleted status of the liquor chest.

Until, finally, after days of mourning, he emerged from his quarters with a sober mind and a cheeky grin. Julianne greeted him with an embrace so enthusiastic she sent him stumbling backward.

"Easy on the old bones, woman." Wombwell dusted himself off. "I apologise for my absence these past weeks. The death of my dearest friend sent me rather into a sour mood. But I am delighted to inform you I have now completely recovered!"

"Completely?" Such a dramatic turnaround could only mean Wombwell was up to something.

"Completely." He wore a wicked grin. "I have realised a new purpose in my life. With Nero gone and my tricorns otherwise occupied, I must find a new companion, another great creature worthy of my friendship, a creature to propel the menagerie into the history books. I must pursue the one animal that has eluded me all these years."

"And what animal is this, Master?" Julianne's smile creased in worry.

"Why, a swamp dragon, of course!"

After this preposterous statement, Wombwell was back to his old self. He spent his evenings performing small monkey shows for the upper-class residences and desperately seeking a hunter skilled enough to procure him that final, trifling curio to replace the hole in his heart left by Nero's departure. Between his mourning and his mania, he had no time to notice the unsettling in London.

However, Lurgo noticed, and it drew lines of worry across his face. On more then one occasion I entered his quarters to find him polishing his barker, muttering of impending war. Many nights I listened at his door as he and Julianne puzzled over Thorn's disappearance.

"If I knew she had reached Graveyard and had rallied the Stokers, I could do something. Instead I just wait and worry."

"You don't have to wait for her instructions, you know. You are a clever man, and I'm sure you have some idea what we should do next. Don't waste this time,

Lurgo. When Thorn comes back, you must be prepared."

"You heard what Sooty said. Practically anyone who shared sympathies with Brunel has become a Sinker. If people are so blinded by his magic that they wish to become lead-soaked vampires, then there's nothing more I can do."

"You give up too easily. You will find others who remember, others who would gladly join you."

"But…what are you doing?"

"Stretching." A simpering tone crept into Julianne's voice.

"Um…can I help…?"

At that point, I left them be.

Often Lurgo would knock on my door at all hours of the evening (sometimes reeking of Julianne's perfume) and bombard me with questions about the Battle for London, about Brunel, about the *Thunderer* and about Nicholas Thorne. I answered as best as I could, desperately trying to cling to what little shreds of truth still remained in my fable of the past.

"How did Thorn's father kill Brunel?"

"I did not see, lad. No one saw, so I suppose it's possible he never killed Brunel, after all. Nicholas pulled himself from the wreckage of the *Thunderer* and raced off to the Engine Ward. He bore a sword at his side and murder on his tongue. A while later, as I was on the boat heading for France, the other passengers' pointed out a pillar of light exploding across the sky. They searched the debris of Engine Ward afterward, of course, but found no trace of Brunel. As I understand, what remained of Nicholas Thorne is buried in a grave at Highgate."

"What made Nicholas turn against Brunel, do you

think?"

"The Boilers, lad. The Boilers did it. Nicholas had the same power as Thorn and Aaron have: that strange affinity for animals that allows them to hear and influence their thoughts. That was why he couldn't stand the Boilers."

"I don't understand."

"Although a Boiler is a machine that works by virtue of gear and piston, inside each metal chest beats the heart of a still-living animal. Some are rats or compies he traps in his lair, some are cats and dogs his minions steal from the London streets, and some are magnificent beasts imported from all corners of the globe."

Lurgo gripped the edge of his seat, his expression drawn.

"It's true, lad. I spent time in Russia and Siberia collecting specimens for Brunel. I have walked amongst the severed hearts preserved within Brunel's cloistered workshop. Nicholas said he could not rest for the noise that assailed him whenever the Boilers drew near. He said the animal minds trapped within called for help, reaching and screaming with their minds for someone, anyone, to free them from their pain. I believe that's why he betrayed Brunel – he could no longer stand to hear them scream."

"When Thorn spoke of the Boiler she encountered within the Wall, she said she could hear its pain inside her head. But the twelve-foot Boilers did not seem to bother her in quite the same manner."

"She has never mentioned this before."

"She was afraid. The Stokers banished her for her power. She did not want the same to happen here."

"It's…disconcerting. Nicholas said that the Version 1 Boilers – the first that rolled off the factory line – were very primitive. They did not affect him as the others did. Perhaps Brunel has thought of some method to refine his machines. Perhaps the hearts of his new Boilers beat with only gears and tines."

"I hope so." Lurgo looked sad. "I wish Thorn were here."

"Me too, lad. I wish it with all my heart."

I took Lurgo to visit Nicholas' grave. I'd never visited myself, and though Thorn had spoken of the decrepit state of it, I hadn't prepared myself for the compie-infested hovel that greeted me. Lurgo knelt on one knee before the shattered facings of the final solid remnant of Thorn's past, and he crossed himself with reverence.

"No man should reside in this broken dream. Nicholas Thorne saved this country. He deserves better." Lurgo rose and dusted off his trousers. "I will repair this."

And he did. He brought supplies from market with the wage Wombwell gave him and every night when he finished his chores at the menagerie, he worked at the gravesite, hammering and scrubbing, working his skin raw.

One evening Julianne arrived in my home carrying a hamper of bacon sandwiches and strips of Dutch liquorice. "I want to talk to Lurgo, *now*. I don't know the way to Highgate, so you're going to escort me."

I set down my novel and checked the mechanism in the mirror above the desk. Since it was night, I lit the tiny wick inside what used to be my temple, and felt the flame flare to life, like a hot tongue flicking across my retina. My study glowed orange and Julianne's fire-red hair blinded me with iridescent strands.

"Doesn't that hurt?"

"Like a thousand broad-range gauge nails piercing my

skull." I dusted off my bowler and settled it atop my head. "Let's go."

Hand in hand we traipsed across London. Julianne chatted aimlessly about this and that, Lurgo's name appearing in every second sentence. I munched on a salty stick of liquorice and thought about Thorn all those miles away, and the immense task that lay before her.

Whatever fate befell Thorn was now completely out of my hands. But Lurgo and Julianne could still hope.

We found Lurgo leaning against his hatchet, his features drawn in a contemplative wince. The tomb itself was unrecognisable; he'd cleared away the detritus, removed the crumbling facing stones and planted rows of hyacinth and poppy to hide the cracked cobbles. He'd melted the glass from the broken bottles into a mottled panel to replace the rusted door-grate.

Julianne presented him with his supper. He bit into a pie, acknowledging the two of us with a nod and indecipherable grunt.

"You've done remarkable work here," Julianne said.

"And now it's over." Lurgo stared at the pie. "Something has been prickling at the back of my mind."

"Lice?" inquired Julianne, indicating the compies with a nod of her head.

Lurgo frowned. "No. Could you two help me with something? It isn't pleasant."

We nodded. He unshackled the lock and gestured for us to follow him inside. "Bring in the lamp and those shovels, please."

The flicker in my eyes lit the tiny crypt. I could see Lurgo had made an effort inside as well, scraping out the compie faeces and patching the leaking roof, though he couldn't afford paint to cover the scribblings on the wall. He pointed into the corner, where a rude symbol had been scratched into the stone. "I think Thorn did this when she stayed here. She burnt this into one of my father's coats once, after he chided her."

My eye-lamps illuminated the etching above Thorn's, where two stick-figures copulated in an avaricious pose that would make even Julianne blush. The female was unceremoniously named 'Lydia', and above the head of the male figure someone had scrawled 'Rex' beside a Williams family crest.

"Ew." Julianne's lips curled back in distaste.

"Help me lift this lid."

Julianne screwed her face up, but she moved to the far end of the stone sarcophagus and pushed her shovel into the lead seal. I moved into the centre, and pressed the blade of the mattock into the seal. When Lurgo gave the word, we pushed and lifted and strained against that stone lid. The acrid lead dust punctured my heaving chest, and trickles of sweat rolled down my spine. Finally, the lead seal crumbled away, and the stone lid slid a few inches off the case.

Lurgo dropped his shovel and pushed it onto the plinth. "Come in closer, Holman. I can't see."

Julianne covered her eyes with her hands. "I don't want to see."

I stooped over the coffin, casting the glow from my eye into that crack of shadow. I bit my lip in anticipation of the horror: I didn't want to gaze upon the skeleton of my good friend.

I needn't have worried. The coffin was empty. Nicholas Thorne had never been buried there.

***

Far from further discouraging Lurgo, this news of

Nicholas' missing body spurred him into a flurry of activity. Over the following weeks, Lurgo spent less and less time with the menagerie, or smoking with me, and instead wandered the streets for hours, always returning encrusted in filth and tracking soot into the carpets. Sometimes Julianne went with him.

He began to return with people. First a boy and girl a little older then he was, who dripped sewer muck through my carpets and stank out my house. Though I presented them with hot soup and inquired of them in my most amiable tones, they would not speak to me but only to Lurgo, and even then they mumbled into their soiled collars. He left them sleeping on the floor in the parlour and retreated back into the night.

The next day there was another seated at the breakfast table. An aging man, at least twenty years my senior, whose greatcoat hung from his shoulders in ribbons, the buttons and stitching long lost to the sewers. He babbled incoherent sentences about train construction and fell asleep in his porridge.

"Why must my home be a refuge for your smatter-haulers and haymarket hectors?" I asked as he scooped the old man off the table.

"These people are Stokers, Holman, left behind when the last trains took us to Graveyard. They're my comrades, my friends. I will hunt every abandoned sewer tunnel and feculent workhouse till I find them all."

And he did. When he could no longer lodge them in the parlour and my housekeeper utterly refused to cook porridge for thirty-six, he began sleeping them in the open field next to the menagerie, and he also began training them, with knives, with irons, and with the animals.

Lurgo had a purpose. He'd found his part in Thorn's

master scheme. I watched him and Julianne each day running their knife drills, rubbing oil into the gears inside my temple with a damp rag. I twined my fingers through the delicate handle of my teacup, and felt deeply ashamed.

***

Now, Igor, jump!

Thorn sensed the tricorn's terror as they approached the steaming contraption. She didn't blame him; she wanted nothing more than to turn away herself. The Boiler's arm lowered, ready to fire.

Sinking as low as she could behind his frill, Thorn gritted her teeth and concentrated on pushing her command out through her mind, through the threads that connected her to Igor. His weight shifted and he leapt, crumpling the mainframe with his thick head and skewering the arm with one of his horns.

Thorn pitched forward, losing her grip on the frill and somersaulting over Igor's downturned head. Her left side crunched into the ground and she wrenched her body away as the Boiler toppled over, scraps of metal flying in every direction. The mud bubbled as the steam hissed from the bent valves.

Joel tugged the boiler upright again, and raced to her side. "By Great Conductor's steaming pistons, are you alright?"

Igor nudged her face, his thick horn grazing her cheek.

Thorn groaned. "I'm fine. Never better."

Joel rolled her over and she saw a long gash where Igor's horn had ripped through her trousers. Luckily, her leg survived, and Joel wiped the few drops of blood away with his kerchief.

"C'mon, up you get." He wrapped his arms underneath her and lifted her from the mud, steadying her against his body so she didn't fall. Igor butted the Boiler again, and it sank further into the mud, emitting a pained gurgling noise. Looking at the broken, mud-caked boiler, she giggled, pressing her face to his chest.

"We did it, Joel. We did it."

"*You*did it, Thorn. Igor and I would be nothing if not for you."

Igor nuzzled her thigh in agreement.

"Do you really think I can fight Brunel? My sense has always been so sporadic, what if I fail?"

"The sense isn't what binds these animals to you, silly. It's *this.*" He tapped her chest, just over her heart. "Whether you call them or not, they'll follow you into doom and destruction. And so will I."

"I'm frightened to face him again, Joel. He has no love for anything. He has nothing to lose, and I could lose everything."

"This is exactly why you *should* be the one to lead the Stokers against him. You represent the worst of everything he's done to our people. And you're wrong, Brunel has much to lose. He's afraid of his own mortality, and it is that which you bring him."

"Joel Williams, what have you done to my Boiler?"

Quartz hobbled across the ridge, followed by Sam pulling a small cart loaded with various contraptions. Behind him jogged a rabble of men, some Stokers, some Navvies, eager to test his new acid weapons on the makeshift training field. They stopped in their tracks, staring gape-mouthed at the flailing Boiler.

"It's okay!" Joel called out to them. "It's not real, a pale imitation of an original."

"I'll give you pale imitation over my knee, boy, if you keep destroying my machines!"

The makeshift Boilers had been Quartz's idea, and – as usual – his astute mind had created a replica so realistic Thorn almost couldn't bear to gaze upon it. He'd built the bodies from the remnants of the machines left in the swamp, beating out the dents made by tricorn horns and mending the gaps with scraps he'd salvaged from the trains. They handled more like a rusted plough and they didn't *live* like Brunel's Boilers, but as always Quartz lavished his every proficiency upon their upkeep.

"I'm beginning to see why Brunel loves these machine so much." Quartz stroked the mainframe. "Poor buggers, what'd they do to deserve this treatment?"

Joel and Thorn looked at each other, and burst out laughing.

***

They fought off the next advance of the Boilers before the month was out. Thorn hadn't expected them to arrive so soon. The tricorns had shot up again, and now stood six feet high. They were an intimidating sight, but their training had barely begun. Thus far only Igor and Lurgette would allow a rider to mount their back.

The attack came during Thorn's watch. Joel had set up a draughts board on the observation deck. She was warming her hands around a mug of broth while plotting the demise of his counters, when she heard the bell for the outer boundary ring.

Thorn dashed to the window and directed the lens over the Narrow. The light found nothing, but upon the horizon she heard a sound that froze the blood in her veins.

Stomping, churning, clanging. The hiss of steam. The gibber of madmen.

The Wall.

Joel eased Thorn's hand from the gear, and pulled her away from the window. He frowned at the wall of levers and gears. "Which one sounds the alarm?"

Numb and shaking, Thorn pointed to a rusting lever.

Joel pulled. Steam rushed from the boilers into the pressure tubes, and erupted from the apex of the Turret with a piercing whistle. Thorn met Joel's eyes, and he squeezed her shoulder.

"The tricorns," she whispered, her voice tight.

They clattered down the stairs, passing a groggy Quartz on their way. He hopped about, cursing as he struggled to pull on his boots. Thorn grabbed the bridles from the hook over the door, and raced to the pens.

The Graveyard teemed with life. Women bustled back and forth, scraping the tinder and lighting the lamps and torches. The men congregated in the alleys, rubbing sleep from their eyes and listening for the distant clanging. Many of them unsheathed knives and tugged pistols from their holsters. The Navvies already gathered outside the turret, their Brunswicks loaded and ready.

Joel and Sam darted behind the Turret and returned dragging a crate. "Grab your weapons, boys!" Joel prised open the lid and they passed around the new weapons; Quartz's elegant Stingers. They helped the men strap the iron tanks to their backs and cock the nozzle-levers. Thorn left them in charge and raced to the pens, kicking wayward chickens from beneath her feet.

She found the tricorns in a state of excitement. Igor and Lurgette danced in lopsided circles around the pens, smashing their bony faces against the walls. The Navvy guarding them shrugged at her – he couldn't control them – and left to join his comrades.

Thorn lifted a set of iron greaves and struggled to strap them around Igor's legs. "Hold still, baby," she cooed, prising her mind inside his. Igor snorted, but ceased his struggling. As quick as she could Thorn strapped the others into their minimal armour. This attack had come too soon; there were only enough greaves for five tricorns, and only Igor and Lurgette had chest plates. *It will have to do.*

She wrapped the coarse bridle under Igor's chin and pulled herself onto his back. Leaning low and clutching the reins with white knuckles, she squeezed her heels into his ribs and uttered the command inside her head.

Go!

Igor barrelled outside the stable carriage, his siblings charging at their heels. She dug her nails into the skin on his frill, letting the reins flap loose by her side. Her heart drummed in her ears.

The Graveyard lay deserted now, but the bobbing lights of the torches disappeared over the crest of the inner boundary. They careened past the Turret, its lens swinging madly from the single pin. She heard shouting, and a woman screamed. She pressed her heels deeper, and Igor sped towards the battle.

As the tricorns thundered into the Narrow and bucked up the slope into the swamp, she saw the thin outline of the encroaching Wall, barely eight feet high and still a skeleton of scaffolding and mechanical limbs. Shadows and Sinkers crawled over the frame, snarling and swiping at the Stokers.

"Out of my way!"

The crowd parted as Igor galloped toward the far end of the Wall, where their real enemy waited. Igor's plate clanked together as he drove his sturdy legs forward.

Stay with me, Thorn commanded the other tricorns. *Stay together.*

The torchlights flew past like shooting stars. Her mind flashed back to her first magical nights in London, where thousands of twinkling lights bathed Wombwell's arena in a peaceful glow. But this light illuminated a much different scene.

Amongst the lights Thorn saw men raising their rifles and readying the Stingers. And – to her horror – she saw the stretching, twitching metal fingers of the towering twelve-foot Boilers, grabbing and twisting and thrusting, pulling more machines out of the Wall. Thorn counted at least twenty of them, and her heart sank. Below the mists from the steam valves that shrouded the battlefield, she saw men crumbling with fear, sinking into the peat in grim anticipation of defeat and death.

Joel stood below the first phalanx, shouting orders at Sam and assessing the challenge with his piercing eyes. His sleek fingers caressed the barrel of his barker, and she knew he had at least two grenades on his belt. Beside him, Quartz struggled under the weight of his Stinger's twin tanks. He grasped the nozzle with crackling, determined fingers and laughed at the enemy with the gusto of the world's finest comedian.

Perhaps this is *a joke, thinking we could beat them.*

No, she must not think like that.

The Boilers advanced first, hissing and cranking, with the Sunken scrabbling behind, licking their blistered lips. The men leapt back in fright, the terror shining in their eyes. Several fired their rifles at the advancing machines. The bullets ricocheted off their iron skin, and they continued to advance, uninjured. She cringed, sensing the waves of panic collapsing over their defeated shoulders. *I have to do something, or we'll lose before the battle even begins.*

"Don't worry about the Sunken!" Thorn cried as she galloped past. "You have to stop the Boilers, they control everything. Use the Stingers!"

Sparks flew overhead and fizzing darts sprinkled the upper buttress like porcupine quills. Joel called them onward while Quartz sent forth a spark shower from his Stinger. As the water and the nitrogen dioxide combined, they pushed a spray of noxious acid into the path of the Boilers. The machines reeled with the rush of acid, which melted their arms into congealed stumps and caused thick crusts to form on their bellies.

Igor slowed. They were in position. Thorn drew his head around, and when she saw an opening she yanked on the reins. Igor barrelled forward, lowering his head and baring his gleaming ivory horns. She could hear the others galloping after her.

The Boilers moaned and trundled back, retreating from the onslaught of acid, but Thorn and her tricorn had other interests. She felt the cords of their minds unravelling inside her head, and she caught each one and sent her command. *Now.*

A thunderous roar erupted from Igor as his horns connected with the frame of the Wall.

Sinkers scrambled for cover as the stampede stove in a section of the scaffold, driving the piles backward into the mechanisms. Thorn pushed her head underneath the crest of Igor's frill and shut her eyes. Her stomach leapt to her throat as all around her metal crunched and the Sinkers screeched.

When she felt air move around her again, Thorn opened her eyes and let out a delighted squeal. Sinkers scrambled from the wounded scaffolding and frantically tried to rescue the sagging pylons. Pipes burst and cogs rolled into the mud. On the flank, the Navvies discharged their rifles, sending several Sinkers crashing into the mud.

They're weak, Igor! Her mind roared. *Hit them again!*

Igor shook splinters of iron and lead piping from his horns, and reared around for another attack. Behind her, the Stokers cheered. The other tricorns thundered past, forming up beside her in a line of razor sharp horns – living, breathing siege weapons. They growled, low in their throats.

Several more Boilers zoomed from the broken scaffold, steam hissing from their valves. Their injured comrades sizzled as they turned to rush their reinforcements. *No, go back!* The puffing steam seemed to say.

"Now, now!" Thorn scraped her throat raw from yelling. She kicked her heels in and the tricorns took off towards the distracted Boilers.

The command exploded inside her head – the pain roasting her eyeballs inside her skull. Every animal for miles around must've heard her command.

Too late, the Boilers realised their mistake. As the first wave of acid poured over their left flank, those who remained un-mutilated turned their backs to the Stokers and their stinging guns and rushed back towards their falling creation.

Joel sprinted before the fray, cupping his hands over his mouth. "Throw the grenades!" he yelled. "We'll smoke the bastards out!"

Fires caught at intervals along the scaffold. As the flames reached the puddles of acid they erupted into engorged firestorms, devouring the Wall and the flailing machines.

The Boilers turned in circles, bombarded on all sides.

Seeing her chance, Thorn and Igor rushed again at the squabbling Sinkers. As he crashed through the debris Thorn bounced forward, grabbing Igor's frill in time to save herself toppling over his neck again. All around her the other tricorns thundered, roaring with triumph as they crushed the encroaching Wall.

A Sinker howled as he fell from the burning scaffold, skewering his belly through Igor's horn. He kicked at Thorn's face as he frantically tried to disentangle his intestines from around the ivory blade. She reached up with one arm and pushed him off, his stomach making a sickening *thwack* as it slid from the horn.

"Run, Igor!"

The acid splashed at their feet, but Igor pranced around the deadly puddles as though he'd trained in the Royal Ballet. The air stunk of burned skin and corroding metal. Boilers sank to the ground in puddles of wasted metal. Steam hissed and gurgled as their fuselages melted into dribbling columns. As Igor carried her across the fens she heard the first explosions as the fuselages ruptured and the superheated steam escaped, casting a dense cloud over the field as flames engulfed the Wall.

The wooden scaffolds buckled and fell, and down came the Sinkers in a pile of wailing, twisting limbs and sizzling flesh. Thorn stared into the wreckage, a calmness settling over her; a victory she could finally own for all eternity.

No more curse, Daddy. I've made my own legacy now.

A figure ran towards her. Thorn lowered her head behind Igor's frill, preparing to run down the stray Sinker, but it was only Joel. He slumped to his knees, his breath heaving and his rifle flapping uselessly at his side. "We...did...it," he puffed.

"We couldn't have, without you."

"Without *you*, Thorn, this would have come to naught. This victory belongs to you."

She rolled off Igor's back and collapsed beside him. Wrapping her shaking arms around his neck, she nuzzled her face into his matted curls.

As Thorn and Joel moved amongst the herd, calming the tricorns and wiping blood from the wounds, they watched the Stokers and the Navvies soak the remainder of the Wall in pitch and acid and set it alight. An orange stripe rippled across the landscape as the symbol of their oppression and poverty and banishment crumbled into the peat. Joel held her hand and squeezed, and though the wind whipped her tangled hair across her face, and her eyes and skin stung from the ashes and the acid, inside she felt warm.

***

JAMES HOLMAN'S MEMOIRS, FIRST EDITION

As I stirred my morning tea and admired the beauty of the cream elixir being devoured into the brown maelstrom, Julianne rushed into the parlour. "James, Lurgo, you must come quick!" She banged her hands on the table for emphasis. "They're at St. Saviour's Dock. He's got one!"

My saucer smashed onto the table. Lurgo spat his porridge over the front of Julianne's pinafore. She wiped globules of oats from her curls and grabbed his wrists, wrenching him to his feet. She stamped impatiently under the lintel while we struggled into our boots.

I knew my way to the docks blindfolded, (sorry, a little ex-blindman's humour) so I allowed Julianne and Lurgo to run on ahead. Clamours of activity seemed to shuffle the crowd forward, pushing sweating bodies into me in an uncouth manner I'd rarely experienced with my walking cane. I stopped at the corner of Fleet Street to get my bearings. As I wiped the steam from the glass bulb of my eye, I bumped a lady forcing her pram between myself and a rotund gentlemen perusing a nearby pie selection.

"Pardon me—" she started to say, but then her eyes rested on my face. My hand was still raised to my cheek and my fingers pressed inside the clockwork contraption that emerged from my temples.

"Ma'am, it's all right—"

The woman gasped, flipping over her pram in her haste to escape me. The pie-seller looked up at me in distaste, and hurriedly turned his cart in the opposite direction.

I sighed.

I pressed on. The path down to St. Saviour's – known to the locals as 'Savoury Dock' on account of the smell – involved a pleasant jaunt through Jacob's Island, London's most deplorable slum. Here, like the great water-neckers of northern Scotland, the poverty of London lurked in waiting, thin necks and slimy tentacles poised to break the surface and ensnare the prosperous city. The leaning, filth-encrusted tenements and workhouses rose stinking from the bleeding streets like festering teeth in the mouths of the dockworkers they housed. Each was stained black from the thick, cholera-infused atmosphere, striped with brown streaks where the upper-storey privies had been emptied into the street below. Human waste gushed through street-cut drains towards the river, and tubs of the filth-filled Thames water sat on crooked windowsills, waiting for the occupants to skim off the solid particles. It was the fluid they drank with their meals, washing down the taste with rotting fish heads and influenza.

Beyond this capital of cholera, the river beckoned. I passed over a rickety bridge that hovered over a swirling ditch of putrefaction, and pressed my kerchief into my mouth, choking back the urge to throw up. I followed the crowd along the shore of the Thames. It was hardly a river at all, but rather a wide, stagnant ditch which boats and barges had to hack through rather than sail over. Animal carcasses bobbed against the pylons and collected at the sterns of the heavier vessels. Here, Rivermen – fellows who made their living fishing bloated corpses from the Thames – hang off the slimed pylons, dangling their iron hooks in the pea-green fungi. Below me, two men tossed sacks of grain into their barge, while another crouched in an empty shipping crate, manoeuvring his craft along the river with a makeshift barge pole. The scene reminded me of my time in Venice. This was a Venice of Drains.

Even this deplorable scene and the mephitic vapour that rose from the putrid water could not scour the joy of my vision. I saw Lurgo's tousled mane bobbing up ahead, and edged my way through the gathering throng towards him. Ladies exclaimed and pointed at Wombwell, who strutted across a twenty-foot high shipping crate that took pride of place on the crowded dock. He wore his finest tailcoat, now flecked with Thames grime, and rapped the beams of the crate with his ivory-tipped cane. His whip rested in a curl over his shoulder.

"Ladies and gentlemen, forgive me for the prolonged absence of my menagerie. It is my delight to inform you that we have returned with an even bigger, more surprising, more delightful and stupendous show than ever before!"

The crowd applauded with much aplomb. Wombwell clambered down from the crate and stood on a rusted dolly. I pushed my way to stand beside him. The two monkeys, Bella and Alberto, lay in the shade of the dolly, their tails slapping against the wet boards and their faces drawn in long pouts. Lurgo scratched Bella behind the ears and she let out a huge yawn.

"So without further ado, I present to you the newest member of Wombwell's Extraordinary Extravaganza!"

Wombwell tossed his cane into the air. Two acrobats leapt atop the crate and removed the pins. They pulled back the lid. Everyone leaned forward, chattering in anticipation. I felt my stomach sink into my slippers.

Out of the box flew a length of galvanised chain, each link as thick as my torso. The heavy bond clanged against the side of the crate, nearly decapitating several people. The crowd fell silent, and it was only then I heard the growl.

It began low, but rose with a rumbling foreboding above the crowd, rattling the dock planks and pulling the chain taunt. An eye the size of a wagon wheel peeked over the edge of the crate and regarded the enthralled audience. It was only when the creature raised its head to the heavens and bared its silvery, sharp teeth that the screams began.

The women were the first to scatter, rushing towards Jacob's Island with an enthusiasm that had never before been encountered. Their screams startled the carrion birds that skimmed the milky surface of the Thames, sending clouds of clattering wings hurtling into the retreating populace, tearing dresses and scratching delicate skin. Dockhands rushed in, swinging deck-plank clubs at the clamorous birds, trying to swipe them away from the unloaded stores. Amongst this calamity stood Wombwell, spinning his cane on his beefy fingers and grinning like the madman he had certainly become.

"Isn't he just darling?" gushed Julianne, her hands entwined over her heart as she admired the roaring beast, who had now dragged his towering body upright and struggled to lever itself free with its diminutive arms.

"He's..." I rubbed my lens, not certain if I were seeing correctly. "No, darling is not the word I would choose."

Wombwell's eyes danced with devilish innocence. "I've named him Boris."

"Of course you have."

He turned to me in concern. "Is everything okay with you, my friend?"

"You said it would be a swamp dragon! Four feet high and basically harmless! Not a giant bloody monster!"

Boris swung its colossal head, and uprooted a shipping container. Onlookers scrambled for safety as several sacks of Indian tobacco scattered across the dock.

Wombwell smiled like a sozzled schoolboy, "I admit, a slight misrepresentation of the facts may have occurred. Won't you come and introduce yourself to our newest attraction?"

***

The house was unusually quiet, so quiet in fact, that I could hear conversations from the street wafting through my open window. A police inspector and the local butcher stood on the corner, discussing the latest disappearances in hushed tones. A few streets over, a woman screamed, and the two men rushed off to investigate.

Wombwell was down on the fields, training his Great Dragon with the assistance of Julianne and Lurgo's motley band of buck-toothed gammys. Lurgo had gone on another of his nightly meanders. Or so I had assumed, until he slammed open the door of my study and stormed up to my desk.

"I'm going out, and you're coming with me."

I glanced out the window, and back at Lurgo, whose face was set with an unusually harsh expression. "I'm busy, tonight, Lurgo. I have letters to write—"

"What use is writing letters when they won't ever be delivered outside the Wall? Come with me." Lurgo insisted.

"Can't Julianne attend you on this jape?"

"She is learning to ride on Boris' back, or some such foolery. I want you to come."

With no chance of peace if I didn't appease him, I pulled on my coat, oiled my eyes, tucked a flick-knife into my pocket and followed Lurgo out the front door.

The cold air bit my bare cheeks, and I pulled my collar up in an attempt to keep out the chill. Lurgo hurried me through the streets, pushing me closer and closer towards the black cloud that marked the now operational Engine Ward.

"Lurgo, we shouldn't be here."

"Why not? You've been here before."

The pressure of his hand on my back increased, pushing me forward, preventing my escape. Fear crept upon me like a great lump in my stomach.

Lurgo stopped. "Look," he said.

We stood in the centre of Bishops Bridge, and as we leaned over we had a view of the Engine Ward. I had never laid eyes on it in its previous state before, and it was more terrible to behold with my restored sight than anything I could have imagined in my blindness.

Smoke billowed from a thousand chimney stacks, which rose from giant holes bored into the street itself. The noisome engines that powered them lay deep within the earth, far from prying eyes. Jutting from amongst these structures were the various spires of the lesser scientific sects, illuminated by ribbons of fire that stretched from spire to spire like hellish Christmas decorations. I saw the Metic church, its spire painted with those cursed metric measurements - centimetres and metres and litres - they wish to impose upon all the world. Christians, too, had built their church in Brunel's shadow; the wooden crosses of their carpenter God charred black in the fires.

The Wall ran through the centre, and spread two arms to encircle the district. It reminded me of the great citadels I'd seen in the East – places of sanctuary, to keep invading forces at bay. But these Walls existed for an entirely different purpose – to keep the populace trapped. The streets crisscrossing the district were littered with debris, and fires burnt in huge metal drums. In the market square the engineers toiled in their workshops, heedless to the hell building up around them. The scientists and engineers stood on the corners to preach, but their words were lost amidst the eternal *clang clang clang* of the Wall. Their audience now were not learned men, but Sinkers, for the snarling creatures prowled every street as far as my eyes could see.

And at the centre, Brunel's Chimney towered over the rest; its smooth steel facade gleaming in the flickering firelight. I knew its perfect curves and symmetrical face could not have been created at the hands of a carpenter – it was a machine palace, a sanctuary for oil and steam.

From the great doors of the structure marched a line of figures. Not men, but machines. An army of Boilers fresh off the assembly line, marching out toward the Wall. It was just as Brunel had always dreamed.

I shuddered under my warm coat. "Never in my darkest dreams had I imagined a place such as this."

"It was not always like this. In fact, it has only become such a few weeks ago, around the time you returned with your new eye."

"The two events are in no way connected."

"You know much that you do not say, James," Lurgo mumbled, so quietly I could have pretended I didn't hear him.

"And you let nothing sneak past your cunning mind, lad."

Lurgo held out his hand. "Shall we?"

Together we followed the road around the perimeter wall, our boots muffled by the clanking within. Frightening warmth emanated from the wall, and we moved to the centre of the road to avoid it. We passed no other man on the road.

I was just about to inquire about the nature of our journey when Lurgo grabbed my wrist and dragged me into a recess. I turned to scold him for wrenching me so, but he held his finger to his lips and gestured for me to follow him. We stood inside the entrance to a narrow tunnel, surrounded by iron on all sides. It was similar to the secret passage that took me into the Chimney, but I did not know where this particular tunnel led. I did not want to follow, but Lurgo's expression informed me I had no choice.

We descended a series of steps into a wide, rank pit, probably the remains of a disused sewage conduit, to judge by the smell. In the distance, water dripped. Down another staircase, and I found myself standing in a wide, high tunnel, the familiar sleepers of a broad gauge railway under my feet. Above our heads, the machinery churned its eternal racket. I walked along the railway behind Lurgo, his steady gait revealing he'd been here before. *What is he doing skulking around the Engine Ward?*

Has Brunel got to him, too? I felt in my pocket for my knife.

"I followed this tunnel yesterday," he whispered, as if he heard my fears. "It finishes underneath the Dirigire clockwork exhibit in the Crystal Palace. I believe it stretches right underneath the Chimney, but I've been hoping to find out why."

His question hung in the air, unanswered. Why would Brunel need an underground railway between the Crystal Palace and the Engine Ward?

Light illuminated the passage ahead, shining from a recess in the wall of the tunnel. Lurgo sucked in a breath, and pointed toward the recess. I leaned my head out, and I saw what he wanted me to see.

Blinded as I have been for the last twenty years, I can honestly say I have never before encountered a horror such as this, and I can only hope that I would never see such a thing again.

I looked not into a recess but a narrow doorway. The light came from a wide hole carved into the ground above us, its sides sloping down into a steep pit. And this pit was filled with men and women, naked, some screaming, some writhing, some still and white as death. All piled together in this horrid hole, crawling and kicking and scrambling over each other, desperately clambering up the slick walls, reaching for the sky, because the sky meant freedom. But from identical doorways spaced around the outer edge, the Sunken swarmed. They crowded the outer edges, digging and pawing at the pit, clawing at the fresh, delectable meat that rushed towards them. Hundreds upon hundreds of howling, rasping, hungry Sinkers ripped at the bodies and gorged on the blood as it poured from the severed limbs of their victims.

I staggered backward, my head spinning from the rancid smell of rotting human meat.

"This isn't the worst of it." Lurgo whispered, grabbing my arm and pulling me to my feet again.

I did not wish to see any more, but Lurgo had already retreated into the passage, and I could not find my way back by myself. The last thing I wanted was to be buried alongside those unfortunate souls. I hurried after him, keeping my head bent low to avoid scraping it on the bricked ceiling. The screams followed us, and I knew their horrible wailing would haunt my dreams.

I could not begin to guess the purpose of that unspeakable feeding pit. *Brunel had always shown disdain for the Vampire King's Sunken. He believed the future lay not in the hands of degenerate, lead-addicted husks, but in dependable, controllable machines. He...oh Gods, those people, crawling in front of my eyes! I am going to be sick—*

"Up here." Lurgo grabbed a mesh staircase and scrambled up, his boots clanging loudly in the gloom. I gripped the railing and heaved myself up.

We climbed for what seemed like eternity, and my head spun from the effort. Or perhaps it was the horrific visions that danced inside my skull. We hunched over and crawled between two metal grates, the space between two floors of a giant complex. Lurgo motioned for me to stop. He reached up and grasped the edges of a metal hatch.

"This." Lurgo opened the hatch.

We peered through the floor grate of a great hall, so enormous in scale that I could only guess at its full size, for it continued on and on into the shadows. A tiny circular window in the lofty ceiling served as the only light, and as my eyes adjusted I could make out long, wide couplings, stacked high along each wall. Attached to these couplings with pinions and bolts were row after row of new Boilers. Thousands of the giant machines sat, immobile, their iron gratings staring forward, while juices ran through pipes attached to their backs. Steam poured from giant engines sitting on the floor of the room.

With a shaking finger, Lurgo pointed to a nearby Boiler. The furnace door in its belly lay open, flapping on two creaking hinges. Black liquid poured from the pipes in the walls into a compartment in its upper torso. I squinted, and raised my hand to adjust my eye.

Inside, nestled into a compartment and surrounded by hundreds of pristine gears and valves, I saw a living organ. It glowed red as it throbbed and pulsed inside the Boiler's belly. With each beat, the blackish liquid pumped its way through the mechanisms. The pistons turned and clicked through their cycle. I could see the liquid sliding into the limbs and pulsing through the pistons that drove the great machine.

I'd spent enough time with anatomists at the Royal Society to realise that organ was a human heart.

I sank to my knees, holding my face. Despair washed over me. Lurgo dropped beside me, and slid the hatch down.

"Now you see?" he hissed. "Now you see why Thorn couldn't hear them? Now you see why Rex couldn't stand a chance? Brunel has made these contraptions from the hearts of the people the Sunken collect. This is the man you entrusted with your eyes. Your eyes, James!"

I could no longer restrain myself. I started to weep. Lurgo glared at me, and he opened his mouth to say more, but something hissed at us from the darkness.

We froze, and listened. The creature hissed again, and inched toward us, making a scraping sound as it crawled over the grating. It came from over my left shoulder.

I whirled around, swirling the mechanism in my eye to send a small beam of light at the wall behind us. In the dim light I could just make out the shape of a Sinker, crouching, ready to pounce.

Lurgo grabbed my arm. There was nowhere to go. I fumbled in my pocket for my knife.

The Sinker grinned, and its sharpened teeth dripped with blood. It raised its arms, and held out an object for us. My iron-tipped cane, the delicate filigree bulb on the handle gnawed away.

Lurgo gasped. "Maxwell?"

The Sinker's head jerked up and down. He was nodding.

"Have you come to eat us?"

Maxwell shook his head vigorously.

"Did you come because of the blood?"

He nodded, and rubbed his tummy. He was hungry.

"Do you want to come away with us? We will find you some food."

Maxwell nodded.

"Okay, but you have to help us get outside without being seen."

He nodded again, turned on his heels, and darted back across the grating. Lurgo raced after him and I crept behind them. I don't remember my exit from the Engine Ward, nor the darting, shadowed trip back through the streets to my residence, Maxwell's ghoulish appearance disguised by Lurgo's Ulster coat, for my mind was occupied with the visions of those poor souls, trapped in that pit of death, being torn apart by the Sinkers; and the Boilers, lined up in rows like a factory floor. Brunel had some nefarious plans to unleash upon this city, of that I was now certain.

Wombwell looked up when we crashed into the parlour, and his expression of surprise quickly turned to one of fear, a rare expression for the proprietor. Maxwell dropped the cane at his feet and rolled on the carpet, leaving a trail of sticky film running along the hall.

"Lurgo!" Wombwell yelled. "This obsession of yours has really gone too far—"

"It's Maxwell, George. He's come to help!"

Wombwell paled. "How did you find him?"

"He found us. He helped us. I'm telling you—"

"And just *where* did he find you? You've gone into the Engine Ward, haven't you? Lurgo, you stupid boy! If Brunel catches you, you could end up as Maxwell here, do you understand that?"

"I understand all right!" Lurgo yelled. "I understand this whole nation is under threat and no one seems to care!"

Maxwell grabbed a candlestick off the table and sunk his teeth into the ornate filigree.

"We do care, lad." Wombwell lowered himself into an armchair, his eyes fixed on the Sinker. "But we have our own lives to live, and while we are helpless, we may as well live them."

"Thorn doesn't think us helpless!" Lurgo yelled. "And she's done more to stop Brunel than the entire country combined."

"We know nothing of what Thorn has managed to

accomplish, or even if she made it to Graveyard—"

"She made it to Graveyard." Lurgo's eyes burned with loathing.

"You don't know that, Lurgo. And if she has, we have only a vague hope that she'll come to London with help. Help against what? We don't even know that."

"Yes, we do. Brunel's new Boilers are controlled by human hearts. The Engine Ward has become a well of bodies as Brunel finds more fuel to feed his Boilers. We're too late to stop him: already he has amassed a great army, one that needs no sleep."

"How has he done this? I don't understand—"

"He has the recipe for breathing life into machines," I said.

Wombwell and Lurgo whirled to face me.

"What?"

I closed my eyes, unable to bear seeing their faces as I finally admitted my part in this horror. "Before she left the menagerie, Thorn gave me a plate – a possession of her father's. She did not know what it meant, but I did, for I had seen it once before. Nicholas stole the plate from Brunel before he went into hiding. This plate contained a key – a code that, when activated, enables a machine to take its instructions from the soul of an animal placed inside it. It activates a chemical process, which imbues life into the metal itself. *Life-that-is-not-life.* Without the plate, Brunel cannot create Boilers that move and think for themselves, that work together to solve problems: he has to calculate precise directions for every one, which was what he had been doing up until this point." Oily tears welled within the mechanism. I wiped them away with the back of my hand. "I traded the plate with Brunel for my eyes."

I opened my eyes, peering through my tears, wanting

to see and yet desperately fearing their reactions. Wombwell's face turned white. Lurgo's fist sailed across the table, and slammed me in my right eye socket. The force of the blow bent the delicate pins back into my skull, and I cried and fell back. My face burned, my head exploded. From far away I heard voices – Lurgo and Wombwell arguing – and a timid female voice calling my name. I blacked out.

***

I awoke hours later with a throbbing pain in my right eye socket. Someone had carried me into my bed, and pulled the covers up, but I was still wearing my jacket and trousers, caked with sweat and soot stains from the Engine Ward. I tried to roll over, but the pain flared again, and I fell back onto the pillow with a sob.

"I don't know if he'll forgive you," a female voice said, soft and sad. I thought it was Thorn at first, but with great pain I turned my head towards the window seat, and saw Julianne stretched across it, her legs bent over her torso at an impossible angle.

"I've never seen him in such a temper." She untangled herself and sat up. "It frightens me, James. So much about this city frightens me now."

"It is a frightening place," I croaked. "And we could have fixed it, but we let ourselves grow complacent. We left that Wall standing, even though we hated everything it represented. We believed if the man was dead, his ghosts could no longer harm us. We wanted to get on with life. Instead, we hastened our own destruction."

"I don't think you have the right to act as though complacency was all that stood in the way of you standing against Brunel, when it is you who has doomed us all. Wombwell says there is no hope now that Brunel can create life from no life. He is making plans to move the menagerie outside of London, probably by sea. But Lurgo is possessed. He thinks Thorn will come to London soon, and he will stop at nothing to keep his promise to her. He does not care what you do; he thinks you have abandoned us for Brunel."

I winced. "What do you think of me?"

"I think you too are frightened, and you wanted only what the rest of us take for granted. I think you did a very stupid thing, James, but I can't hate you for it. It is not in me to hate."

"I wish you could convince Lurgo of the same thing."

"He may come around, when the time comes. You mean so much to him. He loves you, and to think you've deserted him burns him up inside. But I don't believe he would abandon you when this city is overrun."

"Should I speak with him?"

Julianne shook her head.

"How long have I been lying here?"

Julianne glanced out the darkened window, her eyes resting on the smudge of orange light peeking over the red-tiled roofs. "It is nearly morning."

I threw off the covers. "And what of that Sinker, Maxwell?"

She held out her hand. "Come and see for yourself."

***

We housed Maxwell in the larder, the only room of the house with a lock on the outside. He had chewed that lock through, and torn the door to slivers with his lead claws. When we entered the kitchen, we found him hunched over the table, half-buried under a pile of debris, sucking wood splinters from his bloody fingers.

"What have you fed him, thus far?"

"Two candlesticks and that old cauldron in the entrance hall. He's since licked most of the paint off the drawing room walls."

I sighed. "That cauldron was from my trip to Russia." I pushed a sheet of paper and an ink well across the table. "Can you tell us why you came back to London?"

Maxwell grabbed for the paper and ink. A few minutes later he handed me back a scrawled note.

I knew you would come to stop him. I needed to eat. I found my brothers again and I tell them we can be free of him and still have lead. I work in his Chimney so that one day I can be free and I don't have to kill for my food.

"Do you know what Brunel plans to do, and when?"

He plans to murder the Queen and take the throne for himself. He plans to give the city to his machines and take up residence in the Crystal Palace. And it will be soon. He has an army waiting beneath the Wall. They are like no machines I've ever seen before. They are terrible, and he loves them as a father loves his children.

Julianne – reading over my shoulder – gasped. "We have to warn Her Majesty!"

"Of what?" Wombwell leaned against the doorframe, his nightcap obscuring half his sleepy face.

I handed him the paper. Maxwell rolled his eyes at the ceiling.

"I shall go immediately." Wombwell threw the paper back on the table. "I want the rest of you to stay here – don't go into the streets. That means Lurgo, too." Julianne nodded.

"What can we do?"

"I'm afraid there's not much we can do, child, save to keep ourselves scarce and stock up on weapons. I'm hoping to get the animals onto a boat to France today, but they're asking a pretty penny to make it past Brunel's harbour Wall. And even then, they're refusing to take Boris. But tell Lurgo to prepare his army. Oh, and find Maxwell something to eat. He's looking a bit peckish."

Maxwell put down the half-chewed silver terrene, and looked at me with wide, guilty eyes.

***

The winter rains came, and the North winds blew clouds of smoke over the Graveyard. Quartz studied the corrosion on his instruments. "The black soots have passed over. I think Brunel's forces have returned to London," he declared at the war council.

It was now or never. Joel's party left first, a full ten days before the others, to ensure they reached Second Works on time. Sam – who had become like a brother to Joel – insisted on accompanying him, and now waited at the boundary with ten of the Navvies. The Stokers marched out to meet them, their barkers slung on their shoulders and sacks of dried meat and tanks of nitrogen oxide and water strapped to the steam-powered wagon.

Thorn stood beside Joel in the Turret entrance, and pressed Stephenson's cross into his fingers. She tried to speak, but found no words. Her chest, her lips, her limbs hung like frozen lumps of meat from her bones. She managed to squeeze his hand, and he stopped fiddling anxiously with his barker strap and turned to regard her.

"I'll see you in fifteen days," Joel bent over and brushed his lips lightly across her hairline.

At last Thorn found words. "No." She backed away.

"Thorn?"

"Don't—" She wiped the spot where he kissed her. Her skin burned.

"But I—"

"*Don't* say it. That's what Rex said, and he—" She sniffed. "I can't think of that now. It still hurts to hear those words."

Joel gulped. "Right. Fifteen days then?"

Thorn nodded, turning away and hurrying up the Turret staircase. She didn't want him to see her cry.

***

"Drink this."

Brownish liquid sloshed over the sides of the tankard as Quartz slid it across the table. Thorn grabbed it before it toppled over the edge. She licked the sticky mecks off her fingers, and winced.

"Drink it. That's good ole' English courage, that is."

"Are you afraid, Quartz?"

"Naw." He threw back his head and drained his vessel in one gulp.

Thorn sipped her drink. It was just like old times, she and Quartz sequestered together inside the Turret, not talking much, not needing to talk.

"Your father—" Quartz paused. Thorn looked up.

"What about him?"

"He would've disapproved of this. He never could stand war or murder of any sort. How he ended up in the Navy or mixed up in Brunel's madness, we'll never know."

"I may well die out there."

"That is correct."

"It would be a shame to die knowing so little about my own history. You have no relation to me, no debt owed my family. Why it is you took it upon yourself to look after me?"

Quartz regarded the bottom of his tankard with deep curiosity.

"You may not like the answer, Thorn."

"I'd rather hear it, all the same."

Slowly, Quartz pulled the dusty monocle from his eye, and set the lens on the table. He stared at the ceiling, rolling his good eye back as far as it would go. "You and Aaron and your father, you're not the only ones to hear voices inside your head."

Thorn said nothing. After a few moments Quartz continued.

"My voices are of a different sort. Where you hear the voices of the wilderness, I hear the pulsing of Great Conductor himself. I hear the machines of time, turning on their wheels. Day in, day out, I hear the grinding, crunching pulse of mortality crushing in upon our world. Nothing drowns it out, save the drink." He lifted his glass for emphasis. "And you."

"I don't understand."

"I was born in the Americas. My father served in the navy and died at sea. My mother and I lived in a ramshackle farmhouse in New Hampshire, until she met an industrialist and we moved with him to England. The ticking followed me here, as it always did.

"My stepfather loathed me, and month by month he turned my mother against me. He was a deeply evil man, and he did all that he could to make my life as miserable as possible. I was an odd, quiet child, and the ticking permeated my every thought, so I was often slow to respond to commands or questions. This enraged him.

He thought I was slow.

"One day, they sat me down and told me that my stepfather had taken a new job, and we would be leaving our home in London. They packed up our possessions on to the back of a wagon and we set off. But before we left the city my mother took me from the wagon, and told me we were to visit someone in Engine Ward. She walked me through those great iron gates, and I was surrounded by all the noise and bustle. I watched with fascination as several men manoeuvred a large engine across the street toward the Aetherian church. When I turned around, my mother was gone. She had left me behind in Engine Ward. She had abandoned me."

"Quartz, I'm so sorry."

"Don't interrupt. Now, I found the Stokers easily enough, and they took me in as one of their own, as they often did with discarded things. I worked in the furnace rooms beneath Engine Ward, shovelling coal in long shifts to keep the district running. The tick continued unceasing, until one day where my fellow shift-worker introduced me to his newly born son. As soon as I touched his tiny fingers, the ticking ceased, just like that." Quartz smashed his knuckles against the grating.

"The man was Aaron." It wasn't a question. Quartz nodded.

"I spent as much time around that child as I could, and in no time at all he was not a child any more, but a young man of unquenchable morality. After his father died, I saw that Aaron suffered at the hands of his mother and her suitors, just as I had. But then, finally, the drink took her life and Aaron was free. He came to live with me, and that was the happiest day of my life. I spent much time with Aaron and your father, the two men for whom I credit my sanity. As the years drove on, the calm that emanated from Aaron waned, replaced by a terrible sense of restlessness and anger, a rage that ran deep. I didn't like it, but there was nothing I could do."

"When Lurgo brought you into Graveyard from the trains, they wanted to destroy you right then. But I could feel the calm sweeping over me and I knew you had your father's gift. Aaron knew too. Between us we convinced the elders to let you live. Though I knew he wanted nothing more than to raise you himself, Aaron persuaded me to keep you. I'm not much for children, as you've discovered, but your presence kept me sane, and I like to think that I taught you a few things, too."

Thorn smiled, remembering her gruff caregiver teaching her to walk down the rickety stairs, regaling her with despicable stories and fantastical legends, weaning her on the turgid mecks.

Quartz rolled his one good eye at her. "I'm one sorry gammy, what can I say?"

"Say we'll survive this battle, Quartz. Say I'll live to see Joel again."

Quartz leaned over the table and swiped her half-emptied tankard from her hands. Sculling back the bottle, he wiped his mouth on his sleeve and grinned like a demon of the night. He spoke not a word.

***

JAMES HOLMAN'S MEMOIRS, FIRST EDITION

The week after I revealed the true purpose of the plate, Wombwell received an unusual invitation, addressed to him at my residence and sealed with Queen Victoria's crest. He had been in a treacherous mood of late: he had been denied both a ship and an audience at court.

Evidently Her Majesty had more important affairs to attend.

But the letter changed all that. It requested the presence of Wombwell, myself, and all the members of the menagerie at the Crystal Palace two days hence. The Queen would be visiting the Great Exhibition to preside over a ceremony honouring the work of the "Royal Engineer" and wished for Wombwell to provide entertainment in the Grand Transept. Enclosed within the envelope were enough entry tickets for all the menagerie workers and animals combined.

Lurgo – careful to avoid all eye contact with me – drummed his fingers on the table. "She's a foolish woman. She must know by now who her Royal Engineer truly is."

I set the letter down. "Perhaps she has no choice in the matter."

"Perhaps you're right, James." Wombwell held up a scrap of paper. "I found this nestled between our tickets. It reads 'Stay Away', and it was written by Her Majesty's hand. She is trying to warn us; if we show up at the Crystal Palace, we are walking into a trap."

"So we won't be going, then?" Lurgo said, his voice tinged with disappointment.

"Oh, we'll be going." Wombwell smiled. "Wild tricorns couldn't keep us away from that extravaganza."

On the morn of the ceremony, we detached one of my least-favourite stained glass windows, and left Maxwell in the parlour chewing away on the glazing bars. Wombwell packed a selection of animals – not Boris, thank goodness – into ten wagons and strung them with ribbons and flags and tiny variegated lamps. Decked out in our finest linens, we made our way to Hyde Park with much fanfare.

Unlike my last visit to the Great Exhibition, I was looking forward to the fact I could enjoy the sights that had been denied me. Of course, London's atmosphere had changed drastically in these short months, and I doubted there would be any enjoyment to be had at all today. Wombwell and Lurgo had some sort of scheme planned out, but they wouldn't reveal it to me. I could not blame them. Ever since I'd returned with my new eyes, they had treated me as if I could not entirely be trusted, which I suppose was true enough.

Since the season had come to an end, the ticket price had come down to one shilling, attracting school groups and families and even whole parishes taking advantage of Brunel's railway concession tickets. All these country-folk had been trapped within the city when the gates had closed, and their desperation to return to their homes made the streets an unpleasant place to wander. There was a growing tension in the air that hung like a heavy blanket over the city. Word spread about the Queen's appearance at the Exhibition, so hundreds flocked to Hyde Park with malice in their eyes. Though the trumpets blew a gay tune and street vendors peddled their wares on every corner, no one laughed. Children who exclaimed over the passing menagerie were quickly shushed by their parents. The carnival spirit had given way to fear and anger and distrust. Only stony faces greeted us as we rolled into our allocated spaces behind the Eastern Halls and unloaded the animals.

I had passed by the Crystal Palace many times on my walks, but she never ceased to fill me with equal wonder and foreboding. That smooth glass façade stretched across the green for eternity – it seemed all the glass in the world had been employed to create this crystalline prison. It filled the heart with joy just to gaze upon it, for the glass gleamed a thousand dappled colours and danced radiant rainbows onto the trees. And yet I knew behind its beauty hid a figure of darkness, and he had plans for the Crystal Palace beyond simply a monument to England's industries.

And I was about to discover just what those plans entailed.

Lurgo and I left the menagerie to set up and pushed through the crowds milling inside the Western Halls that contained the British exhibits (the Eastern halls were devoted to international exhibitors). We shuffled aimlessly from court to court, passing the Sheffield cutlery display, a chocolate-making machine and a device that wrapped cigarettes without so much as a glance. Though we looked like any other tourists, we had our eyes and ears open for the first sign of trouble.

We saw nothing that should make us suspicious – no Boilers guarding the exits, no Sunken hiding under the exhibition cabinets. And of course, this made me feel even more on edge. We returned to the Grand Transept to find Wombwell. He was in his element, gathering a great crowd around him while he and Julianne led the monkeys and compies through a series of tricks.

Since I had last visited, Brunel had built a railway (broad gauge, of course) through the centre of the Grand Transept, where the Queen would arrive in her newly appointed royal carriage. As Lurgo and I pushed closer to the front of the platform, a great whistle blew and a thousand clocks chimed throughout the entire palace, ushering the patrons to the viewing platforms to witness the arrival of the Queen.

The whistle screeched again, and the train came into view as it slid through the glass entrance. Steam huffed from the engine, soaking the air in thick smoke.

I stared up at the monstrous carriage. It had been years since I'd last been so close to a train, and I couldn't recall them seeming this menacing. Of course, I had never before seen the sleek black body or the ferocious boiler, nor the smoke curling from the stack and clouding the platform like a swamp. Each piston and coupler shone and glistened with fresh black paint and oil and water. The engine hummed and shimmered, as though it were alive.

Maybe it is alive, I thought, remembering that Brunel now had the plate.

With a hiss and a crunch, the carriage came to a stop in front of the makeshift wooden platform. The Queen waved at the crowd from the high window of the first carriage. Though she smiled, her eyes betrayed her terror. She knew she was riding into a trap. Her hand grazed the hyacinth arrangements that framed the window grille. The flowers drooped in the presence of so much steam.

Behind the Queen's flower-bedecked carriage, another had been hitched. Thick black drapes shrouded the windows, and not a single soul entered or exited it. I felt my stomach sink to my knees.

Lurgo sensed it too, for his shoulders tensed and he kept darting nervous glances toward Wombwell and Julianne, who danced with the monkeys on a dais at the far end of the platform. A second crowd had gathered around him, entranced by his display. Even with impending doom approaching, Wombwell could entice a crowd to laughter.

The people surged forward, shouting for the Queen to come out, to explain why they had been locked inside this city, far from their homes. Somewhere toward the rear of the platform, a brass band struck up a jaunty tune.

Everything happened at once. The swell of the people pushing on the platform caught me off balance, and I grabbed Lurgo's arm to prevent myself being pitched into the fray. We could no longer see the carriages over the crowd, but we heard the doors string open, and the screaming began, rising above the shrill whistle – and louder even than the screams were the familiar snarling of the Sunken, licking their lips for the ultimate feast.

The crowd panicked, some still pushing forward and others clawing their way back, away from the trains, screaming and howling in agony as they tore at their fellow countrymen. Women fell and were trampled, children were wrenched from their parents. Gunshots ricocheted off the monstrous locomotive, smashing the glass panels on the ceiling and sending showers of glass shards cascading down on the terrified crowd.

Heedless to the danger, Lurgo surged forward, his face set in a tight line. He dug his barker from the hidden pocket in his coat and held it above his head, dragging me forward with an iron grip.

It wasn't until we broke through the panic that we caught sight of the full horror. Every surface of the first carriage dripped with blood, which clung to the remains of the disgorged flowers in matted clumps. Several Sinkers clung to the tender and swung from the couplers, gnawing at severed limbs and tossing the fresh-chewed morsels into the panicking crowd. More of the creatures poured from the darkened carriage – it must have been filled to bursting with them – and swarmed through the windows, clamouring for more flesh.

"Your Majesty!" I cried over the massacre. "Queen Victoria, are you still alive?"

She was, for she scratched at the blood-splattered

window and cried out. I saw flashes of red sprinting along the platform. Dozens of redcoats pulled themselves up from their secret hiding places under the scaffold and raced to save their monarch. Evidently, Queen Victoria was no fool: she had suspected Brunel's intentions and had not arrived completely defenceless.

The soldiers surrounded the carriage, swords drawn, and tore at the Sunken who clung tenaciously to the windows and roof. Lurgo rushed forward, but I pulled him back.

"There's nothing we can do for her, lad. We must reach Wombwell!"

Lurgo nodded, and we raced down the platform towards the dais, shattered glass tinkling all around us. More barker shots rang in the air, and the platform quickly turned into a stampeding, trampling, screaming nightmare. Knives glinted as they sliced through the air, and puddles of blood stained the wood crimson – and still more Sunken leapt into the fray.

Wombwell had trained his men and his animals well. The menagerie formed a tight circle, each man and beast facing outward, forming a wall against the swarming Sunken. The men drew weapons from secret pockets and forgotten crevices, and set to work dispatching the Sinkers, piling their bodies one on top of the other. Wombwell's whip sliced through the air, severing ears and fingers and causing leathery skin to rip and shred. Julianne stood beside him, her tiny fists flying in all directions, while Bella and Alberto swung from her arms and scratched and gouged at the flailing Sinkers.

Lurgo cried when he saw her. "We can't reach them, and the bastards will overpower them soon!"

"Quick," I pointed. "The tapestry!"

He saw at once what I intended. A great and

magnificent tapestry hung from the roof of the transept, woven by the finest textile workers of India. I ran behind it, unsheathed my knife from my cane, and attacked the thick braided rope that secured it over the strut. Lurgo grabbed a sword from a nearby display, and slashed through the other rope with one swipe. The tapestry lurched sideways as the one remaining rope suddenly bore its immense weight.

"Help me!" My measly knife had barely made a cut. Lurgo marched over and slashed the rope. The tapestry hung in the air for a moment, then the ropes whipped high above our heads and the fabric came crashing down.

"Look out!" I called to Wombwell, just as the fabric buckled in the centre and hit the platform with such force it stove in the wood. The Sinkers scattered; our quick thinking buried a least thirty of their number under the heavy cloth. Wombwell pulled a sword from the belly of a fallen Sinker and ushered his men over to us.

"This way!" Lurgo raced toward the entrance.

"No." I pulled him back. "Boilers are waiting for us there." I grabbed Julianne's trembling hand and pointed back inside the Engineering Hall. "Let's move!"

We scampered through the hall of great machines made by great and terrible men, now deserted save for a few Sinkers feasting on a woman and her child over Shillibeer's expanding hearse. I turned in time to see a horde of the monsters crowding through the entrance to the Hall, their eyes gleaming at the prospect of drinking our blood.

Lurgo raised his barker, but I pushed it aside, urging him forward. We raced through the next court, and the next, till we found ourselves gazing at a high wall of glass: the western wall of the Palace. The Sunken circled around us, licking their blistered lips.

Lurgo raised his barker and shot the glass panel, spewing shards onto the manicured grass. I used a gilded candlestick to clear away the debris from the metal frame, and we flew outside, down the hill, and leapt into our carriages, the Sinkers snapping at our heels.

The neckers could smell the blood and needed no encouragement. They bolted down the path, tails whipping against their churning legs.

I pushed Julianne onto the footplate just as a Sinker leapt onto the roof, his dribbling face hanging down over the roof stays. He bared his teeth.

Lurgo swung his fist up and connected with the Sinker's nose, knocking the creature back. Lurgo gasped and clutched his fist. He wasn't used to hitting anything, much less a creature that ate metal for sustenance.

Wombwell yanked the reins. "Hi-up!" The neckers screeched, and poured on speed.

The jolt of the carriage nearly wrenched my head from my shoulders. The Sinker toppled over the footplate and managed to swing itself onto the roof before the neckers could trample it. Julianne grabbed my cane from my trembling hands and poked the lump on the ceiling. With a yelp of protest the Sinker toppled off the edge and sprawled across the street, where several angry Londoners pummelled it with sticks.

Wincing, Lurgo prised open his fingers and inspected the deep cut across his knuckles. Julianne found a rag to sop up the blood. "It was like punching a train," he moaned.

"Aye, boy, for the Sinkers ooze metal through their very skin. You're lucky to come away as good as you did."

"I want to go home," Julianne whimpered.

"I'm afraid home is no longer safe, Julianne. I'm afraid London's worst days may have just begun."

***

That night, we were left in no doubt that Brunel had returned.

We spent the day barricading the doors and windows to my apartments and piling anything that could be used as a weapon into the front hall. I knew it was only a matter of time before Brunel found out where we were hiding and decided to come for us. There was nothing to do but wait.

Lurgo and I – apparently at peace now – were smoking nargila on the balcony when a great column of fire spewed from the horizon and lit the sky with showers of sparks. Lurgo bolted upright, upsetting the *nargila* and spilling tobacco all over my slippers.

"Can you see it, Holman? What is it?"

"Buggered if I know, lad, but nothing pleasant, of that I am most certain."

Less than ten minutes later, Buckingham Palace burst into flame. I scrambled for my telescope and Lurgo and I watched the palace staff dive from the upper windows in a foolhardy attempt to escape the blaze. Others ran into the surrounding grounds, trying to find shelter amongst the manicured lawns and shaped hedgerows. The great doors opened and hundreds of Sinkers poured into the grounds, their teeth gnashing for a taste of human flesh.

"What will happen if he has killed the Queen?" Lurgo pulled his eye away from the lens, as though he could stand no more.

"We've no time to ponder the answer to that

question. Get your coat, Lurgo. And find Julianne. We're leaving."

"What? But we've fortified the place—"

"And you think the Boilers will be deterred by our defences? It's no use staying here, waiting for death to come knocking. We're leaving the city by any means possible, before we're trapped—"

The door slammed back against the wall, knocking some of my knick-knacks from the shelf. Wombwell stood in the doorway, chewing a fat cigar and holding a crumpled message. Julianne peeked out from behind Wombwell, her expression drawn.

"It's no good, James. I've received word from the dockside. Brunel's got Boilers guarding every gate. They're shooting jets of boiling water at anyone who steps too close to the Wall," Wombwell said. "We're trapped inside. They've shut down every exit from the city."

Lurgo looked to me. "What do we do now?"

"Whatever we can, lad. Mostly we pray, for Thorn is our only hope."

∗∗∗

Thorn and Quartz rode out on the first wagon, which pumped its way along the Narrow, escorted by the remaining Navvies and followed by the ragged line of her Stoker army. The ululations of the Graveyard's women and children folded silently into the night as they travelled further from their home. Her tricorns marched behind, Igoria's seven surviving children were rapidly approaching their full size now, and all would accept a rider. They minded the smaller, more volatile trainees she'd captured from the swamp in the last month.

Less then five miles from the boundary of the Graveyard they found the charred stump of the Wall, abandoned in mid-construction thanks to her Stoker army. A scout of the ruins revealed no Boilers or Sinkers nearby. They weren't long into the journey, however, when the derelict ruins began to show signs of life-that-was-not-life. Another three miles down the road and there was no road anymore, only a cobbled ramp leading onto the Wall, which churned with gears and spewed clouds of smoke into the atmosphere.

Oswald frowned at the markings on his map. "There should be a village here."

"There is." Thorn pointed. "Behind the Wall."

Oswald's lips curled back, and he stared unblinking at that clanking monstrosity for several long moments.

They veered off the road and hid in the surrounding forest. Quartz and Thorn climbed aboard the old steam-powered dray Quartz had dug from the scrap heaps. He had tinkered with the engine until it chugged to life. The men stacked the dray with sacks of porridge and oats. They set off up the ramp, the pressure valve puffing tiny clouds behind them.

Sinkers patrolled the upper buttresses, since the stinging rains were falling and had probably driven the Boilers inside. Thorn's chest knotted, and she pulled her hood even lower down on her face. Two vehicles waited on the road for the gate, a two-person buggy pulled by a team of horses and a merchant wagon pulled by neckers. The animals fidgeted and pulled at their traces.

The Sinkers darted under the buttress, jabbering in their enigmatic tongue as they worked to pull the gates open. Quartz directed the dray to pull up behind the buggy. Thorn noticed glowing eyes regarding her from the shadows of the buttress.

Their dray sagged. Thorn heard a shout, and her head flew around. A Sinker had clambered under the canvas, and moved his dribbling, diseased mouth amongst the sacks of porridge, sniffing and licking the damp sacks with his charred tongue. Satisfied they carried no weapons, he leapt from the dray, and they were allowed to pass through the gate.

The Wall cocooned the village within its own churning, clanking abyss. Every house, every shop and shrine echoed with the sounds of the machine. Sulphur fumes billowed from the chimneys and sewer grates, and the bricks and tiles were stained a coal black. If Meliora was a city inside a clock, then this was a village baking in the bowels of a furnace.

Quartz questioned a pedestrian who pointed him in the direction of the magistrate's house. They passed through the town square – deserted save the cheery pub, where pale-skinned barmaids called out to them between the tables piled high with ale.

Their dray pulled up beside a once stately cottage along the western aspect of the Wall. The blowoff from a nearby chimney had stained the mouldings black and blistered the paint. Tattered stumps and piles of blackened tar and bracken were all that remained of the garden. Quartz rang the bell.

"Sod off," came a muffled reply from behind the peeling wood.

"You're gonna want to open this door, Master Burns."

"Not bloody likely."

With a shot from her barker, Thorn blew a hole in the wood, two inches above the gilded handle. She reached inside and unbolted the door. They stepped into the main hallway. Blotchy wallpaper flaked from the walls and the woven carpet was stained with black footprints. Thorn noticed scratch-marks along the wall, and flecks of red – blood, perhaps – dotted the dresser.

She heard whimpering. Quartz turned into the parlour; stuffed with sagging couches stained with the same black and red prints. An open bottle of cognac and a silver tray piled with miniature pies and sweetbreads sat on the side table. A man and woman cowered behind the piano stool.

"Q-Q-Quartz?"

"Greetings, Burns, you old scallywag. I did kindly *suggest*you open the door." Quartz tipped his head back and skulled the bottle of cognac. He offered the plate to Thorn, who gingerly picked a pie. The pastry tasted of soot. She coughed into her collar.

"We thought...the Sunken..."

Quartz patted the tattered chaise lounge. "Have a seat, we have much to discuss. How is the state of your men?"

"Frightened, and drunk, I'll wager. There's naught to do here now that the Wall bars us from the countryside and pollutes the fields. Old Cooper down at the pub has never had such good business. It's been three score weeks since I've had a sniff of deer or dragon meat."

"We have men in the forest," said Thorn. "Men who have fought the Sunken and won. If you want to end this terror for ever, you and your men should join us."

Burns sat back in his seat, startled by her soft voice. *I guess I probably don't look much like a woman.*

"What do you plan to do?"

Briefly Thorn and Quartz explained the plan. Burns' face remained stoic, but his wife stood up and paced the room near the window, running her hands over the grime on the windowsill and shooting eyes like daggers at Thorn and Quartz.

"It seems awfully dangerous," said Burns at last. "I think that—"

He was interrupted by a loud crash from outside, followed by a clanging bell.

Burns pushed his screaming wife aside and bolted for the door, with Quartz and Thorn at his heels. They raced down the street and stopped on the corner, staring in horror at the inferno that rose like a pyre from the main square.

A hydrogen balloon swung in tatters from the roof of the tavern. Flames engulfed the canvas and licked at the wooden gables. Three Dirigire priests and an acolyte rolled on the pavement, while incensed tavern patrons shouted insults and doused them with spirits.

Another priest crawled from the smouldering basket, coughing and gasping for air. Thorn recognised his drawn, misshapen features. She grabbed him by the collar and dragged him to his feet, shaking him with all the anger in her heart. "What are you doing here, Pierre? What quarrel have you against this town?"

"There's no quarrel, Miss! We lost our way in the clouds and something started shooting at us." Pierre's eyes flashed with recognition. "*You?* We've landed in the swamps where your foul creatures shall devour our flesh! Oh, Mama Helios preserve me!" His charred fingers clasped an amulet: a gilded sculpture of a dirigible wing.

Thorn tore the talisman from his chest and tossed it into the flames. He cried out and dived for it, but she pulled his arms behind his head. Her hand flew to her knife and she held it to his throat.

"You mistake me for your enemy, *Pierre*, though your true enemy is the one who darkens the skies and threatens your borders with his cursed Wall. I assure you, priest, this is not a mistake you'll be permitted to make twice." She pressed the point firmly against his bobbing Adam's apple. He choked out a reply.

"You have been harbouring illegal immigrants and using them to work your land and make you rich, haven't you? You've hidden away all their dirigibles so they can't escape back to France. Well, you will need to find those balloons again, *Pierre*. What was that you speak? Yes, Mistress Thorn, I'll do whatever you say, Miss Thorn. Go on." She increased the pressure of the blade. A droplet of blood marred his pale skin. "Say it."

"...y...y...yes, Miss Thorn."

"Good. Understand that I rule these swamps, and you and your flying machine are trespassing on *my* land. Our army stands five hundred strong, each riding an iron-clad monster, armed with weapons you can't even imagine and *hungry*, so very hungry for revenge. My monsters are just outside, and they never forget a face."

Pierre's eyes bugged. Thorn felt his muscles slacken. He sagged into her, deflating like his broken dirigible as he realised he was beaten.

"I know that you took this dirigible in an attempt to flee Meliora before she is overrun with Boilers. I don't know your plan, but I know you are a coward and a liar. I won't kill you, but I do ask something for my mercy. I will let you down now, and you and your brethren may walk from this village as free men, but I expect you to return to Meliora immediately and send forth to London as many men in as many flying machines as you can assemble. Frederique will lead this squadron. You are expected there in nine days. If I do not see you there—" Thorn frowned. "We *will* return for you. That is my most solemn promise."

She drew away her knife and pushed Pierre to his knees. He scrambled to his feet, his hands clutching his throat, and flew into the nearest alley, blabbering at top volume. His acolytes hitched up their tattered robes and hobbled after him.

Quartz stared at Thorn with incredulous eyes. "You've incorrigible. You're getting as bad as Joel with your fancy words and roguish tongue."

Thorn smiled. "I know."

***

With their pub destroyed and the promise of mechanical bloodshed, the village population were all too glad to sign up. Less then three hours later a motley cohort of a hundred and fifty men had assembled by the forlorn tavern, each loaded down with barkers and powder horns and swinging family swords at imaginary enemies. Perhaps the drink made them fearless, for they did not even seem to mind the tricorns.

The women fetched dried meat and barrels of beer from their stores and loaded their supplies into two dilapidated wagons. One man – his head adorned with an iron cooking pot – declared himself leader and set about organising the men into watches and calculating the daily beer rations.

The next few days brought many similar encounters. They kept off the Wall railway, marching instead through the bogs and forests. With every town they entered, men joined their cause, and their ranks swelled from the original eighty men to near eight hundred by the time they crossed the boundary of Hampshire. Thorn felt better knowing her lie to Pierre was now justified.

The county was unrecognisable. Smoke pressed so thick Thorn could barely see ten feet from her nose. The tricorns whined and pulled on their ropes, refusing to enter the soot-cloaked lands. Their uneasy thoughts mirrored her own.

"Something's happened here," she said to Quartz. "I hope we are not too late." He nodded grimly in reply.

Ten miles up the road they discovered just what that something was. Thorn, at the front of the line, had dismounted Igor and walked alongside him, saving his strength for the road ahead. Suddenly, Igor's thoughts turned to panic, flaring up inside her skull. Through the tricorns she could smell the blood. Rivers of blood, washing over the landscape like a flood.

What's going on? Thorn cast the thought out to her animals.

Suddenly Igor reared up, ripping the reins from her hand. "Steady, boy!" She tried to will him back to her, but his panic forced out all her other commands. He bounded off down the left of the ranks, startling the already cautious men.

"Bloody hell! That monster nearly killed a man. What's going on up there?" one of the Navvies yelled.

"A massacre," Thorn called back, thinking of the blood inside her head. She went to fetch Igor.

A half mile further and they could all smell it, even the Stokers with their numbed senses. Blood on the breeze, blood thick in the air. Shimmers of fear ran through the ranks as the men whispered prayers to their respective gods.

They neared a rise in the road and Thorn stopped short, her breath catching in her throat as she choked on the sight before her. The column came to a silent halt as the men too saw the horror with their soot-cloaked eyes.

A field stretched out below them, over the crest of the sloping hillock and on into the distance. Thorn assumed it was once fresh with grain or potatoes, but now someone had sewn a crop of death. Every inch of the field groaned under the weight of eviscerated bodies, piled one atop the other like discarded industrial waste. Heads ripped off and tossed carelessly away. Disengaged arms and hands – still clutching brownbess and carbine – floated in the streams of blood that ran toward the irrigation ditch on the south side of the field. She could see the bodies of once-regal horses – eyes bulging and bellies ripped open – collapsed under their slain masters.

The smell overpowered every sense, sucking at her eyes, gorging her nostrils, rising bile in her throat. Though Thorn cast her mind over the surrounding landscape, she could sense no life. No cavalry horses remained in the vicinity.

"We're too late," she wheezed, steeling herself against Quartz' body, trying desperately not to throw up.

"They're Redcoats," Quartz whispered. "The bloody English *army*. He's massacred the whole bloody English army."

Thorn whimpered, falling to her knees. She blinked, but the field of blood etched itself onto her eyelids. *We're too late. Brunel has already won.*

A hand rested on her shoulder. Quartz. He was speaking to her, soft words, words of encouragement. Empty words.

"Wait," Oswald called out. "Look over there."

Thorn opened her eyes, squinting at the mists. On the other side of the field, a section of half-finished Wall met the wide road. Half obscured by the fog and the mountains of bodies, a small regiment of redcoats still stood, holding the road against an onslaught of Boilers and Sunken.

We can help them.

The thought sent fingers of fire into her chest. Quartz

met her gaze, and he saw what she intended to do. He reached out to grab her, but she tore herself from his grasp and plummeted down the cliff, her boots sliding over the slick surface.

"Thorn, what in Great Conductor's lead testicles are you *doing?*Get back here!"

Quartz could yell all he liked, for all Thorn cared. She sat down in the mud and slid the rest of the way, splashing into a knee-deep river of blood and gore. A severed human arm brushed past her leg, and she turned and retched, the remains of her stomach joining the bloody river.

Thorn wiped her face, and sucked in a putrid breath. *I can't lose my head now.*

She turned and saw Igor throw his massive bulk over the cliff, skidding in the mud and landing in a big lump beside her. The other tricorns followed. Her men raised their weapons, let out an almighty shout, and charged over the edge.

Stumbling over the first carcass, Thorn reeled from the smell of the already suppurating flesh. Igor stomped beside her, and she pulled herself onto his back. The other riders mounted their tricorns and stomped across the battlefield.

Beside her, men scrambled through the debris, holding their weapons over their heads to keep them dry. The Navvies marched close behind her, hauling their heavy limbs from the mud and clambering over the bodies for footholds. The Stoker regiment lurched at the rear, struggling under the weight of the heavy Stinger tanks.

"Come on, men!" Thorn called to them. "You'll be emptying those tanks in a few moments!" She spurred Igor on, and he galloped over the mountain of bodies and descended upon the unsuspecting Boilers.

Metal crunched, steam hissed, and Igor groaned as he stomped and smashed and tore his way through the Boilers' line. Everything flew by in a blur – limbs, mud, machines, tricorns. Thorn had no idea if they'd even broken through, until Igor slowed his pace and swung round again and she saw the pile of broken Boilers flailing in the mud.

The redcoats yelled and scrambled backward, fearful of the giant beasts that came from nowhere, certain their sharp horns would finish off their defeated ranks.

Thorn held Igor back, counting the tricorns as they fell into formation behind her. The remaining Boilers drew up their line and started advancing toward them, shooting a volley of bolts into Thorn's tricorns. She saw two of her younger creatures go down, but the bolts didn't penetrate Igor's thick hide.

On top of the great pile of bodies, her men drew themselves into a ramshackle formation. The Stokers pushed their way to the front and hit the Boilers with the Stingers.

How the machines screamed as the acid scorched their bodies and buckled their furnace bellies! How the sound sent shivers down Thorn's spine as the mighty machines sank, helpless, into the mud. The Sinkers caught a blast of the acid too, and their bodies contorted and melted into puddles of lead-coloured gore. The Navvies put more down with their rifles.

The redcoats saw this victory, and cheered. They'd long ago tossed away their useless rifles, so they raised their swords into the air and slashed at the front line of Sinkers with renewed vigour. Thorn's army raced from atop the corpse mountain and hacked and stabbed the last line of Sinkers, piling their own mountain of bodies on this field of death. The last Sinkers turned and fled towards the Wall, but the Redcoats and Thorn's men pounced on them and hacked them down, until not one remained who could return to tell Brunel of their weapons.

The redcoats collapsed in the mud, overwhelmed with exhaustion and horror. Thorn slid from Igor's back and approached the panting soldiers. "Who is in charge here?" she called.

The men just stared at her in gape-mouthed silence.

She cleared her throat. "I said—"

Something tugged on her ankle. Thorn reached down and grabbed the wrist of a corpse that had entangled itself around her boot, and pulled. The fingers curled up and grabbed her hand.

Thorn shrieked and pulled away. The hand rose from the detritus and wriggled toward her.

"Help," a voice croaked.

"I don't help corpses," Thorn retorted, masking her distress.

"I'm no corpse, miss. At least, not yet. Help me up."

The fingers wriggled again. Biting back the urge to scream, Thorn grasped the wrist and pulled. This time, she noticed that the skin felt warmer, pliant. She stepped back as a man rose from the mud, his head and right shoulder visible while the rest of him was still buried in the mountain of corpses. His red coat hung in tatters from his bleeding torso, as though a dragon had slashed at him with its claws. Dried blood and mud and gore caked his features, so he appeared to be made of the battlefield itself. He grinned at her, and his white teeth shone in the deepening gloom.

"You're an angel," he croaked.

"No such thing as angels, sorry. Can you move at all?"

"I don't think so. Legs...broken." His face contorted in effort as he struggled to free his torso from the heap. "Yes, definitely broken."

Thorn rubbed her shaking arms; she did not have the strength left to lift him, but she signalled to her men to help her. To distract him from the fact that his legs might not exist anymore, she clasped his hand to her heart. "I'll help you out of here, but I have to know what has happened here." He nodded. "What's your name?"

"Robert O'Malley."

"I'm Thorn. Tell me Robert, what happened here?"

"Brunel, of course. Him an' his stinkin' machines. I've been stationed in London as a Major General in the Royal Irish Guard when this madness began. Brunel built his London railway right through the centre of the Crystal Palace, and Her Royal Majesty and Prince Albert took a journey from the Palace to the Great Exhibition for some ridiculous ceremony. We warned her not to go, but she claimed she had no choice. I was in her private guard with thirty others when Sinkers stormed the Royal carriage, snarlin' and a clamourin' for our blood. Victoria ordered Brunel to stop the train, but he laughed. Laughed right in Her Majesty's face! We lost fourteen men beating those loathsome creatures back, but we managed to rescue the Queen and halt the train. When we searched for Brunel, he'd disappeared back into his fortress."

"He's mighty skilled at disappearing, I've discovered."

"Aye, Thorn. He possesses a dark magic. And my tale gets worse. That very night, the Boilers and the Sunken stormed Buckingham Palace, killed all the staff, and claimed the throne for themselves. The Queen and Prince Albert escaped through one of the underground tunnels. We could not go back to the palace, but we managed to break through the city Wall when we found one of the gates practically unguarded. I had a strange feeling about it, as though Brunel was *letting* us leave. As soon as we were through the gates slammed shut behind us. He's barred every entrance and exit along the Wall. No one can get in or out of the city. We sent Her Majesty and the Prince under heavy escort to her residence on the Isle of Wight, and our remaining regiments fought on this field against the Boilers who followed us from London." Robert swept his arm wide, indicating the slaughter that surrounded them. "You've seen for yourselves the result of that engagement. But even this massacre won't satisfy Brunel. He wants the Queen dead, and the throne of England for himself."

"Brunel has no claim to the throne."

"What need has he of a claim when he commands an army that does not sleep? When we met on the battlefield this morning, our forces numbered in the thousands, but you see what sport they've made of us." Robert gave a rueful laugh as he gestured at the ruin around him.

"My army will defeat him."

"Your...what?"

"That's why I'm here. My army saved your men." Thorn pointed at the still-living redcoats, accepting medical care and mugs of tea from her men.

"You...you command these men and monsters? But how...you must be an angel, or a witch. Where did you come from?"

"I'm no witch, only a girl from Graveyard with a burning desire to see Brunel dead for good."

"Graveyard? So you be Stokers then?"

Thorn paused. "We are English. That should be all that matters."

A hand pulled Thorn backward. She spun wildly, catching her boot under a corpse. She splashed backwards and her assailant spun her round to face him. Quartz's fogged lens stared back at her, his one eye bulging in anger.

"What do you think you're doing, you *stupid* girl?"

"I couldn't just leave them there to die, Besides, Joel could have been here somewhere!"

"And what if he is? By Great Conductor's steam-driven todger, girl, we can't lose you too. You there!" Quartz kicked Robert in the ribs. "Did any Stokers join your ranks? Five men, heavily armed?"

Robert shook his head, wincing. "None, sir. We've met no other soul on the road."

Thorn pointed at the man. "We need four strong men down here and a splint, to pull him out. This is Robert. He's a Major General. He has seen Brunel's assault firsthand."

"Better yet," Robert groaned, "I can take you to the Queen herself. She'll be most anxious to speak to you and your army, Thorn."

"Why would the Queen even take audience with me?"

Quartz shook his head. "This is madness. You've gone crazy, woman, if you're even entertaining the possibility that—"

Robert inclined his head towards Thorn. "Call me a cock-eyed Irish fool, but if what I've seen today be the truth and not some Stoker witchcraft, it appears you've gone up against Brunel with naught but a scratch to show for your trouble. That would interest Her Majesty greatly. Also, you can tell her Brunel's next move."

"No I can't. I've no idea of Brunel's next more."

"Aye, but I do. He's gone to the Royal Society, Thorn. He's calling the Council in session to claim what is his."

***

When they pulled Robert out of the mud he was grateful to discover both his legs were still intact, if bent at horrid angles. It took six of Thorn's strongest men to strap him into a makeshift splint and manoeuvre the contraption back up the slick incline, and he howled all the way to the summit. Quartz – an efficient battlefield doctor if ever there was one – ordered Robert to drink an entire pitcher of mecks while he wrenched his legs back into place and made splints for the wounds. Robert's eyes rolled back in his head and he fell back against the stretcher.

Quartz kicked him with his boot. "Bloody Irish pansy, can't hold his piss. I've given our men instructions on caring for the injured. We'd best be on."

"We need to go to the Isle of Wight. I'm to convene with the Queen."

"By Great Conductor's steam-powered testicles, don't be ridiculous. We'll lose a day at least, maybe more, if we travel to the Isle. You will be late meeting Joel. And we need to get there before the cursed Council gathers. Brunel will be dancing on London's grave before we even cross the threshold of his throne room."

"Joel will wait for me. I must go. She's the Queen of this country and her army is *dust*. I can't walk back into her city and fight without her support."

"It's a pointless endeavour. Whatever support she could have given you lies at the bottom of that cliff. Besides, you're a Stoker. Do you really think she'd take audience with you?"

"She's a Queen first, and a Londoner second. She'll listen as long as I have a means to restore her throne.

We're going, Quartz, and I won't hear a word otherwise."

***

"Eight hundred men? You want to fight an army of deadly living machines and resurrected vampires with *eight hundred men?*"

Thorn blushed. "I did say it was a small army."

"Eight hundred men isn't small, Thorn. It's a joke. It's an—ow!" Robert rubbed his arm. "What was that for?"

"For being a miserable Irish git," grumbled Quartz, flexing his fingers. "We're taking you to see your poxy Queen. So shut up on it, already."

Robert rolled his eyes behind Quartz' back, but he ordered the men to take him below decks. Quartz followed behind them, muttering curses.

Thorn shielded her eyes from the ocean spray as she leaned against the railing, pressing her boot heels hard into the deck in a desperate attempt to keep her balance on the slippery deck. Mean, slick cliffs jutted out along the coast, their faces washed smooth by the vindictive waters of the Solent and streaked with white stripes of dactyl faeces. Around the next head, the port town of Cowes came into view, sliced down the middle by the mouth of the river Medina. The petulant ocean slammed the boat against the waves, as if desperate to expel its unwanted hitchhikers.

Thorn shivered. She'd never set foot on a boat before, and she doubted she'd ever repeat the experience. *I prefer my boots buried in the solid mud, thank you.*

Out on the water the winds took on a mind of their own, battering their merchant vessel like wrathful gods. Thorn looked back over her shoulder, hoping to catch a glimpse of the Hampshire shore, but all she saw was the dense, grey fog.

As they drew into port the fog lifted, and the city came into view – a craggy collection of steepled houses and shabby warehouses, perched on precarious angles between the cliffs. And above it all, the castle loomed. It rose from the surrounding rock as though hewn from the face itself, and each tapering turret bent and twisted at unforgiving angles in an impossible maze of masonry. The castle and every building in the village was strung with thin strands of shimmering fibre, which whipped about in the wind and gave off an ethereal glow.

"Wow," Thorn said, taking a deep breath, awed by the beauty of the place.

The sailors didn't sound nearly as impressed. They rushed about the deck, preparing the boat for docking and shouting jibes at each other.

"What's brown and steaming and comes out of Cowes backwards?" yelled one.

"The Portsmouth ferry!" another chimed in. They all cackled uproariously. Thorn smiled politely – it was clearly an old joke told many times before.

They tied off and Thorn raced Quartz down the gangway. Never had she been so glad to be standing in the mud. She leaned against a dock post and waited a few moments for her stomach to settle itself. Quartz stooped beside her, wringing the seawater out of his filthy hat. He spat on the corner of his jacket and rubbed his lens. "Bloody thing's all salted up," he mumbled.

The sailors carried Robert's stretcher up from the cabin and dumped him unceremoniously in a puddle. He smiled cheerfully, wiping the mud from his breeches and doffing his hat at Thorn.

"I've baked some scones for our picnic!" he shouted, his eyes rolling back in his head. "Now...where did I put them?" He scrambled through his coat pockets.

"Quartz, what have you done to him?"

"I've done nothing except tend to a crippled soldier. It's not my fault he's a fan of my latest laudanum and mecks concoction."

Robert gave her a dopey smile. "Don't cry, Momma. I've got a lovely potato."

"See? He's just being Irish. Bloody potato this, potato that."

"I needed him to get into the castle!"

"Sorry, sorry. Don't worry so much. He'll be fine in a few hours. And at least he's not in any pain."

Quartz called two men to pick up the stretcher again, and they trudged along the dock towards the gleaming village, Robert gibbering nonsense all the way. As they crossed onto the street, Thorn's boot fell into the wisps of silvery string that criss-crossed the cobbles.

"What a nuisance." Quartz shrugged more silvery threads off his shoulder as he wiped sea-spray off his lens.

"I think it's beautiful. Why does it shimmer like that?"

"Oh." Quartz grinned, and rolled his lens around his finger. "You'll love this. The dactyls faecal matter is quite gooey and it turns white in the sun. They come out here to nest, especially up on the cliffs behind the castle – whoever designed that monstrosity seemed to have dactyls on the brain. And so the reason this whole poxy island shimmers like heaven's own lighthouse is because it's covered in bloody dactyl crap."

"Crap crap!" echoed Robert.

"Huh." Try as she could, Thorn couldn't consider the flimsy, silvery string as something disgusting. *If the Queen loves this island too, than at least we have one thing in common.*

The palace grounds seemed deserted. Thorn saw two

guards patrolling the parapets, but they merely nodded at her as she and Quartz passed under the outer gate – perhaps they thought the frightful stone dactyls perched upon the gatehouse served as sufficient warning. Clearly, they feared no threat from their cohort of filthy vagabonds.

They entered a gabled archway hewn in the rock and hung with the familiar silvery strands. More stone dactyls flanked the passageway, their sculpted wings crisscrossing above their heads in intricate patterns. Thorn reached out to touch them, but the look in Quartz' eye forced her hand back inside her coat pocket.

Immediately upon passing into the internal courtyard, a guard waved them down. "You there! What's your business?"

"We're here to take council with the Queen," Thorn said.

"The Queen won't see anyone today. How can you be so insensitive? She's in mourning."

"I told you this was a waste of time." Quartz turned to leave.

"Please?" Thorn grabbed the corner of the man's coat. "I've come all the way from Graveyard to offer my services. If you take her a message, I am certain she will want to speak with me."

"And my potato. Don't forget my potato!" Robert chirped.

The guard squinted at the splint. "What happened to him?"

"That's Robert O'Malley, of the Royal Irish Guard. I pulled him from the battlefield this morning."

The guard's eyebrows arched. "You…what? How did you walk off that battlefield alive?"

"We'd like to speak with the Queen," Thorn repeated.

"We will explain everything to her, not some messenger."

"Of course. Right away, Miss." The guard hurried away. Two more guards approached and escorted them to an alcove off to the left of the courtyard. The sailors rested Robert's splint against a stone plinth and collapsed on the marble flagstones, grimacing as they rubbed their biceps.

Thorn leaned against the garden wall and twined the shimmering strings around her fingers. To calm her racing heart, she concentrated on the two dactyls hopping along the edge of the marble birdbath. Using her sense, she pushed them into the water, and snorted a giggle when they splashed and played.

Time passed. The first guard returned. "The Queen will see you now. Follow me." Quartz stepped forward, but the guard held up his hand. "No, just the girl."

Thorn jogged after the guard, as he wound along the halls and passages. The castle stretched back into the cliff, each corridor and hall carved from the stone itself, supported by stone pillars carved with still more dactyls. Every surface shimmered with the silvery strands.

The guard didn't bother to speak to her. He turned down a wide entrance hall, lined with stone plinths upon which sat hundreds of marble busts, each depicting a royal face – some aquiline and poised, others round and friendly. Still others showed more familiar faces; the royal dactyls – favourites among the sporting Kings who frequented the castle – accorded their own statues in the chamber.

The guard flung open the high oak doors and ushered her into the darkened Great Hall. "Her Royal Majesty," he yelled at the far, gloomy end of the massive room. "I present to you...a dirty Stoker girl."

"Excuse me?" Thorn asked. "I have a *name*."

"Likely so, child," a throaty voice boomed from the shadows. "Step forward and speak it, so that I might address the one who disturbs me on this day of mourning."

Thorn lurched forward, sliding on the slick marble floor. Her breath felt shallow in the cavernous space. Her boots made tiny *clap-claps* that quickly became lost in the darkness. As she passed between rows of fine, tapered columns reaching so high she couldn't see the roof, the rest of the room came into view. A vast space – where several corners might lay undiscovered for centuries – sparsely furnished and all the more imposing for its raw stone and dim light. The throne and dais occupied the entire east wall. Ten tall stone steps led from the floor up to the dark oak platform. Hundreds of tiny argand lamps swivelled in notched alcoves, casting eerie shadows in the gloom and serving as the only source of light. They wreathed Her Majesty Queen Victoria in an otherworldly glow.

And she was truly worthy of such drama, for she was both beautiful and frightening. Poised upon a simple chair of inlaid wood, her black skirts swept the steps below her like a velvet waterfall. Her skin shimmered in the candlelight, translucent as it swam in the black drapery that surrounded her. Delicate fingers rested on a gold lion's head staff, and a golden crown inlaid with black stones perched upon her shimmering hair. Her eyes penetrated the darkness with unflinching intelligence, and her lips curled with...what? Thorn couldn't tell. Annoyance or incredulity, perhaps, or amusement.

Thorn took a deep breath. "I am Thorn, Your Majesty."

"You should bow before your Queen, child."

"I'm not a child," Thorn replied, but she knelt on one knee and touched her forehead to the cold stones.

"Lord Russell informs me you've brought one of my men from the battlefield."

"Yes, your Majesty. Sir Robert O'Malley of the Royal Irish Guard. My army arrived on the battlefield in time to save a small contingent of your men—"

"Your *army*?"

Thorn nodded. "We're marching to London, to fight Brunel and restore our people to England's good graces."

For a minute Thorn thought the Queen would burst out laughing. The corners of her mouth twitched upward, but she held herself. Finally she said, "England's good graces flow from me. You do understand raising a personal army is forbidden in my realm, and is a defence punishable by death."

"With all due respect and reverence, I don't think there's much you can do to stand against Brunel without us."

"The bulk of my army may lie dead on that cursed field, but I still hold five thousand royal guards on this island, and several of my Northern regiments make their way down country as we speak. Explain to me what tactics your nine hundred men—"

"Eight hundred men." Thorn corrected. "And twenty tricorns."

"—*eight-hundred* men intend to employ that my battle-hardened soldiers could not use to greater effect. You'd best choose your words wisely."

As succinctly and carefully as she could, Thorn explained about her journey, how she had come to realise the stinging rain hurt the Boilers, how she had trained the tricorns and helped Quartz design the Stingers. The Queen regarded her with stony-faced silence while she considered Thorn's words. Thorn finished speaking, but the Queen did not reply.

"My quarrel is not with you, Your Majesty," Thorn added, not sure if she was helping her case or not. "But with the man who seeks to usurp your throne. Brunel has been an enemy of my people, disguised as our saviour, for too many years. We have the means to defeat him and his machines. We fought him from our own lands, and we can fight him again in your city."

The Queen was silent for several moments. Thorn shifted her weight nervously from foot to foot, unsure of what to do, where to look. *Should I say something else?* Finally, the Queen spoke, her voice booming through the cavernous room. "You are a brave girl, Thorn. I admire that quality greatly, especially in another woman who has had to establish her place in a world ruled by men."

"Thank you, Your Majesty."

"I will give you four thousand men, and a further eight thousand will meet you in London a week hence, which should swell your ranks a little." The Queen rested her quilted sleeves over the carved chair arm. "But is that enough? Do you truly know whom you face? I was foolish – I realised too late the true identity of the man I'd promoted. Isambard Brunel has ruled this country in all but name since he placed the first glass panel into his cursed Crystal Palace, and now he has brought my city to her knees. We all thought the days of terror were behind us, but once again, the Sunken prowl the streets of London. They massacred hundreds of citizens in the Great Exhibition, and that same evening he razed my palace to the ground. The streets ran red with the blood of my people, and I could do nothing to save them. *Nothing.*"

"It is not the first time Brunel has spilled the blood of people I care about. He murdered my father, and my betrothed. I know of whom I fight."

"I understand that, but you need to understand how this operation will be coordinated. My generals are still in charge. You are to meet with them in camp and explain your weapons, and leave them to decide the battle plan. They will not take orders from a woman, nor fight alongside one."

"They take orders from you."

The Queen smiled at that. "I guess that is so. Very well, I have given you your orders. Now leave me. Upon your exit, Lord Russell will give you my seal. You have much work ahead of you, Thorn."

"Thank you, Your Majesty, for your faith and your men."

"If you rid England of this mechanical usurper, Thorn," the Queen replied, "it is I who shall be thanking you."

***

The boat dropped them back in Portsmouth, where Oswald had marched the Stoker army to wait for them. When Thorn drew up on the beach with fifty boats of red-coated soldiers in tow, their brownbesses resting against their shoulders like porcupine quills, the Stokers hid in the forest, fearing she'd turned against them. She called them back, and explained that the men would fight for her, for the Queen, for all of England.

"There are no more Stokers," she said, as she called the generals together to discuss their tactics. "No more

Navvies. No more Royal Guard, no more enemies of flesh and blood. We are England, and we will not abide this usurper."

That night the camp was alive with stories and song, as the redcoats forgot their ranks and joined with Thorn's army around the campfires. Her tricorns mingled with the army, and those who feared the beasts got to know them as gentle and precocious creatures, and could fear them no longer.

The next day they marched from Hampshire into Surrey, and saw for the first time the swirling funnel of blackened smoke that rose from the maelstrom that had once been London.

A few miles down the road, the smoke rolled over the party, and Thorn reeled as in one swoop the world disappeared into a sea of foamy black soot. The clank and thud of enormous, catastrophic machinery thundered from the maelstrom.

This is a hundred times worse than when I last travelled to London. It really is as bad as the Queen says.

The jovial men fell silent as the full magnitude of their task fell upon them. It would be a three-day trek through this blinding black fog before the final showdown at the Wall of London. For the first time it seemed to dawn on Thorn's army that they fought someone who could obliterate the very air they breathed.

They set up camp on the perimeter of the soot-cloud, and ate their dinner in silence, listening to the deafening clanks soaring over the landscape and shaking the foundations of the earth.

"You should talk to them." Quartz wiped breadcrumbs from his scraggly beard. Behind his foggy monocle, his left eye blinked unceasingly.

"About what?"

"You've been here before, and you know something of this world of steel. Most of these men know only of drinking and farming. Their only knowledge of adventure comes from plays at the harvest festival. Their monsters come from myths told by their mothers at bedtime, from the rantings of preachers who hound them on street corners, or the blood-fever of battles against Frenchmen and natives. You ground these stories in *this*world; you give them truth to fight for. You should speak to them of that truth."

Thorn protested, but Quartz wouldn't take no for an answer. Her stomach churning with nerves, Thorn set down her soot-flavoured meat and stood up. "Excuse —" No one even glanced her way. She cleared her throat and tried again. "Good sirs—"

Quartz slammed his tankard on his thigh and let out a mighty belch. That got their attention. Thousands of pairs of eyes trained on her. Thorn opened her mouth, but all that came out was a croak. Quartz nudged her with his elbow. *You have to say something. It doesn't matter what, just be sincere.*

"Gentlemen." Thorn wiped her mouth on her sleeve. "You are brave for coming so far with me. As I look upon each face around this campfire, I see the terrible consequences of Brunel's deeds. He has destroyed your land, your homes and your freedom. You have lost brothers and cousins and friends to his machines and monsters. You have endured hell, and, unlike our enemy, it has not turned your soul to iron.

"I applaud you, for I alone know that in fact you are doubly brave. I think of the Gods – of Great Conductor and Mama Helios and Meticus and that Christian fellow – and how they command vast armies with only words and feelings and faith. I have no eloquence with words, and in my village I was a pariah. I cannot command loyalty or confidence or love from my own people, and expect no more of you, who do not know me.

"As for faith, I'm no authority on that either. In fact, I find it increasingly difficult to believe in things I just cannot see. But that is because I've seen too much, and it turns my blood cold. And now—" Thorn gestured to the Wall behind her. "—you have seen it too. And if you want it to sod off forever, you'll follow me into the fire tomorrow and help me knock the Metal Messiah off his usurped iron throne."

It wasn't much of a speech, but they cheered anyway, a great roaring wave of applause that rolled over Thorn like the ocean, carrying her along with it until she too believed in herself. A bread roll soared at her face. Thorn caught it in midair and threw it back. This began a short burst of bread catapults, followed by a refilling of the beer tankards and several bawdy tales that made Thorn's ears turn red.

That night she wished for Joel, and dreamt of a land of eternal summer, where the sun rose every morning and set every night, and its light glowed unhindered through lands of earth and stone. Trees and flowers grew in peace, unshackled by the constraints of man or machine, and she and Joel rode their tricorns across the countryside, entertaining villages with their antics and laughing, laughing always at the legacy of the Gods.

***

With gas masks firmly affixed, they marched across Londonshire, following the perimeter of the Wall toward the towering furnace that was London. They stopped at no town on the way, for the Walls here now stretched so high and the smog too thick to allow them to slow their pace. Atop the iron monstrosity, black trains chugged back and forth, their gleaming lights like ghouls flying as they screeched through the darkness.

Thought they had little water and even less food, the generals forced the men onward, anxious to reach the rendezvous point. When they finally stumbled into the familiar rock shelter formed from a circle of dolmens on an ancient sanctuary, Thorn expected to see Joel waiting there, and Sam too, with the army of navvies Stephenson had promised.

But he wasn't. They waited eight hours, sending scouts into the forest to search for signs of his approach. Thorn's stomach grew increasingly tight. Quartz reminded her about their delay on the Isle of Wight. "They could have come and gone," he said, but Thorn did not hear. Thorn climbed abroad the dray and hunched under the dashboard, clutching her hands to her knees and trying to calm her churning stomach.

You thought him dead once before, and he came back to you. Joel is strong and clever and he knows what he's doing. You can't worry about him now; you have to save your strength for battle.

"You were supposed to be here," Thorn choked out into the sick air, unable to restrain herself. "You were supposed to wait for me."

When it became clear she would not budge, Quartz sent the command to move on, and the army hurried to obey. They did not wish to wait one minute longer between the dolmens, blind and deaf inside the black miasma. They could not bear hearing their leader sob.

The soot dried the tears on Thorn's face, and she stared into nothing and tried to clear her head, tried to concentrate on the battle to come. Images of Joel and

Rex tangled before her eyes, melding with the memories of her father and mother – all the people she'd loved who Brunel had taken away. The faces of her friends – Lurgo and Holman and Wombwell and Julianne – trapped inside the blank maelstrom, smiling and laughing and swirling in the haze.

After a few hours they came within sight of London, if you could call the blackened shroud of soot that stung their eyes *sight*. Thorn refused to wear goggles, since only a handful of the men had a pair. Quartz handed around bottles of dandelion salve, which alleviated the stinging for a few precious moments.

The men took long breaks and mumbled amongst themselves, fearful of continuing through the trees without light.

"Follow the sound of the Wall," Thorn called back to them, remembering Holman and his echoes. "Follow your fingers and your boots."

After a time, there were no more trees, and Thorn heard her feet crunch on the field of nothingness, and the wind swirled and shifted the dust around her. She stepped into the submersing haze, opened her stinging throat and called in a voice as loud as she could muster.

"Isambard Brunel, we are here to take back the city! Come out and meet your doom!"

Her war cry was answered by the shifting of dirt and a clap of thunder overhead. Rain began to fall in sheets, the poisoned water flaying her skin.

Finally, something is going our way.

Thorn called Igor forward. The Stokers had already fitted his armour and secured the leather bridle and reins. She rubbed the last of her salve over his cracking eyelids, and climbed aboard his back. Taking a deep breath, Thorn pushed out her own thoughts and fears, and

Igor's mind clicked into place. She felt the press of the other tricorns on the edges of her conscience and she opened her mind further, letting them all inside, feeding them all inside.

I'm ready, Brunel. This time, I'm fighting back.

To her left Thorn saw the faint outline of Quartz, dragging another tricorn forward for its rider. The army scrambled into position, checking the Stinger hoses and performing last minute sharpening of blades.

She tightened the straps of her barker, and pressed her feet into Igor's side. *Forward, now!*

Her head throbbed as Igor thundered into the mists, and she heard the stomp and clatter of his siblings behind. A great clamour ascended from her army as eleven thousand boots pounded against the cracking earth, and knives and swords and rifles clanged against each other in the fray, and six thousand mouths roared a cry of defiance.

Igor slowed. The Wall was in front of them now. Thorn couldn't see it, but she felt it looming, pressing the echoes back upon her. She guessed from the clangs emanating nearby that they were within range. She raised her whistle to her lips and blew.

Quartz responded with two sharp notes. She heard his division march forward. Another bleat of the whistle, and they loosed the first volley.

The night erupted with explosions. The acid attacked the Wall, curling and buckling the iron casing like the flash of a tanner's knife over a fresh carcass. An incredible wave of heat rolled over Thorn, and she shifted on the hot armour. Igor wailed and sank low to the ground.

Inside the inferno, life-that-was-not-life stirred. Sinkers screeched. Bodies raced through the flames, returning their war cry with a maniacal ululation of their own.

"They're here!" Thorn heard someone yell. And from the corner of her eye she saw several men running across the soot field, dressed in the green overalls of the Navvies.

Next thing she knew, Joel was running alongside her, calling his men forward. Though she couldn't distract him with a greeting, Thorn's heart soared as the Navvies met the Sinkers with blades and bullets. She saw a flash of Sam thrusting his bayonet into the belly of a Sinker, and he bellowed in triumph.

Joel is here. He's alive. We have a chance to win this!

Igor whined and ploughed into this horde, scattering Sinkers in his wake. Thorn pinched his frill and squeezed her thighs into the searing metal, stopping herself from slipping. Limbs flew past her face and the firelight danced off slashing blades.

She heard the hissing and knew the Boilers had arrived. Sparks rained on the army from the buttress, and gusts of steam spurted over the ranks. Joel cried, "fall back!" and she saw a man go down screaming, broiled in a shower of steam.

The cries of her men mingled with the Sinkers' tortured shrieks, creating an orchestra of burning – a choir of living corpses serenading their own death-march.

Inside Thorn's head, her tricorns were panicking, tearing at the connections that fused them together, pushing against her skull as they fought to escape.

Stop, she commanded. *Calm down. You're okay. He's not going to hurt you. He has to answer to me first.*

"Come down, you pox-ridden gammys. We've got them!" she heard Quartz yell up. Another volley of acid shot towards the buttress. The Boilers hissed and popped.

Flames curled along the Wall, spreading away from the epicentre. Thorn and Igor raced towards the hole.

Joel shouted at her as they hurtled past, but Thorn couldn't make out the words. Igor flinched as the flames closed in, and his armour scorched, glowing red-hot where it came in contact with the acid. Thorn screamed as flames licked her arms, and squeezed her eyes shut so she couldn't watch her skin turning to ash. Igor didn't slow until they breached the fire and entered the confines of the Wall. Thorn heard a woman screaming, and it took her several moments to realise the screams came from her own throat.

It's all right. You're alive. You're not burning.

Thorn opened her eyes, and as they adjusted to the darkness, the familiar interior of the Wall came into view. Coils of lead hung from dislodged rafters, swiping her puffed cheeks. Igor's scorched feet pounded over steel gratings that buckled under his weight, their gauge nails melting into toxic puddles.

The fire lit the interior with dancing silhouettes, and Thorn saw the outline of a Boiler writhing in the shadows, its belly caved in by a fallen beam, and scraps of its mutilated mainframe littered the path ahead. It flailed its useless arms, and puffs of steam burst from its bent pressure valve. Thorn tugged on Igor's frill, trying to pull him away, deeper into the Wall. He gave the valve a swift kick, and it sagged onto the grating. The steam stopped with a final *pfft*.

Footsteps landed on the grating behind. Thorn looked back over her shoulder, tugging down her barker and aiming it at the shadows.

"Who's that?"

Joel emerged, followed by several scorched navvies clutching spent firearms and knives dripping with blood. Thorn dismounted and ran to him, wrapping her arms around his middle, ignoring the pain that flared from her seared skin.

"Whoa, easy there. I'm a little shaky on my feet." His features looked drawn, horrified. She shied away, but he grabbed her back, pulling her head into his chest. Her ear pressed against his heart, which beat with a frantic pulse. She wanted to ask where he had been, how could he have let her worry so? But they didn't have time.

"There are more inside." Thorn pointed into the gloom, avoiding the words they both wished to speak. "What do you have left?"

"One Stinger, and enough gunpowder for a couple more rounds, and we've at least ten grenades."

The men unslung their barkers and began reloading.

"It'll have to do. The others should be okay outside for now. They will follow when we breach the city—"

A whine echoed off the walls. Something clattered down the shaft behind them. Thorn pulled Joel to the ground as the men aimed their rifles into the dark. "Cursed Boilers," muttered one as he pulled the hammer back.

"Don't shoot!" Thorn leapt in front of him, recognising the silhouette. Lurgette bounded towards them, followed by Verne and Bernard and their limping, dishevelled riders. Igor brushed alongside his siblings, cooing in gratitude.

The men lowered their weapons and sighed in relief.

Joel held up a section of railway sleeper and wrapped it in a scrap of his oil-soaked clothing. He touched the end of the torch into the fire, and tugged on Thorn's hand. "We'd best continue."

Thorn raised her arms into the circle of torchlight and inspected the burns. The skin was splodgy, charred black in some places, yellow and green in others. Stabs of pain needled up her arms, but the pain was oddly insignificant compared to the extent of the injury. She wriggled her fingers. It hurt, but not impossibly so. As long as she could still move her fingers and grip her barker, there was no time to worry about it now.

The deeper into the Wall they travelled the more frigid and sparse the air became. As they left the light of the fires behind, their footsteps became their only company, each footfall echoing through strange and darkened places, shafts and fissures that light had never touched. They followed the series of pipes that crisscrossed the ceiling, listening for the *whoosh* of steam that signalled a Boiler's entrance. Despite the ever-churning gears in the distance, the Wall was silent. Thorn felt a presence on her back, a strange prickling feeling that someone, or *something*, watched her.

"This passage falls off over here, just like before." Joel gestured with his torch. Thorn gazed down, memories bubbling though her head. She scrambled to lift a small section of splintered pipe, and heaved it over the edge. It clattered on a metal grating below.

"There's another gangway, my guess is twenty feet down."

"I don't see a ladder," one of the men observed.

"Last time the gangways were folded up. I guess the Sunken don't need them. Hand me the light." She stumbled along the length of the passage and shone the argand down into the darkness. "There, see. But I don't think we could get over there."

I won't go over there, not this time.

"Me neither." Joel lifted his barker and powder horn

from his belt. "Hand me that torch, and hold onto these, will you?"

"Joel, *no.*"

Thorn grasped his sleeve just as he leapt over the edge. A strip of oily wool tore away, and he sailed below, engulfed in darkness. Thorn's heart was swallowed up into the abyss.

Clunk. He swore. Thorn thrust her head over the ledge, but couldn't see anything.

"Are you okay?" Her chest tightened.

"…mmmm…"

Thorn squinted. A light – faint and flickering – moved underneath her.

The other men leaned over as well, sticking their necks out much further than she dared. Igor pushed his beak into her spine, desperate to be party to the action.

"Stay back Igor, you're too close to the edge." He obeyed, stepping back with the other tricorns.

"…orn…to be pulley system attach …cage…"

"What'd he say?" asked the man next to her.

"Something about a pulley. Joel, see if it works!" She called out. The darkness ate her words, and she heard no acknowledgement from below.

The man next to her cupped his hands over his mouth. Thorn covered her ears.

"WELL, TEST IT THEN, YOU BLACK-TOOTHED GAMMY!" His rasping voice, edged with hard liquor and pipe tobacco, sailed over the chasm and reverberated from the hanging pipes. *Please let nothing dangerous have heard that.*

Thorn heard the crack of a chain being wound. On the wall behind her the gears creaked to life. She trained Joel's barker at the darkness, her hands trembling. Within moments, a rickety platform – ten feet square and clamped in each corner to a rusting chain – penetrated their circle of light. "… on," Joel cried from below.

Thorn held the platform steady while two of the men clambered abroad. They pushed the platform off the ledge and swung into the darkness, the gloom enfolding their bodies as the winch creaked overhead.

When the platform emerged again, she pushed Lurgette onboard. "Stay still." The tricorn whined as the platform wound its way over the edge, but didn't make a fuss.

They made two more trips, one each for Verne and Bernard, and one for the remaining three men. Finally it was Thorn's turn. She pushed Igor on board, and climbed on after him, gripping the guard rail with white knuckles. As the platform lurched over the edge and sank down into the chasm, her stomach plummeted with it. "Does this remind you of Meliora, boy?" she kept her tone light, but inside she was screaming.

Suddenly, someone else was screaming. But that sound came from all around, from inside the Wall, bouncing off every pipe and drum and metal rivet. Igor leapt to his feet, pawing at the chains. Something flew past Thorn's face, and she yelped.

"Hold on…orn…"

The platform ground to a halt. *Oh no, oh no, oh no…*

She heard it breathing, right by her ear.

The gun…where is my rifle…

Something cold clamped over her shoulder. She ducked just as the Sinker snapped his teeth where her ear had been moments before. No time to fire. She swung at it with the heavy barrel. It squealed as her swing landed on target.

Igor snarled. He lowered his horns and moved

towards the Sinker. Suddenly he twisted upward, yelping. Another two Sinkers fell onto his back, squealing as they swiped with their vicious talons.

Steam hissed from above. She rolled under Igor's legs as a jet squealed past her. More Sinkers were up there, and she heard them clambering down the chains. The platform bucked dangerously under their weight. She grasped the edge and flattened herself against the cold steel.

"Joel?" No answer. *Not again, I can't lose him again.* "JOEL!"

She heard squabbling below. The hollow room erupted into a shower of sparks. A wave of heat rushed over her. The chain clinked and let go, hurtling the platform through the flames.

No, no, no ...

Thorn landed with a jolt, pain searing through her limbs. Igor moaned. Above them, the Sinkers leapt from the beams, swinging down the chain winch like misbehaving monkeys. As they fell Thorn saw the flames glinting through holes in a mesh crate.

The mesh crushed down upon her, knocking her to the ground. She landed hard on her side, and the ground moved. *Not the ground, Igor.* He was groaning, rolling beneath her. *What's going on?* Thorn pushed her hands out, but all she could feel was mesh, all around her, on every side.

"Joel!" Thorn couldn't see or hear him. All she saw were Sinkers, crawling and simpering from every pipe and tunnel and crevice. All her men were gone. Panic welled in her chest.

Sinkers grabbed at the corners of the cage, dragging it further into the bowels of the Wall. Suddenly, they all scattered. Thorn and Igor were left alone in the darkness.

But not for long. Boilers rolled down from secret places, and surrounded the cage. They hooked it to a trolley and trundled the contraption along winding pitch-black corridors, fires flaring within their furnaces as though they signalled to each other. Thorn backed into the centre of the cage, away from the whispers of steam that reached for her through the wire. She pulled off her rifle and fired at the nearest one.

Her shot bounced off its belly, denting the iron and rolling harmlessly away. She didn't bother to reload.

After an eternity in the gloom, the Boilers pushed her and Igor through an arch and into a cobbled London square. The city had changed. What was once a vibrant, jewel-toned metropolis, Brunel had reduced to a charred, dissolute ruin. Flames leapt from building to building, engulfing the terraced housing and the old, rotting rooftops. Terrified citizens clung to the windows, too afraid to jump, howling as their skin roasted on their bones. Smoke billowed from the fires atop the Wall, shrouding the city in an arching dust that made it seem no different to the Wall itself.

Thorn tore strips from her tunic and soaked them in the London rain. She tied them loosely around her arm, to keep the burn cool and protected from further damage. It hardly hurt at all now, just a numb ache that mirrored the ache of her chest.

People dashed past, carrying heaped parcels of their possessions with wildfire in their eyes. Boilers set fire to buildings. Sinkers flooded every corner, darting and snarling after the fleeing citizens. Hoodlums slunk in and out of windows, dragging out unlawful merchandise. Thorn saw the blue jackets of Scotland Yard over by the bank office, doing over one unfortunate sinker with their truncheons. She screamed at them to notice her, but they didn't look up from their work.

The streetlamps faded into nothing. They passed Hyde Park and Thorn saw the Crystal Palace, lit by a thousand shimmering lanterns and patrolled by a regiment of Boilers. Ahead of her loomed the iron stack of the Chimney, a monster among the lesser spires and alight with a thousand flames, burning with a scalding light. They passed through the wide stone gates of Engine Ward and raced toward the Chimney. Smoke poured from the foreboding Chimney, soaking the air with soot.

Thorn's blood turned cold. They were taking her to Brunel.

***

JAMES HOLMAN'S MEMOIRS, FIRST EDITION

We felt the explosion before we saw it. Lurgo and I were in my study, poring over plans of the Crystal Palace – Brunel's new seat of government – and sucking the bubbling tobacco from my *nargila*, when the house threw my nib from my hands and sent Lurgo reeling into the bookshelf. The books rattled and my exquisite King James Bible with illuminated chapter headings and marginal notes from notable biblical scholars cascaded from its place and clattered onto Lurgo's head. He rubbed his temples, and his eyes grew wide.

"Are you injured?"

"No, look!" Lurgo pointed a shaking finger out the window. I leaned over my wobbling desk and peered outside.

A funnel of smoke billowed from the Wall, expanding over the surrounding districts like a poisonous field mushroom. Flames licked the nearby roofs, and I could hear choruses of women screaming. The bells from every fire department in the city clanged on full alert.

I covered my ears.

Lurgo leaned out the window. "It's Thorn! I know it!"

"We don't know that. It could be another horror wrought by Brunel. We must wait until Maxwell returns."

Lurgo couldn't sit still after that. He paced the room, clenching and unclenching his fists. I shared his nervousness – my stomach twisted in knots, and a great lump built in my throat.

Wombwell wandered down the hall, carrying a candle sconce and wearing a confused frown. "What's all the commotion?"

Lurgo made a half-turn at the hat-stand and resumed his pacing, ignoring Wombwell's question. Wombwell frowned at me. "It's been a long while since I resided in a house that wasn't on wheels. Are the walls supposed to shake in this manner?"

"No, this is a peculiarity of my residence—"

"If we could *not* make this situation into another joke," Lurgo snapped. "Thorn is out there and I—"

The door flew open. Maxwell stumbled inside, his ruined skin charred an even deeper black. Pieces of his facial tissue fell away and floated to the floor. He looked as if he'd been squatting in a bonfire.

"By the Vampire King's blackened soul, Maxwell, what happened to you?"

"Where is Thorn?" Lurgo barked.

Maxwell made a gasping, croaking noise in his throat. I had set the paper and inks ready for him, and he collapsed against the table and scrawled his message with haste.

I snatched up the paper and read it aloud. "They have taken Thorn to Brunel," I read, "The Stoker army have breached—"

Lurgo wasn't listening. He stumbled into the hall, tripping over the rippling carpets. "Julianne, sound the bell! We're marching out!"

Suddenly and quite without warning, my head exploded.

I doubled over, dropping to my knees and holding my head with my hands. My tongue flapped against my jaw. The pain tore at my mind, I didn't know if the world still shook or if the feeling was only inside me.

Wombwell bent over me. "James, what is the matter? Is it your eyes?"

"Mmmmmmmgh!"

As I screamed and writhed I felt something rattle inside my socket. The shaking had dislodged a gear inside the mechanism. The vision in my left eye clouded into a haze of grey.

Wombwell pulled me to my knees and wiped the tears from my cheek. When he drew his hand back I saw with my right eye that his fingers were coated with blood.

At the end of the hall Lurgo thumped into his boots. "If you're not coming, I'm not waiting!"

Wombwell sighed, and pulled me to my feet. "Can you walk? Do you wish to remain in the house? I'm not certain we can find a doctor in this carnage."

"Brunel." My breath wheezed with agony. "You must take me to Brunel."

***

With much hissing and traction-manoeuvres on behalf of the Boilers, they pulled the heavy trolley up the steps and through the entrance of the Chimney. The cavernous church, deserted now, spread out in squidlike tentacles from a narrow, vaulted nave. The candles smoked as they dribbled wax from their sconces onto the riveted mosaic floor.

The Boilers clipped the cage to a pulley system and lowered it into a dark shaft. Igor backed up and slammed the cage with his nose horn, bending the wires and rocking the entire mechanism. A Boiler jammed a jagged pipe through the grate, slashing Igor's cheek. He howled as blood pooled from the wound. Thorn reached over and cupped Igor's face with her hand, trying to stop the bleeding and to calm him. She didn't have much luck: Igor pushed her away and backed up to charge the cage again. Thorn didn't blame him – she didn't feel very calm herself.

The Boilers hissed their goodbyes as the cage descended into the gloom. Thorn clutched Igor's frill and cried silently into his warm skin.

We were so close.

Long after she'd expected to hit solid ground, the cage continued its steady trundle into the centre of the earth. *Maybe this is my punishment for failure…to forever travel the tunnels of Hell, always gazing up at that pinprick of light and hoping they will come for me, and wondering what I might have done different to save us…*

It was not to be. The cage jerked to a halt, though Thorn's heart continued to plummet through the gloom. She could see nothing save the minute speck of flickering light above. She pressed her hands against the mesh, trying to think of a plan. But nothing came to her, only the bleak darkness of her fear.

"Who have we here?" A panel slid open, and bright flames rushed her eyes. A misshapen silhouette framed by a halo of fire leaned in and puffed fetid breath into her face. Igor growled and shuffled to the rear of the cage.

Thorn didn't reply. Her useless rifle felt like a lead weight in her hands. Now she wished she'd reloaded it when she had the chance. *I could have shot him in the head, and ended this madness.*

Her eyes adjusted. From the darkness emerged two yellow orbs. Eyes, or a mockery of eyes. Brunel blinked, staring her up and down. "I've seen you before."

"Set me free, right now!" Her words sounded hollow, childish. She felt a weight against her leg. Suddenly, she remembered Joel's barker. She backed up inside the cage, moving her hands behind her body as she tried to pull it out with Brunel noticing.

Igor, distract him. Igor obeyed, pawing at the steel, ramming his beak against the cage, his eyes fixed on Brunel.

"You're both brave and foolish, girl, to make an enemy of me." Brunel crouched on his knees and peered into the cage, not even flinching as Igor once again crashed against the steel bars. "An armoured tricorn… how remarkable. Aaron Williams would have approved." He pressed his fingers through the mesh and caressed the iron gauntlets. Igor lifted his foot and stomped on his fingers. Brunel frowned.

Thorn whipped out the pistol, aimed it at Brunel's chest, and fired.

The weapon jerked in her hand as the shot rang out. Her ears hummed with the sound. She peered into the gloom, her heart hammering, trying to see if she'd landed her shot.

Please, let him be dead—

"Now, that's not very nice." Brunel got to his feet,

drawing back his hand from the cage. He peered down at his shoulder, where Thorn noticed a hole had been torn through his clothing. Brunel drew back the fabric of his vest, and grinned.

She started to scream.

He had no right arm, only iron rivets moulded around clunky gears. A tuning key drove the mechanism, vibrating between a drive-shaft that ran the length of this hand-that-was-not-a-hand. Brunel flexed and unflexed the fingers, his thin face brightening as he delighted in her horror.

"Now you see, girl," Brunel whispered. "Your plot to destroy me is pointless. I am not like you anymore, made of flesh that can be destroyed and blood that can be spilled. I am gears and springs. I am the engineer of all things. I cannot be unmade."

Thorn spat at him. "You're insane."

"An archaic notion, indeed." He wiped away her spittle, admiring the stain. "Insanity is merely unrealised brilliance. Tell me – for I could not extract the answer from James – did you Stokers decipher the plate?"

"The plate...you have that?"

Brunel walked to a bench and lifted it off; dangling it before her eyes the way Aaron would tease the dogs with juicy cuts of meat. "It is, after all, my property."

Thorn grabbed for it, but Brunel held it just out of reach.

"It's mine! My father wrote that message."

"Your father..." Brunel smiled, replacing the plate in his pocket. Thorn's stomach sank. She had a bad feeling she'd just given something away she shouldn't of.

"So you must be Ophelia. I've heard *so* much about you. My dear girl, you're in for a treat. Tonight, you shall see a true God at work."

My birth name? Save for Holman, no one outside the Graveyard knew that name, not since she'd abandoned it fifteen years ago for the moniker of her father. *So how does he know?*

Brunel reached into the inferno and pulled down a lever. Thorn's cage lurched sideways, sliding along a track on the ceiling to rest on the far wall of a long, damp room. Every inch was filled with strange and eldritch devices that hurled flames in all directions like Corinthian columns being thrown up from the hounds of hell. One entire wall consisted of a round-bellied furnace that grinned at her, steam leaking from slitted eyes.

Brunel faced a panel of dials and gears. He pulled a lever, than another. Steam gushed into the pistons, and a metal frame swung outward and cranked open, revealing a human torso. Armless, legless, the lump of noisome, malodorous flesh stood suspended within the iron box. An enamel clock-face was set in its belly, and hundreds of wind-up keys punctured the cachexic skin.

Time froze.

Thorn lost all sense of fear and place and danger. All emotions died inside her as she stared at that disfigured, dehumanised lump of flesh, ichorous sap oozing from its loathsome appendages. Her eyes locked on its frozen, lifeless face, and memories from some long forgotten time pressed against her temples. Perhaps they were not even memories at all, but dreams of what might have been. Her heart fell into her boots and she *knew...*

Brunel smiled.

"Now, watch."

He dug the plate from his pocket and pressed it into a slot below the clock, the calculating smirk never leaving his cracking, gold-plated lips.

As Thorn watched, her body numb, the hands on the clock began to tick. Between the stumped legs, a pendulum swung on its escapement, a mechanical mockery of the torso's manhood. Thorn clamped her hands over her mouth, choking back the bile rising in her throat.

"The mathematician Charles Babbage – Great Conductor rest his soul – designed this system with the plate as the activation key. It brings my machines to life. Your father stole it from me during the Gauge War, and irreversibly altered the course of history in the process. If I had been allowed to continue my work, England would be the most powerful country in the world right now. But, that is no matter, for I have been patient, and the plate has found its way back to me." Brunel paused in front of the rows of keys. "Forgive me, young Ophelia, this process is a little archaic. I have had to rebuild much of the knowledge lost after my death, and I do not have the precision required to recreate Babbage's calculating machines. This is the best I can do. But watch, I give the gift of speech." Brunel turned three keys by its throat. Steam-driven pistons thumped at either side of the box. A tuba-shaped horn protruding from the ceiling vibrated with the tension.

I will not cry, he wants to break me. I will not give him the victory. I will not cry...

"Uuuuuuh..." A sound like sludge emptying from a privy emitted from the horn.

"That's...oh, *Daddy!*"

Images flooded her mind; thoughts so strong and intense they felt like her own, even though they weren't. For she saw herself in the memories, felt the gentle softness of her newborn skin against coarse fingers. She held a baby aloft, drinking in the buttery, sweet scent of that new person she had created. She held the child against her chest, feeling that tiny heart beating against her own, pulling her little hands away from a fountain pen, carrying her around his office, rocking her to sleep. Then she was laughing as a small, strange-looking dragon rubbed its snout against that baby's cheek. More and more of these memories assailed Thorn – she was speaking in a soft, soothing voice as she read a book of fairy tales by the fireplace. She was handing the baby off to a beautiful black-haired woman who gazed up at Thorn with eyes filled with love. *My mother,* she guessed, but the feelings that welled up in her chest were not for a mother. *My wife.*

The tears fell now, cascading down Thorn's face like a ruptured water pipe. The strangled, rasping breath rolled through that horn and bounced from every pipe and lever and furnace in the workshop of hell, amplified by the years of pain and loss and lifelessness. Worse than death, worse than dying a thousand times, worse than eternal torment in the hands of the Vampire King, worse than punishments by a thousand fire demons with a thousand whips of glass was staring at the visage of her father, now alive-but-not-alive and bedecked with blasphemous implements, like a lump of meat hung at market. Thorn wanted to look away, oh how she prayed to Great Conductor and to every God she'd forsaken to tear her eyes and ears from her skull and cease the agony that tore her limb from limb.

But she could not. She was glued in place and there in front of her was her father, and she had no idea what to do.

Brunel regarded her with that same mocking, knowing expression. He paced the room, talking to her in a low, calm voice, as if she were a student of his taking notes rather than a captive sobbing and heaving as he tortured her undead father before her very eyes.

"For the past nineteen years Nicholas Thorne has been a continuing experiment of mine. When he came to kill me, we fought, and he fell alongside me into the abyss. I had already taken steps to ensure that my mind would survive long after my body decayed, and luckily, I was able to preserve Nicholas' mind as well. My Boilers came for us, and they kept us alive, but unfeeling, unseeing, un*knowing*, for many years. Finally, I was strong enough to crawl back from the abyss of death, and I brought Nicholas back with me. When I could extract no more information from his tortured brain I turned over his body to my machines. I wanted to explore the human organism from the inside out. A remarkable design, at once complex and easily faulted. By simplifying it into its base parts I can harness the essence of what it is to be human. What keeps our gears moving, what causes our hearts to pound and our teeth to chatter.

"You have seen the fruits of my labours. *Change and Adapt*, that's what the great scientific minds impress upon us, Ophelia my dear. *Change and Adapt.* Whereas once I used only animal hearts to power my Boilers, I now harness a much more sophisticated engine. My new Boilers can think, they can change and shift, creating new life from the shards of their departed. Because of their success, my Wall marches over every territory, claiming this country as my own. You have your father to thank for all this."

The new Boilers...they're human. That's why I cannot hear them...Oh God, I'm going to be sick...

Brunel's eyes glowed with pleasure as he watched the understanding dawn on her face. "Of course such experiments are doomed to failure without the information on that plate. The flesh rots, the veins weaken, the equipment runs down. But since your friend James so dutifully placed the key to my salvation into my hands..." Brunel smiled again, and rapped his mechanical fingers against the frame. "But you're not interested in this technical talk. You only wish to talk to your old pops, yes?"

Thorn tried to protest, but her voice had gone. Brunel reached up and turned one of the keys.

"Opheliaaaaaaaaaaa..."

Thorn's head exploded with pain. She did not know if it was pain sent through her father's thoughts, or if it was her own agony. But it was excruciating, nonetheless. She clutched her head, straining against herself to force out the terror.

Oh God oh God oh God stop the pain, please stop the pain. Thorn did not know if she screamed aloud or only inside her pounding, fissuring skull. *Please Great Conductor lord on earth anyone who can hear me stop the pain stop the—*

The door buckled inward, and two figures crashed into the room. Thorn tore her eyes away from the horrific visage of her father, and recognised the men. Holman hunched over as he ran toward Brunel, his hands pressed against his face. A strange sound, like a strangled scream, came from behind his hands. Wombwell barrelled after him, his usually jolly expression set into a grim line.

Brunel spun around in surprise. "James?"

"Take it out, take it out!" Holman collapsed to the floor, clutching his head and writhing as though possessed by malevolent spirits. Blood squirted between his fingers.

Wombwell stormed in behind him and noticed the cage. "Thorn, what's this—"

"Thorn's here? Thorn's *here?* No, no, no." Holman lifted his face from the floor, and for the first time Thorn saw the flickering bulbs and saw-tooth gears that turned inside his molested skull, weeping oil and blood.

She let out a strangled cry, forcing herself to address them, forcing herself back to the present. "We breached the Wall. Our army is pushing into the city…but the Boilers, they're human…Omigod, they're *human*…" Thorn's thoughts trailed away as she stared at Holman, and her mind processed what he had said. She dared herself to meet Brunel's glowing eyes once more. "*You* did this to him?"

Brunel threw his head back and laughed. Her rage collected in her limbs and she flung her body against the mesh, no longer content to writhe within. Again and again she pounded the cage, screaming incoherent curses at the tormentor of her father and her friend. Every muscle screamed to be free; every finger ached to be wrapped around Brunel's neck, squeezing the life from him before he could collect it from another.

Finally, she collapsed in exhaustion. Her bandage had fallen off and blood dripped from the crackling skin of her burn.

Brunel watched her and smiled. "I did only what he asked. Go on James, why don't you tell her about the plate?"

But Holman could only weep. Wombwell grabbed his shoulders and dragged his screaming body across the room, dropping him in a lump at Brunel's feet.

"Thorn…" Holman choked. "The plate…I'm sorry. It is a formula…for bringing metal to life…"

At the sound of his voice, a long, sorrowful warble emitted from the horn. Holman turned his head toward the torso, and his body convulsed in horror.

"...*frieeeeeend...*" echoed through the room.

"Nicholas? Oh no, no, no." Holman sobbed.

Wombwell crouched over the shuddering man. "James, James, can you hear me? Its okay, did you hear what Thorn said? We won. We've defeated him. Brunel is nothing without his precious machines. That plate means nothing."

"Oh, *contraire*." Brunel settled into a wingback chair, resting his boots on the sill of the roaring furnace. He needed only a pipe and a folded newspaper to appear a genteel lord at rest. He leaned towards Thorn's father and tapped the plate, stroking his fingers lovingly over the protruding surface. "With this plate, I am *everything*.I am earth and sun and sky and sea. I am life and I am death. With this plate—" He cradled his metallic hand to his chest. "I am God."

"A God is nothing but the value of his followers," Thorn spat, her sadness flicking to rage. "We *made* you this...monster, and we will unmake you. Did you hear that, James? He is *nothing*. Don't you let him touch you!"

Holman moaned softly, his feet battering the tiles like a child in a tantrum. Wombwell dragged him upright and manoeuvred him into a chair. "Take it out," he ordered, pulling Brunel by his shirt collar. "You've no business tinkering inside a man's head. *Take it out.*"

There was a flash of light as Brunel swung his mechanical arm, and Thorn screamed.

Wombwell slumped to the floor. He didn't move.

It was more than Igor could stand. He flung himself at the grate, and several wires bent and snapped. He reared up and smashed again. The cage creaked, and the rivets wriggled in their slots. Again he crushed his head against that metal. A flake of ivory snapped from his horn and skidded across the floor.

The rivets snapped, and the cage collapsed. Brunel barely had a chance to turn in surprise when Igor barrelled into him, sending the man sailing across the room. He crashed into a bank of temperature gauges and slid to the floor with an inhuman crunch.

Brunel began to laugh.

"You think you can kill me!" He chortled deep in his throat, coughing black spittle down the collar of his fine coat. Raising his metal hand, he brushed slivers of mercury from his lap. Despite Igor's blow, Brunel seemed to be uninjured, and extremely amused.

"You think...you think I am some monster? Oh dear Lord forgive me." He wiped oily tears from his cheeks. "You should know better, young Ophelia. Why, not too many months ago now you probably ate the mother of that creature you call a friend. You devour flesh to survive – are you any better than a Sinker? But have you ever eaten a machine? No, you have not. But I have. So tell me, who is more moral? Who is more just? I am the best of all things – I am life without death, I am machine without rust, I am above you in every...what is this nonsense?"

Sparks rained from the ceiling. The Chimney let out a low moan, as though the entire structure buckled on its foundations. Brunel looked to the roof in concern.

Now it was Thorn's turn to smile.

"French men of science have named it nitric acid, and it can destroy metal at a most alarming rate. Our stingers made short work of your Boilers, and I've put them to work on your Iron Palace."

"No, that can't be!"

For the first time since she'd arrived in the Chimney, Thorn detected a hint of concern in Brunel's voice. She stepped aside as he raced into the darkness in the corner of the room, and disappeared. She heard clattering as his steel boots raced up a flight of stairs. She squeezed her eyes shut, trying to shut out the quiet moan of the...of *her father* as sparks flew from the machine. Slowly, achingly slowly, she reigned in her horror and pushed it deep inside her. She took a deep breath and rushed to Holman's side.

"Can you walk?"

He nodded, and rose slowly. "George?"

Thorn bent over Wombwell, and dragged his heavy body into a sitting position, carefully avoiding looking over her shoulder at the whirring machine. Wombwell didn't move, didn't register her touch, though he still breathed shallowly and she felt a faint pulse at his wrist. Igor sniffed his fallen master, whining softly as he nudged Wombwell's limp arm with his beak.

"Help me drag him on."

Together they dumped the overweight proprietor onto Igor's back. "Where would Brunel go?" Thorn asked.

"There's a secret railway tunnel above this chamber that connects the Chimney to the Crystal Palace." Holman turned a lamp around so it shone in the darkened corner, and Thorn saw the staircase shrouded in shadow, leading further into the depths of the Chimney. "It's wide enough to manoeuvre machinery in and out – which means it's wide enough for Igor. Lurgo and I discovered it a few days ago. I bet Brunel's trying to escape through there. I can show you the way."

"You must go ahead, James. Take him into the tunnels. Igor will protect you. Here." Thorn grabbed her rifle, reloaded it, and thrust it into his arms. She tugged on Igor's frill, and he took off towards the staircase, tugging at the strings in Thorn's mind. The horrors had erased her previous connections, but gradually she felt her way back into Igor's mind. *Protect them,* she told him, *and bring them safely into the light again.*

"Miss Thorn—" Holman's lolling orbs rolled between the distraught girl and the mangled torso of her father.

"I said go! I have something to attend."

He reached out to her, but seemed to think better of it and stumbled after Igor. She heard his footsteps clanging up the metal rungs.

"Heeeeelllp meeeeeeeeeeeeeeee…"

Eyes on the floor, Thorn tore a strip from her shirt and wrapped that around her burns, sobbing with pain as the coarse wool scraped the charred, weeping flesh. Staggering to her feet, she took another deep breath and looked up at her father, the full horror of what he was sinking into her, becoming part of her.

"I love you, Daddy," she whispered. "You will sleep at last."

Thorn raised her leg and smashed her boot into the clock face with all the force she could muster. Glass and gears flew in all directions. A curdling hiss echoed from the horn, crushing her head under the weight of its sorrow and sending her heart plummeting to her boots. She sank to her knees and sobbed as the torso twitched on its silver tines, and the misshapen head leapt back and forth on its steel mount. The keys sprung from their casings with a series of metallic *pings,* and clattered on the floor. With a final howl of agony the monstrosity slammed against the box and fell still.

Pushing aside dangling pieces of the broken mechanism, Thorn pulled the plate from the slot and threw it into the furnace. She watched it melt into a formless lump, returning to the void of fire and soot.

She stood there a long time, longer than she should

have with sparks flying from the ceiling and the sound of the metal pylons giving way above her. In her head whirled silent conversations, words and feelings and unanswered prayers that she sent with her father's spirit. She didn't cry. She was bereft of tears.

When her senses returned to the present and she felt the heat of the flames cascading down the wall of instruments, she scrambled around Brunel's workbench until she found a long, thin dagger, which she shoved into her belt and thundered down the stairs. From the tunnel above, Igor's thoughts pushed on her temples – he was frightened. He wanted to come back for her. *No, Igor, you stay with Wombwell and Holman. I'm coming. I'm right behind you.*

Other thoughts pushed against her mind. A chorus of voices, quiet at first, but growing louder, all calling to her through an intense wall of pain. They were the voices of the old Boilers, the ones that were animals. *Help us,* they cried, and again. *Help us. Free us, as you freed your father.*

"I wish I could!" Thorn cried, clutching her aching head and pushing the thoughts away. She couldn't have them in her head now. She needed to think her own thoughts.

After she ascended several flights of stairs – the only sound her feet on the staircase, the faint voices inside her and her heart hammering against her chest – she emerged into a wide, arched tunnel. Her feet thudded across gauge rails and wooden sleepers. Water dripped from the walls and filled the air with syrupy damp. Thorn could hear footsteps, a long way ahead. Sucking in a deep breath, she jogged down the passage.

Above her, the earth rumbled, and dirt and ash cascaded down the walls. Thorn ran faster, her chest heaving with the effort. She swallowed and tasted blood.

After a mile or so, the passage ended at another stairwell. Smoke seeped from above, choking the stairwell in grey fumes. She pressed her coat over her mouth, closed her aching eyes and scrambled for the Palace.

The staircase ended with a trapdoor, which opened into a glass room filled with Dirigire clocks. She pushed aside the curtain and stepped into the next hall, following the sounds of shouting men. Huge sections of the outer glass walls had been smashed, and she saw men, Sinkers and Boilers fighting across the lawns. The voices of the Boilers' intensified, until her skull filled with screaming. *Go away, please. I need my own mind right now.*

Thorn figured Brunel must have run outside, but a flickering light danced across the exhibit of farm equipment, leading her deeper into the Crystal Palace.

Fire. The light was fire. She raced through the exhibits, following the dancing light.

When at last Thorn entered the Grand Transept, she found it alight. Most of the glass had blown out and the great trusses creating the arch of the transept had almost entirely caved in – the only thing keeping the entire structure from collapsing were the great oak trees lining the promenade, and these now crackled with orange flames. Sparks flew from the precarious beams that sagged under the weight of the collapsing structure. Everywhere she looked, exhibits burst into flame – cabinets made of precious woods burning to ashes, and beautiful tapestries shrivelling to nothing. The treasures of the empire laid to waste. Smoke from the fires inside and out mingled together in the air, and Thorn flailed about for her bearings.

As Thorn stumbled across the room she found

Holman and Igor hiding behind a wall of toppled statuary, sheltering themselves from the falling debris under the torso of Olympian Zeus. As she crouched beside them she saw the outline of Brunel, pulling himself up onto one of the great altars and calling to a figure that emerged from the shadows of the exhibits. The stranger approached Brunel, and the light of the fire danced off his drawn sword.

The shadow circled the altar, the blade held awkwardly in front of him. Brunel darted away from his feeble thrust, and held something shiny aloft. Thorn squinted. It looked like the plate...

But I just destroyed it! He has made a copy. Of course he has. He probably has several copies by now. Bloody hell, now what will we do?

"I have it!" Brunel cried. "I have the secret of life! Cease your feeble attempts to cut me, boy. You can't kill me. I am your new God."

The figure laughed. "God? There is no God in this place, only reason and intellect. You do not belong here."

He stepped into the flames and swung. Thorn leant forward, heart soaring. *It's Joel!*

Thorn's heart erupted with joy. The connections in her mind drew closer, and instead of pushing them away, Thorn pulled them to her, drawing power from their pain. The screams of the Boilers amplified as other minds joined with hers – animals for miles around gave her their thoughts, their power.

Joel swung at Brunel, but the engineer reached out a steel boot and kicked the sword away.

"Joel, *no!*"

Thorn's joy turned to horror as she realised Brunel had trapped Joel between a wall of burning tapestries.

Defenceless, Joel backed towards the flames as Brunel pointed his great mechanical arm and fired a sharpened bolt at Joel's head...

...a great surge rose in her veins and welled over. The power left Thorn's body, toppling from her pores and casting out into the world. The gossamer threads rolled and fished and searched for a receptacle for her hope. And they snagged and caught on a black shadow with razor sharp teeth, and she *pulled*...

Joel ducked and rolled away, grabbing for his discarded sword. Darting forward with surprising speed, Brunel leapt from the altar and stomped on his outstretched hand. Joel screamed...

...Thorn's mind pulled harder, drawing the shadow close...

Brunel raised his mechanical arm high above his head. "You dare to defy me, boy? I am the ruler of England. I am a God. I *am* God!"

From the shadows of the falling building something leaned down and snapped his arm off.

"Boris!" Holman exclaimed.

Brunel screamed. Black, sludgy oil spurted from the wound. He staggered back against the stone altar and sank to his knees, cradling his amputated stump and wailing like an infant. His arm crunched between the dragon's teeth, and the perturbed look in the creature's eyes faded to anger as he realised the flesh tasted unusually cold and gritty. Mangled, saliva-coated gears rained down on their hiding place.

Joel stared at the dragon with gape-mouthed horror, his fingers closing around the hilt of the sword. Thorn felt the dragon's rage mounting, filling her with the urge to destroy. She fell to the ground, clutching her head.

"Joel," she yelled. "Don't move!" She pushed the

dragon away from Joel, back to Brunel. The dragon leapt down from the disfigured rafters and cut off Brunel's escape. The Messiah reeled, skidding in a pile of his own viscous fluids and collapsing over a broken statue of himself. Thorn heard the crunch of metal as he crashed to the floor. He writhed in a pool of oil, his legs twisted beneath him in an uncomfortable manner. Jagged gears poked from gaping wounds in his thighs.

"Call him off, call him off!" the Metal Messiah screamed.

"You're a God," Thorn sneered. "The engineer of all things, I heard you say. *You* call him off."

"That's Wombwell's dragon!" Holman cried. "Thorn, you're controlling it!"

Joel dropped to one knee, the curved blade trembling in his grip.

Boris leaned in, and Brunel's final, wrenching scream was cut abruptly short as a mouth of serrated teeth penetrated his chest.

Thorn felt Boris' teeth sink into metal and flesh as though she herself took a bite from Brunel. She *tasted*the blood, sucked at the metallic juice, revelling in the joy of the feast, in the sanctity of her revenge. She felt his body go limp and the last vestige of life-that-was-not-life leave his body forever. The connection snapped away, leaving her feeling hollow, and the taste of blood in her mouth.

Joel turned away, covering his eyes. Thorn dropped Holman's hand and raced across the transept, taking a wide berth around the feasting dragon. Crouching beside his hunched figure, she reached her arms around him and squeezed. The joy swelled in her chest, erupting from her eyes in a flurry of fresh, triumphant tears.

"Don't *ever* threaten a maniacal engineer again," she sobbed. "I thought I'd lost you."

He grinned wildly, stroking her hair with his soft hands. "Nah, I would've been fine. I had my trusty sword."

"Do you even know how to use that thing?"

He shook his head. "If it's older than black powder, it confuses the hell out of me. I picked this up off a dead redcoat. I figured I'd give Brunel death by a thousand cuts."

"Thank Great Conductor I sensed Wombwell's dragon—*oh no, Wombwell!*"

Thorn dropped Joel and rushed back to Igor. Wombwell had slid off Igor's back and lay sprawled in an impossible position across the tiles, his legs bent under his body at an angle only Julianne could articulate. Holman bent over him, slicking his matted hair back from his face. Thorn knelt at his side, clasping his beefy hand in hers. The skin felt cold, and when she held her hand over his mouth, she felt nothing.

"No..." It seemed too much.

Joel clasped Thorn's shoulder, trying to pull her away. Boris stalked down the aisle, spitting mangled screws onto the tiles. Above them, the pylons crackled and crashed over the altar. Flames leapt through the wooden pews, devouring the ornate carvings on the kneelers and arm-rests.

"Thorn." Joel tugged on her sleeve. "We have to get out."

"No..." She rested her head on Wombwell's belly.

"Thorn...for God's sake..."

"*There are no Gods!*" She felt panic rising within her. "No God would do this to his people!"

"There's no time to panic now. You two, grab his legs," Holman struggled to his shaking feet, pulling Wombwell's shoulders. "We'll have to get him back on

Igor. Thorn, we'll need your help."

"Who the hell are you?" Joel narrowed his eyes at the strange man with the mechanism on his face who was dishing out instructions.

"James Holman, Esquire. Pleased to make you acquaintance. Joel, I presume?"

"Thorn said you were blind."

"Yes, indeed I was. If you don't mind, I feel that's a story best saved for another day. Now *pull!*"

Thorn wiped off her tears, tugging her panic down into her belly, and pushed her hands underneath Wombwell's corpse. The three of them lifted together, straining under the weight – Holman's eye gushing blood – and dumped the body on Igor's back. The tricorn sagged under the weight, but looked up at Thorn with wide, understanding eyes. He bounded off down the transept

They raced down the transept after Igor and out the grand entrance, dodging falling rafters and showers of glass shards. Boris finally spat out the mangled metallic skeleton of Brunel and lumbered after them.

Outside, the rain splashed on the cracking cobbles, sizzling as it attacked the flaming Palace. Thorn rubbed her eyes, unable to believe the sight that greeted them.

The old Boilers had turned on their new masters, and tore down the twelve-foot machines, bending and jamming their pressure valves so they spluttered and fizzed, then pushing them over and crushing their mainframes beneath their whirring belts. They hissed steam from their double chimneys, as though calling in triumph to each other as they raced between the mangled bodies of hundreds of Boilers that littered the once-pristine lawns. Thorn realised she could no longer hear their cries inside her head. In fact, she couldn't hear anything at all.

Joel stared at Thorn in awe. *"You* did this?"

Stunned into silence, Thorn nodded.

Several of Joel's Navvies jogged past the marble steps, their Stingers pouring streams of acid over the edifice. The rabble of her army had congregated in the park, feeding the flames with debris and barrels of oil. Sinkers wailed from within the inferno, but the Stokers met their anguish with more fire.

In the distance, a high plume of smoke rose from the mangled Engine Ward, and the sky bobbed with bulbous shapes that trailed black clouds behind them. They pitched over the city and spread out, bobbing in formations of ten and twenty. As they neared, Thorn saw they were Dirigire balloons, their baskets weighted down with men who leaned from the sides and punctured the streets below with lead-tipped bolts.

"That froggy bastard kept his word!" She pointed to the balloons. "Look!"

A squadron flew overhead, and the clatter of bolts as they hit the Palace sent cheers through her ranks of men. A balloon broke away from the formation and fluttered to the ground. Thorn ran over as Frederique scrambled over the wing, helping a staggering Quartz to the ground.

Quartz ran to her, his face criss-crossed with weeping cuts, and shook her firmly by the shoulder. He grinned like a salacious clown. "I never thought I'd see this city again. Thorn, you've made a grizzly old blagger very happy."

His embrace felt strained, empty of emotion. Everything – the end of their suffering, the beginning of forever – felt tainted by her father's and Wombwell's deaths. Thorn nodded, her face numb, as he let her go.

She shook Frederique by the hand.

"You came," she whispered.

"I wouldn't have missed it." He smiled, hefting a complex weapon over his shoulder. "Pierre sends his regards. He's taken ill in recent days, and had to remain behind."

"Of course he has." Thorn managed a weak smile.

"He did manage to 'recover' all these balloons, though, so we can't judge the bastard too harshly. We've razed the Chimney, and most of the Boilers are gone – it seems they turned on each other. It's been great sport, and an honour to fight with you. Until we meet again, Miss Thorn." Frederique smiled at her one final time, and waved his men forward to assail the burning Palace.

As she watched him join the fray, Joel's men drew back and a rabble of Londoners marched in to hack at the last of the Boilers and Sinkers with knives and pipes. To Thorn's surprise, a thin line of Sinkers led this charge, calling to their brethren in their harsh, snapping tongue. Several of the creatures tossed aside their human dinners, and joined the ranks of London. Confused, the remaining Sinkers retreated into the wreckage, where their lead-soaked skin cracked and bubbled. The old Boilers did not attack, but seemed to welcome their destruction and soon fell under the onslaught of men.

A familiar figure darted from the fray, leading a party across the square, back towards the burning Engine Ward. He screamed as he swung his rapier and black curls whipped across his back. "Lurgo!" Thorn cried, but the figure did not turn around.

She lunged forward, but Quartz pulled her back. "You're done, lass," he said, and she felt the pains throb in her arm again. "We've won. Let them finish it off. Your work is done."

Fatigue washed over her. Thorn collapsed to her knees, her eyes locked on the figure of her friend stomping through the flames like a god of fire. Julianne followed him, her bare legs gleaming as she whipped and danced, two daggers clutched in her tiny hands. She'd painted her skin with swirls of silver, and she shone like a firefly called to the light. Lurgo shouted orders to his ruffians, who advanced through the flames, dislodging the scattering Sinkers with sword and dagger.

"Who are those people?"

"Lurgo's army." Holman stuffed a crumbled scrap of fabric around his bleeding eye. "They're the London Stokers, although many of them are not Stokers in the true sense of the word. He's spent the past months flushing every one of them from hiding, finding anyone clever enough to see through Brunel, to be brave enough to fight against him when the time came. He's been waiting for your return."

Thorn smiled at that, and squeezed Joel's hand.

"Even Maxwell returned. He said the Sinkers would join us, if we could promise them food and kindness. It seems he was right."

We won.

Thorn collapsed on the pavement, every limb in her body aching. Her heart ached most of all.

***

After the three days of public mourning for the partial destruction of London, and when the private sorrows of those who'd lost loved ones had dulled in their hearts, the crowds gathered at the smoking precipice of the Wall, torches burning and hatchets and hammers slung over every shoulder.

Queen Victoria and Prince Albert rode nonstop from Portsmouth to be there on this day. They sat under a makeshift tent – made from torn scraps of iron from nearby houses, all the finery they could salvage. Victoria donned her black mourning robes, and gave only a brief address.

"My heart weeps for this city, and all that we have lost. But amongst all this sorrow you must take solace in the fact that you've won a great victory, not just for yourselves, but for all of England. We can learn much from Brunel's evils. Namely, that we shall never again be so foolish as to allow the pursuit of mechanical perfection to distract us from what is truly important. We must never forget that we are the makers of the machines, and the Gods of our own destiny. London will see no days darker than this; from here until forever she shall be a city of peace and light."

Every tongue lashed vitriol against Brunel. Wrath lurked in every eye. The air was thick with their vengeance. The crowd jostled for space, each person banging shoulders with the next, eager to be in the front, to take the first swing at Brunel's monstrosity.

Joel and Sam stood ready with their men, stingers poised in case any Boilers emerged. They didn't know what horrors still lurked within the darkness of the Wall. Behind them waited the Sunken, ready to claim any lead that came from the wall. They were bedecked in their new uniforms – for the Queen had given them a new task; they were to patrol the cities and towns, keeping back the dragon population. Maxwell saw her staring, and he gave her a wave, his epaulets shone in the midday sun.

The Queen commanded the crowd to move forward and begin the attack. As one squabbling, raging unit they pushed at the base of the iron structure, swinging with their tools.

Thorn – her burnt arm in a sling – sat with Lurgo and Holman on top of an abandoned carriage, and watched. She couldn't muster her emotions to feel the anger, to share in their joy. The task seemed insurmountable. The Wall towered over them, casting the crowd in shadow. Though they tore sheets from the casing and pummelled the struts with all their might, they hardly seemed to make a dent in the towering structure.

Next to the pie sellers, Julianne stood by a cart piled with whetstones, ready to sharpen the weapons of the anti-Wall brigade. She waved at Thorn and cheered.

"How will we destroy it?" Thorn's eyes followed Joel's darting figure.

"Exactly as it was made," answered Holman. "One rivet at a time."

"I don't understand," said Lurgo. "If they can destroy it with hammers and fires, why did they wait until now? I wouldn't have stood by and let Brunel take over this city. Why did they need us to lead them against him?"

"These people lived with that Wall for more than twenty years. It became such a part of their lives that each new horror Brunel visited upon them went unnoticed next to the problem of sourcing their next meal. People are like that, Lurgo. They didn't see this Wall as a barrier, because they were *happy* here. They didn't want to go outside, not till they saw the hell this paradise really was."

Thorn stared at that Wall and thought of Rex. Like the Londoners, she'd been happy not because he was good for her, but because she had known no other. And now she saw him for who he really was; marked in the face of every Sinker, because to her he *was* one, a demon of her past lost to his own madness. If London could burn down its barrier, she could burn hers.

She jumped down from the carriage and dodged around the outskirts of the crowd. Lurgo called after her, but she ignored him. Like so much else, he was behind her now, in her past.

Joel saw her running towards him, and he smiled. She vaulted a smoking pile of debris and folded herself into his arms.

"You should stay with James and Lurgo," he scolded, pulling her hair back from her face and stroking her cheek with rough fingers. "You must let your wound heal."

"Yes." Thorn grinned. "I must let all the wounds heal."

Joel bent down and scooped up a large hammer and handed it to her. She tested it in her hand. It felt reassuring, thick and heavy and cool against her blistered skin.

"For your freedom," Joel said.

"Freedom!" Thorn cried, and swung the hammer behind her head, smashing it down on the iron wall with all the force she could muster.

***

Queen Victoria accorded Wombwell a state funeral. Thousands travelled from all over the countryside to line the streets of the newly free London, waving black kerchiefs and whetting their tears with sweet wines purchased from unscrupulous street vendors. It reminded Thorn of her first days in London; now, as then, her heart weighted heavy with sadness.

The procession began at the Smithfield Green, where

Wombwell's Travelling Menagerie had held court during the annual Bartholomew Fair celebrations. Many of the pie-sellers and proprietors of chance had set up shop to take advantage of the crowd, calling their sales pitches over the lamenting ululations. But today not even the scents of roasted chestnuts and hot, pastry-wrapped mutton could permeate the fog inside Thorn's head.

She crouched beside Lurgo on the rotting gallows planks, swinging her legs over the platform and watching Joel and Holman help the handlers lift the oak coffin onto the royal hearse. Dozens of children threw in garlands of lilies and carnations, so the entire coffin was buried under a mound of flowers. To the dirge of thirty sombre violins the carriage left the Green and rattled through the streets of slaughterhouses. Throughout the afternoon it would wind its way through all the major London streets, finishing at the gates of Highgate, where Wombwell would be escorted to his tomb for life's final great adventure.

"Do you want to follow?" Lurgo asked, leaning back against the wooden upright.

Thorn shook her head.

"Would you like to walk to Highgate?"

"Okay."

They waited until the procession disappeared down the road and the gloomy notes of the band blew by on the breeze, then leapt down from the gallows and cut across the field, heading through the deserted streets towards Highgate.

"Lurgo, I meant to say thank you, for raising that army."

He shrugged. "I kept my promise, and nothing more. I had to do *something*. You left me alone here."

"I know. I'm sorry." Thorn stared at her hands,

tracing swirls on her palm, like the swirls on Julianne's dancing legs. "But you're not alone anymore."

"No." Lurgo smiled. "And neither are you."

They continued in silence. London enveloped them in her gloomy magic. Soot and ash streaked the buildings, and every now and then fireman's bells punctuated the hushed air. The Engine Ward still smouldered – the remains of a great bonfire offered up to the gods – and the Crystal Palace stood no longer. Fires still burnt along the length of the Wall, burnishing the sky with plumes of smoke and coating the city in a husky, burnt bread smell. The streets were empty; those who weren't following the parade cowered indoors, watching the shadows and not believing the nightmare was really over.

They passed through the cemetery gates hours before the procession was due to arrive. Lurgo had one of the officers on duty direct them to Wombwell's grave. Thorn recognised the surrounding plots; she'd walked here the year before, searching for her father. To be here with Lurgo seemed strange, out of order.

The tomb stood between two hornbeam trees, the wide plinth towering over the nearby plots. A stone Nero sat atop, eyes cast toward the exact spot where they stood, regarding them with his characteristic kindness. One paw hung lazily over the edge of the lintel.

"It's a good likeness," said Lurgo.

"Yes," said Thorn. There didn't seem to be anything else that needed saying.

"You can't hear them anymore – the animals?"

Thorn shook her head. "The sense is gone. It left me after I sent Boris after Brunel. I don't know how I feel about that. I am trying to untangle who I am from my connection to the animals. Maybe I should be glad to be rid of it, but I do not yet feel glad."

"Do you want to see your father's grave?" asked Lurgo, his voice hopeful.

Thorn shook her head. Lurgo started to say something, but stopped himself. He looped his arm through Thorn's and they left Highgate.

At the public house it was as if nothing unusual had transpired. The mutton pie still tasted of heaven, the ale warmed her stomach, and the conversation erupted into frequent bouts of laughter as one person or another retold tales of Wombwell's legendary deeds. Thorn let the mood of the place wash over her, cleansing her of guilt and sadness. Wombwell was gone, but not forgotten. He would've liked it thus.

***

In a charred, crumbling room in Somerset House, Queen Victoria called a meeting of her war council. Brunel had been defeated, but the work was not yet finished. This time, they could not leave Brunel any hope of resurrection. Every trace of the Chimney and the Wall had to be eradicated. There was no telling how many Boilers and Sinkers still stalked the countryside.

Along with much of London, Holman's apartments had been razed to the ground, and many of the menagerie's carriages had been destroyed in the battle. The Queen graciously offered a suite of rooms on the lower floor of the palace for Thorn and her friends to use. Besides the smoke damage to the exquisite paintings and drapery, this wing had escaped the fire, and all the workers and animals of the menagerie – including Thorn and her tricorns – took up residence in the vast halls and gilded throne rooms. All except Boris, who was too large to fit through the doorways, so the soldiers built him a makeshift pen in Hyde Park.

Somerset House had been looted during Brunel's occupation, so the chamber had no table or chairs. The council sat on delicately embroidered cushions. Brunel had murdered several of Victoria's most trusted ministers and generals – all those unfortunate enough not to escape the city in time. In their places she appointed Joel and Sam and Lurgo and Robert and Holman and Julianne and Thorn.

The remaining lords and generals conversed with Holman, Joel and Sam in low tones, heads bent toward each other as they exchanged news of lives lost, assets destroyed, and a countryside laid to waste. Lurgo helped himself to the scones.

Thorn and Julianne settled themselves into the windowsill – the monkey Bella perching between them – and watched the sun rising over London. Streaks of grey and orange soared across the sky, a fitting ode to the battle of lead and fire. Plumes of smoke climbed from the rubble of the Wall, punctuating the serenity with whispers of death.

Thorn stroked Bella's fur and watched the sun battle the soft grey clouds for possession of the city. As the light settled over the city, the Queen cleared her throat.

"Before we address the matters of state," Queen Victoria said. "I am in haste to settle Mr. Wombwell's estate. This menagerie cannot live in the palace forever. I'm not certain straw and tricorn dung in the reception rooms is the best visage to present our foreign ambassadors."

Lurgo leaned forward, dropping his scone in his lap. Thorn couldn't read the expression in his eyes. Julianne gave a little gasp, and squeezed Thorn's hand.

The Queen folded her hands on her lap. "Mr. Wombwell's will was – like many of our court documents – burnt in the fires that swept the city. As you know, this means his property automatically passes to the Crown."

"But—" Lurgo leapt to his feet, his face red.

"Sit *down*, Mr. Riley," Victoria barked. "I have not finished. As the new owner of Wombwell's Travelling Menagerie, I am passing the entire estate – along with a full retinue of refitted carriages – to Mr. James Holman, Esquire, to deal with however he sees fit."

"And I," said Holman, a mischievous smile playing at the corners of his mouth, "am gifting the menagerie to Lurgo and Thorn, with my sincerest wishes they continue Wombwell's legacy."

His statement was greeted with stunned silence. Thorn glanced at Lurgo and saw her own surprise reflected in his eyes. *How can Holman do this? What do we know about running a menagerie?*

Finally, Julianne spoke, furiously wiping tears from her eyes. "I've already spoken to the performers and handlers. We see no reason to cease operating Wombwell's Travelling Menagerie. It brings such joy in a land wrought with terror and toil. We would be honoured to keep Wombwell's legend alive, and I think Thorn and Lurgo are just the people to do it."

Thorn gaped at her friend, still not trusting herself to speak. *But how will we do this? We have never even had jobs before, let alone operating something as complex as the menagerie.*

Lurgo was the next to speak. Though he stood and spoke to everyone, he addressed his speech to Thorn, his pale eyes shining with renewed energy. "If Thorn and James agree, I would like to employ the menagerie for a noble task. Though the Wall has fallen in London, it still criss-crosses the countryside and pollutes the air and water. There are still Boilers and the hungry Sinkers seeking to make more of their own. I wish to return across the countryside, to revisit the towns and hamlets and all the kind people who supported Wombwell's endeavours and Thorn's army. We could take Boris and the tricorns and our other animals, and help tear down the Walls and plant new crops and spread hope where there has been only darkness. And I want you all to travel with me."

"I applaud this noble idea, and I will give you an escort of two thousand redcoats," Prince Albert added. "You will need many hands to tear down the Wall."

The council nodded its approval. Lurgo turned to each face in the room, his eyes expectant.

Sam spoke. "With Brunel finally gone, it's time to introduce a standard rail gauge throughout Britain, and enable all people to easily move across the country. If the Queen agrees, I would oversee a team of workers—" he smiled at Joel, "—both Navvies and Stokers, of course, to tear up London's rail network and replace it with a working, *un-living* standard gauge circuit. We will connect once and for all every major city in England by rail."

Queen Victoria nodded her approval, than glanced at Joel. "What say the Stokers to these proposals?"

Joel stood and paced the room, his brow furrowed in thought. Finally, he leaned against the windowsill and squeezed Thorn's hand, placing his other on Lurgo's shoulder. "I am not sure it's my place to speak for all Stokers, but I think this is a fine and admirable mission, friend. I would accompany you and the menagerie, but I am needed in London with Sam, overseeing the Stokers and the Navvies in their work. There is much here that still needs to be rebuilt, much damage still to undo within our own people. But Thorn will go."

Thorn looked at him in alarm. She was still reeling from the news that she'd inherited Wombwell's business; she hadn't even *considered* that being with the menagerie might separate her from Joel. "I'm not leaving without you!"

"Yes you will. No, don't cry." Joel wiped away a tear that escaped her eye. "The Gods are kind to us. We have many days left to enjoy each other. Go with your animals and your friends. I'll be here when you return. Of that you have my word and my heart."

Thorn nodded, too stunned to speak. Behind her, Lurgo beamed.

Joel turned to him, and clasped Lurgo's hand in his. "Take care of her, Lurgo, as you have always done. And if I might ask one more favour of you. When you pass through Graveyard on your travels, collect my daughter. She would greatly enjoy a jaunt in the countryside before coming to London for the wedding."

"The...wedding?"

Joel nodded.

Thorn smiled so hard her face hurt.

Thorn looked to Holman, her eyes wet with unfallen tears. "What of you?" she asked, her voice barely audible. "Will you travel with us?"

Holman took her hands in his. "Though it would please my old heart more than you could know, Miss Thorn, I cannot. I have a duty now to undo the chaos I have made. Brunel's Palace and Chimney may be destroyed, but his crimes will fall into obscurity if I do not record them. I have documented Brunel's rise and fall over the last two decades in my own private journals. It is time I sought to publish these works, so that future generations may learn from our mistakes."

"Will I see you again?"

"That is not for me to decide." Holman tapped his mechanical orb. "But I have seen you. And that is a blessing I had not foreseen and did not deserve."

Thorn wrapped her arms around the once-blind man, and as he lifted his hands to her shoulders it seemed that he also lifted a great weight from her. For nineteen years she'd endured the wastelands of Graveyard, and she'd wrapped her own arms around her heart to prevent the cold seeping in. Now she had a fire roaring inside her, flames licking behind her eyes, desperate to leap forth and engulf the world.

I'm only just beginning.

EPILOGUE

JAMES HOLMAN'S MEMOIRS, FIRST EDITION

The following week Joel and I stood on the platform at Paddington Station and waved goodbye to the menagerie.

The Stokers had already reclaimed the rail yards and surrounding district as their own, tearing down the rotting slums and erecting scaffolding to build new homes. Queen Victoria gifted them with building materials and food stores as a gesture of thanks, though she ordered them to get to work rebuilding the rail network in standard gauge and finishing Paddington Station so the railways could run again. By unanimous vote, Joel had been elected foreman of the project, with Sam as his deputy, and for the first time since the Gauge Wars began, they will command a joint workforce of Stokers and Navvies. The ancient rivalries had begun to mend.

The statue of Brunel was gone, the stone plinth cracked and bare. Joel wanted to put a statue of Thorn there, but the thought horrified her. "Plant a tree," she said, and he said he would. London needed more trees.

S.C. GREEN

Spectators crowded the platform, jostling each other for the best view. I reeled as a lady brushed past, the tip of her parasol knocking the delicate mechanism that served me for eyes. A brand new STEPHENSON & COMPANY locomotive waited on the tracks, every wheel ridge and cylinder gleaming in the sunlight. The engine was of Crampton design, with 4-2-0 wheels and a low-pitched boiler. It would convey Thorn at great speed across the countryside, away from me.

The carriages sagged under the weight of the animals. Boris had an entire railcar to himself, so heavy had his bulk grown under the steady diet of Hyde Park rosebushes. Three days ago, Thorn's sense had finally returned to her, stronger than ever, and it was her thoughts that kept the animals from panic as the train prepared to leave. There was just one animal who still struggled against her control; from the back of the train I heard the familiar whine of Igor, amplified inside the hollow carriage.

Thorn and Lurgo sat on the first carriage, two cups of tea and a plate of mutton pies nestled between them. They waved at us through the window, and Lurgo pressed a button at the brim of his proprietor's hat. He'd ordered Julianne to make it for him, and he wore it with pride despite the unbearable weight of the mechanical dragon that tottered around the rim, puffing steam from its nostrils and chewing on unwary flies. Wombwell would be proud.

The whistle sounded and the boilers roared to life. A cheer rose through the crowd as steam gushed through the cylinders and the train pulled away.

Thorn leaned out the window and waved frantically at us. "I love you both. I'll see you again soon."

"Get back inside before you lose your head!" I yelled

back.

Joel tipped his hat to her and flashed a broad smile, but his eyes betrayed his concern. "I'm beginning to regret my decision," he whispered.

"You are needed here." It was true.

"And she is needed there, if for nothing more than to keep Lurgo and Julianne out of trouble." Joel smiled again, a real smile this time.

With a puff and a hiss the train pulled away. Joel stared after it until it rounded the corner and disappeared from sight. He squared his shoulders, sighed, and took my arm. "What do you say we go grab a pint?"

***

Thorn has been gone now for eleven months. Joel shares her letters with me, but I do not write in return. My words must be saved for a more arduous task.

Her news is always bright. Julianne and Lurgo continue their romance. There is talk of a wedding next spring. The tricorns are growing at an alarming rate, with Igor now standing twice the height of Thorn. By all accounts, age hasn't tempered his delightful nature. She wrote that just last week he was shifting Wall debris from a clogged riverbed when he swung around and dropped his load on top of a riverside cottage. I wish I could be there to see it.

Thorn has asked for us to go to her. Joel has packed his bags and bought his train ticket. He will meet her in Bristol this Sunday. He wishes me to accompany him, but I refuse. Though the idea of escaping into the countryside tempts me beyond all reason, I cannot accept. I feel Death's caress on my ankles and fingers, and it will soon spread. Some sickness within the mechanism has spread through my body. Soon it will claim me, and I have work still to complete. I had this last chapter still to write.

And now my work is finished. This manuscript records for eternity my most horrific betrayal. And yet its creation has also been my greatest joy. In Thorn's eyes I see happiness, and to see the spark of her life ignite from the midst of her sorrows delights me. It seems that no evil wrought by man or god can extinguish the fires of the human spirit.

Post Tenebras Lux – after darkness cometh the light. And with this last press of the pen, my work is complete.

THE END

THORN

S.C. GREEN

A NOTE ON THE TEXT

Fiction is a reworking of established truth. All things subtly shift under the author's pen, and even the most infallible facts become relative. As the *Engine Ward* series is set in an alternate history, I have taken certain liberties with the historical evidence. For your interest, I've listed some of the more blatant fallacies below.

Both Wombwell and Holman are historical figures, although whether the two met in life is not recorded. Wombwell died in 1850, not 1851, and did not live to see the Great Exhibition. Any curious persons can view his monument in Highgate cemetery, guarded by the ever-vigilant statue of Nero.

The cemetery itself, which is a prominent feature of my London landscape, first opened in 1838, and would have been quite empty when Thorn first visited.

Many other historical figures make an appearance in the series, including the mathematician Charles Babbage, (who really did harbour a hatred of organ grinders and write to Lord Tennyson about the mathematical inaccuracy of his poetry), Charles Darwin, William Buckland, Joseph Banks, and the remarkable Ada Byron, the so-called enchantress of numbers.

George III's mania was believed to be caused by prolonged exposure to arsenic, resulting in the malady *porphyria*. Victims of porphyries suffer from abdominal pain, vomiting, seizures and mental disturbances. Porphyries affect heme (a vital molecule for the body's organs), causing the skin to blister when exposed to sun and the gums to retract around the teeth and the canines to become pronounced. Many scientists have speculated porphyria accounts for historically documented cases of vampirism. Canadian biochemist Dr. David Dolphin has popularised this theory with research suggesting ingesting human blood relieves the symptoms of porphyria. Scientists tested follicles of George III's hair and found large amounts of arsenic, known to be a cause of porphyria. He was not – to the knowledge of any historian – actually a vampire.

Isambard Kingdom Brunel was appointed chief engineer of the Great Western Railway (affectionately known as the *Goes When Ready,* to its rather loose interpretation of a "schedule") in 1833, and the first train ran in 1838. He built several notable English bridges, including the Clifton suspension bridge and the Royal Albert Bridge – and two of the largest and most innovative ships of his time – the *Great Western* and the *Great Britain* (the first iron-hulled steamship to cross the Atlantic, the SS *Great Britain* was a passenger vessel, not a warship). Brunel's atmospheric railway was completed and abandoned in the 1840s, not the 1830s as I have led you to believe. He had no delusions of godhood. Probably.

Lastly, the widespread occurrence of dirigible flight has been altered dramatically. All these decisions were not made lightly. Thorn's world called for these divergences and each was necessary to create the story and anchor the Victorian world. I did not lead you down a false path. I am a spinner of tales. I hope you have enjoyed this one.

S C Green

ABOUT THE AUTHOR

S. C. Green is a New York Times and USA Today bestselling author of dark urban fantasy and science fiction. Her popular Engine Ward series explores a steampunk Georgian London where dinosaurs still survive. Her latest series, The Chronicles of the Wraith, is co-written with bestselling urban fantasy author Lindsey R Loucks.

Steff lives in an off-grid home in rural New Zealand with her husband, two mischievous cats, and a medieval sword collection. She also writes paranormal romance under the name Steffanie Holmes. Find out more about Steff's work on her website: steffmetal.com.

***

Want to be the first to know when new novels are released? Want access to exclusive previews and fan-only stories?

Sign up to the mailing list at steffmetal.com/subscriber.

OTHER BOOKS BY
THE AUTHOR

WRITING AS S C GREEN

Engine Ward Series
The Sunken
The Gauge War
Thorn

Court of the Litterfey

WRITING AS STEFFANIE HOLMES

Crookshollow Books
Art of Cunning
Art of the Hunt
Art of Temptation
The Man in Black
Watcher
Reaper
Digging the Wolf

Witches of the Woods
Witch Hunter
The Coven
Curse

www.ingramcontent.com/pod-product-compliance
Lightning Source LLC
Chambersburg PA
CBHW031024030726
47497CB00004B/996

* 9 7 8 0 4 7 3 3 5 1 3 5 9 *